THE IMMORTAL GAME

THE
IMMORTAL
GAME

TALIA ROTHSCHILD & A. C. HARVEY

NEW YORK

A SWOON READS BOOK

An imprint of Feiwel and Friends and Macmillan Publishing Group, LLC

120 Broadway, New York, NY 10271

swoonreads.com

Our books may be purchased in bulk for promotional, educational, or business use. Please contact your local bookseller or the Macmillan Corporate and Premium Sales Department at (800) 221-7945 ext. 5442 or by email at MacmillanSpecialMarkets@macmillan.com.

Library of Congress Cataloging-in-Publication Data is available.

First edition, 2021
Book design by Liz Dresner
Printed in the United States of America

ISBN 978-1-250-26290-5 (hardcover)
10 9 8 7 6 5 4 3 2 1

For Ethan, who shares my fantastical heart
and joined me on epic adventures
—SPLASH

For Anesa. May you grow to be as gracious as Galene, as brave as
Iyana, as loyal as Braxtus, and as wise as Kostas.
—MAMA

1

GALENE

Galene trailed her fingers over the hilts of weapons lining the dark stone walls.

The worn, wrapped leathers and freshly sharpened blades spoke of battles, and heroes, and gods crowned with immortality. Stains darkening wooden shafts told stories of desperate, bloody fights—some of which she'd witnessed.

Today the fight for immortality was hers.

In the gleam of an ax-head, she caught sight of bright blue eyes watching her.

Galene turned to look at her best friend. Iyana wore a stunning set of soft blue robes, her long white-blonde hair—loose as always—adorned with a gilded silver comb. In contrast, Galene's wavy brown hair was already slipping free of her braid, and she was dressed in light armor, her scimitar and throwing daggers on the belt at her hip.

Iyana's face was drawn with tension. "Are your weapons sharpened?"

Galene gave a strained smile. Of course she'd sharpened her blades. "I'll be fine."

Her friend's expression tightened. "You're not immortal yet."

Galene let out a breath, trying not to think of the last death at an Immortality Trial. What her brother had done in response to that death, and what her life had become afterward. But the Olympians hadn't allowed anyone to die since. She'd survive. No, she'd win.

Failing wasn't an option.

A horn blared, echoing through the tunnels beneath the stadium.

Iyana reached out and gave her fingers a squeeze. "Go prove yourself a goddess fit to be worshipped."

Galene gave a single nod, then turned, crossed the preparation room, and stepped through the door into the dark passage.

Torches lit the limestone walls, a rich, earthy breeze guiding her toward open air. She passed a small group wearing tunics embroidered with Apollo's laurel—healers waiting to see how the battle would end. Galene kept her eyes ahead, focusing on the beat of her sandals hitting the floor to lull her frantic mind.

The tunnel brightened as an archway of light came into view. A steady hum echoed down the tunnel, growing continuously louder.

Her heart banged against her rib cage. Every cruel word, every suspicious and disapproving glance she'd received over the last three years crashed through her mind. This was the day she'd overcome it all. She'd sketched plans for the temple that would be built for her, spent nights awake at the prospect of introducing herself to the humans. She'd dreamt of the day her father would look at her and see *her*, and not the shame of her brother.

I will walk off that battlefield a victor.

She crossed into the stadium.

The crowd erupted into a roar, and Galene blinked in the sunlight.

The massive amphitheater stretched one hundred and fifty feet wide and twice as long. A wall encircled the dirt grounds, and above it, packed stands rose into the sky, a mosaic of dully colored tunics with spots of shining armor. It roiled as the crowd rose and fell, waving arms and cheering. Every god on Mount Olympus must have been there, along with visiting gods and goddesses who'd turned up for the event.

The sound was deafening, exhilarating. Jeers mingled with the revelry, but Galene ignored those. She pulled back her shoulders and lifted her chin, turning to find the small section of her fellow Unnamed—the young gods and goddesses who were still mortal. Iyana would take her seat there soon. She raised her hand toward them in acknowledgment.

In the front rows of the stands closest to her, on elevated seats, were the most powerful of all the gods: the Twelve Olympians. The rulers of both Mount Olympus and the humans below.

They watched her, glowing with power, the only silent spectators. Four decks of cards sat on a table before them, glowing like the Olympians themselves.

The Decks of Fates.

Despite the clear sky, a crack of thunder echoed throughout the stadium.

The crowd hushed instantly, and the King of Olympus, God of the Sky, stood. Above his trimmed, dark beard, Zeus's storm-gray eyes scanned the crowd.

"Six months ago, the council of the Twelve Olympians enacted a new requirement: Poseidon's children and my own are to take their Immortality Trials three years early, at the age of eighteen." Zeus did not shout, but his words carried clearly to all listening. "With the powerful gifts bestowed upon our children, they are fit for this greater challenge." He fixed his eyes on Galene. She inclined her head in deference. "Galene Unnamed is the first to face this new requirement. Today she will prove whether she is worthy to join the pantheon."

The crowd cheered once more, and chills raced down Galene's arms. She was ready—this was an *opportunity*. The Fates were giving her a chance to prove herself.

"Choose your terrain," Zeus commanded.

Galene held his gaze. "Water."

Zeus nodded, unsurprised, then turned to Poseidon. "If you will."

Galene's father stood. The Earth-shaker, God of the Seas, was tall like his brother, but not as broad. His long hair and beard were dark gray and unkempt, and a wild spark kindled in the sea-green eyes Galene had inherited. He looked at her only for a moment, offering barely a nod before turning away. She steeled herself.

Poseidon raised his arms, and the ground shook.

Widening her stance, Galene looked down. The dirt fractured, creating a circle around her a few paces in diameter. Cracks shot outward, webbing across the arena floor to break up the smooth, packed dirt. Clumps and boulders of loose earth trembled beneath Poseidon's power, then tumbled downward into the gaping fissures.

Piece by piece the arena floor fell away, crumbling until Galene stood on a pinnacle, staring into an abyssal pit. Her stomach lurched at her sudden height, but Poseidon was not done. Through the rubble far below, water rose. It sloshed over the rocks and boulders, climbing rapidly until it surrounded Galene, leaving only a short drop between her and its settling surface.

She looked back to the Olympians. Her father's face was grim as he retook his seat.

"Now let the Fates choose your opponent." Zeus flicked his hand, and one of the Decks of Fates scattered forward, as though blown by the wind. Tumbling through the air, the golden cards spun toward Galene, slowing as they approached. Most of the deck came to a stop, hanging in the air like leaves on an invisible tree. Five cards, however, came closer, aligning themselves at Galene's eye level.

"Choose three," Zeus reminded her.

Galene reached up and hesitated. *Don't overthink it.* She touched two on the left and one beside the far right. They glowed brighter, hanging there until all the other cards drew back, returning to a neat pile on the table.

The gold coating on the first card dissolved to reveal an image and printed words.

It depicted a whale-like sea creature with a gaping mouth lined with rows of long teeth.

Body of Cetus, the card read.

Galene swallowed. She had expected one of the cards to be monstrous—at least now she'd gotten the worst out of the way.

She turned to the second. Its golden coat, too, disappeared.

A giant gryphon was emblazoned on it, the fur and feathers shining with gold.

Hide of the Gryphiekin.

She blinked in shock. The King of the Gryphons' eagle-and-lion hide was like armor, nearly impenetrable. This card was as bad as the first—drawing blood would be formidable, let alone *killing* whatever hybrid creature these cards would create.

Turning to the third and final card, Galene sent a silent prayer to the Fates. *Please be something to balance these out—sight of a cyclops or something.*

The gold disappeared, and she felt the ichor drain from her cheeks.

Heads of Scylla.

No.

Galene looked between them again. She had to have misread them—there had to be a mistake. But no: *Body of Cetus, Hide of the Gryphiekin, Heads of Scylla.* Each individual card could change any two basic creature qualities into a deadly beast, but all three together . . .

She clenched her fists, digging her nails into her palms. This six-headed monster would be huge, smart, and nearly impossible to wound. *I don't know if I can do this.* Her legs trembled, and she hoped the Olympians couldn't tell.

The cards flew back, presenting themselves to the Twelve. Behind them, gods and goddesses leaned forward to get a look at the cards. Shocked murmurs rose, rippling around Galene as the word of her opponent was passed around the stadium.

Excitement began to vibrate through the crowd, people realizing that if nothing else, they were about to get a show. There had *never* been three creatures of this caliber combined for an Immortality Trial.

She looked to her father. His mouth was a thin, pressed line. The other Olympians didn't look at all fazed—some merely sat forward to watch her more closely, disdain in their eyes.

The sight lit something inside her. She choked down her fear, forcing herself to stand straighter. *Losing isn't an option.*

The three cards, settling now on the table, began to glow.

The Fates had given her these cards. They must believe she can do this.

I'm strong, powerful, and a good daughter. When I beat this thing, there will be no doubt of my honor, despite Chrysander's actions.

I am worthy of being a deity.

Renewed determination surged through her, and she looked out across her element.

Under the water before her, a speck of light appeared. Glimmering like a star, it flickered once, then began to grow. As it spread out, shifting and shaping, the light faded to something dark and solid. Several feet below, the sea creature came to life.

Gasps and exclamations rang around her. Spectators rose from their seats, pointing and moving for a better look.

The giant shape dwarfed her. Half of it was large and thick, four powerful fins stroking, propelling it through the water as a fanned tail steered with surprising agility. The other half split into six thick necks, snaking below the surface in search of prey. The necks alone were thrice Galene's height.

The beast circled her island, swimming out of the shadow of the arena wall. Sunlight struck it, and hundreds of shimmering rays bounced from its golden hide, shooting through the water.

Anticipation was thick in the air, the hundreds of eager eyes distracting, but she did her best to ignore them. She rarely practiced with spectators and doubted many of the gods here today had seen her gift in use. She was about to show them exactly what she was capable of.

Raising her hands, Galene called on her first gift—manipulation of tides. She reached out with her mind until she had an intangible, mental grip on the water around her. Sensing its slight, natural flow, she pushed the water to the far end of the arena, bracing it there, adding more. Pressure built against her, a captured wave waiting for release. Fighting the pull of gravity was never an easy task; it took all of her focus to hold it. As the water level sank on her side of the arena, so did the creature. The monster circled once more, crossing between Galene's rock and the growing wall of water.

She unleashed the wave.

As it fell, she pulled, forcing the water forward with extra speed. The swell crashed into the beast, and it slammed into the rock. Her bones rattled as the ground beneath her shook, and the tidal wave battered her with water, sloshing past to break against the opposite arena walls. Outcries sounded as the crowd, too, was doused.

Using the water's returning momentum, Galene threw it back to the far end of the arena, but knew she didn't have the same amount of time. Only giving it a moment to build, she hauled it back. Again, the monster struck the rock. A chorus of bellows resounded beneath the waves.

Gambling that she had one more use of the trick, Galene pushed the water again, but as she forced it to build up against the wall, the monster's cry became deafening.

Six heads had burst from the water. The crowd screamed.

Galene staggered back, squinting against the dappled hues of gold and bronze that caught the sun. Droplets beaded and dripped off the interlocking feathers that created a scaly armor. The heads of Scylla reared over her, snarling with razor teeth and tongues that flicked like whips. On each head, two sets of cunning, blood-red eyes locked on her.

Terror threatened to overwhelm Galene. She could almost see each mind working, reeling with whatever instincts had been set within it, savoring the delicious moment of tension before its attack.

Galene took a slow step back, feeling the edge of the rock with her heel.

The three center heads seemed to grin.

It thinks I'm trapped. A spark of confidence ignited in her. *But I have a second gift.*

As the three heads struck down, she turned and dove off the rock. She fell, exhaling every bit of air from her chest. She hit the water and sucked in a breath. The cool, salty liquid filled her lungs, her body adapting seamlessly.

Galene looked to the surface to see the beast refocus on the rock, heads twisting as they searched for her.

Perseus had used Medusa's head to kill Cetus—not a possibility here. No one had ever done anything more than escape Scylla, and the Gryphiekin had bested all challengers. She ground her teeth. Her blades would be of little use against the Gryphiekin hide. She'd need something much stronger to injure this beast. She looked up through the water at the gleam of Scylla's ferociously sharp teeth—teeth that could penetrate any armor.

An idea formed in her mind.

She dove for the beast's belly, pulling a tide forward to propel her. With a powerful wave of its front fins, the monster drew back, its heads falling into the water.

Galene willed the water to push her faster before the heads could find her. The waters darkened as she moved beneath its belly, but she could still make out the lighter gold underside, where the feathers morphed into a thick, bristly lion's coat. She shot along, moving to the tail fin.

Heart quickening, Galene kicked up. She dug her fingers into the fur, clamping her legs around the swishing fin. She let go with one hand, drew her longest dagger, and slammed it down to claim its attention.

The blade ricocheted off the impenetrable hide, sending a shock wave up her arm. All six heads snapped around, four crimson eyes on each finding her. With a cacophony of roars, they struck.

Galene released the beast and propelled herself between the necks, barely missing razor teeth as the first head snapped down where she had been, scoring itself. Too quickly a second head was there, jaws ready. Crying out, she pushed herself back with a swell of water, almost straight into the mouth of another.

Galene tumbled away, pulling the tides to rush out of reach. *Too close.*

Would anyone even notice if it killed her? Could they even see her down there?

The heads were still leering over its back, and Galene flicked her eyes to the tail of the beast. A thin line of blood oozed into the water.

She dove again, back to the same spot, seizing the hair with her free hand, brandishing her dagger with the other.

Four of the heads turned around and snaked forward, launching the creature back into motion. Galene almost flew off the tail as it swiveled, beating the water, and she redoubled her grip. The other heads snapped at her from each side. She prepared to leap from its back again, then paused, noticing their lack of effort.

It figured out my plan.

They tore through the water, up toward the surface. Two heads continued to snap at her as Galene's mind worked, thinking of any possible strategy to overpower or outsmart this thing.

The creature breached, launching into the air.

The sudden jerk dislodged Galene, her dagger slipping through her fingers as the creature arched back toward the water.

Galene tumbled downward. The shouts from the crowd, almost as loud as the crashing water, rattled through her. She choked back her shriek. Olympus couldn't see her fear.

The creature hit the water first, creating a maelstrom of frothing waters. Galene curled up and braced for impact.

The water stung as she hit and sank, bubbles and foam obscuring her vision. Throwing out her arms, she frantically pushed the churning water away, bringing clear water to replace it.

Six heads shot toward her, mouths open.

She screamed, heaving on the water, but a jaw snapped onto her side. The teeth pierced her breastplate, driving into her flesh.

Vicious pain tore through her, and she grabbed the length of a tooth still exposed above her armor. The creature reared back, whipping its neck up through the surface.

Terror pounded in her veins as she was flung through the air in the beast's jaw, a blur of colors racing by. Distantly, she heard the stadium screaming.

Crack! She slammed down onto rock, stars erupting into her vision. Her body vibrated with the force of the creature's bellow, and the teeth began to retract from her side. The crippling pain resurged as she was pulled with the retreating head, sliding along rock. There was a loud snap, and a tooth broke off, still lodged inside her.

She jerked to a stop, coughing water from her lungs until she could breathe air again.

Water hissed and sloshed, and the crowd hummed in tense anticipation. Her pulse thrummed in her ears. Fire burned through her abdomen.

For a moment, she could picture what Olympus must be seeing—a bleeding, broken young goddess on a lonely rock, barely moving. A failure.

No.

Galene tried to push herself up, but the pain flared, blinding her. She fell back again.

If I can't even sit up, how am I going to win? Despair struck her at the thought, almost as painful as the tooth still protruding from her side. *I'm not going to. They'll stop the Trial any second now.*

Anger bubbled up with the tears. She'd worked so hard.

Still clutching the tooth in her side, Galene dared to look down at her torso. Golden blood streamed from rows of holes in her armor and leaked around the single tooth remaining. Tightening her grip, she squeezed her eyes shut and ripped the tooth out.

Agony tore up her throat in a scream. Striking the ground, she forced herself up.

She opened her streaming eyes just as six jaws filled with jagged teeth lunged for her again.

Flinging her hands up, she willed the water to obey her desperation. A wave slammed into Cetus's body, lifting the sea creature as the heads converged. She gasped, falling back as the necks plunged, the heads striking the ground a mere arm's length above her head.

Her lungs shuddered with ragged breaths as a new fear gripped her . . . not the fear of losing, but the fear of *dying*.

They haven't stopped the Trial. They should have stopped it by now!

Fueled by instinct more than anything, she thrust the tooth up, burying it into a thick, golden neck above her.

The creature screamed and writhed. Scarlet blood rained down as she yanked the tooth out and slammed it back in. *Stop the Trial.* A single tooth against six heads—the odds were impossible. *Stop the Trial!*

More jaws came at her from either side. She wrenched the tooth out again, screaming, swinging . . .

An explosion of sound accompanied a searing flash, the air

crackling with electricity. The beast burst into light, disintegrating before her eyes. Water crashed down, leaving behind nothing but a ringing silence.

Beyond the water Zeus was on his feet, hand still outstretched from directing the lightning bolt.

Galene uncurled her fingers from the tooth and let it clatter to the ground.

A sob cracked against her ribs, sending another lance of pain through her. Shame crushed her as she pressed a hand to the gaping wound in her side.

She hadn't proved herself worthy to be worshipped—hadn't erased the shame of Chrysander.

She'd done nothing but fail.

2

KOSTAS

The emotions of everyone in the arena washed over Kostas, but Galene's struck him the hardest.

He leaned forward, watching her carefully from his seat beside his mother, Iris. As the son of Hermes, one of the Olympians, he was privileged to be positioned close to the Twelve. From this angle, he could see Galene clearly. A colored aura of tumultuous blues and grays pulsed around her. Her face was screwed up in pain as she pressed her hand into her side.

Poseidon was back on his feet. With a wave of his hand and a deep rumble, rocks rose from the water, forming a path from the tunnel to Galene's island. A few waiting healers rushed out, hurrying to Galene's side. One of them, a son of Apollo, put his hands on Galene's torso, calling upon his ability. The others helped Galene sit, then stand, pulling out bandages.

Galene's face relaxed slightly, and a dignified expression settled there.

Few would suspect she was feeling anything other than what she displayed, patiently waiting for her judgment. Kostas, however, could see more than everyone else.

The somber colors around Galene contradicted her poised demeanor. She was simmering with hurt, anger, and crushing disappointment.

No one can blame her.

He looked to the Olympians and the Decks of Fates laid before them. The cards Galene had chosen were absurd. His mind ran over the math again.

Between the options she was presented with and the ones she selected, she had a less than one percent chance of getting those three particular cards. Either the Fates truly don't think she's meant to be a deity now, or this was deliberate sabotage. From what he knew of Galene's power—which she had just proven—and her notable intellect, Kostas had a suspicion.

With narrow eyes, he looked over the Olympians. A mixture of hues swirled through their auras. Surprise and relief was the most prominent in all of them, followed by dark regret. And throughout a few of them he caught flashes of the deep purple he was looking for. *Shame. They* must *have done something.* He checked himself there. *There are many reasons they could feel guilty. They could have stopped the Trial sooner, or not allowed a beast that cruel to battle Galene. Or they could simply be ashamed that Galene wasn't powerful enough to beat it.* Kostas ran a hand through his dark curls and scratched his neck, absorbed in this new riddle.

"Galene Unnamed," Zeus called out. "You have failed to pass your Immortality Trial."

The colors around Galene flooded blue. She bit her lip, but kept eye contact with the rulers of Olympus.

"In ten years' time, you may request to retake the Trial to prove yourself worthy of immortality."

"Ten years?" Kostas muttered. "She almost got the thing."

His mother set a pale hand on his dark brown arm, her hazel eyes urging caution. "Ten years is standard."

Even so, she'd be much older before she stopped aging.

Galene's blue colors started to taint, creeping darker until they reflected not just misery, but anger and humiliation. As he stared at her, he began to feel those same emotions creeping into his own heart. He blinked them away.

"You fought valiantly and well," Zeus said, "but you need more training and discipline before you are to join us in immortality. Tend to your wounds, then return to the Common Temple of the Unnamed."

Galene dropped her head in a shallow bow, unable to do more as the healers worked on her. The Olympians rose to leave.

Kostas stood with everyone else, waiting respectfully for their twelve leaders to exit first before the masses began to shuffle out of the stadium. He glanced once more at Galene, now being guided toward a pair of gods approaching with a stretcher.

Parting from his mother, Kostas made his way to the other side of the stands where the Unnamed children of the gods had been seated. It didn't take him long to find the god he was looking for.

Braxtus stood taller than most, his thick, curly blond hair adding an extra inch or so to his height. But Kostas wouldn't have needed eyes to find his best friend. The loud, endless chatter would have led him there.

Braxtus was in a deep conversation with Iyana. Kostas was surprised to see them together and—he glanced through the surrounding gods to be sure—without Iyana's boyfriend.

Though Braxtus primarily radiated shock and concern, Kostas couldn't help but notice the flashes of yellow and rose gold that danced across his aura as he looked at Iyana. Her aura was a raging scarlet, flashing with dark blues of grief to break up the fury. Her arms flew as she vented to Braxtus.

". . . *completely* unjust, and . . . well, *barbaric!*"

"Keep your voice down," Kostas muttered as he approached.

"It *was* crazy!" Braxtus turned, seamlessly including Kostas in their conversation. "I thought for sure Galene would win, but did you *see* that thing?"

Kostas nodded. "It was nothing like I've seen in the Trials before."

"I thought *your* beast was nasty."

"It was." Five months ago, Kostas had battled a winged creature

15

at his Immortality Trial: a mix of a harpy, boar, and sphynx. It had been a mean combination—agile with a tricky tongue. He had eventually shot it down, gaining immortality and his official title as God of Games.

It was appropriate, as he had practically built his life around games already. His ability to see and feel others' emotions gave him a substantial edge in competitions and made his natural intuition that much more accurate.

"The Fates always give us more difficult tests," he said, referring to the children of the Twelve. "At least Galene was able to use her power over the tides."

Iyana scoffed. "I bet Poseidon himself would have had trouble with that thing."

Braxtus scratched his short beard, brown eyes squinting in the sun. "Is this how they're going to be from now on?" His aura swirled to a worried gray as he glanced at Iyana.

Iyana went pale, and he felt her flutter of fear. Iyana was the daughter of Zeus. She, like Galene, had to take her Trial early. In fact, they were currently the only two Unnamed impacted by the Olympians' new rule. And Iyana only had three more months to prepare.

Kostas looked at her seriously. "I surely hope not, but if I were you, I'd start training much harder."

Her eyes widened, her aura suddenly suspicious. "Did you see something? From the Olympians?"

He tilted his head. "That might be a conversation for later."

Iyana pressed her lips into a thin, wobbly line. "I need to check on Galene."

She raced away, Braxtus's eyes following her.

"How did you two end up talking?" Kostas asked.

"We sat together. Demitri"—Braxtus flared with both frustration and jealousy at the name—"was on duty patrolling the stands with some of his brothers."

Kostas nodded. Braxtus had a special dislike for the handsome son of Aphrodite and Ares. Braxtus and Iyana had been close—practically inseparable for over a year, with something obviously more than friendship there. So really, it had come as a shock to everyone when Demitri pursued Iyana and when she returned his advances. Soon after, the two had established a public relationship. Kostas winced, remembering Braxtus's relentless hurt and anger that had lasted weeks before shifting to unyielding determination to keep her in his life.

On occasion, Kostas had felt Iyana's love for Demitri, along with her confusion surrounding Braxtus. He didn't have the heart to tell his best friend either of those things.

Feeling others' emotions certainly had its disadvantages.

"I have a rotation of guard duty around the arena all night," Braxtus told him, "but I'll come visit you in your temple tomorrow. I'd like to hear about what you picked up from the Olympians today."

"Yes, I'll see you tomorrow." Kostas didn't miss guard duty, or any of the rotations across the mountain. As a recent Immortal, he had been granted a break from the shared duties of Olympus to get used to his new responsibilities as a deity.

Braxtus raised a hand in farewell and jogged off. Kostas turned down a small path, heading up the mountain toward his home.

Kostas's temple was built to resemble three tossed dice, the two on the bottom serving as a base for the one on top, allowing space for balconies and checkered patios. Kostas strode through the front gate and pushed open the double doors. Passing over the narad-i-shir board that made up the floor, he wandered around tables of his favorite games, toward a room in the back.

Jewels, carvings, and gold littered several tables. He raised his eyebrows as he looked around his Linked Chamber. It was more than he had expected after only being an official deity for five months.

Every Immortal's temple had a Linked Chamber that connected to their corresponding temples and shrines in the human realm. The chambers replicated each offering the humans presented as payment or plea.

Kostas made his way to a cushioned chair at the center of the room. Settling in, he listened to the echoes of those praying for his help.

I need to win this game . . .

Bless me with luck in my tournament . . .

Give me the intuition to understand my enemies . . .

He tried to focus on one at a time, letting himself become connected to the individual in prayer, but Galene's Trial kept festering at the back of his mind. Each time he tried to tune in, he was tugged back to Galene's cards and the likelihood they had been tampered with. His mind soon swam with equations and different methods for rigging the outcome of the Deck of Fates.

Grumbling, Kostas pushed himself up and walked to a table full of heavenly food that had just appeared. Picking up an apple, he took a bite as he wandered out of the chamber. *Even if the Olympians had cheated, what on Gaia could anyone do about it?*

3

IYANA

Iyana's sandaled feet struck the cobblestones as she raced up Mount Olympus, robes bunched in her fist. Wind rushed around her, giving her a slight push forward, swirling her long blonde hair around her face. She combed it back. Calling upon the wind hadn't been intentional—it just responded to her urgency.

Just as she passed the God of Medicine's temple, the infirmary came into view: short and long, lined with white pillars. Iyana cut off the main path toward it, then pushed through the pristine doors. Her stomach knotted as she hurried to the wing reserved for the most serious injuries.

Gods and goddesses moved in and out of the rooms, instruments in their hands. One caught sight of Iyana and paused.

"She's in room two, but you'll have to wait." She adjusted the tray in her arms. "She was just bitten by one of Scylla's heads. Give us a while."

Iyana opened her mouth to ask if she could just sit quietly in the room, but the goddess gave her a severe stare. She closed it again, leaning against the wall.

The goddess looked like she wanted to send Iyana farther away, but just sighed, hurrying into Galene's room with her supplies.

The minutes dragged by. Iyana was just considering finding a chair when footsteps echoed down the hall behind her. She turned to see a familiar face, and her breath caught in her throat.

It was obvious from Demitri's looks that he was the son of Aphrodite and Ares. His mother's beauty and his father's ferocity seemed to have merged perfectly into the imposing figure that walked toward her. He had the kind of face that stopped people in their tracks. Iyana supposed he must be used to it—the sudden pause in a goddess's natural expression when she looked his way, followed by overcompensating with an unconcerned air. Of course the blush that always accompanied it was a dead giveaway.

Iyana had long since stopped feeling jealous—Demitri, it seemed, only had eyes for her.

He brushed his dark hair back from his forehead, clear blue eyes finding Iyana's.

She gave him a tense smile, and as he reached her, he gathered her small frame in his powerful arms. He smelled like the wood of his weapons. Despite everything, she relaxed into him.

"I knew I'd find you here."

"Where else would I be?" she mumbled into his tunic. "I have to see her."

"I know."

"She had so much confidence. She seemed so *ready*." Tears burned at the corners of her eyes.

Demitri pulled back, trying to look at her. "No one expected an Immortality Trial like that."

She nodded, but buried her face back into his shoulder. He tightened his arms around her, and Iyana let herself be soothed by the safety of his embrace.

They waited outside the room for several more minutes before they were approached.

"You can go in now."

Iyana stepped into Galene's room to see her best friend propped up on pillows, staring out the window. Her coppery brown hair had been loosed from its tight braid, hanging in damp waves around her shoulders. She wore a light shift, and Iyana could see the bulk of bandages around her middle.

"Galene!" Iyana rushed over to the bed, but caught herself before she flung her arms around her.

"Hi, Iyana." Galene's voice was hoarse, her sea-green eyes a bit puffy. She shifted to the side, and Iyana sat, clasping her hand.

"How . . . how do you feel?" She cringed at the terrible question.

Galene shook her head. "Those were the three most powerful creatures in the Water Deck of Fates."

Iyana let out a breath. "I knew it. That's completely unfair! The Olympians shouldn't have made you fight something like that."

"There was always a chance to get all three," Galene mumbled. "I should have trained harder."

"No." Iyana squeezed her hand, partly in comfort, partly in anger. "I don't think even Demitri could have beaten that beast, and he's the son of the War God."

"Then it's just not my time to be a recognized deity. Even the Olympians can't oppose fate."

"You think this was fate?" Demitri said from the doorway, voice incredulous. They both looked over at him, and he pushed himself off the doorframe toward them. "The Fates may influence the direction of our lives, but they don't manipulate events that directly."

Here we go. Iyana fidgeted, unsure how Galene would take to this conversation. Galene didn't respond, but she kept her eyes on Demitri, expression cool. She'd never been overly fond of him.

"The Olympians decide when it's your time to be a deity, not fate," Demitri continued, lip curling in disgust. "They required the two of you—specifically the two of you, since there's no one else who fits the criteria of the new rule—to take your Immortality Trials three years early. They've already proven they don't want to play fair."

Galene pulled her hand free from Iyana's to sit herself up

straighter. "That was supposed to make it *more* fair. I'm the daughter of Poseidon, Iyana's the daughter of Zeus. The two most powerful Olympians."

"Yes, and they're so intimidated by your potential that they gave you less time to train and a brutal test. They don't really want you to pass your Immortality Trials."

"You think they stacked the Decks of Fates against me," Galene said, voice laced with disbelief.

"Absolutely."

"They wouldn't do that."

"Wouldn't they?"

Galene looked to Iyana for backup, but she bit her lip, feeling sick. She glanced around, then leaned toward Galene, lowering her voice.

"Demitri has been telling me for a while that the Olympians consider us a threat. He thinks they're worried we'll draw away those who worship them. That's the reason why we rarely get to train with the actual Olympians, or any other skillful warriors. I haven't been believing it, not really, but after what we saw today, well . . ." Galene started to protest, but Iyana hurried on. "It's just hard to believe that you would get all three of the hardest beasts when you already had to take the Trial early. They didn't seem surprised, and they didn't even stop it when you were bitten."

A mixture of anger, fear, and hurt swam in her friend's eyes. "You two are starting to sound like Chrysander."

Her tone wasn't accusatory, but a pang went through Iyana's chest. Galene didn't normally talk about her brother. She used to be close to him, but he'd left Mount Olympus years ago.

Demitri shifted. "Sometimes I think your brother had the right idea."

Iyana shot him a warning look, but he ignored her.

"Don't say that." Galene pressed her hands to her temples.

"Why not?"

22

"I know you two were best friends, but my brother nearly committed treason for his crazy ideas."

"Maybe they weren't so crazy."

"Excuse me?" Galene narrowed her eyes at him. "Gathering the exiled? Open rebellion?"

"I thought he was crazy then, too, but look at what the Olympians have done to you. I'm starting to think he was right."

"No," Iyana snapped, rising to Galene's defense. "That's too far. Chrysander wanted to rally the most wicked of gods and goddesses. They were exiled for good reasons."

"There's got to be something better than this," Demitri muttered.

"Do you really think Chrysander found something better, Demitri?" Golden heat had risen to Galene's cheeks. "Out there alone, never worshipped, never able to return?"

Chrysander had broken one of the most important laws of Mount Olympus, deserting the mountain before his Immortality Trial. The consequences of leaving without an Immortal escort had sentenced him to a life as an outcast.

Demitri opened his mouth to argue more, but Iyana caught his arm. "She doesn't need this right now."

He shrugged, but Iyana could tell he wasn't satisfied.

Galene slumped back against her pillows, getting a faraway look in her eye that only appeared when she wanted to be alone.

"We'll let you rest." Iyana leaned forward to give Galene a gentle hug. "I can come back when you're ready for more company."

Galene nodded distantly, and Iyana eased herself off the bed, leading Demitri away. She paused at the door, looking back. "No one would have done better. You're a hero, and I love you." She blew Galene a kiss and closed the door softly behind her.

They were silent as they left the infirmary. Dusk bathed the mountainside in golden light as they walked down the path toward the Upper Common Temple. Anxiety continued to twist Iyana's stomach, and once again, the wind responded to her feelings, whipping around them. Demitri caught her hand, pulling her up short by Persephone's gardens.

"What's on your mind?"

She smiled ruefully. "What isn't?"

"Something specific is bothering you." His piercing eyes studied her. "Is it your upcoming Trial?"

She nodded, throat tight, thinking of what Kostas had said. "I'm not as powerful as Galene, but I don't think the Olympians believe that. If they stacked the Decks of Fates against her, they're going to stack it against me, too."

"Yes," he agreed, not bothering to sugarcoat reality.

Her anxiety mounted. "As the daughter of Zeus, they'll probably make it just as hard. But I have such limited control over wind. I can't even fly!"

"If you could get the wind to guide your throwing spikes, that could increase your chances—"

"Demitri, my Immortality Trial is in three months. I don't have the control, or the time." Panic squeezed her throat tight. "What if . . . what if I don't even walk out of there? Telamon didn't."

"Listen to me, Iyana." Demitri grasped her shoulders. "I'm not going to let that happen."

"You can't interfere."

"But I can teach you survival tricks. The Olympians haven't let a Trial end in death since Telamon, and it's been a few years now. If you can't defeat the beast, they will stop the Trial eventually and kill it for you. You just need to stay out of its way."

She blinked against the tears that threatened to rise again. "None of this is fair."

He pulled her against him and pressed his lips to her forehead. "I know. It's not."

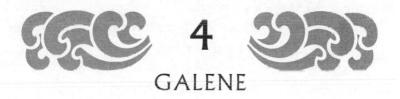

4

GALENE

The sun had hidden itself beneath the horizon hours ago. Lit torches in various temple grounds offered the only sources of light to guide Galene's way.

She breathed shallowly, holding her side. With careful footsteps, she made her way toward the outskirts of Olympus, taking smaller paths that wound to the Northeastern slope. The scattered temples of lesser Immortals were quiet with sleep, and she saw no one.

Feeling a little more secure, she pushed through the pain and walked faster. It was a trek from the infirmary to where she was headed, but she had an appointment to keep.

She wasn't looking forward to it. After every meeting, she left angry and resentful. Still, she always went back. How could she not? He was family.

Cutting through an ancient olive orchard of Athena's, she left the path, slipping into the trees and passing a small lake that marked she was close to the border of Olympus. There would be guards patrolling nearby, but Galene knew their routine and where to hide.

Between two of the boundary line towers within the growing wilderness of trees was a large, leafy bush. Galene wrestled her way through the thick branches until she broke through to a tight, empty pocket within. The shimmering, magical barrier that ran between the towers cut the hollow bush in half. On the other side, two sea-green eyes gleamed at her. She felt a rise of anger, of resignation, at the sight of him.

"So?" the young god's voice inquired, forgoing any greeting. His voice was muffled through the barrier.

She closed her eyes. "I failed."

There was silence, then, "Tell me everything."

Galene relayed the events in the arena, the dark figure across from her listening to it all. She felt sick as she spoke. She'd intended to tell him of her success, a bitter part of her wanting to show him what he'd missed out on by leaving. Instead, she admitted her failure. She waited for his reply, but he remained quiet. "Chrysander?" she urged, though unsure she wanted to hear his thoughts.

"I told you not to even take the Trial, Galene," he said, clearly trying to keep quiet. "I told you what could happen. Scylla, Cetus, *and* the Gryphiekin? That's not fate, Galene, that's trickery. The Olympians, our *father*, tampered with those cards to set you up. You're far too powerful for their liking, everyone knows it. I can't believe—"

"Please, stop, Chrysander, I just had to listen to all of this from Demitri."

Her brother was silent for a moment. "I knew he'd see through the Olympians eventually. He should have come with me. Still could. The same goes for you, sister."

"I'm not like you," she ground out. "I won't betray our leaders or abandon my home." Normally, she could keep her anger with him in check. Not tonight, not after the opportunity to overcome his legacy had slipped through her fingers.

"But everything I'm saying is *true*, Galene, can't you see it?"

"No!" she snapped, then paused, checking her volume. "I have been blessed with a great ability, so clearly the Fates believe I should be more prepared, more in control of it before I can become a deity. I won't fail next time."

"In *ten years*," he reminded her. "And what makes you so sure they won't just give you something even worse to fight?"

Galene gave a dry chuckle. "I don't think there is a worse combination to get."

"You know that I left hoping to one day change bigoted traditions like the Immortality Trials."

"The Trials bring order," she protested. "Not just *anyone* should be able to influence the lives of the humans. Why do you think we have such a strict law about who crosses the border?" It was the simplest and most exacting of all Olympian rules: If you left before you were granted immortality, the consequence was exile. And the exiled were forbidden from going near humans, under threat of death. "There has to be some sort of test to prove that you can protect and lead the humans before you can contact them."

"So you're supporting the Olympians? You really think your ability to slay a ridiculously overpowered monster—one that's not even *real*—should determine whether the humans should know and worship you?" he challenged.

Galene clenched her teeth. "Maybe not. But your leaving didn't do anything except make my life harder. So what good have you done?" She didn't give him a chance to defend himself. "The Olympians banished the Titans and organized chaos. They know what they're doing. We should trust their wisdom and be grateful for their guidance."

"Guidance? Galene, how have any of them helped you in your life? What have they done but try to keep you down?"

"They're trying to make me strong."

"You *are* strong!" He let out a breath and leaned away. "Maybe it *is* for the best, then. Maybe now you'll finally start to see."

A cool fury enveloped her. "You're glad this happened? That I failed, that I still have to suffer your shame as my own?"

"I'm trying to fight for something *better*, can't you see that?

27

If I had to exile myself for the cause, so be it. I'm sorry you got caught in the crossfire, but I wouldn't take it back."

Her anger slid down into grief as she thought of the biggest thing he had lost. "But you'll die," Galene whispered. She had never cried so hard in her life as the day he left three years ago. Choosing to leave Olympus before his Immortality Trial had ensured that he would die within the infancy of her own immortality.

"Perhaps," he replied. Galene blinked at the odd response. "But I have never felt more free, and isn't freedom more important than eternal life?"

She didn't answer. They were silent for a long moment, long enough for Chrysander to pull a few drops of water from the earth, staring into the small pool he created with his power. Galene nudged the water with her gift, making it ripple back and forth. They'd often played together like this as children, but that was long in the past.

"I'm not the only one who feels this way, either, Galene."

"A few rebel fanatics don't help prove your point."

"There's more than just a few of us out here."

She scoffed. "How many, then? Ten? Twelve?"

He scowled. "Over fifty now, actually. With more coming to our banner every day. With what's happening next, we'll soon have hundreds. Maybe thousands."

Galene frowned. "Your *banner*? Chrysander, what are you talking about?"

"Why don't you come and see for yourself?"

She sighed, suddenly incredibly tired. "No, Chrysander. This is my home, my family."

"Am I not your family anymore?"

Galene bit her lip. "I love you, brother, and I wish you'd never left. But once I get my immortality, I'll be free to leave Olympus without escort, and I can come and visit you whenever I like. We can see the world together. All of the oceans and seas, like we used to talk about."

He gave a short, warm laugh. "In ten years, if all goes according to plan, we'll have already done all of that."

Galene's heart skipped a beat. "According to plan?"

"I already told you, Galene, come see for yourself. I can't risk telling you here, not when you refuse to see the truth."

She shook her head. "What you're saying isn't truth."

"Only time will tell who's right. But if you do change your mind, little sister . . ." He shuffled forward slightly. With her eyes now adjusted to the dark, she could make out the faint copper and gold streaks in the hair that mirrored hers, their waves falling down across his brow. He raised a hand up close to the border and Galene copied him, their skin tones matching perfectly, her hand only slightly smaller than his. ". . . you can find us in the heart of the Land of the Taraxippi."

A primal warning flashed through her. "The Land of the Taraxippi? Chrysander, that place is dangerous!"

"Not for us. We've claimed territory there, where no one will bother us. Galene, come and see. You could help right all of this mess. You have no idea what good you could do."

Galene opened her mouth, words faltering.

Three short horn blasts echoed faintly across Olympus.

She whipped around, but could see nothing through the thick foliage.

Another warning call, this one louder.

"Sounds like trouble," Chrysander muttered.

"I have to go," Galene said, turning. "Fates be kind to you, brother."

"Stay safe, Galene. You know where I'll be."

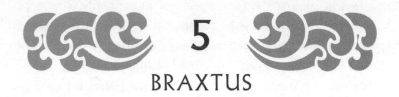

5

BRAXTUS

Braxtus yawned widely, then pinched himself.

Night watch is the worst, he thought as he reached a tower, turning around to pace back the other way. He tripped over a loose rock in the grass and grumbled under his breath.

Normally he didn't mind guarding the boundary—but *normally* he was scheduled during the day, when he had a nice view of the mountainside. During the day, he'd actually reported beasts and humans wandering a little too close.

At night you couldn't see much. A fire glowed softly at the top of each tower that ringed the boundary line, but even that light only stretched so far down the mountain, doing little more than making the translucent, magical barrier that ran between the towers glimmer slightly. Tonight's moon was dark, which made Braxtus's vision all the worse, and he'd been prohibited from lighting his own fire.

On top of that, he was exhausted. With the excitement of Galene's Immortality Trial, he hadn't bothered to nap before his shift. Now he was paying for it.

His eyes fluttered, and he pinched himself again. If he didn't pay attention, he could wander straight through the barrier instead of alongside it, and it would seal behind him forever.

Braxtus *had* passed through the barrier a few times, but always supervised. When his father, Apollo, needed to answer prayers in person, he'd occasionally brought Braxtus on excursions to Megara and Eretria—two of the human cities that primarily worshipped his father. Braxtus was really hoping Apollo would take him to Sparta soon, but his father had grown distant lately, and it'd been months since Braxtus had left Mount Olympus at all.

In a couple of years you'll pass your Immortality Trial, he reminded himself. *Then you can explore as much as you wish.*

Careful to stay well away from the barrier, he picked up his pace, hoping that would drive back his exhaustion.

A shout cut through the night.

Braxtus stopped, squinting up the mountainside. *It's bound to be Leander up with too much wine.* Still, he waited a moment.

Light beamed near the arena, powerful and golden, then faded away.

What on Gaia was that?

Another shout, sounding surprised and angry. More golden light flared to life, then disappeared.

Braxtus hesitated, unsure whether to leave his post. *Does Diantha see this?* He looked up at the closest tower. The head deity on guard duty was leaning out to get a better look.

Braxtus finally made sense of the shouting as it rose in pitch and volume. *"Backup!* Help!"

His heart leapt to his throat.

"Guards, go!" Diantha yelled to the scattered gods below her. Braxtus unsheathed his sword and took off running, shield thudding against his back. To either side of him, other guards along the boundary rushed to join.

Light flared up again, so bright it left spots behind in his vision as he ran, circling the arena to get to the far side. The shouting cut short, and he pumped his legs faster.

Only to grind to a halt, his heart stopping.

Before him, uncurling from the ground, were dozens of monstrous beasts.

Light twisted around their legs, wings, snouts, showing him their deadly features with painstaking detail before fading as the creatures solidified, one by one. A few loose cards scattered along the ground between the beasts, glimmering with gold.

Someone had created monsters from the Decks of Fates.

The creature closest to him lurched to its feet, and Braxtus stumbled back a step as all three heads towered above him, eyes coating its entire body.

Heads of Cerberus, horns of a satyr, eyes of Argus. He listed the characteristics in his head, dumbfounded.

Four other guards ran around the side of the arena to join Braxtus. "Kronos!" one of them cursed.

The three-headed dog before them snarled, wheeling their way, and other solidifying beasts looked up. Braxtus leveled his sword, adrenaline coursing through his body as he flicked his eyes between each of them. A ghostlike drakon, an enormous silver fox, and a few others launched themselves toward the summit. A half-woman, half-snake with crab arms slid down toward the boundary line.

"Cut that thing off!" Diantha ran up, shouting at two of the guards. "Don't let it cross the boundary line! Unnamed, raise the alarm!" And with that, Diantha threw herself at the hundred-eyed canine. Two other guards rushed to Diantha's aid, the others sprinting for the snake woman.

Raise the alarm. Braxtus took off toward the arena entrance, weaving between the snarling monsters. A centaur with a scorpion tail reeled into his path, eyes rolling, but Braxtus drove his sword into its leg. It howled, and he yanked his weapon free, trying to push onward, but the centaur swung at him. Braxtus leapt to the side, but his foot caught on something heavy, and he went sprawling. He rolled and raised his sword in defense, but another charged in to engage the beast.

He caught sight of what he'd tripped over—a young god with

dark hair. His heart lurched. Grabbing the god's shoulder, he flipped him over, only to see his glazed, dead eyes. It was Endymion, one of the most recent gods to gain immortality. A short dagger was buried in his chest, and ichor pooled beneath him.

Braxtus let go and staggered to his feet. Though they never aged, no Immortal was invulnerable. Only the Twelve Olympians were truly unable to die. Still, Braxtus had never seen a dead Immortal before.

It was one thing if the Olympians engaged these beasts, but if others, especially the Unnamed, had to face them . . . He snapped his gaze to the Common Temples. Disfigured beasts careened and galloped up the mountain, getting closer to the most vulnerable of the gods and goddesses.

"*Unnamed!*" Diantha bellowed as she fought.

Braxtus sheathed his sword and threw himself back into action, sprinting for the archway. This time, when a riled, deformed manticore lunged for him, he called on his element and shoved his hands out in front of him. Fire raced to his fingertips, shooting toward the creature, who screeched and reeled away.

Braxtus snatched the horn from the wall and put it to his lips, blowing three short blasts. The volume of the horn had been magnified by someone's gift, and the powerful tone thrummed through the air, sure to be heard much farther up the mountain.

Monsters screamed and stamped at the noise. A few scattered guards tried desperately to hold them at bay. One of the smaller, uglier beasts leapt at a guard, and the god turned to stone under its gaze.

Kronos! Braxtus kept the horn fisted in his hand as he tore up the path toward the Common Temples. He blew the horn again as he ran, three more short blasts.

Another horn echoed in response, and torches lit around a few of the lower temples. A third blared, then a fourth as more people took up the warning. Braxtus began to see gods and goddesses rushing out of their respective temples, responding to the call to congregate at the summit.

A harpy-like creature swooped overhead, landing on the roof of the Upper Common Temple. Someone screamed as its powerful barbed tail swung through the roof, sending granite and slate flying.

Bleary-eyed young gods and goddesses stumbled through the doors. They gaped and pointed at the enormous fox that tore through Persephone's flower fields, shrieking at the dark shadows of other beasts. A few of the older Unnamed pulled out weapons, herding the others up the path. Braxtus let out a breath of relief as he saw Demitri among them, taking charge. The son of Ares might be at the bottom of his friends list, but he was more than handy in a fight.

Braxtus skidded to a stop. "Is everyone out?" he shouted to Demitri.

"I think so!" Demitri called back, eyes sweeping over the group as he lifted a young boy into his arms.

"Where's Iyana?" Braxtus looked through the faces for her, and Demitri groaned.

"She was with me a minute ago. I grabbed her from her room—"

Braxtus turned and looked along the path, scanning frantically. His eyes locked onto a spill of white-blonde hair, a small, determined figure racing not up the path, but *down* it.

He threw his hands up. "Where are you going?" he said aloud. Without bothering to mention Iyana's location to her boyfriend, Braxtus charged back down the mountain, leaving Demitri to take care of the other Unnamed.

Iyana was fast, but Braxtus was faster. He gained on her until he got close enough to catch her attention. "Iyana!"

She paused, glancing back over her shoulder. "Braxtus?"

He caught up to her. "What are you doing? It's not pretty down there."

A roar split the air so loudly that the ground trembled. Hermes came sweeping down the mountain in his winged shoes, the first of the Olympians to engage the beasts.

"Galene is in the infirmary!" Iyana said. "I think the healers left her behind!"

"What? Why?"

"I saw them evacuate. Galene wasn't with them, and she isn't even supposed to be *walking* alone." Without waiting for his response, she raced along the path, taking the fork that led to the infirmary.

Braxtus pounded after her. "I'm coming with you!"

They burst into the infirmary, and Iyana made a beeline for the right wing, throwing open one of the doors. The bed was unmade, and a few linens stained with ichor had been laid on a table, but other than that the room was empty.

Braxtus sensed Iyana's mounting panic and caught her elbow. "This just means she headed up the mountain on her own. She'll be fine. She's around here somewhere."

Iyana nodded, her eyes flicking down to the hand on her arm.

He flushed and dropped it. Casual contact between them still came naturally to him. It stung that he'd have to work on that. "Come on, we have to get to Zeus's temple. It's dangerous out there."

"What happened?" she asked as he led the way from the infirmary. "I saw a few of the creatures, but—"

"Someone tampered with the Decks of Fates," he explained. "There are dozens of them, and they all have to be killed to disappear."

"Who? *Why?*"

"Don't ask me, all I saw was—"

A harsh squeal was the only warning they had before something dark and hulking erupted onto the path before them. Iyana let out a surprised shriek, and it locked its tiny eyes on them. Vampiric teeth curved around its snout. *Body of a Calydonian Boar, fangs of a mormolykeia* . . .

It pounded the ground once with its hoof, then charged them, head lowered.

"Look out!" Iyana ran into him, shoving him aside, and it stormed past. She reached for the spikes on her back as it spun around on nimble feet. Hefting one, she threw it at the beast, but it skittered off its thick hide. She cursed colorfully, wind swirling her hair.

Braxtus swung his shield from his back and unsheathed his sword. "Just like old times, right?"

"The practice beasts were never this size!"

"Maybe not, but we had our fair share of fun."

Under any other circumstance, he was sure he would have gotten a laugh from her, but she just palmed another throwing spike, going shoulder to shoulder with him.

The creature raged toward them. Braxtus and Iyana both waited, then sprang to each side at the last second, swinging their weapons at the creature. Braxtus put all his strength into the stroke, but his sword bounced away. The boar reared and spun toward Iyana, but a gust of wind swept her out of reach. She started running.

"Braxtus!" she shouted over her shoulder. "I think this boar has the hide of a Nemean Lion!"

"Maybe we can just outrun it!" he yelled back, running after her.

A magnified voice boomed across Olympus. "The boundary is on lockdown to prevent the beasts from escaping to the humans. Those fighting, search for the goddess responsible: Galene Unnamed, Daughter of Poseidon."

Braxtus's stomach lurched, and he stumbled to a halt.

Iyana seized his arm, crystal-blue eyes wide in horror.

Rhythmic pounding rang on the path. He turned, breaking her grip as the boar rushed them.

Leaping in front of her, he raised his shield. It crashed into the boar's jaw, and both he and the monster staggered. Braxtus went down, rolling to keep his shield above him as the hooves descended, pounding into the metal.

He cried out as the edge of the shield drove into his stomach, cutting through skin, crushing him. Pain exploded through his torso.

"Braxtus!"

Through streaming eyes he watched as Iyana charged the monster, slashing at its face. It squealed and backed up, then turned and fled.

"Help!" A strong wind whipped to life around them as Iyana summoned it, snatching her voice to carry it away. "Braxtus Unnamed needs help! We're by the infirmary!"

He groaned, gritting his teeth against the brutal pain, but even as Iyana dropped to her knees beside him, darkness spotted his vision.

6
KOSTAS

Plumes of smoke rose toward the roiling red storm clouds above. Below on the mountain, dozens of temples were already wrecked, a few utterly demolished, only pillars and rubble where proud edifices had been.

Kostas stood between the temples of Demeter and Hermes at the top of Mount Olympus, bow at the ready for any monsters that got past the barrier of fighters. Auras of black fear and red anger clung to both the Immortals and Unnamed clustered in the shadow of Zeus's massive temple. Even a few dryads, the tree spirits of Olympus, had joined the place of sanctuary, ghostly green forms wailing as they huddled together.

The creature two temples below reared its horned head, fire erupting from its maw, the force and heat incinerating leaves in the grove.

Zeus dropped from the sky before Kostas, a frighteningly calm expression on his face. The air cracked with electricity as he raised his arms, then pointed at the beast.

Boom! Lightning splintered from the sky, blinding Kostas for an instant as it struck. When the spots faded from his vision, all that was left of the creature were a few dusty trails of light. Zeus closed his eyes and raised his arms to call for more.

The ground shook, and Kostas staggered, turning to watch as Poseidon ripped a hole in the mountain just beyond Aphrodite's temple. A snarling three-headed dog with countless eyes tried to scramble free of the chasm, but plummeted, swallowed by the earth as Poseidon wrenched the ground together again.

A shadow passed overhead, and Kostas pulled back on his bowstring, following it before letting the arrow fly.

It pierced a wing of a scaly pegasus, which careened in the air, screeching. Kostas's keen eyes made out the dark figure of his father, catching up to it on winged sandals. Bringing his golden sword down, Hermes skewered the creature. The pegasus burst into light, disappearing, and Hermes nodded once at his son in appreciation. Kostas saluted back with his bow, and his father returned to the hunt.

Kostas looked around again. Though the destruction was horrible, almost all the creatures had been killed. Ares seemed to be taking care of one of the last, tearing into the creature with an ax.

A beam of light appeared, like a comet streaking at him. He snapped his gaze toward it, and a moment later, a beefy Olympian with long, golden curls came into view on a chariot pulled by two pegasi. Apollo, God of the Sun, Prophecy, and Healing, was spattered in gore, with the most intense red aura of anyone Kostas had seen tonight. He was livid.

A moment later, Kostas recognized the two Unnamed who sat next to him. Shouldering his bow, Kostas ran to help as they landed on the singed grass before Zeus's temple.

"Braxtus," he groaned. His best friend was slumped against Iyana, unconscious and soaked in ichor. Iyana's aura swirled gray in worry, and Apollo stood in the chariot, snapping for healers to tend to his son. They broke free of the cluster of gods and hurried over, Demitri on their heels.

Kostas helped them lift Braxtus from the chariot, and they nodded their gratitude, staggering off under his weight through the open doors of Zeus's temple, which had been turned into a temporary infirmary. Demitri gave Iyana his hand to help her down, then pulled her into a hug, his aura showing mixed anxiety and irritation.

"Last one, Apollo!" the goddess Artemis called to him from her own chariot, pointing at a massive silver fox that leapt over a small temple and streaked for the Eastern boundary line. Apollo snapped his reins and took off after his twin sister.

"Continue the search for Galene Unnamed!" Athena shouted to all within earshot.

Galene. He would have been furious, too, after a Trial like hers, but this? From what he knew of her, the destruction around him seemed far from her character. *But if the Olympians are so sure, they must have proof.*

A few minor gods and goddesses broke free of the group at the summit to join the search, moving down the Southern slope in the direction of the arena.

He snorted. If Galene truly was guilty, she would have fled the scene of the crime. He turned his back to the search parties and rounded Zeus's temple, stopping to look down the Northern slope. Though still cast with a red hue, there was much less clamor and destruction on this side.

Crossing his arms, he narrowed his eyes, searching for an aura that might not match the fear and anger of the others around him. A few long minutes later, he caught sight of the glow of dark green. Confusion. He almost passed over it—it hadn't been an uncommon hue that night—but he paused, looking back. The color was hardly tinged with fear at all, and certainly not anger.

A moment later, with the crunch of staggering footsteps hurrying up gravel, he could make out the owner's face—sea-green eyes and a smattering of freckles across her cheeks.

Got you.

He waited in silence as Galene drew closer to him, limping toward Zeus's temple. She didn't seem to notice him waiting in the shadows until Kostas rushed forward and seized her arm.

"Hey! What are you doing?" she protested, eyes widening.

"Come with me." He dragged her forward. She let out a groan, clasping her side, and he slowed their pace a little.

"Kostas?" she questioned. "Let go of me. What's happening?"

Kostas didn't answer as he pulled her back around the side of Zeus's temple. She resisted him, but the green hue around her intensified as she took in the destruction.

"I found Galene Unnamed," he said loudly.

The few around him who heard repeated the call.

"What is going on?" Galene's tone suddenly had an edge of panic in it, orange flaring in her aura. "Kostas, tell me what's happening!"

"You tell me." He raised his eyebrows at her. "Apparently, you're responsible for this."

She blanched, jaw dropping, and uneasiness settled into his gut. Her aura bloomed with bright green—genuine shock. Something wasn't right.

The Twelve Olympians swarmed, running up or landing from the sky with eyes full of fire.

Kostas pushed her into their midst, and she turned around, stunned as they formed a circle around her.

7
GALENE

Twelve pairs of eyes bored into her, each Olympian emanating their strange, ethereal light. Behind them, silhouettes of the crowd pressed in. Embers danced into the night from the burning land and temples behind them, reinforcing the nightmare.

Through the smoky darkness, she found her father's eyes. His wild beard did nothing to hide his disappointment and disbelief. Turning slowly, she searched for one among the Olympians who hadn't already condemned her for the chaos she could see. Her courage shrank with every grim face.

"How *dare* you?" Aphrodite, Goddess of Love and Beauty, spoke first, face screwed up in fury.

"We should have known," Hephaestus grunted. "It runs in the blood."

Rage spiked through her fear and confusion.

"Galene Unnamed." She tried not to flinch at the anger behind Zeus's voice. "The lives lost, the shrines, temples, and grounds you have destroyed, all call out for justice. We condemn you for your crimes."

"I—" Her throat closed up.

"Strike her down now!" Ares bellowed. The God of Bloodlust and War sent a jolt of fear through Galene. His brown eyes were tinted dangerously red. Those eyes were famous for shifting to the color of blood when the Olympian lost control.

"No, let's hear what she has to say for herself!" Athena snapped. Despite her short stature, the Olympians fell silent at the Goddess of Wisdom's demand.

Galene found her voice. "What do you think I've done?"

Ares snarled, a couple of others muttered. Apollo stepped forward. "I'll lay it out," he said. "After your humiliation in the arena today, you decided to retaliate. You broke into the arena vault to steal two Decks of Fates, then created the beasts that have wreaked havoc upon our sanctuary."

The ground seemed to become unsteady, and Galene staggered, the pain in her side a distant throb. *This can't be happening. This isn't real . . .*

"You murdered an Immortal and are responsible for the injury or death of several dozen other gods and goddesses," Athena added.

"Galene wouldn't have!" a familiar voice shouted, and Iyana pushed her way to the front of the crowd, firelight flickering on her pale face.

A crack of thunder and a threatening look from Iyana's father silenced her, but her wild blue eyes found Galene's.

"No," Galene choked out. "She's right, it wasn't me, I wouldn't—"

"We have proof," Hera snapped. She stood with a tall, gilded scepter in hand, chin held high, blue eyes blazing.

How can they have proof? Galene looked back to the king of the gods. Zeus waved a hand, and the God of Prophecy took a menacing step into the circle. Galene resisted the urge to retreat.

"Tonight I had a dream!" Apollo announced, sweeping a hand around him. A moving image glowed to life in the air, showing the scenes of destruction across Olympus. "A vision of Galene's crime."

The image blurred and changed. Galene watched a shadow running up a path she knew well—the trail that led from the Common Temples to the arena. The arena stood ahead, and a second building came into view.

43

The armory could easily pass as a squat temple sitting in the shadow of the arena. The bright fires surrounding the armory and arena cast a flickering light on the phantom, who wore a dark brown, almost black cloak, the cowl pulled low over their face.

The figure crouched, moving swiftly until they were between the two buildings. There they slowed, stalking past doorways until they reached the far end of the armory. A lone guard stood around the corner—Valence, the Immortal.

The figure lashed out with incredible speed, snaking a hand around the guard's mouth and slamming the butt of a dagger into his temple.

Galene almost choked. She knew that wave pattern on the hilt, the blue leather tied around it. The dagger was hers—the one she'd dropped in the arena today. The one she hadn't retrieved.

With only a muffled grunt, the guard fell.

The figure eased the body to the ground, searching for the keys at his belt. Once they had the keys, they retreated behind the building, moving to one of the doors, sliding a key into the lock, and listening for the click.

The door swung open, the figure leaping into the shadows.

The room was small and empty save for a narrow marble table. Four sets of golden cards were carefully stacked on top. The figure grabbed two decks, then ran back out the door, leaving it wide open behind them. Fleeing back toward the trees, the rogue began pulling cards free three at a time.

Barely glancing at each set they drew, the figure threw them into the night. The trios of cards tumbled through the air, then froze, glowing before setting off the growth of a misfigured combination of monsters.

Dozens of them began to rise from the ground.

"Hey!" someone shouted. The figure turned to look at Endymion, God of Youth, who watched with wide eyes. "What are you doing? Stop!" Endymion raced forward, trying to grab at some cards. He was too late; they had already started the creation of another beast. "Make it stop!"

The cloaked figure rushed Endymion, and the young god threw up his hands, trying to dodge. *"Backup! Help!"*

Galene's dagger flew from the figure's fingertips, burying up to the hilt just below the young god's heart. His face went white, and he tumbled to the ground. The figure took off running, then slowed in the outskirts of the Western Woods, turning to watch the havoc they had unleashed. A breath of wind caught the hood, and it fell back. The copper and gold highlights of her hair gleamed in the moonlight, and the smile that touched Galene's lips was small, cold, and satisfied.

Her mouth went dry. "No."

It was impossible, but there she was, every detail identical, from her sea-green eyes down to the last freckle. A furious outcry erupted from the spectators. "No, I didn't do it. It wasn't me!"

The image dissipated, leaving only a pit of panic and nausea in Galene's stomach. She searched for any show of support from the assembled gods beyond the ring of Olympians, and found Iyana again. Her eyes were wide, horrified almost, and a shock of disbelief went through Galene. *She thinks I'm guilty.*

But no, Iyana was shaking her head, her expression conveying her words. *Of course I know you wouldn't!* Relief sapped Galene's strength.

"Here's your proof, Galene." Zeus waved his hand, and a guard stepped forward, raising Galene's dagger, stained with ichor. "We found this still in Endymion's body. It matches the God of Prophecy's vision."

"I—" What could she say? She couldn't accuse Apollo of lying. Dread squeezed her heart as she doubted he even would. Galene's eyes burned. "I would never do such a thing."

"I am the God of Truth!" Apollo bore down on her.

"I just meant, there's been some kind of mistake—"

"Galene, where were you then, right before the beasts were set free?" Poseidon's words were pointed, but hesitant, as if he dreaded the answer.

With Chrysander at the border. She squeezed her eyes shut. If she told the truth, that she was fraternizing with the exiled, she would have no chance of mercy. "Walking through the olive groves below Demeter's temple. No one was with me. But I swear on the River Styx that I am innocent!"

There were a few shocked outcries at her statement.

Ares let out a biting laugh. "And now she takes a sacred oath in vain. Long after it would have been most honorable to confess, she still denies the proof we hold right before her arrogant eyes!"

"She is as cunning as any one of us." Hera studied her. "Her whole plan tonight wasn't rash. It was a well-thought-through and skillfully executed scheme to get back at her judges, simply because she wasn't mature enough to handle our verdict. It is only thanks to Apollo's vision that she has been caught." She glared around at the Olympians and the silenced crowd.

"She is the cause of destruction and death," said Aphrodite, tears gleaming in her bright blue eyes. She swept her strawberry blonde hair over a raised shoulder to shun Galene. "Your soul has no beauty in it, for causing so much loss." Galene nearly broke at the grief that flashed in those eyes.

Demeter jutted out her chin. "What should we do with her?"

Most of the Olympians began talking over each other. Galene could barely make out any one god's words, and their voices steadily got louder and angrier in unified hatred toward her.

"Death with death!"

"—labor rotation isn't *nearly*—"

"The *avyssos* was created for such situations . . ."

"Imprisonment . . ."

"Exile . . ."

"Like her brother . . ."

The crowd around them was just as loud. Cries of agreement overlapped until Galene's head rang with them.

"Silence!" Zeus called. He stared down each Olympian until they quieted, the crowd following suit. "We seem to have come to a mutual agreement. All in favor of Galene Unnamed to be exiled from Mount Olympus."

The world spun around her as the words slowly registered.

"No!" Iyana's voice rang clear through the night, followed by the sounds of a muffled fight.

At first there were no hands. Then they all went up at once. Ten of the twelve voters, her father and Hermes the only ones with their hands down.

Galene swayed. Poseidon covered his ashen face with a hand.

Zeus looked around. "It is decided. Galene Unnamed, Daughter of Poseidon and Amphitrite, you are hereby exiled from Mount Olympus. You are never to return. You are stripped of the potential to receive your official title and temple. You will never gain your immortality, never become a worshipped deity.

"Tomorrow at dawn you will be escorted to the boundary line. You may take your belongings—no horse, no other supplies. And I will remind you that interacting with humans is strictly forbidden. If you do, we will hear about it, and you will be hunted and killed. You better start saying your goodbyes."

8

IYANA

*E*xile.

Fear clutched Iyana's heart. She stared past Poseidon at her closest friend, somewhat aware of Demitri holding her back, speaking soothingly in her ear. Galene took an uncertain step away, clearly dismissed.

No no no no—

Roaring filled her ears, wind swept around her, and she twisted out of Demitri's grip.

"Wait!" She threw herself between the Olympians, into the circle. If possible, Galene's face went whiter. Iyana planted her feet, standing between her best friend and her father. She threw out her hands as though she could shield Galene from her sentence. "You can't!"

Twelve pairs of eyes burned into her. Iyana's wind whipped around her, stinging her cheeks and sending everyone's hair dancing.

"Do not presume to tell us what we can and can't do, Iyana Unnamed." Hera spoke, cold as ice. "Stand down."

Galene touched Iyana's arm. "There's nothing you can do. Don't get yourself into trouble, too—"

Iyana shook off Galene's hand, keeping her eyes on Zeus. "No. Hear me out, Father, I beg you."

A few of the Olympians hissed at her nerve. The King of

Olympus looked at her long and hard, then gestured with his hand. "Speak."

"Iyana—" Galene groaned.

"Let her speak for you, Galene." Kostas, God of Games, stepped into the circle, nodding in respect at the Twelve Olympians. He took Galene by the arm and pulled her back outside the ring. Galene didn't protest, but held Iyana's gaze as she left her alone in the midst of the Twelve.

Iyana tore her eyes away, swallowing. She had one chance.

"This is not in Galene's nature. She is not her brother, and if anyone ever bothered to get to know her they'd see that." She looked to Galene's father. "Poseidon, you know your daughter. She's had nothing but respect for you and the rest of the Twelve her whole life."

Poseidon did not answer.

"I'm her closest friend. I *know* she would never do this."

Ares snorted. "She had a bad day and snapped," he said, eyes still tinged red.

"That's right," Dionysus chimed in to agree with Ares. "One thing breaks and their whole mind turns upside down." The God of Wine and Madness spoke with a thoughtful, intrigued tone.

Iyana shook her head. "But Galene is clever, too! Why would she strike against Mount Olympus on the *very night* she failed her Immortality Trial? And why would she leave her dagger in a body? No one would do that unless they *wanted* to be caught—of *course* fingers would point to her!"

"Anger can impede anyone's logic." Athena cast a sideways glance at Ares.

Iyana turned to her. "Athena, Goddess of Wisdom—you honestly don't think it looks like a setup, do you?"

She pursed her lips. "I might have considered it, but Apollo's vision is solid evidence to the contrary."

"All right, then . . ." Iyana wheeled around to face Apollo, then immediately wanted to recoil from his powerful bearing. She clasped her hands in front of her to avoid flinching. "Apollo, God of the Sun . . . if I may . . ." His thunderous expression conveyed *no you may not*, but she plunged onward. "Every gift is fallible, is it not? Couldn't it be possible that your vision was incorrect?"

"My gift has never failed me," Apollo growled. "And the night's events confirm it."

"But we only saw Galene's face once in your vision. Couldn't that part alone have been wrong?"

Athena cut in again. "It is possible, perhaps, but *very* remotely so. Putting an innocent face in place of the guilty is an incredibly specific way Apollo's gift would fail him."

"This is pointless. You cannot disprove Apollo's vision." Hera's threatening expression sent chills up Iyana's arms. She had a seething hatred for all of Zeus's children birthed to a different mother. As Iyana was currently the only one on Olympus under that criteria, Hera had always seemed to channel all of her animosity toward her.

"But . . . but Galene said she was walking through the olive groves." Iyana did her best not to sound like a whining child. "We can search for witnesses among the dryads and naiads. One of them may be able to confirm Galene's location at the time of the attack."

"Most of the dryads and naiads have fled the destruction," Artemis said. "They are in poor condition, and no one should waste time hunting them down and questioning them while they recover."

"Not even for the sake of an innocent goddess's future?" Iyana demanded.

"Now is not the time," Hera said.

"Then we *wait!* Wait for your judgment until you can search for confirmation of Galene's story!"

"We have no need to question the proof that has already been brought before us!" Hera gestured to Apollo. "Stop your mindless arguing, Iyana Unnamed. You're wasting our time."

"I have proposed a valid compromise!" Iyana fired back, curling her hands into fists. "Hate me all you want, Queen Hera, but do not dismiss what I'm saying because of it."

Zeus raised a hand, and Hera closed her mouth, eyes blazing. "She's right, Iyana," he said, voice soft. "Your loyalty is admirable, but we can't ignore Apollo's vision. Is there any last thing you wish to say?"

Iyana looked around but saw no sympathy. *They've already made up their minds. Nothing I say will change that.*

"Galene has her whole life ahead of her." Her voice trembled. "You're taking *everything* from her. Her home, her honor—"

"We are not taking her life, Iyana," Artemis pointed out.

"But you *are*. You're taking away her future immortality." Iyana's vision blurred with tears, but she was beyond caring. "She will die."

"She failed her Trial anyway."

Hera's words put a searing knife in Iyana's chest. The wind around her fell still. "So she's worthless now? Will I be worthless, too, in a few months, when you set it up so I have to defeat Typhon himself?"

Murmurs ran around the circle of the Olympians.

"Enough!" Hera struck the ground with her scepter, and it blazed with a brief light. "You do not speak to an Olympian like that!"

But hot fury and hurt raged in Iyana's heart, forcing her mouth open again. "I think you *want* Galene gone so she's no longer a threat to you."

"My daughter, you're shaming yourself," Zeus said. "Your anger has blinded you, just as Galene's anger blinded her. You will leave now."

A gentle breeze returned as she made a decision. "Yes, Father. But when I leave I will not come back. I'm going with Galene."

The Olympians stared at her in shock. There was a long moment of silence.

"You would exile yourself?" Aphrodite asked incredulously. "You love her that much?"

She didn't answer.

"You know the law, Iyana," Zeus said. "If you leave Mount Olympus before your Trial, you, too, will be stripped of your potential to be a deity, and you may never return."

The tears finally tumbled to her cheeks as she looked her father in the eye. "So be it."

She turned and pushed her way back out of the circle.

The surrounding crowd burst into conversation.

". . . exiling *herself*—?"

". . . still can't believe . . ."

"How could she—"

"Did you see—"

An Olympian shouted for order, and people moved forward to be assigned a cleanup shift.

Someone grabbed Iyana by the shoulders, and Iyana had to blink away more tears before she could make out Galene's face in the darkness.

"No." There was a brightness in her sea-green eyes. "I won't let you."

Iyana gripped her arms back. "I'm not staying here, Galene."

"Do you think I could live knowing that you cast yourself out because of me? You will regret it the moment you step foot across that border. This is your home." Iyana started to speak, but Galene cut her off. "What about your friends? What about Braxtus?"

A swell of emotion rose in her, but she shook her head. She couldn't be close with him anymore anyway. It was probably for the best.

Galene ground her teeth. "What about Demitri?"

Her breath caught in her throat as she saw Demitri standing off to the side with Kostas, watching the exchange with hooded eyes.

Sensing a victory, Galene grabbed Iyana's wrist and started dragging her toward the Twelve Olympians, now breaking apart. "You're going to go apologize, tell them you will accept their chastisement, and *stay*!"

"No!" Iyana planted her feet, leaning back. "I'm not letting you go out there alone."

Galene pulled harder and winced. She was still weak from her injuries. "Someone help me!" she snapped at Demitri and Kostas.

Iyana shot them the sharpest look she could muster. "Galene, you can't stop me. You can't change my mind. I'm coming with you whether you like it or not. We're in this together now."

Galene dropped Iyana's wrist and turned to face her. Iyana saw the tears rising in her eyes. "How could you do this, Iyana?"

"Because I love you, and *someone* needed to stand up for you."

"This isn't the way to do that. Stay, try to prove my innocence. When you earn your immortality you can come visit me on your trips to the humans."

Iyana shook her head, desperate to make her understand. "This goes beyond missing you, Galene. This is about making a statement. It's about being downtrodden and unfairly judged and tested and everything Demitri was talking about. I don't fully understand it myself, but I know that I have to go with you."

Balling her fists, Galene pressed them to her eyes, as though trying to convince herself this wasn't real. Iyana stepped forward and wrapped her arms around her. "It's okay. This is my choice, Galene. Neither of us will regret it, I promise."

Galene couldn't seem to form any more words over the sobs that shook her body.

Four guards approached and surrounded them. Iyana looked

up, and one of them stepped forward to take Galene's arm. Even through her tears, Galene's jaw hardened.

"We're to escort you to the Upper Common Temple to gather your supplies," he said, ignoring Iyana.

"I'll come to get my things soon, too," Iyana whispered.

Galene gave a nod, tears flowing down her face as she let them take her away.

Demitri was in front of Iyana in an instant. "What has gotten into you tonight?" He took her face and tipped it to make her look directly at him. His piercing eyes swam with anger and hurt.

"I . . ." She quavered. "I thought you of all people would understand why I chose this."

An expression of disbelief crossed his face. "Is it *my* fault you've made such a rash decision?" When she didn't respond, he let go of her. "What on Gaia is going through your head? Just earlier tonight you agreed with Galene that Chrysander was wrong and crazy."

"I said Chrysander's *solution* is wrong and crazy," Iyana corrected. "I'm not leaving to gather the exiled and revolt. But after this, I have to make a stand."

Demitri groaned, looking skyward.

"Don't you think this is unjust?" Iyana challenged. "Don't you think Galene is innocent? She defended the Olympians today when we talked to her!"

He paused. "Yes," he admitted. "It wouldn't surprise me in the slightest if they still felt threatened by her. Apollo could have made up that vision to get her exiled."

"If you're right, this further proves your points against them. I have to go."

"But what about me?" Demitri gestured to himself. "I'll have been left behind by my best friend *and* my love."

Iyana buried her face in her hands. A moment later, his arms wrapped around her, and he lowered his lips to her ear. "Stay with me."

"You won't change my mind." Iyana didn't surface as she spoke, her voice coming out muffled. "You'll just make the heartache worse."

"Iyana, it's dangerous out there. You could get hurt." He ran his fingers through her long hair, his breath brushing her cheek and neck as he spoke. "You belong here, where I can protect you."

She looked up, and he drew her face to his, lips coming down on hers. His kiss was fervent, protective. She kissed him back, gripping the fabric of his tunic, trying not to think, trying not to cry.

He pulled away, his nose still touching hers. "Please, Iyana."

"Come with me," she whispered.

He went as still as stone. "What?"

"*Come with me*. If enough of us leave, that's a powerful statement. The Olympians won't be able to keep ignoring us."

Demitri pushed away from her, turning his back and running his hands through his hair.

"You know how much you're asking of me, right?"

"I know," Iyana murmured. "I . . . I don't mean to be selfish. But it sounded like you were considering a move like this anyway."

"Not with any serious thought." He turned back around, a whirl of thoughts and emotions in his blue eyes that pinned her in place. "Not *now*, anyway."

"What were you waiting for?" she probed. "Something like this?"

He stared at her for a long moment.

"Kronos," he finally cursed. "I guess I'm coming."

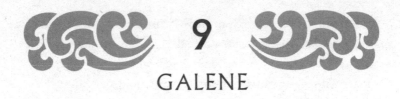

9

GALENE

Not many of Galene's possessions had survived the attack on the Upper Common Temple, but that didn't matter. The satchel across her back had no room for unnecessary items.

After she'd gathered her things, she'd been escorted back to the infirmary, where Apollo himself expedited her healing. The look on his face had left nothing to the imagination—she was the last person he wanted to heal. If it wasn't protocol to treat the exiled before sending them away, she knew he would have been more than happy to leave her to suffer her wound for months in exile. It still ached, and he'd left her with a scar, but at least she had full range of motion again.

With puffy eyes and both emotional and physical exhaustion, Galene, Iyana, and Demitri were escorted to the boundary line. Walking as slowly as she could, Galene took in every detail, imprinting the beauty of home in her memory. Despite the wreckage, it was stunning. Orchards and fields lay still, like artwork. The sunrise sent light shimmering off temples and lakes.

She would never see it again.

There was only a small group at the Southern boundary, gathered on the main road to say a proper goodbye. Surrounding the group were a handful of gods on guard duty, watching to make sure everything went smoothly. Zeus, Poseidon, and Aphrodite were the only Olympians there. One parent each. Kostas, to Galene's surprise, had come as well.

Demitri went to his mother, who threw her arms around him. Galene knew he was coming for Iyana, but still, she couldn't completely wrestle away her wish he wasn't.

Iyana paused as Kostas approached.

"Braxtus would kill me if I didn't come and say goodbye for him," he said.

Iyana's lips trembled, and she pressed them together. "I wish I could have told him goodbye in person. Tell him . . . tell him I'm sorry."

Kostas nodded slowly, dark curls shifting at the movement. He flicked his onyx eyes toward Galene.

She expected his gaze to be accusing, but it was more curious than anything. She returned his quizzical gaze for a moment, then looked away, feeling her cheeks warm. She didn't know what to think of the mysterious god. He'd been the one to throw her in the midst of the Olympians, but also the one who pulled her out so Iyana could stand up for her.

Not that it matters. I'll likely never see him again.

"Daughter."

It took effort to lift her eyes to Poseidon as he stopped in front of her. "Thank you for coming."

He nodded, scratching his beard. "I do not know what happened last night, Galene, but whether or not you are guilty . . ." Galene didn't even try to protest her innocence another time. ". . . you are my child, and you have, in the past, made your mother and I very proud. We hoped for great things from you." He cleared his throat, then held out his hand. On his palm lay a small white cone shell. "A gift for you and your companions. A boon from the oceans to be used in your time of need."

Shock bloomed in her chest. She swallowed it and bowed in

gratitude, then took the unassuming shell. An ocean boon could manifest itself in many different ways. She didn't have any idea of how it could be useful to them, but she knew it was the best gift her father could give. She hadn't even expected him to be here.

"Thank you, Father."

"And," he added hesitantly, his voice audibly softer, "if you should ever enter one of my temples, I will hear you."

Hot tears pricked Galene's eyes. *How did it come to this? Will I even be welcome in the sea?* But again, she bowed. "Thank you." It came out barely over a whisper.

Iyana was speaking with her father now, Kostas walking back up the road. Demitri was still being fussed over by his mother, who had tears sparkling in her blue eyes. She seemed to be checking his weapons and satchel, her son patiently readjusting everything she touched.

They had elected to wear their armor rather than carry it—breastplates, pteruge skirts over their tunics, arm and leg guards. Demitri had a javelin and staff over his back—the staff, she knew, split into twin swords. At his belt hung a hunting knife, and she knew he had all manner of supplies in that bag of his. Iyana also had her weapons strapped across her back—a quiver of throwing spikes she was mastering. Galene wore her scimitar and knives, though she had left behind the one they found in Endymion's body.

Shaking the image from her head, she moved up to the border. Gods and goddesses carefully steered out of her way, and she made sure not to meet anyone's gaze. Instead, Galene looked once more back up the mountain. Smoke still rose in places, but Galene tried to ignore it, focusing on the trees, lakes, and gardens, on the rivers and waterfalls that tumbled from lush, green ridges.

Iyana stepped to her side, taking Galene's hand in her own. The warmth and security of that grip sent a much-needed wave of comfort through her. Demitri took Iyana's other hand.

I'm the reason they're leaving, Galene thought with a heartthrob, *and they're more prepared for this than I am.* But then, she couldn't help feel a touch of jealousy that they got to choose this fate for themselves.

The sun broke the horizon line, spilling more light over the mountain. "It's time." The King of Olympus waved a hand.

Beyond the shimmering barrier lay the clear, faraway world.

The ring of guards began to close in.

Squeezing her hand, Iyana guided her around to face the new road ahead. To either side of the path, scattered rocks gave way to trees. As tears leaked onto her cheeks, Galene took a steadying breath.

This injustice will not stand with the Fates. The scales will balance out in the end.

"Galene?" Iyana asked. The guards moved closer.

She took a step forward between the main two towers.

The air rippled as they passed through the magical barrier. The sound of marching guards and final farewells became muted, like the conversations Galene had with Chrysander.

Galene kept a tight hold of Iyana's hand, watching the expression on her best friend's face. There was a shadow there, but Iyana gave her a tight-lipped smile as they walked away from their home.

When they were far enough away from the border to be safely out of earshot, Iyana asked, "So . . . what's our heading?"

Galene knew of one person who would be happy to see them, though part of her hesitated to suggest it. "How would you feel about finding my brother?"

A smile grew on Demitri's face. He looked to Iyana, whose eyebrows furrowed.

"You want to see Chrysander? Galene . . . he . . ."

"I know" Galene put up her hands—"but he's my family and the only connection we have out here now. We don't have to get involved with whatever he's up to." Galene swallowed as she remembered his words from the night before. "We probably *shouldn't* stay long. But it would give us time to breathe, to get our bearings."

Iyana's mouth twisted in concern. "How would we even find him?"

Galene steeled herself. "I know where he is."

Two sets of eyes snapped to hers.

"How?" Demitri asked. "Did he tell you where he was going? It's been a long time, I wouldn't be sure that—"

"He told me yesterday."

Iyana gaped. "Excuse me?"

"He was here?" Demitri's eyebrows shot up.

Galene focused on the road beneath her feet. "I wasn't walking through the olive groves when the beasts were created, I was meeting with Chrysander at the border."

Iyana halted. "You *what?* Galene!" She grabbed Galene's arm and spun her around. "Why didn't you tell the Olympians? You had a witness to your innocence!"

She shook her head. "Do you really think telling them about Chrysander would help my case? It would have made it worse. He was nearly exiled for conspiring against the Olympians before he exiled *himself*. They probably would have claimed he helped me do it."

Her best friend bit her lip so hard it turned white.

Demitri shook his head. "Apollo's vision *was* wrong."

Galene's stomach turned. Every time she thought of it, seeing her dagger killing Endymion, seeing her face as the murderer, she wanted to be sick.

"It was your dagger, though," Demitri mused. "Someone wanted them to believe it was you." He refocused on Galene. "So where is Chrysander?"

That's the other thing . . . Galene tried not to wince. "The Land of the Taraxippi."

Iyana looked like she might faint. "Taraxippi?"

Galene hurried on. "He says they've claimed territory there and they're safe. If we can find him, we'll be just fine."

"*If,*" Iyana repeated.

Galene didn't know what else to say, so she said nothing, waiting for them to make their decision.

Demitri took Iyana's hand. "I would love to see him again. We're all in the same boat now, right?"

"But taraxippi . . ." Iyana stopped herself, meeting Galene's eyes. She still looked like she wanted to argue, but her eyes moved between the two of them. "All right. Fine." She squeezed Demitri's arm. "Just for a visit."

THEY SOON TURNED from the main road of the gods, picking their way down the south side of the mountain, Galene guiding them to curve east.

"Why can't we just follow the trails?" Demitri complained, whacking a tree branch out of his way.

"We could," Galene replied, "but I don't particularly want to spend an extra two days on unnecessary travel."

"But it would be easier."

"Horses would be easier," she mumbled, "but we don't have those, do we? You know what else would be really nice? Not getting exiled in the first place."

No one made any more comments for the next few hours.

From the mountainside, the view of the Aegean Sea was stunning. Galene only wished she was in the mood to enjoy it. *I'll see it from the shore,* she promised herself. *And then I'll travel around the whole Mediterranean.* She could build her own house on the coast somewhere, Iyana and Demitri nearby. *Maybe with Chrysander.*

Chrysander.

She sighed. No matter how happy she was at the chance to get their relationship back, she couldn't shake the sinking feeling that accompanied it. What was he up to? Whatever it was, he would try to rope her into it. Would there even be a chance to go back to how things were between them? Despite being exiled, she had to stay out of trouble.

They reached the base of the mountain late that afternoon and decided to set up camp in the shelter of the foothills. Demitri helped find food for the night. Galene searched for water and Iyana set up the fire. They went to sleep as soon as the sun set, still not speaking about the morning's events or their destination.

The next day they crossed the foothills of Olympus, walking until they reached a plain stretching out to the sea. In the distance, the grasses turned yellow—a clear indicator of where the Land of the Taraxippi began.

They stood, staring out across the open field.

"Are you sure we'll have enough daylight to travel through the Land of the Taraxippi tomorrow?" Demitri asked. "If night falls before we find Chrysander we'll be in trouble. That's when the taraxippi will be at their strongest."

Iyana shuddered, and Galene judged the distance. "If we push on until dark, we should be close enough to the boundary when we make camp. We can get up and enter taraxippi territory in the light of dawn to give us the most time to find him."

"All right, then." Demitri nodded. "Let's get going."

Iyana still looked unsettled at the haunted land in the distance, but nodded as well, and they set out across the grasslands.

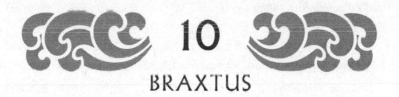

10

BRAXTUS

Braxtus rolled on the cot to catch the eye of a passing healer, and pain shot through his middle. He groaned at the ache, then again at being ignored for the fifth time. He let his head fall back onto the pillow to stare up at the vaulted ceiling. For whatever reason, he wasn't in the infirmary but in an open chamber of Zeus's temple, easily recognizable by the storm-blue and gold trimming.

There were several rows of wounded in this room, and as far as Braxtus could tell, he was in the best condition of all of them. The god a few cots to his left had multiple healers attending to a large burn up his arm and neck, and there was a goddess close by who was frozen, stiff as a board, in a fighting stance. *Paralyzed. Not many cures for that.*

There were no windows to see outside, which only made him more anxious for news. *Maybe I'll just . . . go.* He sat up gingerly, pulling up his tunic to examine his stomach.

A deep gold bruise bloomed under his skin from his own shield driving into his gut, but the wound had sealed up nicely under the healers' care.

He let his tunic fall and cautiously swung his legs over the side.

"Lie down, they haven't released you yet."

Braxtus looked up to see his best friend approaching.

"Kostas!" He half-stood, then fell back on the bed. "I've been awake for over an hour, and no one has told me *anything*! What happened? Is Olympus okay? Was Galene actually responsible for creating the beasts?"

Kostas dragged a stool over to the cot with his foot, then sat on it heavily. "You might want to sit back."

Braxtus obeyed, shoving the pillow behind his back and gesturing for Kostas to speak.

As Kostas explained finding Galene, her impromptu, vicious trial, and Apollo's vision, Braxtus's heart sank. He was unsurprised but sickened by her sentence of exile.

"Wow." Braxtus shook his head. "That's insane. I can't believe Galene would do that."

Kostas paused. "I'm not so sure she did. Her emotions didn't line up with the story the Olympians told. She was too sincere in her plea of innocence."

"What, do you think my father's vision was wrong?"

Kostas furrowed his brow. "I'm not sure, but something strange happened. Between her stacked Trial and this, someone seems to be out to get her."

Braxtus watched him, curious. As God of Games, there wasn't much Kostas was unsure about. This mystery was going to drive his friend crazy.

And Iyana. She was sure to be going ballistic.

"Where's Iyana?" he asked. "She can't be taking this well."

Kostas jerked back to the present. He looked at Braxtus warily, sympathetically. "Well . . . that's the other part."

Braxtus's heart stopped. He leaned forward. "What other part?"

"Iyana defended Galene. She fought against the Olympians on her behalf. When they didn't change their minds, she got angry. She decided to exile herself with Galene."

"She *what*?"

Kostas hurried on. "And Demitri agreed to go, too. As a statement, and to be with Iyana. They left two days ago at dawn."

He fell back in shock. *She's gone. Forever.* He tried to picture it—her shouting at the Olympians, her stepping over the boundary line, it sealing behind her. His mind reeled, but then hurt crept into his shock. This was the second time she'd forgone an explanation, a goodbye. The second time she'd blindsided him and left him behind. The first had been for another god, but this . . .

He clenched his jaw and blinked hard against sudden tears.

"I'm sorry." Kostas reached out and clasped Braxtus's hand. "I know you two were close."

"Were." Braxtus couldn't keep the bitterness from his voice. "We haven't been nearly as close since Demitri came into her life. She didn't even wait to leave Olympus until she could say goodbye."

"Her decision was to leave with Galene, and Galene was forced to go the very next morning." Kostas kept his voice gentle. "She *wanted* to say goodbye to you in person, but she couldn't. She told me to tell you she's sorry."

Braxtus covered his face with a hand. "Kronos. This is so messed up."

"I saw her off. I told her you would have wanted to be there."

"Thank you." He rubbed his eyes. "I don't even know where she's going. I'll probably never see her again. Even after my Trial how could I find her?" He had a sudden thought and jerked his head up. "Kostas, your mother. Goddess of Messages. We could look for Iyana in her Rainbow Glass!"

Kostas straightened, eyeing him. "Are you sure that's wise?"

"What?"

"Looking for her might make things harder than a clean break, Braxtus. She's made her decision."

"Kostas." He swung his legs over the edge of the bed. "I just want to see where she's going. Please."

Kostas let out a long breath, then stood and helped Braxtus gingerly to his feet. "Can you walk?"

"I'm fine."

They walked right out of Zeus's temple, none of the healers even glancing at them.

Braxtus's eyes widened as they stepped outside. The sun dipped toward the horizon, casting an orange glow on the destruction that was Mount Olympus. The earth appeared as though it had been ripped apart, then slammed back together. Everywhere he looked were toppled statues, wrecked temples, heaps of stone and mortar. "You said it's been two days since all of this happened?"

"You wouldn't believe the cleanup shifts," Kostas said dryly as they picked their way down the path. "We've been clearing out rubble, putting out fires . . . The Common Temples are in the worst condition. The Unnamed have been staying at their parents' temples, or wherever there is room. Hestia and Athena have been organizing the rebuilding efforts."

They took a smaller path that wound through trampled gardens to a small, elegant temple. For being made primarily from glass, it was in good shape. Prisms cast rainbows at their feet as they moved to the front door.

Kostas knocked twice, and it swung inward. They strode into the glittering entryway.

Iris, Goddess of Rainbows and Messages, stepped out of her Linked Chamber to greet them, long red hair flowing behind her. Braxtus caught a glimpse of the treasures inside before the door closed quietly. She looked between the two of them.

"Kostas." She smiled. "How can I help you, my son?"

Kostas just looked at Braxtus, eyebrows raised, so he stepped forward. "Iris, I came to request—"

"You want to see Iyana Unnamed," she guessed.

He rubbed his beard uncomfortably. "Yes. Please."

"Are you sure that's wise?" she questioned.

Braxtus scowled, glancing at Kostas.

Iris pursed her lips but beckoned them. They followed her through the temple and out the back door.

She led them down a path and through a garden of olives. Braxtus held his breath as they skirted old, twisted trunks and ducked under silver branches. He'd never seen the Rainbow Glass before.

The leaves thinned, opening into a small clearing. Braxtus's mouth moved to a small O of wonder.

Around the outer edge, twelve olive trees stood behind twelve marble pedestals, each with a silver amphora perched atop. Glowing torches hung from the branches, filling the clearing with dappled light. In the center of the clearing, three miniature metal trees sprung from the ground. The gold, silver, and bronze trunks climbed up to the height of Braxtus's torso, then melted together, colors swirling to form a metallic rainbow cradle for a glittering bowl.

It was beautiful in both a reverent and haunting kind of way.

Braxtus shifted his weight as Iris lifted the amphora from the marble stand bearing the symbol of Zeus, then poured the contents of the jug into the basin. Crystal liquid sloshed over the edges and dripped down the metal stand, but Iris didn't seem to mind. She emptied two other amphoras into the glass, those of Poseidon and Ares.

Iris took a step back and opened her arms, welcoming them to look. Braxtus stepped forward and leaned over the ripples, heart thumping. The liquid and glass were clear, showing the swirl of metallic color beneath. The water shimmered, and an image began to form.

Rocky ground raced past, as if the glass was in swift search. It slowed all at once, showing an overhead view of three travelers. Slowly, the view dipped down, until they were watching them from behind. An eerie evening fog from the land beyond was rolling in.

The figures were downcast, walking somberly toward the unnatural mist. Braxtus's eyes locked on Iyana, the setting sun glowing against her white-blonde hair. He swallowed the sudden lump in his throat.

"Where . . . where are they?" he asked, trying to identify the terrain. He turned to Iris, but her wise eyes were lost in the glass.

Kostas stepped closer. "Why would they be traveling there? That place is dangerous."

Iris shook her head mutely.

"Where are they going?" Braxtus looked between them.

"They're heading almost directly northeast," Kostas explained.

Braxtus scrambled to put a map in his head, then a new fear crept into his stomach. "They're heading into the Land of the Taraxippi."

Kostas nodded, and Iris touched her finger to the center of the liquid. Braxtus gripped the sides of the bowl as the vision began to ripple away. "What are they *thinking*?" he asked through gritted teeth.

"This whole situation keeps getting stranger," Kostas muttered.

Braxtus whirled on him. "They could be killed. Easily."

"Once you walk into that fog, there's very little chance of ever getting out again," Iris agreed, voice quiet.

"Thank you for allowing us to look in your glass, Iris." Braxtus bowed, mind racing. Iris nodded, watching them intently as Braxtus turned to lead Kostas out of the grove of trees. A short way up the path, Braxtus planted his feet and gripped his friend's shoulder.

"We have to go after them."

Kostas's eyes bore into him. "I knew you were going to say that."

"Hear me out," he said in a rush. "By going with *you*, an official deity, I will not be exiling myself. I can come back. Call it training for my Immortality Trial. We can go, help them, return, and no one here will be able to say we did anything wrong!"

"You're forgetting how delightful the Land of the Taraxippi is," Kostas said dryly. "Filled with malicious ghosts and the dark gods who will be there to welcome us."

Braxtus lit his hand on fire. "Fire scares off ghosts."

"It's still dangerous." But Kostas had a glint in his eye, and Braxtus could see his mind working through it. It was one reason Braxtus had always liked Kostas—as logical as he was, he had a wild side. The God of Games wouldn't be able to resist a quest.

"If we leave tonight, we should catch them before they're too far in."

"And you could say goodbye." Kostas raised his eyebrows.

Braxtus narrowed his eyes. "And *you* could talk to Galene and figure out more of what's been happening."

They stared at each other challengingly for a long moment, but Braxtus knew he'd hooked him.

Kostas jerked his head, mouth quirking up in a smile. "Let's get packing."

They left that night, cloaked and armed, riding into the darkness at the fastest speed their stallions could sustain.

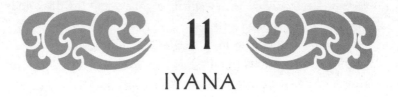

11

IYANA

The sun's morning rays shone over the horizon line in the distance and glowed against the prairie. Birds chirped in squat trees and rodents scurried through tall, yellow grasses. A warm, earthy scent reached Iyana on a breeze.

She scowled at the welcoming atmosphere. The land ahead of them had been nothing like this the night before, with thick mists and unearthly sounds that kept her from sleep. "We just walk right in?"

"As deep as we can. Before we run out of daylight." Demitri, too, seemed wary, narrowing his eyes at the Land of the Taraxippi. They would be fairly safe in the day, but when night fell, the ghosts would fully emerge.

Iyana glanced at Galene. "You're sure we can find Chrysander before the sun sets?"

She breathed out. "We better." She led the way into the fields.

They moved at an urgent pace, the morning hours creeping by. The landscape remained constant, but Iyana didn't relax, staying close to Demitri and Galene.

Around midday, a patch of dry grass caught Iyana's eye. She stopped and stared. Strange white rocks peppered the earth, and she squinted at them before realizing with a chill what they were. Bones.

Old rusted armor was half-covered in dirt and grass. The

plating was dented and dull, smaller than what was forged for the gods.

"Galene. Demitri."

They turned and followed her pointing finger.

"Human." Demitri said what she was thinking.

"Come on," Galene urged. "Let's keep going."

They moved faster, silently agreeing not even to stop for food. The farther they traveled, the more bones and old armor they found buried in dirt, until they had to pick their way around them. The scent of decay overpowered the earthy smell, and Iyana swallowed her bile.

The land darkened, the afternoon sun muting to a dull red glow. Shadows grew longer than they ought to have been. The air turned humid. Wind whispered among the leaves and grass.

Iyana focused on her ability and hushed the wind, trying to settle it. It pushed back, rustling the trees all the more loudly. Her heart gave a pound of panic—she hadn't mastered her ability, but the wind had never *fought* her before.

A rodent's chatter turned to a bony laugh—a bird's cry to a warped scream.

Iyana quickened her step.

As they walked on, a light mist descended.

"It's getting late." Iyana pulled her sweat-dampened hair from the back of her neck. "I haven't seen anything. No camps, no people, nothing but grass and trees and bones."

Demitri took her hand.

"We're close." Galene kept her eyes fixed ahead. "We have to be."

Iyana swallowed, looking behind her to eye the diminishing distance between the sun and the mountains. *Why did I agree to this in the first place? We could have gone to the sea.*

"Never," an icy voice whispered in her ear.

Iyana shrieked. Drawing a spike, she swung at empty air.

"What is it?" Demitri whirled, staff in hand.

Iyana breathed heavily, searching the surrounding shadows for signs of movement. "Nothing." But she curled her fingers tighter around her spike.

Red-streaked clouds bled across the mountains fringing the flatland, and the mist thickened into fog that swept over the ground. It forced them to slow down, their feet disappearing in the cloudy blanket. Iyana brought up her hands, pulling a southern wind to life. It responded, sending their hair flying, but as hard as she tried to sweep the fog away, the wind danced right over it, leaving it intact.

She let it die out, sick to her stomach.

An hour later, the sun was almost hidden behind the mountains.

Iyana stopped, catching her friend's arm. "Galene, he's not here. I don't see anyone."

Galene turned to look at her. Her face was drawn, tight with fear.

"He has to be close. We're in the heart of taraxippi territory." Demitri paced in a circle, scanning the area.

Iyana shook her head. "No one is here."

The last rays of sun winked away.

They went still, looking at each other. A breath of chilly air fluttered down Iyana's back, and the hair on her arms stood on end.

Figures appeared around them: pallid and translucent, with robes and hair that undulated like vapor in a breeze and black, soulless eyes.

"*Run!*" Galene took off. Iyana tore after her through the swirling clouds, Demitri right by her side.

Under cover of darkness, the land transformed, revealing its true nature. Unnerving chanting, sinister drums, wails, choirs, howls, and cold laughter rose in incessant disharmony as they fled. Iyana caught only a few more glimpses of the taraxippi, but the images burned into her mind. They laughed at the intruders from the shadows, streaking across their path, reaching for them.

Iyana ran blindly, trusting Galene was going in the best direction. The trees that had looked so short now towered above them, some appearing out of nowhere. She weaved with the others, breath coming in stitches.

A short wall materialized before her in the darkness. Gasping, Iyana crashed into it, tumbling over and rolling as she hit the ground.

Galene and Demitri skidded to a stop, spinning to check on her. She looked back. The wall was gone.

Trembling, Iyana pushed her arms against the ground to stand up, but something grabbed her ankle and hauled her backward.

She screamed as she was dragged a few feet, then released. Scrambling back toward her friends, Iyana drew a spike, turning to face her attacker.

A white face appeared in front of her, inches away. Its jaw hung open, the translucent flesh decayed. She could see to its bones.

With a shriek, she brought her blade up, right into its heart. It wasn't just vapor—she felt her spike hit the creature, slowing and stopping as it entered the ethereal body. With all the power she could muster, she sent a blast of air tearing at it, but its tattered robes only fluttered.

Heart pounding, she looked into its black eyes. The loose, gaping mouth drew up into a sickening smile. It pulled back, moving through the metal harmlessly.

"What do I do?" Iyana whispered.

"Run," Demitri replied. "On my count. One . . . two . . ."

The taraxippi lunged. Iyana spun and ran. Demitri let his javelin fly. It whistled past her ear, and she heard it clatter to the earth behind her. Demitri swore. He leapt for her, hand outstretched. Iyana reached out. Their fingers touched.

Icy hands seized her legs and yanked her backward.

"No!" he yelled.

Iyana slammed onto her stomach. She tore at the grass as she was pulled back, desperately trying to get a hold of something. Demitri and Galene charged after her.

Sharp nails dug into her calves. She kicked and twisted, but cold started to creep through her legs, paralyzing them. The icy, numbing sensation reached her stomach, and her insides began to freeze. She gasped, struggling for air, tears turning cold on her cheeks.

A flash like lightning tore past her and the thing released her. Warmth flooded through her legs, and her body became her own again.

She didn't stop to think, leaping to her feet and sprinting toward Demitri. He reached out but was thrown backward by an invisible force, striking a tree across the glade with a dull thud. A taraxippi converged on him, but another streak of light cut through the night, slashing through the spirit. With a wail, it evaporated.

Iyana looked around for the source of the light, but only saw more pallid faces in the darkness. She and Galene backed toward each other, clutching their worthless weapons.

In the near darkness, a small flame sprang to life. It shot forward and struck another taraxippi. The spirit bellowed and backed away, a smoking hole in its chest. More missiles of flames exploded from the darkness, and the taraxippi fled, dissolving into the night.

Hooves pounded, then two figures erupted through the fog.

"Iyana!" a familiar voice called.

Iyana blinked, gaping at the tall figure that swung down from his horse. *"Braxtus?"* Her legs moved of their own accord, and she ran and flung her arms around him. He caught her in a hug. His warmth enveloped her, and fresh tears flooded her eyes. "Braxtus, what—?"

"Seems I'm always chasing after you, aren't I?" Though his words were lighthearted, his voice sounded strained.

"But—you didn't—" She jerked back, scanning his face. "You're not *exiled,* are you?"

"No, no," he assured her. "I'm supervised."

Iyana glanced over his shoulder to see Kostas, a flaming arrow nocked as he surveyed the territory from atop his horse.

"What in Tartarus are you two doing here?" Demitri asked, rubbing the back of his head as he stumbled over. A dark expression settled on his face as he looked at Braxtus and Iyana. Her face heated, and she stepped toward Demitri.

"We saw where you were headed in my mother's Rainbow Glass," Kostas explained.

"We came to help," Braxtus added. Demitri leveled a stare at him, and Braxtus raised his eyebrows in return. "I know you sons of Ares can usually take care of yourselves, but fire is the best weapon against the taraxippi."

"I think we frightened them off for now, but it won't last forever." Kostas swung from his horse.

"Thank you." Galene looked at them with a mixture of relief and curiosity.

Braxtus turned his eyes back on Iyana. Even in the dark, she could make out so much on his face—fear, hurt, concern, caution. "What on Gaia are you doing out here?"

She heard the other question behind this one: *Why did you leave?* She stared at him, guilt tugging at her heart. As happy as she was to see her dear friend, she'd anticipated this being the clean break she'd needed from Braxtus. It'd been hard, seeing him consistently when she used to have such strong feelings for him. She was with *Demitri.* And Demitri was smart and handsome and made her feel wanted . . .

Demitri put his arm around her, and she leaned into his

touch. "We're looking for Galene's brother. He claimed some territory out here."

Braxtus searched her face, clearly wanting to ask more, but hesitating under the scrutiny.

Whispers echoed in the trees. Branches snapped. Demitri withdrew his arm to snatch a weapon, and Iyana spun toward the new threat.

Braxtus lit his hands on fire, letting the flames shoot toward the sky.

Four hooded figures stepped into the flickering light.

12

KOSTAS

Demitri had his staff poised before Kostas had fully drawn back his still-burning arrow, but Demitri faltered. "Chrysander?"

The god leading the group pulled back his hood, and Braxtus's firelight glowed against his coppery-brown hair. Kostas blinked at the striking resemblance to Galene, recognizing her older brother.

The god grinned, joyous yellow dancing into his aura. "Demitri?" The two ran to each other, clasping hands and embracing. "What are you doing here?" Chrysander clapped Demitri's shoulders. "Did my words of wisdom sink into that thick skull of yours?"

Demitri rolled his eyes, shoving him off with a smile, then stepped aside so Chrysander could see the rest of them.

Chrysander's gaze fell on Galene, and the bright yellow swirling around him settled into a still, sky blue. His sea-green eyes lit up and he ran to her, arms outstretched.

"Galene!"

Her eyes sparkled as they met, and she buried her face in her brother's shoulder. "It's been so long since I've hugged you." Her voice was muffled.

"By the Fates it has!" He pulled back to look at her more closely. "You came!" He threw his arms around her again. Though the smile on her face was genuine, her own aura shone more dully than Chrysander's. "I can't believe I actually convinced you to come! What changed your mind?"

Like a blown-out candle, Galene's aura flooded dark blue. "I'm not exactly here by choice, Chrysander." She described what happened.

Kostas watched the shifting colors around Chrysander, analyzing the feelings of sympathy and frustration rolling off him. There was no hint of shock or surprise.

"Wait." Braxtus ran a hand through his curls. "You were talking to *Chrysander* when the beasts were created?"

Galene nodded. "I was with him at the Northeastern boundary line. We've been meeting every new moon since he left," Galene admitted, toeing the ground.

Iyana sighed but wasn't surprised. *Galene already told them about her alibi.*

"And you didn't invite me." Demitri shook his head at his old friend.

Chrysander grinned apologetically. "Sorry. But she is my sister, and the meetings were risky enough as it was."

"You confirm she was with you that night?" Kostas asked Chrysander.

"Yes." The glowing amber sincerity that accompanied those words satisfied him.

I'm convinced. She's innocent.

"But your dagger . . . ," Braxtus said, "and the vision . . ."

Kostas nodded. "It doesn't make sense."

Chrysander shrugged. "For all we know, Apollo could have made up that vision. The Olympians, they . . . well, you know what I think." Chrysander closed his eyes and clutched his sister's hands. "You're better off here anyway. We're your family now, Galene"—he turned to the rest of them—"all of you. Come, we'll take you back to camp. We have hot food and warm tents for you to rest in."

Galene nodded her thanks and looked questioningly at the others.

"This is what we came for, isn't it?" Demitri grinned and slapped his friend on the back. "Let's go." He was all joy, with a smidge of self-satisfaction. Kostas pulled his mouth into a thin line. *He probably thinks he's the reason we found him.*

Iyana followed her best friend and boyfriend. Braxtus gave a sigh, but trailed behind. Taking the horses' reins, Kostas took up the rear.

The three other gods Chrysander had come with had lowered their hoods but watched them all warily, glancing frequently at himself and Braxtus. Kostas kept his eyes on them as well. Though their weapons were lowered and their posture casual, he knew these gods were kept away from Olympus for a reason.

The nine of them wove through thickets and ruins, Kostas's mind a storm. Galene had been set up. That could be the only explanation. Though Chrysander was clearly not an ally of Olympus, he was truthful. He and Galene had been together while the Decks were stolen. She would not have had time to create the beasts and meet with her brother.

So someone had stolen one of her daggers and framed her, but Apollo had seen her in the vision.

None of it sat right with Kostas.

Through the misty darkness, specks of light began to appear in front of them—campfires and torches. Dozens of tents were set up throughout a large clearing. Fires blazed between each, but the sentries seemed fully at ease. There must have been a vicious territorial claiming—the taraxippi hadn't bothered the group at all since Chrysander found them.

Chrysander's companions stopped at the edge of the camp, taking up their posts. *Sentries,* Kostas realized.

Eyes followed them as they were guided through the tents. Gods and goddesses, some Kostas vaguely recognized, wandered throughout the complex, busy with what, he couldn't imagine. Though the rebels and exiled watched them all, most of their haunted eyes lingered on Galene. Everyone's emotions stayed mostly between red-orange curiosity and pale turquoise hope.

Hope, he considered. *They probably think we're joining them.*

Someone intercepted him and offered to take the horses to water and rest. He silently handed the goddess the reins, keeping an eye on where she took them. Chrysander himself led their group toward the back of the complex, where the largest tent now came into view.

"I must introduce you to someone before we can really catch up." He pulled back the flap of the tent, disappearing inside.

Galene swept after her brother, Iyana and Demitri on her heels.

Braxtus hung back, meeting eyes with Kostas. "Tell me I'm not the only one with a bad feeling about this."

Kostas nodded, glancing around. "Keep your eyes and ears open."

They entered the tent.

Furs and fabrics hanging from the ceiling split the space into compartments. Even though the main area was smaller and the floor covered, it wasn't anything Kostas would have described as cozy. The colors were dark and there were few comforts.

A single chair was placed against the far canvas. In it sat a stunning, forbidding goddess draped in purple robes. Her flawless pale skin looked to be carved from stone. Unnaturally silky, ink-colored hair fell around her shoulders and arms. Black eyes ringed with long lashes stared at them, but the aura around her was one of pleasure and surprise.

"Well, Chrysander." The woman's full lips curled up in a smile. "How ever did you manage to get her here?"

Chrysander bowed. "Galene, this is the commander of our movement, Poinê, Goddess of Retribution."

A shock ran up Kostas's back. *Goddess of Retribution.*

Poinê had been exiled for a serious revolt. Though the Olympians couldn't retract immortality, her temples, both in the human cities and on Olympus, had been destroyed.

Galene nodded at Poinê, caution in her aura.

"She has been forced off the mountain, wrongly accused of causing great destruction on Olympus."

"Well, I'm sorry to hear that you're not responsible, but unsurprised that you were framed." Her voice was sickly sweet, and she closed her eyes, shaking her head in supposed remorse, but her aura showed no sign of pity or sympathy. "Hopefully, my dear, you will now be able to see what your brother and I have been trying to accomplish out here. Perhaps, after Chrysander explains a bit more, you will also be willing to join us. And who are"—she dragged her eyes across the five of them—"the rest of you?"

"Demitri Unnamed." He stepped forward.

Poinê's focus seemed to sharpen as she appraised him. "We do not use that term here, Demitri. It was established by the Olympians as a way to elevate themselves."

Demitri nodded slowly. "I am Demitri, Son of Ares."

"Welcome," she said softly, turning her eyes on Iyana.

"Iyana, Daughter of Zeus." She took Demitri's hand. "We chose to exile ourselves with Galene to protest the injustice."

Braxtus cast Kostas a wary look. "Braxtus, Son of Apollo."

Poinê's eyes turned to Kostas, and he returned her gaze calmly. "Kostas, God of Games."

"An Immortal." She cocked her head, a flicker of maroon suspicion rippling around her.

"Like yourself," he returned with a small smile.

"And why are you two here?"

They'll never let us go if they think we can return and report them to the Olympians. "Braxtus chose to exile himself as well, and I left without any favor in the eyes of the Olympians. Even on

Olympus, there is much unrest about how things are run. We joined the others later due to an injury Braxtus attained during the attack."

To their credit, no one showed the surprise or admiration he could see in their auras.

Poinê paused. "Well then, I am glad you are here. I'm sure you will all be great assets to our cause."

Chrysander nodded, a satisfied smile on his face, aura now reflecting Poinê's pleasure. "With your permission, I will take them to settle in for the night. They've had a long journey."

Poinê nodded, eyes sliding back to Galene. "I am sure. I trust, Chrysander, you will keep them out of trouble. For your own safety, my friends. As you know, this is dangerous territory."

"Of course. Thank you." He bowed again and turned to exit the tent.

Galene kept her eyes on the goddess, giving the smallest dip of her head, before turning after her friends. Kostas waited for her at the entrance, getting one more look at the Goddess of Retribution. Her eyes were fixed on his, her aura calm as ice.

The canvas flapped shut behind them.

Chrysander and Demitri took the lead, an old friendship instantly renewed.

Kostas strode beside Galene, analyzing her downturned eyes and muted orange aura. "What are you thinking?" he asked.

Galene blinked up at him. After a moment she turned forward again. "I'm nervous to hear what Chrysander has to say. What are you thinking?"

Caught slightly off guard by the return of his question, he hesitated. "I . . . am still taking in everything."

"There's a lot to sift through. I imagine you're still wondering about my part—how much of this is my fault." She looked at him from the corner of her eye. "I *am* sorry for what happened, especially to Braxtus."

Despite everything that has happened to her, she still shows only sincerity and kindness. "You have nothing to be sorry for. I believe you."

Her aura flared with surprise, then melted into the light colors of gratitude and relief. "Thank you, Kostas. That means a lot." She glanced away, but not before he caught the glimmer of tears in her eyes.

His footsteps faltered. He reached for her, then stopped himself. *Galene cannot spend the rest of her life with Olympus's condemnation.*

He cleared his throat as she dashed away the tears. "It *is* quite the mystery, though. Which intrigues me. There's not much I wouldn't do to solve a good riddle."

She pulled her mouth to the side. "My life isn't a game, Kostas."

"Everything is a game, Galene." He raised his eyebrows. "But believe me when I say, I do not take any of this lightly."

He watched her think through that, appreciating her careful consideration.

Chrysander led them to a bonfire where sizzling meats roasted and incredible smells rose from a steaming pot of stew.

"Refreshment as promised. I'll have some wineskins brought, but for now, sit and rest."

Braxtus didn't wait before sinking onto one of the logs circling the fire. Demitri and Iyana sat opposite him, Demitri seeming completely at ease, joyful to be reunited with his friend. Kostas took a seat beside Braxtus, and Galene settled herself between him and Iyana. After Chrysander made the request for wine, he walked around, ruffling Galene's wavy hair before sitting next to Demitri.

Beside the fire was a stack of bowls, which he began to pass around, and by the time the stew was ladled out the wineskins had arrived.

"Thank you for your hospitality, Chrysander," Galene said. "I knew we would be able to stay with you for a few days while we decide on what to do next."

"Why not just stay here? Now, Galene," he hurried on, "before you say anything, let me tell you exactly what we're planning."

Galene shifted uncomfortably. "Say your piece."

"For the benefit of everyone"—Chrysander looked around—"I'll start from the beginning.

"The Twelve Olympians were once the only gods the humans worshipped. They were all-powerful, all-encompassing. But naturally, as they had children, there became more deities to ask for guidance, *other* gods and goddesses to send sacrifices and payments to. Power began to slip away from the Twelve, and they have taken action to steal it back.

"I saw it years ago. I requested audience after audience with the Olympians to improve things for the Unnamed. I tried to get better mentors for us to train for our Trials, more supervised outings from Olympus, better weapons . . . When those requests were brushed aside, I started gathering others to petition against the Olympians. When the Twelve got wind of it, those meetings were forcibly shut down, and I was punished for 'disrespecting authority.'" His eyes darkened. "I began to explore and study and quest as much as I could, trying to train myself to be stronger against them, but there is only so much you can do within the boundaries of Mount Olympus. I was considering running when . . ." He faltered, dark, painful blue smothering his aura. "The unthinkable happened."

"Telamon," Galene murmured.

Chrysander nodded. "He was a gifted son of Dionysus. He was . . . my friend. They didn't stop his Immortality Trial when things went badly, and he didn't make it out of the arena alive." Red anger sparked. "I left the next day. To see if anyone out here would listen. Here, I found my people."

Kostas looked around at the gods and goddesses settling in their own groups around the campfire. Beneath dark auras, they looked weathered, eyes continually shifting, seemingly permanent scowls on their faces. None of them looked like allies he would want to keep.

"I found Poinê, and together, we began planning for the new future of Olympus." He leaned forward. "The Olympians' regime must come to an end."

Iyana's and Braxtus's jaws dropped. Galene pressed a hand to her face, and he felt her frustration, her patience shaking.

Chrysander's aura radiated confidence.

"Why do you think that you and this Goddess of Retribution will be better rulers than the Twelve?" Kostas kept his voice calm and flat, simply a question out of curiosity.

"If you promise to hear me out until I've finished speaking, I'll tell you everything you wish to know."

Five pairs of eyes moved to look at Galene. Hers stayed fixed on Chrysander, aura simmering gray with worry, but she nodded at him to go on.

"We have found a way to retrieve the *avyssos*."

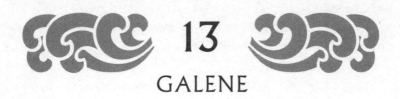

13

GALENE

Silence fell.

Galene gaped at her brother, unsure if she'd heard him right. "The . . . the *avyssos*?"

Chrysander held up a hand. "You promised to let me finish."

Though a feeling of foreboding ran through her, Galene pressed her mouth shut.

"Leading through the Aegean Sea is a trail of markers, directing those who follow it through tests and trials meant only for an Olympian to pass. At the end of the trail is the *avyssos*. All of you know what it is, yes?"

"I've heard the name," Iyana murmured.

"It's an orb with the power to draw gods and goddesses in. To draw anything in: people, creatures, objects . . ." Braxtus kneaded his knuckles on his forehead. "The *avyssos* keeps them captive inside, preserved. Only the person who holds the *avyssos*, with the knowledge of how to open it, has control over what goes in or out."

"It keeps things inside of itself. So it's large?" Iyana asked.

Braxtus shook his head. "No, I don't think so. No one really knows where they go. They're just . . . drawn in because of the *avyssos*'s power. So maybe it's a gateway to a place only the *avyssos* can reach." He dropped his hand and looked around. "It doesn't matter. Either way, when its power is directed at someone, they vanish. They can be held captive for eternity."

Chrysander nodded. "This is the key to everything we hope to achieve."

Galene clenched her fists in her lap.

"You're going to trap the Olympians inside," Kostas said gravely, voicing her thoughts.

"That's not all." Chrysander smiled. "The Olympians used to use the *avyssos* for crowd control, when there were too many monsters running rampant. They trapped hordes of them. Now they only use it on occasion, when there's a god or a beast that poses a real threat to the humans. So within the *avyssos* is an army of Olympus's enemies. Poinê and I will release those who pledge to fight, and together, we will lead them in an assault of the mountain. Then, when we've captured all who oppose us, Poinê will set a new rule over the world."

"I'm sorry, what?" Braxtus demanded.

Chrysander ignored him and turned to Galene, eyes shining. "Galene, it will be a rule of balance and freedom, where no one is pushed down because they have potential for power. And when we have taken the mountain, you and I can return. We can build our temples! Travel the world as Gods of the Sea. We will be worshipped and loved!"

He sounded giddy, almost drunk on the thought. But Galene's imagination tumbled with visions of a battle, the downfall of her home, their parents and leaders. Even if they could return, what would they return to? What would the world look like after that?

"And now that you're here," he went on, "you can help us get it."

She straightened. "What?"

"Galene, you are one of our father's most powerful children. You have been given power over tides and the ability to breathe water. Reaching the *avyssos* will be easy for you."

"Why can't you go?" Braxtus asked. "You're a son of Poseidon and Amphitrite, too."

Chrysander shook his head. "My power is limited to drawing

water from the earth. I can't even do anything with it once it's there. And not all the children of Poseidon can breathe water. It's a rare gift."

"You said there were tests and trials only an Olympian could get through." Demitri watched his friend with unreadable eyes.

Chrysander leaned forward. "Yes, but only Poseidon is truly meant to be able to reach it. Galene, with you we could achieve everything we've dreamed and planned within the month."

Even as he spoke, Galene shook her head. "How could you think I would ever agree to this? That I would join you in"—she struggled with the words—"destroying Olympus!"

"We'll rebuild it better!"

"You're talking about killing gods and goddesses, about trapping the Olympians for *eternity*—"

Chrysander shot to his feet. "About restoring justice!"

"Are the Olympians so unjust you feel the need to overthrow them?" Galene raised her voice to match his. Nearby gods turned to stare, muttering.

"You're saying they were right to exile you for the crime you didn't commit?"

"No, but—"

"Have you considered it was them that set you up? They're growing more desperate, cheating us out of what we rightfully deserve!"

Galene threw her hands up. "They did *not* set me up. And even if they did, do you realize what would happen if the Olympians were gone? Have you thought about it? The seas would rage, storms would ravage the land. Earthquakes and volcanoes would tear this earth apart. Do you have people with power enough to keep this planet in check? Do you have people to take over every facet of each Olympian's power? Poseidon: God of the Sea, Earthquakes. Apollo: God of the Sun, Prophesy, Healing. Athena: Wisdom, Warfare, Strategy. And that's not *close* to all they do and represent.

"And even if you did," she continued, overriding his clear desire to explain himself, "what about the humans? If everyone they worship suddenly disappears, who will they pray to? Who would offer them guidance and blessings? Eventually, the offerings would stop coming. The Linked Chambers on the mountain sustain Olympus. Whatever you're planning, this is not the way to fix things."

Gods and goddesses were moving from nearby groups to surround them, listening in on their conversation. Good. She wanted them to hear.

"Poinê has everything figured out," he assured her, palms raised. "We've mapped out plans—"

Her temper flared again. "And Poinê, Goddess of *Retribution*, is your first choice to rule?"

"The Olympians have taken away everything, Galene," he snapped. "You just got exiled, wrongfully. They wouldn't even listen to you, didn't even try to consider looking at other evidence or proof. How can you still stand behind them? *Beneath* them?"

Galene's face grew hot. She stood. "We are all fallible, even the Olympians. How can you damn hundreds of lives only to bring this cosmos back into chaos? You haven't thought this through!"

"I have." He stepped toward her. "*You* need to."

"No I don't. I would never participate in this . . . this coup, this mutiny."

"Galene, how can you be so blind? So passive? How can you refuse to stand up for what's right?"

"I *am* standing up for what's right!" she yelled. "I won't be party to this, Chrysander. I will not."

They held eyes, glaring at each other until she saw the fire die from within him. He sighed, shoulders slumping.

"I think . . ." She glanced around at her friends. "I think we need to leave."

Kostas gave her an almost imperceptible nod.

"Fine. This will happen with or without you, Galene. Your refusal means nothing but a longer time line."

Fear shot through her. "Who else can retrieve the *avyssos* for you?"

A tall goddess stepped forward from the crowd, eyes cold, dark hair cropped close to her scalp. "Me."

A bitter smile crossed Chrysander's lips as he turned to the new speaker. "Anyss. Descendant of Oceanus. She has a raw power over the water—in any form. Staying underwater will require some creativity, but we have no doubt she will be just as successful, if slower."

Anyss stared Galene dead in the eye and raised a hand. From the lightly clouded sky, rain immediately began falling, padding the soft ground everywhere but the circle in which they stood.

Galene's mind raced. "You can't do this."

"Oh, little sister," he cooed, stepping around the logs, "tomorrow, due south to the seashore, the *mutiny* begins. If any of you have opinions of your own, don't let Galene sway you. You're welcome to stay. If, however, you're all just as blind"—he waved his hand dismissively as he walked away—"don't get in our way."

As Chrysander left, so did the crowd. Gods and goddesses gave them final, nasty, or awkward glances as they disappeared between tents.

Galene dropped back onto the log, legs shaking. Their little group waited a long moment before speaking.

"What do we do?" Iyana's face was ashen.

"Their plan is solid," Kostas said. "Depending on the obstacles they face, they have a real chance of securing the *avyssos*."

"We can't let them get it," Galene ground out. All eyes turned on her, but she just shook her head, unable to say more. She focused on controlling her breathing. Iyana slid over to her, linking her arm through hers.

There was silence for a while, then Kostas spoke. "This is perfect."

Galene's stomach lurched, and she shot Kostas a fierce glare. Chrysander's insane, traitorous plan was *perfect*?

Kostas met her eyes. "Listen. We can use this plot to prove that you are trustworthy and honorable. This can be your chance to get back to Mount Olympus."

Her heart stopped, then leapt in hope. "How?"

"Chrysander clearly thinks you are the best person for this." His eyes shone. "If you leave now you can get a head start toward the *avyssos*."

After a moment of stunned silence, voices cried out in protest. Surprise crossed Kostas's face at the sudden, fierce objections.

"Galene is not going out there alone . . ."

"—unbelievably dangerous!"

"Chrysander and *Poinê* . . ."

"Okay, quiet!" Kostas snapped, eyeing the scattered gods around them. "We have to keep this quiet." He huddled closer. "Galene is the only chance to get ahead of this. Iyana and Demitri, you can stay here and watch Chrysander's group from the inside. Braxtus and I will return to Olympus, where I'll look for a way to help you, Galene."

Galene perked up, holding his gaze.

"If there really are tests and trials," Kostas continued, "you'll probably want some assistance. I might be able to find out what they are, and perhaps even get a blessing from Poseidon to join you underwater . . ."

"Why not just return and tell the Olympians what Chrysander is planning?" Iyana asked.

Demitri shook his head. "Because as soon as the Olympians hear that Galene came straight to Chrysander, they'll *never* clear her name. They might not even trust Kostas's word because of it."

"Exactly," Kostas confirmed.

"And you are siding with us?" Galene asked Demitri skeptically. "Not Chrysander?"

He paused, deliberating. "I'm not saying I don't agree with his motives. Things *are* wrong on the mountain. But you're right, this is extreme."

"Okay, but even if we do everything you're saying, Kostas, how would getting the *avyssos* first prove anything? I can't just hand it to my father and say, 'Chrysander is trying to overthrow you; put this somewhere safer.'"

"No, but we *can* use it to capture the people responsible for trying to overthrow Olympus. And then the Olympians can question them to verify our story. If they were to realize how big of a movement this is, maybe it would even improve things on the mountain."

Galene considered it, then her tangled thoughts landed on a painful truth. *They would kill Chrysander.* Despite what he was plotting, she didn't want him to *die*. Meeting Kostas's eyes, she somehow knew he had the same thought. Her bottom lip trembled, and she bit down hard.

Iyana pursed her lips. "That's all well and good, but if anyone is going with Galene on this trip, it's me."

Kostas shook his head. "No one else can breathe underwater, and you can't return to Olympus with me."

"What about me?" Braxtus demanded. "You're not going to dump me back on the mountain while you feed your quest addiction."

Kostas scowled at him. "That's not what this is about, Braxtus. Galene needs to clear her name. You can help me with the research, and perhaps we can even find evidence that Galene was framed."

Tears in Galene's eyes threatened to start flowing. This god hardly knew her, and he was so convinced of her innocence. "Thank you, Kostas."

"There has to be another way." Iyana frowned. "It's *dangerous*—we can't just send her out there alone, and there's no guarantee you'd be able to get to her at any point, Kostas."

They've already gotten into enough danger because of me. "I can do it myself. Without you, too," she added to Kostas.

"No, Iyana's right; you're going to need help. After I get your father's blessing, I'll catch up to you. As soon as I can."

"*If* you get—" Galene started.

"What about me?" Iyana asked, furious.

"*You're* not going anywhere without *me.*" Demitri gave Iyana a fierce look, and she meekly pulled in closer to his side.

"I told you both," Kostas emphasized. "You'll be helpful on the inside here."

"Make Braxtus do it!"

"Why am I suddenly the disposable one?" Braxtus looked at her accusingly.

"He has to go back to Mount Olympus."

"No way!" Braxtus argued.

"You can't be alone and you can't come with us underwater." Kostas took his arm. "The longer you're away from home, the more trouble you're going to be in. If they check in on you and find you unsupervised or swimming in the sea with Galene the exiled, they might very well exile you, too."

"Not if your plan works and we save Olympus," Braxtus countered. "Then we'll all be heroes."

Kostas groaned.

I might just have to sneak away, Galene thought, heart sinking. *Kostas is the only one with a clear head about this. It's better if I go alone, if . . .* She paused as a thought struck her, and she slipped her hand into her pouch, curling her fingers around the small cone shell. She looked around at her friends, still arguing quietly. She didn't have to tell them. She could still sneak away, keep them safely out of this and handle it herself. *Can I, though? If I fail . . .*

Tentatively, she withdrew the shell and held it in her palm.

"What's that?" Braxtus asked.

Galene waited for everyone else's attention. "Before I left Olympus, my father gave me a boon."

Iyana's mouth fell open. *"What?"*

Braxtus whistled appreciatively.

"What kind of boon?" Demitri asked.

Galene looked at each of them. "Whatever we need from the ocean."

"Why didn't you tell us sooner?" Iyana demanded. "We can *all* go with you! We can use the boon to breathe underwater!"

"I really don't want to put any of you in danger, but I think . . . ," she sighed, "this is bigger than me."

Iyana smiled, her eyes bright. "Galene! We can do this!"

Kostas was smiling, too. "Iyana, Demitri, and I will accompany you, then."

Braxtus threw his hands up. "If you're all going, I'm going, too!"

"Even though you could be exiled for staying out here with us?" Kostas asked him, eyebrows raised.

"This is *important.*"

"What about your issue with water?"

Braxtus's cheeks flamed gold. "Kostas," he snarled. "I'm going."

Kostas raised his hands as if to say, *just remember, this was your choice.*

A smile tugged at Galene's lips. She might have a way home. But even if she didn't, she would risk anything to save Olympus. "Thank you," she said, meeting each of their eyes, "all of you, for believing in me and supporting me."

Iyana squeezed her in a tight hug. "Don't worry, Galene, we're going to make all of this right. Together."

"We're with you." Demitri nodded.

Galene let the smile grow. "So what's our plan?"

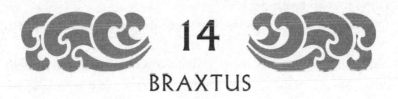

14

BRAXTUS

Braxtus didn't sleep.

Despite his heavy lids and the muscles that ached from hours of hard riding, he stared blankly at the tent ceiling. His mind raced as he tried to process the events of the day. They'd fought off taraxippi. Found a rebel camp. And now they were going to race a jumbled group of vengeful gods and goddesses to the *avyssos*.

In the sea.

Underwater.

Braxtus sent a rush of small flames across his arms, warming him against the thought.

Sometime in the middle of the night, Galene slipped inside the tent.

"Wake up, it's time."

Braxtus rolled out of bed and cracked his neck, waiting as the others roused themselves. Iyana stirred in Demitri's arms, then sat up, rubbing her face until her cheeks were rosy gold. Demitri kissed her head, and Braxtus looked away, moving to Kostas.

"Is everyone ready?" his friend asked. Braxtus looked around the crowded tent. Faces turned grim, determined. They nodded.

Braxtus jerked his head at Kostas, and the two of them stepped through the canvas into the night air. Tents clustered around theirs. Above them, the sky was cloudy, threatening rain, but when Braxtus looked to the distance, fog encircled the camp, rising to blend into the clouds.

They wound through the tents, avoiding the more direct path Iyana and Galene would take to the stables. Kostas chattered uncharacteristically, as though they were merely on a late-night walk. Braxtus glanced back at their tent once, just in time to see Demitri slip out and move in another direction. He fixed his eyes forward again. Iyana and Galene would wait a few more minutes before making their exit.

Braxtus was rather impressed with Kostas's pointless, one-sided conversation. Though he didn't see anyone standing guard, he was sure it was effective in drawing attention to themselves, away from the others.

They circled back around to the tent, Kostas tapering off his conversation, swishing the tent flaps as though they had returned.

Then they ran for the stables. Braxtus tried to keep his feet quiet, a rush of adrenaline coursing through him as they passed close to more tents. Stealth was not his strength, but with any luck, they'd be out of there soon.

He pushed the stable door open, and it struck something. As they stepped inside, he glanced down at an unconscious guard slumped in the corner.

Just as planned, Galene and Iyana were already there, saddling horses with quick fingers.

"Any trouble?" Kostas asked.

"No." Galene handed them their weapons, and Braxtus accepted his sword and shield gratefully, arming himself. They followed as the goddesses led the horses out the back door.

Iyana guided an Olympian stallion to Braxtus, passing him the reins with a tense smile.

They waited on horseback for Demitri. Though Braxtus and Kostas's Olympian mounts stood quietly, the other three horses jittered. Iyana ran a hand down her mare's neck, but her eyes kept darting back to the stable. A breeze rustled through the grass, and Braxtus knew it came as a reflection of her emotions.

Finally, footsteps. Someone spoke from inside the stables. Another voice responded. Braxtus tightened his grip on the reins. If they were discovered, what would they say? Would they leave without him?

Demitri appeared at the back door, Chrysander by his side. Braxtus's hand flew to his sword, his whole body tensing.

Galene's brother froze. "What's this?"

Demitri swung his staff, slamming the butt of it into Chrysander's temple. He crumpled.

"Sorry, he caught up with me." Demitri ran for them, and Iyana threw him the reins of the fifth horse. He seized them and swung up. "Go!"

Braxtus wheeled his horse around and kicked its flank. All of them took off into the grasslands, Galene in the lead.

"Braxtus," Kostas called, "light the way!"

Braxtus snapped, and a spark sprang to life, blooming into a ball of flames between his fingers. He held it up, holding the reins in one hand.

A single horn blasted behind them, and he looked back to see a few gods emerging from tents, running for the stables. "They know!" he shouted. "I think they're coming after us!"

"Faster!" Galene commanded.

He gave his stallion more rein. Wind stung his eyes and whipped his fire backward. An unnatural chill burnt his throat. They pounded into the fog, and dread rose in him. Whatever had kept the taraxippi at bay in Chrysander's camp was gone, and Braxtus sensed them returning to the hunt.

The trees reached for them, whining and snapping in the sudden wind. A scream of a tortured beast pierced the night, echoed by other faint cries that sounded unnervingly human.

Braxtus pressed his heels into his stallion, moving up in the group until he reached Galene's side. He flared the fire in his hands.

"We're not far!" Galene said.

Pale figures appeared in his peripheral, but whenever he looked they were gone. Shrieks and chatters rattled through the night, raising the hair on Braxtus's arms. Galene guided her horse with unwavering certainty, eyes set forward.

"How do you know where we're going?" He could hardly even make out the stars through the mist.

"I can feel the sea."

They charged on until all at once, the mist evaporated. They rushed into clear air, the haunting sounds of the taraxippi falling behind them.

He looked back, slowing his horse. The mist rose in a distinct wall.

"We must have crossed the boundary." Iyana rode beside him, eyes wide with relief. Braxtus closed his fist, putting out the flames.

"We can't slow down," Galene called over her shoulder. "We'll be easier to follow without the mist."

Braxtus gritted his teeth and urged his horse on. They rode through several knolls, the land lowering until it opened into a dark, shifting expanse glimmering with reflected starlight.

The Aegean Sea.

The horses' hooves hit sand.

"We need to find the first marker!" Galene stood in the stirrups, squinting along the shore. "It should be close. We came due south, like Chrysander said."

"What does it look like?" He jumped down from his horse and dropped the reins, lighting both of his hands. He focused, and the flames grew large, casting flickering light across the beach.

"I have no idea, but it would definitely stand out. It wouldn't be called a *marker* for nothing."

The others leapt off their horses as well, scanning the scattered rocks and shells. Braxtus moved down the shore toward a cluster of craggy gray rocks, beaten into strange shapes by stormy waters. *Something different.* Keeping his hands aloft to share the light as much as possible, he dragged his eyes along them. *There!*

Almost touching the water was a stout, silvery granite stone, worn smooth and half-buried in sand. It was striped with fissures of a different rock Braxtus didn't recognize, but the golden hue stood out, even in the dark night. He ran to it, sliding to his knees in the wet sand. Putting out the fire in one hand, he touched it.

As soon as his fingers met the cool stone, the surface began to glow.

"Over here!" he bellowed.

The others came running, guiding their horses with them. Iyana dropped to her knees beside him, bending over to read the silver and gold writing that appeared across the marker.

Take to King Aegeas's realm and sail toward winter's dawn.

Two days on.

"King Aegeas's realm. That's the Aegean Sea. But toward 'winter's dawn'?" Iyana looked up and stared out at the water. "It's summer, we can't wait—"

"Southeast," Galene interrupted. Braxtus turned and caught Kostas shooting an appreciative glance at her. "The sun rises farther to the south during winter. We sail for two days southeast."

"Sail on what?" Demitri studied the marker. "We don't have a boat."

"We don't need one." Galene turned to her horse and slapped its rump, sending it fleeing across the sand. Then she sprinted into the water.

"Galene!" Iyana stood. "What are you doing?"

"You'll see!"

Kostas sent the other horses after Galene's. Braxtus swallowed as he watched them go.

Galene stood knee-high in the sea, digging through a pouch at her belt. Pulling something free, she began whispering to her cupped hand. Her fingers lit with a green glow, light blazing between the cracks. She pulled her arm back and threw the object out into the waves.

"What was that?" he asked.

"My father's boon!"

"But we needed that to breathe underwater, not to travel." Demitri pushed out after her.

"I did use it for you to breathe." She turned to them, eyes glowing. "Leave the traveling to me, and get in the water!"

No one moved.

Galene looked at them desperately. Braxtus met eyes with Iyana, mutual apprehension running between them. Underwater. Away from air, away from fire. His flames danced a little brighter on his fingers.

Galene threw out her hands. "Fine, I'll go by myself." She turned to run deeper into the sea.

"Wait!" Iyana leapt forward at once. "Just . . . just tell us how this works."

Galene shifted, eyes flicking toward their pursuers as she answered in a rush. "It's a magical shift of your lungs breathing water instead of air. The transition can be jarring. The air or water already in your lungs doesn't just disappear when you change elements. The best way to do it is to exhale everything so your lungs are empty. Then you can take in the new element without having to choke anything up afterward."

"What if it doesn't work?" Braxtus asked, heart racing at the thought of intentionally sucking in a chest full of salt water.

"Then I'll be here to pull you up and make sure you're okay."

Her words didn't do much to comfort him. Galene's obvious impatience grew.

Kostas blew out a long gust of air, then ran into the waves.

He dove under, and Braxtus shuddered, staring at where he disappeared. They waited in silence.

After what felt like eternity, Kostas's head popped out of the waves. He sputtered a little, staggering to his feet, but his eyes were alight.

"It works!" he exclaimed, voice hoarse. "Don't worry, it's easy. Come on."

Fear squeezed Braxtus's chest, but it seemed to be enough for the others.

Iyana quickly braided back her hair. Casting one more look of anxiety at Braxtus, she took Demitri's hand and dove with him under the water.

Braxtus couldn't bring himself to move. His memories of the water weren't fond.

Shouts of Chrysander's comrades sounded in the distance. He looked back. Lights sprang into view at the edge of the tree line.

Galene stretched her hand out to him. Smothering his flames, he swallowed and accepted her gesture, letting her lead him into deeper waters.

She breathed out, signaling for Braxtus to do the same. He did so, glancing at the night-black water around him, lengthening his exhale as much as possible. He could see nothing. *Anything* could be down there.

"Ready?" Galene asked.

No. He nodded.

Galene sank down, guiding him with her. It took all of his strength not to suck in a breath before his head went under. He kept his eyes closed, knowing the salt water would sting.

"Braxtus?" Galene's voice sounded strange as it rippled through the water to his ears. He held his breath.

"Braxtus!" someone else called.

He shook his head. He couldn't do this. Hands grabbed his shoulders and he opened his eyes to see Kostas, hair undulating, tunic flowing around him. The water felt fine against his eyes—he could see clearly, and it didn't sting at all. But he could taste the salt pressing against his lips, wanting to flood his lungs. His chest ached and his head swam.

Kostas shook him. "Breathe."

He shook his head, starting to kick upward.

A fist slammed into his gut. He gasped.

Cold liquid flooded his lungs. He clutched his chest, but the water moved smoothly and easily. He took another breath.

"See?" Galene said. "Easy."

"But not pleasant," he coughed, testing out his voice as he shot Kostas a glare. His friend didn't look at all apologetic for punching him.

"You'll get used to it. Now, let's get moving." Galene swam farther out.

Braxtus blinked a few times, keeping his breathing slow and cautious as he looked around. He could see his feet and the sandy floor, and the others around him. Iyana and Demitri were floating farther off, Iyana's eyes understanding. Beyond them was only darkness.

"We'll need to swim for a bit," Galene explained, striking out into that abyss. "When we're deep enough, I can use the tides to speed us along."

"Won't you get tired?" Iyana asked.

Braxtus pushed himself forward, kicking toward her.

"If my plan works, I won't be using my power for long." Galene put her fingers to her lips, then a loud whistle cut through the water.

Braxtus didn't ask. He focused on Iyana, her hair shining like a silver beacon in the night. He tried to ignore the seafloor dropping away into nothing.

Sooner than he would have thought, pressure built around him. Galene stopped swimming, but she didn't stop moving, the water now towing them along.

It took a minute for Braxtus to stop trying to swim with it, letting Galene's tide just push him. Iyana picked it up fast. She and Demitri remained linked at their hands, gliding along.

At least Kostas didn't look nearly as graceful.

"Here they come!" Galene smiled.

Braxtus snapped his eyes ahead. There, in the distant, midnight waters, a clump of shadows began to appear. Racing toward them.

He threw his arms out, trying to stop moving forward, but Galene's tide wouldn't release him. The shapes began to form, fins standing out.

Sharks? He floundered.

Galene slowed their approach, but the things were almost upon them. In the dim light, he made out the long, slender faces of horses.

He blinked. "What . . . ?"

Galene swam forward, waving at them to follow.

"Great Gaia!" Iyana struck after Galene, Kostas close behind.

Braxtus stayed back, watching as the sea horses spun and whinnied, acting delighted to see them. They were just as large as the stallions they had left behind. Their manes swirled in the water, and their wide horse eyes were bright with curiosity. Their front legs were strong and muscular, but instead of hooves, wide, powerful fins pounded the water. About halfway down their backs their bodies shifted into thick, sleek tails like sea lions. At the end of the tail was another wide fin. The skin by each fin was pearly and translucent, the webbing in the fins a startling white.

Galene and Iyana greeted them warmly, catching their manes and twirling around with them. Demitri didn't get close enough to play with the beasts, but hovered near Iyana, watching her glee as she and Galene played with them.

"My father's creations!" Galene said. "We'll ride them so we don't have to keep using my powers!"

"Brilliant!" Kostas grinned. "And they're gorgeous!"

Braxtus considered this alternative. If they were riding sea horses, would they even have to breathe water? Hesitantly, he kicked forward. He had to admit they were beautiful. Majestic, even.

As if reading his mind, Galene said, "We won't even have to stay underwater. We'll ride over the waves with them as long as possible."

"Are we far enough away that we won't be spotted from shore?" Demitri asked.

Galene nodded. "We've traveled farther than it seems."

"So how do we mount?"

With one swift movement, Galene took hold of a mane, swinging a leg over and settling onto the sea horse's back where it melded from horse to fish. "Above the waves, it feels just like riding a horse."

Iyana took hold of one and glided onto it. Kostas and Demitri took a little longer, but were soon astride. Galene looked to Braxtus and he felt his cheeks warm. She whistled, and a larger sea horse appeared from the back of the group. It swam fearlessly up to Braxtus, who cleared his throat and did his best to look composed as he laced his fingers into the slippery hair and pulled himself onto the mount.

Galene nodded her approval, then kicked her horse. It struck for the surface.

"Remember to breathe all the water out of your lungs!" she called, then her head disappeared into the open air.

Grateful for the idea of air again, Braxtus urged his mount after hers.

He broke through the surface, water streaming off him, and sucked in a breath of the cool night air. Though it was summer, goose bumps rose on his skin.

Iyana emerged beside him and rubbed her arms.

"Here," he said, guiding his sea horse over to her as Demitri and Kostas surfaced. Lighting as bright a fire as he could within his palms, he held it beside her.

She smiled and closed her eyes. A strong breeze whisked through his fire, almost guttering it. He shot it brighter.

The now warmed air swept over them, drying their skin.

"Don't keep that lit too long." Demitri rode past him. "It's a beacon to the shore."

Braxtus gave him a narrow look, but let it die.

Galene waved to the rest of the herd, now disappearing back under the waves. Then she motioned for the four of them to follow her once more, farther into the Aegean Sea.

15

IYANA

Breathing air again was blissful. The winds off the water were crisp and playful, and though they chilled her still-damp clothes and hair, the feeling was freeing. The sea swelled and rocked, stretching out to the horizon. Skipping above the surface, the five of them rode swiftly. Waves shattered over their knees, breaking into glittering foam that drifted away behind them. She dropped back, leaning over the side of her sea horse to trail her fingers through the water.

"It's a beautiful night." Braxtus slowed his sea horse and joined her. Combing his wet curls back with his fingers, he nodded toward the brilliant sky. Thin clouds veiled the familiar constellations, but light still glimmered through.

"It is," she agreed. "The water makes a stunning reflection, like the sky wraps all around us."

"You like it out here."

A pang went through her. "I already miss the mountain. But what we're doing is important."

Braxtus glanced at the dark water. "Still . . . I'd prefer the *avyssos* to be somewhere else."

"I know. I would, too." She lifted her lips into a smile. "Thank you for coming anyway."

"You mean despite the dark, bottomless, airless pit stretching out below us?"

"Why, Braxtus, I didn't think you were afraid of anything," she teased.

He returned her mischievous grin, but it shifted into a wide yawn. Iyana looked more closely at him. Dark gold ringed the underside of his eyes.

"Did you sleep at all before we left Chrysander's camp?" she asked.

He grimaced. "No."

"When was the last time you slept?"

He rubbed his beard. "On Mount Olympus two days ago."

"Braxtus!"

"We had to push hard to catch up to you. I'm fine—"

"No you're not." Iyana leaned forward, and her sea horse sped up. "Galene! We need to find somewhere to sleep."

Ahead, Galene let out another whistle, and the sea horses all slowed to a stop, rocking in the currents. She turned hers around. "We have a good head start on Anyss. If there are another two days of riding ahead of us, resting now would be a good idea." She looked to Braxtus. "But we'll have to sleep underwater. There's no way to anchor ourselves up here and no islands for miles."

Iyana frowned, but Braxtus rubbed his eyes. "At this point, I don't care."

Galene nodded, reminded them once more to breathe out, then submerged. Iyana hardly had time to bid a mental farewell to the wind before her sea horse followed suit, lurching below the surface. She exhaled, then drew an uncomfortable breath of water.

Galene guided them down through the darkness to the sea bottom. Iyana could hardly make out Demitri beside her, but with Galene's help, she managed to tie a long strand of seaweed around her waist.

"This way the tides won't carry us off in the night."

Drifting weightless turned Iyana's stomach, but finally exhaustion won out and tugged her into a restless sleep.

In her dreams, black, soulless eyes and grinning ghosts chased after her. She ran through a cold, dark night in search of Demitri, and when she found him, he threw flaming javelins into their hearts. As the taraxippi scattered, Demitri wrapped her protectively in his arms.

She woke to rippling, weak sunlight. Clear blue waters stretched all around them, reeds waving in the currents. Galene had already gathered seaweed for a measly breakfast, and Iyana tried not to mimic Demitri's disgusted faces as she choked it down.

As soon as they finished, they rode to the surface, the light growing increasingly bright until she burst into open air. The glare of the morning sun on water stung her eyes, and she had to cough some liquid from her lungs before she could breathe normally. Still, warm air felt wonderful and she immediately sent it flying through her hair.

"Did you say there were islands around?" Braxtus asked Galene as she surfaced.

She smiled at him knowingly. "There's one directly in our course, actually. We should reach it by evening."

His visible and audible sigh of relief made Iyana giggle. "Thank Gaia. I'm going crazy with nowhere to put my feet."

THEY ARRIVED AT the island just after sunset, weather-battered, burned, and sore from a long day on the waves.

The "pile of rocks," as Braxtus noted, was "hardly worthy to be considered a landmass." But he seemed happiest of all as they tested their weak legs on solid ground.

As Iyana clambered among the rocks and coral, working her legs, a glimmer of gold caught her eye. She focused on the sparkling granite stone tucked away by some tide pools.

"Is that a marker?" she asked. It looked almost identical to the one they had found on the beach the night before.

Demitri, close behind, followed her line of sight. "I guess we were supposed to end up on this island."

"Between the tides and the sea horses, we traveled faster than a ship." Galene caught up to Iyana and bent to inspect the rock. The friends glanced at each other, then together reached out to touch it. Words glimmered to life.

Sink beneath the horizon to the realm below
Hold the course
Through surviving the insatiable thirst.

"The whole thing is a riddle," Kostas said, joining them, "split up into markers along the route."

"What's the 'insatiable thirst'?" Braxtus asked.

Everyone looked at each other, but no one seemed to have any answers.

"Well, sinking below clearly means traveling underwater," Galene offered.

"Clearly." Braxtus shuddered.

"I'll think it over," Kostas said, stringing his bow. "Let's scout the island and find some food."

They found a small plateau that overlooked a long, rocky beach and split up to make camp. Kostas spotted a couple of cormorants and shot them for dinner. Demitri took a look around, and when he returned with a confirmation of its "perfect dullness," they cooked their food over Braxtus's fire.

Iyana devoured her meal, then licked her fingers clean with a happy sigh.

Across the fire, Braxtus caught Iyana's eye. He looked skyward and raised his hands, mouthing *thank you*. Iyana giggled. Beside her, Demitri looked over at Braxtus with raised eyebrows, but he was innocently poking at the flames again.

"You've never liked him much," Iyana whispered.

Demitri draped an arm around her, not answering at first. "He's annoying, but fine, I suppose." When Iyana gave him a skeptical look, he pressed his nose to her cheek, admitting, "I don't like why he's *here*."

"Demitri." Iyana shifted uncomfortably, turning to face him. "We're just friends. He knows that. Besides, he might have come for my benefit initially, but that can't be why he's still here. He must believe what we're doing is the right thing." She looked into his eyes. "Clearing Galene's name, saving Olympus, showing the Olympians that we're capable and worthy . . ."

He looked unconvinced.

"Think of it this way," she pressed, taking his jaw. "Between all of us we have"—she glanced around the circle—"tides, a brilliant mind, fire, wind, your insane combat skills . . ." He smirked. "My point is, we have a lot of power and ability on our side. We should be grateful for all the extra help to get the *avyssos* before Anyss."

"Yes, because fire will be *really* helpful underwater."

She elbowed him, and he unapologetically pulled her in for a kiss, then stood, moving toward the other side of the fire to shed his armor.

Iyana watched the flames for a minute, then called for her wind to make them dance higher. The air responded more readily than usual, sweeping in with a solid gust. The fire jumped, and Iyana smiled. The wind seemed to have more natural movement out on the water, making it easier to manipulate. *I wish it was this easy all the time.*

"Careful there." Kostas leaned back. "Wind and fire make a feisty combination."

Iyana quirked an eyebrow at him, a sudden blush heating her face, but released her hold on the winds. The flames settled, and Iyana walked over to Galene.

Together they lay down a short distance from the gods, where they could still feel the warmth of the flames. Iyana got as comfortable as possible on the hard ground, gazing up into the sky—a midnight backdrop with a thousand glittering diamonds faceted onto it.

She rolled onto her side to look at Galene. "How are you doing with all of this?" she whispered.

Galene's green eyes were glassy in the starlight, and she rolled to face Iyana, too. "I'm grateful you're here." She kept her voice low. "And I'm grateful things lined up so I don't have to attempt this alone."

"I said you wouldn't regret me coming."

"It's still so dangerous."

"Um . . . you're a deadly warrior." Iyana tapped Galene's heart. "You fought your Immortality Trial beast and nearly had it. Nothing could be worse than that sea creature, and now there are five of us. We can take anything on." She worked to keep her voice confident. It wasn't that she didn't believe what she was saying, but the taraxippi had been frightening enough.

"You're right." Galene smiled, then leaned closer. "I can't believe Braxtus followed you out here." She paused. "Actually, I can. Especially if he thought you were in mortal danger."

"I *was* in mortal danger."

"It's still a big move." Galene paused. "I always thought you two were good for each other."

Iyana let out a breath from her nose. She already knew how Galene felt, and it only tightened the knot of conflicting emotions inside her. She was genuinely almost frustrated that Braxtus was with them. It complicated things. Her face still got hot when he came too close. He was sweet and funny and they had great memories and . . . and Furies she *missed* him. But he'd had his chance, and now she'd chosen Demitri. She loved him—Demitri was good to her. He took care of her and loved her deeply. She wished Galene would come to like him as well.

She shifted to look at the gods. Demitri had just settled down to sleep, isolated from Kostas and Braxtus, the two lost in a deep conversation.

Iyana turned back to Galene, who had followed her gaze to the gods, a soft expression on her face. Iyana glanced back and forth between her and the three of them before realizing who she was watching.

"Kostas is handsome," she said slyly.

Even in the dark, Iyana could see Galene's freckled cheeks blush. She gave Iyana a wry smile. "He's decent, I suppose."

Iyana poked her for the lie, and they hid their giggles before Galene spoke again. "I'm trying to figure him out. He keeps saying things that surprise me."

"That's a good thing, right?"

"Yes."

Iyana smiled. "Hopefully, we'll be back on Olympus, cleared of all charges after this is over. Then you'll have all the time you want to get to know him."

Galene went quiet. Tension settled across her face.

"Talk to me," Iyana probed.

"I'm worried about Chrysander," she whispered. "If we follow Kostas's plan and trap the rebels in the *avyssos*, the Olympians will kill him for this."

Iyana found Galene's hand and squeezed it. "Then you convince him to run. We can trap the others to confirm our story. Without his people he can't hurt Olympus."

"He's stubborn and passionate about what he's doing. Convincing him to run is going to be difficult."

"You're going to have to anyway. His life depends on it."

They lay in silence by the fire until it burned down low and the others went to sleep. Finally, Iyana closed her eyes.

She stood in the training arena, battle-gear strapped on. With a click and a thunk, an arrow came flying at her.

Iyana caught it on her raised shield, and dread raced through her as she remembered this moment. She turned, throwing a spike at the automatic crossbow to disarm it, but missed by a good foot.

Two more arrows launched themselves at her.

She ran, dodging one, but the other cracked on her shield powerfully enough to make her arm tremble. She knew this, remembered what was going to happen, but was unable to stop herself from reliving it.

Her foot caught on a loose stone and she stumbled. The shield slipped down her arm as she tried to catch herself, leaving her exposed as two more arrows sliced through the air toward her.

But it was okay, because this is when Demitri saved her. She could see him now, coming as though in slow motion, diving at her from the wall of the training arena, ready to knock her to the ground . . .

He turned to mist, vanishing a second before impact.

The arrows slammed into her.

Iyana jolted awake, sweating, the cool rock beneath her reminding her where she really was.

She sat up and wrapped her arms around herself. Her dreams were becoming increasingly more realistic. She shivered at the memory of that humiliating day on the training grounds. But Demitri had been there to save her. And he was still with her, keeping her safe.

She looked over at him, sleeping peacefully with his arm outstretched. *Maybe I can steal some of his body warmth. It might chase away the dreams, too.*

Just as she decided to move to him, a sound grabbed her attention. She stiffened, straining her ears. Above the crashing and hissing of the waves, a scatter of sweet laughter rang out. Iyana rose from the rock, moving to find the source. Her bare feet pressed against the cold stone as she picked her way along the most silent path. Reaching the edge, she peered down.

The ground sloped away onto a rugged beach with tall, stone pillars shooting from the earth and water. The waves swirled around and crashed against them, sending spray shooting into the air, sprinkling the four beautiful figures perched atop.

Iyana recoiled at the sight of the women. *Humans. I can't be seen.* Then she hesitated, squinting at them. They weren't small enough to be human women, so they were . . . goddesses? Out here on the same lonely rock?

They sat in flowing, cream dresses, rich-colored shawls draped over their shoulders and arms. Though they all had perfect skin and long hair, each looked completely different from the others, with varying skin tones and hair colors.

One hummed a starting note, then sweet, velvet voices rang out in perfect harmony.

The sound struck Iyana to the core, stoking a powerful sense of yearning.

Sirens! Panic shot through her and she jerked her hands toward her ears, but then the blonde hit a high note that rang pure and clear. It drew her in—she longed to reach it. She let her hands fall to her sides.

As the ethereal tones built in intensity, the redhead rose from her rock and dropped to the ground below, her bare feet splashing in the tide. Lifting her rich green shawl from her shoulders, she twisted her hands around the fabric for a better grip and began to dance.

She flew across the sand, hardly seeming to touch the ground as she moved with the music, spinning her shawl around her.

A moment later, the woman with ebony tresses and bronze skin leapt down to join her, still singing. She raised the deep violet shawl above her head and mirrored her friend. The two of them danced together, circling, twisting those shawls and catching hold of each other's.

Their music grew more compelling, pulling at Iyana's heart, urging her to join them. She teetered for a moment, then, confused at her own hesitancy, started down the slope.

At her step, stones broke loose and rolled down to the shore. Their heads snapped in her direction. The dance slowed but didn't stop, and they kept their eyes locked on her, appraising her coolly until as one, they beckoned.

She hurried down the side of the plateau, but stopped before she got too close, aching to join them, strangely self-conscious. She swayed to the haunting, thrumming melody. The third goddess dropped from the rock, landing in front of Iyana.

Cowed by her unearthly beauty, Iyana took a step back. Rich brown locks spilled over the crimson shawl, and her almond eyes gazed at her. A tiny smile of approval formed on the brunette's perfect lips, and she untied an extra shawl from around her waist, extending it to Iyana.

The music thrummed in her ears and heart, and she reached out to take hold of the blue satin. She ran her fingers along it, marveling. The goddess took her own scarlet shawl and wrapped it around her hands, showing Iyana how it was done.

Together, they began to dance, first stamping to the rhythm, then rotating and spinning with their shawls. The goddesses took her arms, moving her until she picked up speed. Throughout it all they sang, never losing their breath. Iyana hummed to the haunting melody in ecstasy, and the world turned to a blur as she danced.

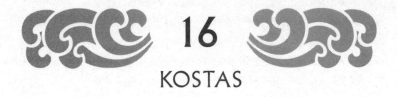

16

KOSTAS

Kostas woke suddenly, unease crawling down his spine.

It took a moment for him to orient himself. He was lying on his back. Their small fire had gone out. And he was alone.

A soft beat thrummed behind a wistful melody. It tugged at his heart, teasing his emotions.

He clapped his hands over his ears. "Kronos!" he cursed, leaping to his feet. "Sirens!" The notorious sea monsters used their song to lure any being within earshot, lulling them into a stupor so the sirens could kill and eat them. They preyed mostly on humans, but would happily take a god if they could catch one. *This is bad.* If their song had coaxed his companions away, they could already be dead.

A shadow moved, and his heart leapt. "Galene!" he called, starting after her. She was walking away, silent in her bare feet and tunic as she moved toward the edge of the plateau, unresponsive. Her aura rippled sky-blue calm and pale green longing.

He started running, hands still over his ears. "Galene, stop!" Catching up to her, he hesitated, then dropped his hands and grabbed her. He spun her to face him, and the music flooded back into his mind. Though he could feel it coaxing him, he pushed it back out.

Galene's eyes were distant. She tried to turn back toward the sound, but Kostas slapped his hands over her ears, shaking her head slightly.

After a few moments, she blinked, eyes focusing. Then fear ripped through her aura, the emotion washing over him as she gasped. She reached up to cover his ears. "Kostas! You—"

"I think I'm immune. Mostly," he quickly assured her. "Their magic seems to focus on overwhelming the mind with emotion. My gift resists outside influence."

She nodded in relief.

"Where are the others?" he asked.

"They're not here?" She moved her hands to her own ears, pressing on top of Kostas's hands. Once they were firm, he slid his away. She looked around frantically, her alarm rushing against him. "Kronos, they might already be on the beach. We have to go after them."

"But you'll get transfixed again! You stay here, I'll go. I can help them snap out of it."

"No!" Her eyes were wide. "I'll keep my ears plugged. I'll yell. But Iyana's down there!" She didn't wait for his permission, turning and racing to the edge of the plateau, then starting down. He leapt after her, heart pounding.

Down on the beach, five beautiful figures danced. He could tell instantly they were neither gods nor humans. Their auras were muted, with basic colors fluctuating sluggishly. The dominating feeling emanating from them was a greenish brown: hunger.

The sirens laughed and sang in incandescent harmony, loose hair shining in the starlight. Kostas's breath caught at the emotion in the music, but he tore his eyes and mind away, scanning again for his companions.

Braxtus and Demitri were at the bottom of the plateau, both moving toward the charming sirens. Kostas swore under his breath, moving faster to keep up with Galene as she hurtled toward them. If he could get to them before they made it all the way . . .

One of the sirens let out sweet laughter, spotting Braxtus and Demitri. She held out a hand, beckoning, and both of them eagerly picked up their pace.

Galene skidded to a stop, and Kostas collided with her. "What?"

"It's Iyana," she whispered.

He looked around again. "I don't see her yet, but that doesn't mean—"

"No. It's *Iyana*."

His eyes fell back on the sirens, and he understood. The one who had beckoned to Braxtus and Demitri danced for them again, familiar white-blonde tresses spinning as she moved.

His stomach dropped and he broke into a sprint, skidding down the slope. The intensity of the music climbed, and he had to grit his teeth against the influence. "Don't forget to yell if you have to!" he called over his shoulder.

Two of the sirens moved to meet Braxtus and Demitri, reaching out and clasping their hands, still singing.

"Braxtus!" Kostas yelled. "Stop!"

Braxtus didn't seem to hear him, but the tall brunette dancing with Iyana jerked around. Her eyes narrowed at him, a touch of dark orange caution leaking into her aura.

He forced himself to slow down as his feet touched the sand. *Pretend to be entranced,* he told himself, letting his eyes glass over. The brunette still watched him, but she let him approach.

The redhead was singing sweetly to Demitri. He stared at Iyana, but the siren tugged him away, and he followed her toward the tide. The black-haired siren cajoled Braxtus, trying to pull him away, too. Before Kostas could reach his friend, the golden blonde cut him off.

She smiled, raising a soft yellow shawl and looping it around his neck. She sang, and a nearly irresistible longing penetrated him. He gaped at her.

No. The thought surfaced. I *am God of Games. Emotions are my realm. I control how I feel.* He forced the feelings back. She paused, but it wasn't long before she smiled again, pulling him along. When they were close to the others, Kostas grabbed the shawl, ducking out from under it and spinning toward Iyana. He grabbed her shoulders mid-twirl.

"Iyana, it's a trap!" he hissed.

She pulled away, not looking at him. The two sirens close by watched, unsure of what he was doing.

He seized Iyana again, this time ducking his head until she looked directly into his eyes. "They tricked you!" he tried again, giving her a shake. "Come on!"

She shoved him, hard.

Kostas staggered away.

Iyana's eyes were cold as she turned her back on him and kept dancing.

"Kostas!" Galene cried. "They're going to kill them!"

Kostas spun, looking to see Demitri and Braxtus up to their knees in the water, oblivious to their state as the sirens pulled them farther into the sea. Galene stood on the shore, hands over her ears, face screwed up in concentration. The tide slunk back, keeping the gods from getting deep fast, but it seemed to be all Galene could do against high tide.

Kostas started to move again, but a cold hand closed around his arm in an iron grip. He twisted, bringing his elbow up to slam into the brunette's jaw. Her aura snapped red. She hissed, letting go, and Kostas sprinted into the water.

"Braxtus! Demitri! Wake up!" The water slowed him down, but he forged on, cursing himself for not bringing his bow. The siren with Braxtus looked up, the melody on her lips transforming to a snarl. She left Braxtus—who stood there, stupefied—and lunged at Kostas, anger dominating her hunger.

He raised his hands to block her first strike, but her second took him across the temple, and he stumbled. Lowering his shoulder, he tried to ram her, but the dark-haired siren twisted aside, using his momentum to pull him past her. She struck with open hands and brutal strength. Kostas barely kept up with the bludgeoning—his skills didn't lie in hand-to-hand combat.

The siren shoved him back, then seized his arm, twisting it painfully until he lost his footing. His head went under the water, and she forced him against the sand.

They think they can drown us, Kostas realized, staring through the seawater. To his right, he could see Braxtus's bare feet, standing still in the sea. He struggled for a moment, then let himself go limp, breathing out bubbles into the water.

The siren's grip loosened.

He kicked her, then launched himself at Braxtus, swinging a fist at his blank face. The punch landed hard, and Braxtus toppled backward, falling into the currents. He looked up in shock, and his eyes lost their dazed expression. Kostas grabbed his arm and yanked him back to his feet. "Fight!" he commanded as the siren screeched, leaping at them again.

Braxtus turned and caught the siren's hands with his own, bringing his knee up to sink it into her stomach. She screamed louder, writhing and wrestling to break free of Braxtus's grip.

There was a large splash behind Kostas, and he flipped around to look for Demitri. He and the redhead were nowhere to be seen, but bubbles rose to the surface a good distance away.

"Demitri!" Kostas left Braxtus and the siren to their fight, splashing through the water to try to reach him. *He can breathe underwater. He can fight. If he's not still entranced. Kronos, what if he's . . .*

A figure erupted from the water: tall, dark-haired, and dripping. One hand grasped his javelin, the other was tangled into the red locks of the siren, dragging her head above the water. She screamed with rage and fear, raising the hair on the back of Kostas's neck at her inhuman cry. All the entrancing music had stopped.

"Get out of here," he yelled. "I'll deal with this."

He pulled his javelin back. Braxtus ran into Kostas, pushing him to the shore, so Kostas didn't see the javelin fall, but he heard the scream cut short.

Snarls and splashes from behind them sounded that Demitri had engaged the dark-haired siren as well. On the shore, Galene faced the blonde siren, a few paces apart. The blonde tied her yellow shawl around her waist and raised her hands, as though ready to stop Galene from passing. Behind the siren, Iyana still danced with the brunette, oblivious to the screams, somehow still entranced despite the lack of their bewitching melody.

Kostas stumbled onto the shore, then reached down and hefted a rock, hurling it at the blonde siren. It struck her shoulder, and she shrieked. Galene tried to take the opportunity to run past, but the siren was faster, dashing into her path and striking.

Galene ducked and backed away, looking desperately to Kostas and Braxtus. "Don't let her drink that!"

"What?" Kostas asked, running in her direction.

"The goblet!"

Kostas slowed, following Galene's pointed gaze. A clear goblet was clutched in the brunette's fingers. She offered it to Iyana, tantalizing her with it. A pearly blue liquid swirled inside.

"It will turn her into one of them!"

Iyana reached for it.

Braxtus sprinted around the blonde, who was still focused on Galene. "Iyana, stop!" he yelled. "Iyana!"

But Kostas knew he wouldn't make it in time. Iyana accepted the glass, delight and curiosity alive on her youthful face. She raised it to her lips.

Something dark sliced through the night.

The goblet shattered.

Iyana let out a surprised squeak, stumbling back as glass and droplets of the liquid scattered everywhere, and a black javelin struck the ground only a few feet away.

The brunette turned, eyes and aura full of fire. Demitri tore in her direction, drawing his staff from his back, pulling it apart into two swords. He charged, glowing with confidence and resolve as he leapt into the air and kicked her in the chest.

She fell, snarling and swiping at him.

"*Go!*" he yelled at the others. "I can handle this! Get out of here!"

The blonde siren turned from Galene and Kostas, sprinting up the beach to help her sister. Ahead, Braxtus reached Iyana, who stood in a stupor.

"Come on!" Kostas urged Galene toward the plateau. She hesitated, watching Iyana, who wouldn't move. Braxtus swept an arm behind Iyana's knees and lifted her.

"They're coming, now let's go!"

She nodded and ran beside him, followed closely by Braxtus and Iyana, leaving the son of the War God to take care of the mess behind them.

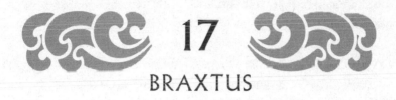

17

BRAXTUS

Rocks dug into Braxtus's bare feet as he ran up the side of the plateau, carrying Iyana. White-blonde hair spilled over his arm, her head lolling against his chest as she stared at the sky, face blank. He swallowed, the fear of losing her to the sirens still lingering.

He allowed himself a glance back at Demitri.

He moved like a dark whirlwind—the sirens didn't stand a chance. Fierce joy lit Demitri's face as he fought.

Braxtus focused on the climb again, feeling a strange wave of jealousy. There weren't many people he envied when it came to combat, but with the abilities Demitri had inherited from his father, he was in a league of his own.

Iyana groaned and shook her head as though to clear it. Her crystal eyes focused on him. "Braxtus?"

His heart skipped a beat, her warmth pressing against him. "It's me."

"What's going on?"

"We ran into trouble." They reached the top of the plateau, and he cautiously set her on her feet. "But we're all safe now, thanks to Kostas. And Demitri," he admitted.

A lost expression settled on Iyana's face. Galene squeezed her hand, then turned for her armor and weapons.

Braxtus joined Galene and Kostas, strapping on his armor and sword with quick fingers, keeping an eye on Iyana. She followed suit slowly, almost like she was still in a trance. Her face grew more and more pale, and Braxtus could tell she was starting to piece things together.

They laced up their sandals and made their way down the other side of the plateau, where they first landed.

Starlight reflected on the water, illuminating the heads of the sea horses waiting for them close to shore, whinnying anxiously. Braxtus gritted his teeth and waded in the cool water.

Iyana stayed on the shore. "Where's Demitri?"

"He's coming," was Galene's only hurried reply.

Braxtus motioned for her to join them, then steeled himself, mounting his sea horse again. Iyana stepped into the water and straddled her own.

They waited a few tense moments, listening to the lapping water.

A figure appeared, leaping down the rocks, staff on his back and javelin in hand. He mounted the sea horse waiting for him, holding his javelin underwater to clean it off.

Iyana spoke. "They were sirens, weren't they?"

Kostas, Demitri, and Galene exchanged glances, looking surprised that she hadn't figured it out earlier. Braxtus scowled at them as Iyana flushed. *She was in a trance like the rest of us, and didn't wake until after the ordeal. Of course she wouldn't have known.*

"They tried to turn you into one of them." Demitri fixed her with an icy stare.

Her eyes widened. "What? I've never heard of that before!"

"Me neither," Braxtus put in.

"They don't breed." Galene shivered. "They all started as humans or gods. Usually, they just kill and eat who they can, but occasionally they'll grow their numbers."

"Why would they target me?"

Kostas scratched his neck. "I don't know, but you were so entranced. I couldn't snap you out of it like I did with the others."

Iyana's cheeks flamed gold, and she ducked her head. "I'm sorry if I made it harder to get out of there."

"It's not your fault," Braxtus said flatly.

Demitri glanced over at him with an unreadable expression.

Kostas shrugged. "It doesn't matter."

"He's right. We're safe now." Galene guided her sea horse away, urging all of their mounts to start moving again.

Demitri nudged his sea horse closer to Iyana's. Braxtus just caught his quiet words. "I'm glad I'm here to protect you."

A spike of anger went through Braxtus as Demitri surged ahead. Iyana lowered her gaze, and he thought he saw her wipe her eyes. Looking over at Demitri's impassive expression, he seethed.

"We should dive," Galene called back to the others. "The marker said 'Sink beneath the horizon to the realm below.'"

Braxtus's anger was switched with choking dread.

"You're right," Kostas agreed. "If we're heading out now—"

"Um . . ." Braxtus's voice went hoarse, and he cleared his throat. "Now? Apollo hasn't even brought the sun up yet; it will be pitch-black under the water."

Galene gave him a sympathetic glance. "I feel like we should follow the riddle exactly."

"Can't we just dive when we get closer to the next part of the riddle?"

Galene looked over at Kostas, who frowned. "We're going to have to dive eventually, you know that."

Braxtus lit his fingers on fire and put them out again. "Of course I know that. But we will spend less time underwater if we dive *later.*"

Demitri smirked. "Let the kid keep his candles lit a while longer."

Braxtus ground his teeth, urging his mount to round on Demitri, but Galene said sharply, "All right, let's just go. They said to 'hold the course,' so it shouldn't make much difference whether we're at the surface or not."

"'Hold the course through surviving the insatiable thirst,'" Kostas reminded them. "I haven't figured out what that means yet."

Galene nodded and took off. Braxtus forced himself to follow, the water around him turning to steam from the heat of his legs.

The sun rose steadily as they traveled. The others winced and splashed their burnt faces as it climbed into the sky, and he felt a twinge of guilt. He couldn't burn. His father's domain wouldn't harm him, but it was no wonder the others were eager to dive.

No one spoke, their faces lined with exhaustion from the extra-early start to their day. Iyana stayed at the back of the group, her blue eyes swimming with the insecurities he'd often seen. Demitri rode up front near Galene and Kostas, giving her space. Braxtus kept shooting glances at her, then finally slowed down to ride beside her.

"Hi."

She looked at him sideways. The shutters closed behind her eyes, as though trying to hide her distress. "Hi, Braxtus."

He studied her for a moment. "If you're thinking you're weak, you're not."

She stiffened, then a wry smile quirked her mouth. "You're insufferable. You always act like you know what I'm thinking."

"Am I wrong?"

"No." She fidgeted, glancing at the others. "Why didn't I have enough willpower to snap out of it?"

"You don't know if it has anything to do with willpower or weakness," he pointed out. "They could have tried harder with you because they found you particularly pretty, or good at dancing. Both of those seem to be required qualities of a siren."

"But part of me still feels bewitched . . ."

"So the mysticism spoke to your soul," he teased. "That's not necessarily a bad thing."

She allowed a smile, and her shoulders relaxed a little. "Thank you."

"I'm always here to talk some sense into you."

"I just wish I was more help than hindrance." She frowned. "I wish my ability was stronger." Even as she spoke of it, a breeze ruffled through her long hair. She always wore it loose, she'd once told him, because she loved how it felt when the wind caught it.

"Your ability is amazing." He tipped his face into her wind.

"I can make a strong headwind at most. Not a storm. I don't have the accuracy to even guide my throwing spikes, which is why I chose them as weapons to begin with." She grimaced. "I'm probably the weakest of Zeus's children. Even the Gryphiekin has more of Zeus's power than me."

"The Gryphiekin?" The name rang a bell. "King of the Gryphons, right?"

"Yes." She cocked her head. "Do you know much about him?"

"Just a little. There are cards in the Deck of Fates with different attributes of the Gryphiekin. They're some of the best cards to get in Beast Maker."

"You still play that?" She grinned at him, and he grinned back. The game used a Deck of Fates to create creatures that battled each other. Of course, he had only ever played with a mock Deck of Fates, creating miniature beasts. If you used a *real* Deck of Fates to play, the beasts were life-size and the consequences of losing much more extreme.

"Kostas and I are best friends, remember? We've played every game out there, but Beast Maker is one of his favorites. Of course"—he shrugged—"it was more fun with you. Then I could actually win on occasion."

"Only on occasion." Her eyes sparkled in amusement. "But yes, the Gryphiekin is in the Deck of Fates. Galene's creature for the Immortality Trial had his hide, remember?"

"That's right." He recalled the golden feathers, the lion's hair.

"How does it have more of Zeus's power than you? It's just a beast. You're his daughter."

"Zeus created him. When he did, he put a piece of his power inside the creature. Apparently, that power is manifested as perpetual storms that follow him."

Braxtus let out a low whistle. "Has Zeus ever shown you the creature?"

"No," Iyana sighed. "He hasn't been seen for a long time. I've just always hated that I don't even measure up to a *bird*."

Braxtus considered this, rubbing his beard. "The Olympians must have seen potential in your abilities. You were about to take your Immortality Trial three years early, like Galene."

"Or merely assumed it, since I'm the daughter of Zeus." She eyed him. "If you haven't noticed, the Olympians don't pay too much attention to us as individuals. You can conjure fire, Demitri is a natural fighter. Both of you would do better than me in the arena three years early."

She's right. Another indicator of their unjust system. He let out a breath. "Well, you don't need the Immortality Trials *or* a powerful ability to prove you're a hero. Being a hero is about fighting for something bigger than yourself, despite the obstacles, despite the fear." He caught her gaze again. "You did that for Galene. You do that every day."

A smile bloomed on her face. "And is that why you're still here? To become a hero?"

He paused. Why *was* he here, in the middle of the sea, risking exile? He searched himself for an honest answer. "Maybe. I want to protect Olympus from Poinê and Chrysander. I want to help Galene get home. But more than that I just . . . I have a hard time letting those I care about face danger alone." He held her gaze for a long moment. Was the gold on her cheeks the sun or a soft blush?

She cleared her throat. "Thanks for always being such a good friend."

His heart panged. "Don't do that, Iyana."

"Do what?"

"Act like we're just friends. Like that's all we've ever been."

She opened her mouth, the color rising more intensely to her cheeks. She closed it again, and the gentle breeze whipped into a stronger current. "I don't know what you want me to say."

A sea horse suddenly swung around in front of Braxtus, cutting him off, and he veered. Demitri, riding it, raised his eyebrows at Braxtus, a touch of contempt in his sharp features. Iyana looked away as Demitri took his place beside her.

All right, then. Conversation over.

Braxtus felt his own face burning as he heeled his mount to swim up to Kostas.

Kostas kept his eyes on the horizon. "Did you know attraction is an emotion?"

Braxtus stared at his best friend.

Kostas brushed a speck of dust from his tunic. "Most assume it's a physical reaction, but there's an emotional side to it as well. An appreciation of someone. Desire, intrigue, longing. It's all in there, swirling around. I can feel it all. I see it as a rose gold."

"What's your point?"

"Well, I'd ask what your conversation with Iyana was about just now"—he grinned—"but from all the emotions that just assaulted me, I think I can take a pretty good guess."

Braxtus raised a fist to slug him in the arm, but, as Kostas probably intended, his curiosity was piqued. "How is she feeling?"

"Confused. Stressed."

He pressed his knuckles to his forehead. "You think I should back off?"

Kostas paused. "Look, I don't want to be the reason for a heartbreak, but . . . I think you have a chance." Braxtus's heart leapt, and Kostas gave a wicked smile. "What's your strategy?"

"Kostas, it's not—"

"*Everything* is a game," Kostas insisted. "Everything."

"All right, then, what do you—"

Braxtus's sea horse suddenly whinnied, pumping its fins and rearing its head. The other sea horses reacted similarly, and Braxtus grabbed his mount's mane as Galene called out to them.

"Something is wrong!"

Now what? He eyed the waves as he patted the sea horse's slippery neck, guiding it closer to the others. "Do you know what it is?"

"No," Galene held her hands out on either side of her, balancing on her sea horse's back with her eyes closed. "But we're moving fast. The tide is powerful."

Only then did Braxtus notice the subtle change—rather than the lap of rising and falling waters, it rushed past his legs, towing him and his sea horse with it. "Can't you slow us down?"

"I can try . . ."

"We should pull back to decide what to do," Demitri said.

Galene turned her mount, the rest following, pounding the water with their powerful fins. They gave a few more whinnies of alarm, eyes wide and rolling. With water in every direction, Braxtus couldn't tell for sure, but it didn't feel like they were making any progress.

"*Look!*" Iyana pointed behind them, and Braxtus squinted to see what Iyana's sharp eyes had caught.

His stomach lurched. In the near distance, the sea was a white, shifting, turning mass of rushing water—a force of nature that dwarfed them. Even as he stared, he and the others drifted around it. Toward it.

The vortex was pulling them in.

18

GALENE

Surviving the insatiable thirst.

The answer to the riddle struck her like a bolt of lightning as they sped toward the maelstrom. "Charybdis."

"What?" Sudden terror drained the color from Braxtus's face. "Did you say *Charybdis*? The sea monster?"

Beneath her she could feel the terrifying, godlike strength of the waters ripping past them in a fury unlike anything she had experienced before. The lines of the riddle seemed so obvious now. Too late. "It has to be! There's no other reason for a whirlpool this size so far from land."

Charybdis had been a sea-nymph who flooded land to grow Poseidon's terrain. Zeus, angry that she encroached so far inland, turned her into a monster and bound her to the bottom of the sea. She was cursed with eternal thirst, and her frenzied drinking swept the currents into a mighty whirlpool, stronger than any natural force. Entire ships had been swallowed in her greed.

Charybdis had an equal—a sister in the sea. The image of the six heads of Scylla flooded through Galene's memory. She'd fought Scylla in her Immortality Trial and had lost, dreadfully. Now she was supposed to face that monster's counterpart?

Cold fear clutched Galene's heart.

This time, no one will save us.

The sea horses swam in a frenzy, whinnying and tossing their glossy manes.

"We can breathe underwater!" Demitri struggled to control his mount. "Let's just dive now. We'll be fine if we can break straight through this storm!"

Galene shook her head, panic rising. "From here, these currents will pull us directly down into Charybdis's jaws! This is why we needed to go underwater—to pass between the strongest currents at the surface and the monster beneath."

"How did you not sense this earlier?" Demitri demanded.

"I did! I mistook the pull of the water for an island!" She pushed loose strands of hair back from her face, trying to see to the other end of the whirlpool. Too far.

Galene whistled at the sea horses, urging them to resist getting pulled into the eye of the storm. The others struggled along beside her, mounts swimming as hard as they could toward the outskirts of the maelstrom.

"Galene!" Iyana cried. "It's already too strong!"

Galene heaved on the waters, but her grasp suddenly seemed miniscule, her ability swallowed in Charybdis's might.

Her hands shook, and she clenched the sea horse's mane tighter. Her mind raced, flooding with thoughts and ideas that she discarded as the tides grew in strength.

The horses shrieked, fueling her fear.

"Galene!" Iyana's scream pierced her.

Galene shielded herself against a spray of water, then looked toward the center of the storm. The roiling white waters sloped away, curving down into a yawning, dark hole.

A cold wave struck from behind. Kostas let out a yell as his sea horse reared. He slipped, tumbling off its back and into the surging waters.

"No!" Galene dove after him.

Willing the biting water to push her faster along its spiral, she reached him, seizing him around the chest and pulling him up to the surface. She wiped the water from her eyes, looking for the others.

The rest of the sea horses had fled with the first. Braxtus, Iyana, and Demitri all swam, fighting to keep from being pulled under. They lurched, the currents dragging them all in a tighter spiral toward the abyssal darkness.

Kostas grasped her arm, kicking furiously to stay afloat. "Galene! You can stop this!"

"I—" She pulled at the currents again, trying to make just a pocket of calm around them, but the storm crashed right through it.

How could she tell him she couldn't?

Another powerful lurch of water caught them. Her fingers slipped and Kostas ripped away from her, sweeping directly into the funnel of the storm.

Kostas! Horrified, she battered the waters, pitching, trying to keep herself upright. Braxtus shouted, striking out after his best friend. Within seconds, his head disappeared in a blur of white. Demitri went careening after them.

Iyana looked at her in panic—then she, too, was sucked into the raging tides.

A dry sob escaped her throat. Not knowing what else to do, she let the storm pull her under to follow her friends.

Galene was snatched, pummeled by thousands of pounds of seething water. Tumbling and reeling, she lost all sense of direction. She could see nothing but white fury, hear only the roar of a million rushing waters. Her skin stung with the whips of the fierce, hungry whirlpool.

Salty water swirled in her mouth and nose, a choking mixture of water and bubbles. Her lungs shuddered as they attempted to switch back and forth between water and air, causing an agonizing ache to build in her ribs and chest.

Fear like nothing she had ever experienced swallowed her whole. For the first time in her life, she could not breathe.

Her body convulsed as she attempted again and again to suck in a breath, but all she could inhale was the frothing swirl that *hurt*. She tried to clear her mind, to reach out to the sea, but sucked in another painful breath and panic resurged. She tried again. Her throat burned and her lungs screamed. Dizziness threw dark spots into her vision. *I can't do this, I can't . . .*

But you have to, another voice inside her said. *Your friends are suffocating, too.*

The thought came down like a hammer. Somewhere, tossed around her, they were dying.

I have to.

She forced herself to ignore the fire in her chest and the pounding in her brain.

Mentally she reached out, past the surging, churning waters, until she sensed the steady current of the sea beyond. With a monumental effort, she pushed off it.

Lurching backward, her body broke through a swirling wall of water into air, then plummeted through the empty eye of the maelstrom.

Heart in her throat, she dropped toward the base of the funnel, a dark, gaping abyss stretching out below. Gagging on the last of the stinging water, she gasped, the full weight of her situation striking her.

Somewhere in that darkness at the bottom of the sea, the monster sucked in hungrily.

Galene flung out her arms to gain control of the water swirling around her. It spilled from the maelstrom's walls, filling the base of the funnel. She yanked the water up as fast as she could. It rose in a column, then stretched up as fingers, ready to catch her.

She braced herself for impact, then crashed into it. Hard.

Every inch of her burned. The water below started spiraling

out into the whirlpool again, and her stomach heaved as she dropped toward the creature's mouth.

She grasped at the tides. *Stop!*

The water around her stilled. Gritting her teeth, she pictured her friends' faces. *I can do this. I have to do this.*

She shoved against the water below her and shot up through the pillar until she was out in the air again. Spitting the water from her lungs, she threw out her arms, feeling the roiling storm.

I am the daughter of Poseidon, God of the Seas.

The words vibrated through her.

I will save my friends. I will clear my name.

The strength of the maelstrom rose around her power, threatening to overshadow it.

I will tame the sea.

She seized the speeding currents.

A scream tore through her lips as she felt the full force of the maelstrom crash onto her, the water's momentum hitting her like a mountain. She fought to reverse Charybdis's tides, but it felt like she was holding back a great, toppling wall.

Wind howled down through the tunnel, snatching her hair and tunic, spitting water at her. She pinned her eyes shut. The enormous pressure built, raging to be set free as Galene battled to bring peace. Nature pushed back with all the logic and strength of the universe.

No! She drew upon every drop of her ability, power coursing through her, tearing at her.

The currents slowed, then stopped.

Galene opened her eyes. For a fraction of a moment she marveled at the storming waters, frozen like glass.

Then she shoved with all her might.

Galene screamed again. The waters surged backward, the resulting tidal waves crashing away. The pressure around her released, and she tumbled into darkness.

19

KOSTAS

The world rocked.

The motion pulled Kostas from the brink of uncon-sciousness, forcing him to again acknowledge his fast-approaching end.

He'd stayed on the outskirts of the maelstrom, sometimes tossed into clearer waters before he was sucked back into the funnel. The occasional breath had been just enough to keep him from blacking out. He'd caught glimpses of the others as they streaked past him with flaming orange auras of panic, but could do nothing as they'd ripped around the circle toward Charybdis's jaws.

Kostas choked again and again, and a new tongue of flames erupted through his chest. His vision flashed. *Make it stop. Just make it stop.* He gasped again and . . .

~~Cool, soothing liquid filled his lungs to the brim.~~

His mind sharpened. He took another breath. Easy.

Kostas tested the motion of his limbs and found no resistance.

His eyes shot open. The sea thrummed with settling waters, rocking him. But the maelstrom was gone.

In a rough circle above the seafloor, his friends floated, bodies convulsing.

Where's Charybdis? He raked his gaze over the rocks below, but there was no sign of the monster. He struck out for Braxtus.

"Kostas!" Utter relief flooded his best friend's face, so strong the emotion slammed into him. They met halfway and embraced. "That was . . . that was . . ." He swallowed and clutched his chest. "Why aren't we dead?"

"Galene!" Kostas whirled, searching, but around him were only three still-terrified auras. *Where is she?*

"There!" Braxtus pointed down.

Galene floated below them, only feet from the jagged seafloor. She was a swirl of dark hair, limp and still.

She had no aura.

Fear seized Kostas and he dove. "Galene!"

What had she done for them? What kind of energy had the feat taken from her? He kicked harder, scooping water to propel him toward her.

The rocks below them shifted, then rumbled.

Those aren't rocks.

An enormous crack split the earth, slowly opening to a dark maw.

The abyss gaped just below Galene, the monster's teeth grinding apart.

Panic clenched his heart. *Faster.* He reached out to Galene and caught her arm. She didn't respond.

Above him, Iyana screamed. "Galene!" She dove toward them.

Kostas seized Galene around the waist and kicked.

Not daring to look back at Charybdis's widening jaws, he held Galene close to him, swimming with every fiber of strength that remained in his body.

"Swim!" Demitri yelled from ahead. "Swim, damn it!"

Iyana caught up, seizing one of Galene's arms to help tow her deadweight through the water. Kostas just swam. He wasn't even sure if Galene was still alive, but he had to get her to safety. All of them had to get out of there. Now.

Another vibration jarred the waters followed by a deafening, hungry moan.

"Faster!"

"Where are the horses?"

Kostas gritted his teeth. His lungs strained, his arms and legs already aching. Iyana kept pace with him, breathing heavily.

A sound like an earthquake deafened them, the sea around him pulsing with the force of it. How large was Charybdis? How far had they even been able to travel from the maelstrom?

Not far enough.

A sharp whistle cut through the waters.

Kostas didn't know if the others were close above him, or behind. *Just swim, just swim.*

Galene didn't stir. He wasn't even sure he could feel her breathing.

Please, he begged the Fates. *Please, let her have survived. Please let us survive.*

The water thrummed by his ear, and he cried out a second before shining scales and pearly fins jumped into his vision. The sea horses.

His heart didn't slow as one of the creatures swerved in front of him. Together, he and Iyana pushed Galene on its back. He threw himself on behind her. "Go!"

Iyana leapt onto her own steed, and Braxtus and Demitri appeared beside him, riding their own horses. They shot off, and he lurched forward, putting his arms around Galene to seize the mane in front of her.

"Is everyone all right?" he yelled over the growing thunder behind them.

"Is *she* all right?" Iyana cried.

Kostas couldn't answer. The sea horses tore through the waters, and after a few deep breaths, he allowed himself to look back.

A dark shadow rose from clouds of rock and sand. All he could

138

make out was a massive, wormlike shape and a huge, gaping black mouth. Charybdis roared.

THEY DIDN'T STOP until the monster was less than a speck behind them. The sea horses pulled up on the green seafloor, so deep the surface was barely visible.

Kostas had found a pulse in Galene's wrist and assured the others that she was alive, but his chest was still tight with worry. He kept his arms around her, throwing a leg over the horse to dismount. He lowered Galene, cradling her as Iyana and the others rushed over.

"Is she waking?" Iyana touched Galene's face, pushing her flowing hair back so she could examine it.

Kostas shook his head.

"She stopped it." Braxtus gaped down at her. "She reversed the *entire maelstrom.*"

Demitri whistled, the sound carrying well underwater, and Kostas realized it must have been him who called the sea horses. "That was an incredible display of power."

"It almost killed her." Iyana retied one of Galene's sandals, hands trembling.

Kostas brushed more of Galene's hair away. "Her body and mind have to recover. She'll sleep as long as she needs to."

Iyana looked like she was fighting tears, but nodded. After a few seconds of heavy silence, she retreated into Demitri's embrace. "I thought we were dead."

Braxtus's face crumpled, and Kostas felt the same trauma, fear, and disbelief radiating from each of them. Demitri reined it in admirably, but his aura couldn't fool Kostas. They were all wrecked and shaken.

He held Galene tighter, discovering comfort in her closeness and warmth, in her light, liquid breath he could feel on his face.

Her Trial had made it clear that she wielded enormous power, but this was a new level.

Kostas thought of her diving into the maelstrom after him, how she'd gripped him, horror and fright enveloping every part of her—her face, her aura, her emotions that swelled against him, that he felt *with* her.

She'd been through so much, too much, in the last few days. Looking at her peaceful face, he was glad that—despite the nightmare they just went through—at least now she would have time to properly rest.

"What do we do now?"

Kostas looked to Braxtus, then Demitri and Iyana. They were all quiet, but their eyes kept going back to Kostas. He cleared his throat. "'Sink beneath the horizon to the realm below. Hold the course, through surviving the insatiable thirst.'"

"We've done that." Braxtus shuddered.

"We've traveled a long way," Demitri said, looking back. "Do you think we passed the next marker?"

More worry tainted their auras.

"It couldn't have been too close to Charybdis," Kostas thought out loud, adjusting Galene in his arms. "You'd get sucked into the maelstrom just trying to read it. The follower of the riddle was supposed to pass the maelstrom underwater at a safe distance, then continue on the path."

"But for how long?" Braxtus asked.

Kostas shook his head. "The riddle is placed for people to find and follow it. The obstacles are to trap any unwanted pursuers of the *avyssos*, but the *markers* wouldn't be hidden. The sea horses have kept us on the southeastern course we've been following, so . . . I say we keep going. We should find it."

"*Should.*" Demitri crossed his arms but didn't say more.

Kostas looked to each of them for their thoughts. No one said anything for or against the idea.

Finally, Iyana said, "I'll gather some of this seaweed for rations. We should eat now and be sure to have some for Galene when she wakes. We don't know what's coming next."

They didn't linger, all of them agreeing they still felt too close to that monster. He mounted, holding Galene in front of him again. Though they rode fast through the waters, it was clear none of them were too eager to get to the next challenge.

20

GALENE

Her muscles ached.

It was the first thing she became aware of. Her whole body pulsed with it, and her mind immediately tried to submerge her back in sleep. She nearly let it, but then she noticed the rocking, and the pressure of an arm around her waist. All thoughts of sleep fled.

She jolted, eyes flying open, the sudden blue light blinding. Blinking and squinting, she tried to make sense of where she was. A sea horse's head bobbed in front of her, and the open sea stretched ahead. She looked down. There was indeed an arm around her waist—dark-skinned and strong.

"Welcome back." Kostas's words brushed her ear, sending a shiver through her shoulders and warmth to her cheeks.

She twisted to look at him. "What . . . where are we?"

His dark eyes softened in a smile. "A few days on from Charybdis."

Memories flooded back, and an echo of fear resonated through her bones. *Charybdis. The maelstrom.* She'd almost drowned.

But I stopped it. Despite herself, a smile sprouted.

"You *should* be proud," Kostas told her, no doubt reading her emotions. "You bested Charybdis's maelstrom, one of the strongest forces throughout the oceans." She heard his grin and her smile grew wider.

"You're awake!"

She looked out to see Iyana, Braxtus, and Demitri riding around them, Iyana's face lit up with a smile.

"Finally." Braxtus grinned. "We were starting to worry we'd have to face the next task without you."

The next task.

"Here." Iyana approached, guiding a riderless horse.

Kostas's arm slipped away, and she felt a twang of disappointment as he helped her onto her own horse. Then, remembering he could see and feel her emotions, it turned immediately to embarrassment.

She ducked her head and avoided his gaze. "So what is the next task? Did you find the next marker?"

"Not yet, but it has to be along this route somewhere," Kostas said.

Galene nodded. They had probably discussed this days ago, and she trusted him. Instead of questioning further, she closed her eyes and reached out, testing her ability. It felt like stretching a sore muscle, but she could sense everything within the tides. She could almost see where the waves of motion were broken up by coral, rocks, and fish. She kept that part of her mind open as they continued on, waiting for something similar to the last markers—smooth, bare rock.

Staying close to the seafloor, they rode a dozen feet apart from each other, trying to cover more distance in their search. But as the day stretched on, sea life began to disappear, and the waters darkened.

"What if we don't find it?" Braxtus asked once.

No one elected to answer him.

It was almost too dark to see, when something alerted Galene's senses. She focused back on the currents as they washed over the seafloor ahead of them.

"There's something ahead." She took the lead, riding toward the mass. *It might be nothing. It's large, and not all of it is smooth . . .*

They were almost upon it when a golden glint caught her eye. "There!"

They flew toward it. A giant chunk of granite squatted in the sand. Gold and silver streaks glittered across the surface, and it was haloed with waving plant life, sure to be housing schools of resting fish. Kostas leapt off his mount and swam toward the bare peak, spooking a few creatures out of their holes to dart into the night. Without hesitation, he pressed his hands to its surface.

It glowed with writing, and Kostas read aloud, "'The Craftsman's game calls from the depths.'"

Game. The Fates must have had a hand in Kostas ending up on this journey. Galene couldn't think of anyone better than the God of Games to be their companion for the next task. He looked up at them, a smile pulling on his face. "Daedalus. He was named the Craftsman."

She nodded. Glimmers of understanding and recollection showed on the others' faces.

"Is that all?" Demitri asked. "It doesn't say anything about where to go."

"It says 'the depths,'" Braxtus corrected.

"Very helpful."

"We must just keep heading the way we are," Galene said. "We are probably supposed to hold the course until something clearly changes."

"Aren't we already in the depths?" Iyana glanced around her.

"The sea will naturally start to get deeper," Galene explained, "but if I remember correctly, there's a trench somewhere at the bottom of the Aegean Sea. I'd bet that's where we're going to end up." She caught the look of horror that Braxtus and Iyana exchanged.

Demitri cracked his neck. "Goodie. Well, now that we have that to look forward to, shall we get some sleep?"

AS THEY ROSE to the watery light of morning, Galene drew up a map in her head. If it was correct, they should reach the trench that evening. With that in mind, the day was filled with a tense apprehension.

Braxtus looked miserable—he clearly hadn't slept well. Iyana didn't look much better, but she and Demitri stayed close together, talking softly.

Kostas kicked his sea horse over to hers.

"Are you feeling better?" he asked.

She nodded. This morning she had woken feeling almost completely back to normal, the aches in her joints mild. "Iyana told me you practically snatched me out of Charybdis's jaws. Thank you."

A smile tugged at his mouth. "You saved me first."

She'd failed to save him first, too, when he was ripped away from her by the maelstrom, but she didn't mention that. They rode beside each other in silence. She noticed his attention flickering to Braxtus, riding alone. His face was haggard, and he kept his gaze fixed on his hands, fisted in his horse's mane.

"How long have you and Braxtus been friends?" She kept her voice soft.

"Several years," he replied. "He's one of the best gods I know."

Galene smiled. "Iyana had endless fun when she spent time with him. She was always *happy*. I always thought the two of them . . . I wish, really—" She shook her head, cutting herself off. "It says a lot about you that you two are so close."

"Thank you, Galene. I think it says a lot about Iyana that she's such good friends with you. Getting to know you has made me feel rather foolish about not spending time with you before."

The warmth within her grew and she tried not to blush. She hadn't interacted this extensively with many gods. She thought a few were handsome, but when was the last time she'd *felt* something for someone? Had she ever? "I believe you kept your circle quite small." She made a face. "And my own has shrunk in recent years."

He looked around at the others. "They're getting a little bigger, though."

"We're a good team." She nodded. "If I had come alone . . ." She trailed off, imagining how far she would have gotten—probably not even past the sirens.

"The Fates intended this."

"Do you really think we'll make it? These trials have almost killed us twice already, and Anyss is sure to be close on our tail."

He didn't do her the dishonor of lying to bolster her confidence. Instead, he told her, "We're moving as fast as we can. The sea horses give us an advantage."

Galene wasn't so sure. That depended on how strong Anyss was. Galene didn't want to underestimate her. "Anyss can manipulate water to her will . . . What if we have to face her at some point?"

"Then we'll win, together." His eyes shone like a starlit midnight, and her heart fluttered. "Look how much we've already accomplished, how much *you've* already accomplished. Don't forget that. We won't get anywhere if we let fear and doubt corrupt us."

"Should we send Braxtus back, then?" Demitri's voice cut through the water.

"Do you have something you want to say?" Braxtus ground out, turning to look at him.

"You've expressed nothing but misery at being down here." Demitri eyed him coolly, despite Iyana's pleading expression. "And if we hadn't stayed on the surface, then we wouldn't have been in so much danger from the whirlpool in the first place. We'd probably be much farther ahead and able to worry less about Anyss."

Galene opened her mouth to defend him, but Kostas rounded on Demitri first.

"The only help *you've* been, Demitri, is killing those sirens, and we could have done that without you."

Galene debated the truth of that statement, but wasn't about to refute it. Demitri shrugged, gave Braxtus a smirk, then turned away. Galene shared an uncomfortable glance with Iyana, then she sighed and tried to turn her thoughts elsewhere, staring back into the shifting waters.

21

KOSTAS

A great, stretching pit marred the seafloor. The sides of the trench cut down into swallowing darkness and stretched out so far Kostas couldn't see where it ended. When they had found it the evening before, he thought that might be because of the fading light, but now, in the brighter morning waters, he marveled at the sheer size of the trench.

"Tartarus itself could be down there." There was a quaver in Iyana's voice.

Galene practically glared into the blackness, her emotions tense and focused. Kostas knew she was attempting to scout it out with her gift. "I don't sense anything out of the ordinary. But something tells me we're in the right place."

"How are we going to find a game in that darkness?" Iyana questioned. "How would we even play?"

"Or win?" Demitri muttered.

"We will." Galene smiled at Kostas, all confidence and courage. He paused, touched and grateful for it—their group needed it, that little spark. Braxtus's and Iyana's auras were nearly black with fear, Demitri's mere shades lighter. Kostas wasn't exactly jumping at the idea of diving in there, himself, but he took a breath.

"What are we waiting for?" Kostas asked. With the feeling of stepping from the roof of a tall building, Kostas urged his horse forward . . . and down. His stomach rose. Somewhere behind him Braxtus let out a groan and someone else sucked in a breath.

Galene urged her mount beside his, brown waves of hair rippling out behind her.

"You're not scared," he stated.

She eyed him. "I'm not exactly excited, but . . . I can't help feeling pretty good after what I just accomplished." Despite the fading light, he could see her blush. He smiled. He hadn't needed to see it to know how she felt, but it was sweet all the same.

"You don't need to be so modest. Like I said yesterday, you should be proud."

She flashed a grin. "Along with that, I've never been underwater this long before. It feels so right, like it's giving me life, energy. I don't really know how to explain it. I've never been able to test my gift this much." The joy in her aura lit his heart and soothed his worries. "I know terrible things have happened and still will, but . . . I'm going to try to enjoy every moment of this"—she threw out her arms—"that I can."

He shook his head, amazed. "You are quite the character, Galene."

Yellow, pink, turquoise, and rose gold made her aura a bright rainbow. Kostas let her emotions sink into him, pushing out the rest of his lingering fear as they descended into darkness. He focused on that blushing gold and pondered what his own emotions reflected. If he had an aura, what would it be showing right now? He hid a smile at the thought that it might just mirror her own.

IT WASN'T LONG before the dusky, deep seawater faded into midnight shadow. The dimming light stifled most conversation, and the figures of Galene and the others were barely visible, their auras the main thing keeping Kostas oriented to their whereabouts. Glowing colors of their varying emotions faintly illuminated them, from Demitri's tension to Braxtus's panic. Galene pushed confidently downward, the other sea horses following.

"It got dark pretty fast," Iyana said. The tremble in her voice hadn't improved since the beginning of their descent.

"We're diving fast," Kostas said. "Can you feel the pressure building as well?" No one answered. A human probably would have been crushed by now. He glanced at Braxtus, making out his clenched jaw. Everyone's auras were dark—even Galene's grew cautious now. After a moment longer, Kostas felt his sea horse slow. "What is it?"

"A wall," Galene replied. "I can sense it up ahead."

They pushed on, forward now instead of down. His sea horse whickered nervously as they moved into a suffocating darkness that Kostas had a feeling wouldn't have eased even on the brightest of days. Goose bumps ran down his arms. He could sense the yawning emptiness around them, but still feared what he might feel if he reached out his hand.

"Something unnatural is here," Galene breathed. "I don't think the sea horses can stay with us anymore."

Kostas heard her slide off her mount and reluctantly did the same.

"Thank you," Galene murmured, "and goodbye."

There was a swift current as the sea horses abandoned them. Kostas took in a deep breath, then kicked gently forward to Galene's side, reaching out until his fingers met stone. From their auras of curiosity and anxiety, he saw the others reach the wall, then start feeling around.

"So if this is it, what do we do?" Demitri asked, his voice floating to him from the right.

Kostas's thoughts started moving. "Spread out," he ordered. "'The Craftsman's game.' Try to feel for something matching that part of the riddle—grooves of a game board, or a doorway or tunnel."

"But this thing could be huge—" Demitri started.

"If you have any better ideas, let us know."

Demitri clicked his tongue, but then moved away, feeling the wall with the others. Kostas went to work.

He traced his fingers along the wall, moving back and forth and up, cursing the darkness. The search went on, done in complete silence, Kostas mindlessly keeping track of where everyone had wandered to when . . .

His fingers brushed over a deep, deliberate crevice in the wall. His heart leapt, and he followed it. It ran a few feet horizontally before sharply cutting up and back in on itself, then back down to rejoin the first line, making a clear triangle.

"I found something!" he called. "Up here, come on!" Soon they were all clustered around, feeling the engraving.

"It's the letter *delta*," Iyana said as she moved away.

"Daedalus's symbol." Kostas nodded even though she couldn't see him.

"Wait—is this a labyrinth?" Demitri asked. "He's the man who made the Labyrinth for the Minotaur, right?"

"That's what I was thinking," Kostas replied.

"But how do we get in?" Iyana asked.

Kostas thought, then propelled himself forward and threw his shoulder into the triangle, gripping the grooves in the wall to anchor himself. A low, quiet grind started, then faded.

"A little help?" he asked. The others moved around him, clinging to the wall and pushing at the triangle in any way they could. He felt the water shift, Galene using her power to aid them. The grinding started up again, this time louder. Rocks scraped over each other. Kostas grunted as his fingers slipped, but regained his grip and kept pushing.

Light seared through cracks. Silhouettes of the others backed away from the blue-white glow of the *delta*. It grew brighter as the cracks widened. More appeared, outlining a huge square around the triangle, big enough to be the door to Zeus's throne room.

Kostas felt himself getting giddy. *I get to experience the work of the Craftsman firsthand. To test myself against it.*

Scrawling words lit up against the stone inside the triangle.

The only way out is the least likely route.

Kostas committed the words to memory. The grinding noise didn't cease as the entire section of the wall inched backward, then slowly slid left, behind the rock wall.

A long, square tunnel stretched before them. The walls were silver rock emanating a soft glow: Like an Olympian, it was a light source in and of itself.

Even through the majesty of Daedalus's creation, the hall seemed to sneer at them, challenging and cold. Kostas tore his eyes from it and looked to his friends. The light of the walls reflected in their eyes as they each looked to him.

He checked his quiver strap, took a breath, and crossed over the threshold. The others followed.

The wall slid out and closed itself again, sealing them inside.

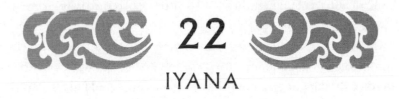

22

IYANA

The unyielding chill grew stiffer. Every muscle in Iyana's body tensed, and stress lined everyone's faces. Galene closed her eyes.

"What do you feel?" Iyana asked.

"All the currents have stopped flowing. I suppose it's to be expected in a labyrinth, but I thought . . . well, I thought I'd feel a little bit, enough to guess where the exit is."

Kostas nodded. "That would have been easier, faster, but"—he gave them a smile—"I'm God of Games, remember? All we need to do is figure out the rules of this place. You saw the next line. 'The only way out is the least likely route.'"

"There's only one way to go right now." Demitri gestured at the huge tunnel that seemed to stretch on endlessly before them.

Kostas nodded. "We can't waste any time." He kicked forward, and the others followed his lead, Demitri taking Iyana's hand.

It took more time than Iyana would have thought, but they reached the first fork, branching off to their left and right. They stopped, staring down both shafts.

The shaft to the right looked identical to the one they had just traveled down. The shaft to the left seemed to grow smaller, and the light from the walls was less bright. Everyone glanced at each other. There was no discussion. They chose left.

Iyana kicked through the water with the others, searching for miniscule differences in the passageways. Sometimes the choice was obvious, but it became less and less so. Many passages, though different in lighting and width, looked equally grim to Iyana.

With one particularly difficult choice, Braxtus suggested picking a passage at random. Kostas immediately stomped out that kind of thinking, explaining that a wrong turn could significantly set them back. No one mentioned that possibility again. From then on, voices were raised to debate whether *this* tunnel looked dimmer than the next, or if *that* one gave a more forbidding feeling than another.

Iyana kept quiet, letting the others work out which way they thought was best.

A few hours into the maze they hit their first dead end. Iyana's stomach tightened. This meant they had chosen the wrong path at least once. How many mistakes had they made so far? Kostas hurried to reassure the others it was to be expected, that they needed dead ends to understand the maze, but it was clear the puzzle gnawed at him. They backtracked and tried a different tunnel, Demitri muttering that he had *said* that shaft was the spookiest. But it, too, led to a dead end.

Nerves running high, they backtracked even farther to a three-way split. Iyana squinted at it, perplexed by the unfamiliar sight. But the others seemed to remember, so she followed them down another shaft. They didn't get far, however, before they stopped at another dead end.

Iyana pressed her lips together and looked at Kostas. His brow furrowed. "This doesn't make sense."

Galene took his arm and gently turned him around. "There's nothing for it. Let's keep going."

Iyana struck out ahead of them, then stopped dead, staring through the dim waters.

A silver wall blocked her path. Another dead end.

"Impossible," she breathed.

She felt the realization hit the others like a physical force.

"The walls *move!*" Kostas gaped, swimming toward it.

"It's a giant trap, that's all it is!" Braxtus turned in circles, eyes raking over the glowing walls. "This whole labyrinth can't wait for us to die—I can feel it!"

Panic rose in Iyana. "What . . . what are we supposed to do?"

"Well, we're not going to wait around for death!" Demitri pushed toward the wall and swung his staff at it.

There was no crack—the weapon *sank* into the wall. Iyana gasped, and Demitri stared at his staff, halfway in what appeared to be silver stone. He kicked to move through the wall.

"Wait!" Iyana rushed to get to him, but the stonework swallowed him up. She stared. It looked as real as every wall around them.

Demitri's head popped back through the structure, and she squeaked. "Come on, it's just an illusion!" He seized Iyana's hand and retreated, disappearing again. The rock rose up to greet her, and she flinched, then passed through to the other side.

Kostas, Galene, and Braxtus erupted through behind her.

They were all silent for a moment.

Galene turned to Kostas. "This makes more sense."

He nodded, eyes glinting. Iyana could practically see the wheels spinning in his head.

Braxtus cleared his throat. "Maybe it makes more sense, but now we're lost. We didn't feel every wall on the way here to make sure it was real. That first dead end—we might have been going the right way. That wall is probably fake."

"It was *probably* right at the start." Kostas raked a hand through his tight curls. "'The only way out is the least likely route.' To either side."

Demitri cursed. "We could have passed dozens of entrances, swimming right past hidden shafts."

"But now that we understand the concept, can't we logic our way out of here?" Iyana took Demitri's hand, and he squeezed it.

"I believe so," Kostas said. "Let's backtrack farther along this path, feeling for hidden openings. I think I can work us back around to where we were."

With no better options, the group split—Iyana, Braxtus, and Demitri trailing their hands along one side of the tunnel, Galene and Kostas along the other. Iyana's fingers slid along the smooth stone, ungiving as she swam back through the shafts where Kostas directed them.

Just as she debated suggesting they turn around again, Galene's hand vanished into a wall. Without much discussion, they went through.

The shafts here looked exactly the same as the ones they'd just been traversing. Iyana swallowed her disappointment and resumed testing the walls.

They found several more hidden shafts and passed through most of them, trusting Kostas's decisions. It was unsettling, traveling through seemingly solid stone.

"I'm looking for a specific shaft," he explained. "It takes a sharp left, then splits into three directions. If we find it I can lead us back to the start of the maze."

"How are we supposed to find it?" Braxtus pressed his fists over his eyes. "We've been moving through walls that we hadn't before. We could be in completely different tunnels now."

Iyana silently agreed with him.

"I've been doing it deliberately," Kostas assured him. "I have a good idea where we are. We're moving back toward the entrance."

A muscle in Demitri's jaw twitched. "We're supposed to just trust your sense of direction? Does being God of Games somehow enhance that?"

"Keeping things straight is definitely an attribute of a good game player." Galene leapt to his defense. "Have some trust in someone other than yourself for once, Demitri."

"What's that supposed to mean?" he demanded.

Kostas cut off Galene's answer. "She means we all have different strengths, and smashing people with swords isn't currently the most useful one."

Iyana saw Demitri's temper flare and caught his arm. "Demitri—" He shook her off.

"Well, *your* strength was supposed to be with water, right?" He turned on Galene. "We're underwater, and you've been useless for the last three days."

She growled.

"She saved us from Charybdis, Demitri . . . ," Iyana moaned.

"I'm hungry," Braxtus muttered.

"We're all hungry!" Demitri and Galene fired back together.

Braxtus threw his hands up. "I'm just saying we're running low on time, too—" The others began arguing on top of each other.

A surge of anger and frustration rose in Iyana as her friends bickered. *We don't need this right now.* She turned and swam several feet away for some space.

She paused. A short distance down the shaft on her right, it made a clear, deliberate cut to the left.

Maybe this is the one Kostas was talking about. The one that splits into three.

She glanced around at her friends, whose frustrations were mounting in volume. She wouldn't go far; just enough to see if this was it. It was easy enough to come back.

She kicked into the passageway.

The tunnels were all so similar it was hard to tell, but she thought this one looked familiar. The walls seemed to open up, giving her a little more space as she traveled. Confidence growing, she allowed herself a smile as she turned the corner.

Then came to a stop, heart sinking. This shaft split not three times, but four.

Tartarus take you, Daedalus. Your trickery is going to get us killed. She turned around and froze.

A dead end.

"It's just an illusion," she reassured herself, ignoring her pounding heart. "I came through this way." Swimming forward, she stretched a hand in front of her.

It pressed into solid stone.

Her stomach twisted into a knot. She hit it again. And again.

Panic rose higher with every strike on the barrier. Her throat constricted—her breathing grew shallow. She threw herself to the right, ramming her shoulder into the other wall, then launched off it to cross to the opposite side, crashing into that, too. *Why did I ever leave my friends? I might never see them again! I might die here!*

The thought was terrifying enough to unstick her throat. "Demitri! Galene!" She automatically reached for her wind to carry her voice, but nothing responded. The first sob escaped her. Would they even hear her underwater, through a wall? She struck her fist against the wall again. "Help, please help!"

She cast an anguished look over her shoulder at the branch-off of four passageways, but immediately discarded that thought. If she moved from where she was, she most *certainly* would never find her friends again. Maybe, just maybe, the wall would disappear after some time. Maybe all the walls rotated from being an illusion to solid to nonexistent . . . but in that case they'd never find their way out. The thought made Iyana's head spin, and another sob burst from her lips.

No one had seen her slip away. They would have no idea which direction she'd gone. Still, on the off chance they would hear her, she called again and again between her sobs.

"Demitri! Please help. Please." Her words trailed into whispers, and she clamped her arms around herself. Her tears mingled with the water around her.

Why did I ever think I could do this alone?

"Iyana!"

Her head snapped up at the muffled cry.

"Iyana, *where are you?*"

Hope seared through her chest. She threw herself against the wall and pounded again, terrified she'd lose this opportunity. "Braxtus!" Her voice cracked with the force of her cry. "Braxtus, I'm *here*! Can you hear me?"

"Iyana!" This time it was Galene's voice, and her heart took flight. She was close, very close. Muffled by the wall, but definitely there. "Hang on, we'll find a way to you! Keep shouting!"

"I'm here! Can you get through? Oh, thank Gaia—I'm right here!" She continued smacking the wall.

"We might be able to get to her if we go down this shaft!" She heard Kostas's urgent voice.

The panic resurfaced. *"Don't leave me!"*

"We're not going to leave you! Iyana, do you understand me? We're coming for you!" This was Demitri.

"Yes, yes, I trust you!"

"Iyana, keep shouting!" Braxtus's voice suddenly seemed to come from the right wall. She moved over to it.

"I'm here! Can you hear me? Braxtus, don't lose the others, either!"

"Shout louder!" His voice came from even farther down the wall.

"Braxtus!" she bellowed. "I'm not *kidding*, don't lose them—"

But suddenly he came barreling through the wall, into one of the four shafts ahead of her. He looked around frantically, brown eyes wide with alarm, and an enormous flood of relief crashed over Iyana. She launched herself at him. *"Braxtus!"*

He caught her in a hug, shaking. Still hysterical, she sobbed into his shoulder, letting his warmth flood through her. He just held her, seemingly unable to speak.

"Braxtus?" Galene's voice was strained and still muffled by the wall. "Get back out here *now*!"

Holding Iyana all the tighter, Braxtus pulled her back through the illusion.

"Iyana!" Demitri grabbed her shoulder. Reluctantly, she let her arms slide free of Braxtus, turning to Demitri. But before she could embrace him, he gripped her upper arms and held her back, fury alight in his eyes.

"How *dare* you scare me like that?"

Iyana squeezed her eyes shut, still shaky. "I'm sorry. I thought this was . . . and the wall . . ." She trailed off, not bothering to make her story clearer. Nothing had been worth that risk.

"You constantly getting into trouble makes everything so much harder. First the taraxippi, then the sirens, now this!" His hands tightened around her arms, and she gasped.

"Demitri!" Galene growled.

Demitri ignored her, eyes burning into Iyana's. "You cannot handle these things alone. This is why I came, Iyana!"

Something in her chest crumpled. "I'm sorry. I know, I'm sorry, Demitri—"

"What are you doing?" Braxtus knocked one of Demitri's arms away from Iyana, and she jumped, looking at him. *Oh no. This will only escalate things.* She raised her hands to pacify Demitri, but he ignored her, turning slowly to Braxtus.

Galene took Iyana's shoulders and pulled her away from the two gods. They both tensed for a fight.

"She was terrified!" Braxtus seethed.

"Well, since *you* seemed to have covered the comfort part already, I thought I'd get to the root of the problem." Demitri's eyes flashed his warning. Iyana's heart thundered.

"The *problem?*" Braxtus swelled in outrage. "So Iyana's a burden?"

"I never said that."

"That's how you act."

Demitri pushed off the wall, getting in Braxtus's face. "Everything I do is to protect the goddess I love. What are *you* trying to do here? Prove yourself a hero?" Demitri cocked his head, blue eyes scorching. "You're a little late—Iyana didn't see anything in you. She chose me."

Heat rushed through Iyana, a mixture of humiliation, guilt, and shock.

Braxtus went white with rage, hands balling into fists. "Furies take you, Demitri."

"Hey, let it go!" Kostas gripped Braxtus's arm. Braxtus snarled, trying to yank free, but Kostas gave him a rough shake. "I said let it go!"

Demitri's hand shot out and grasped Braxtus's tunic. "You need to back off, Braxtus."

Braxtus glared wordlessly at Demitri, refusing to look in Iyana's direction.

Iyana still trembled, but she pulled out of Galene's grip, swimming between the two. "Demitri," she murmured, placing a hand on his chest. "It's all right."

His eyes slid to hers, and he released Braxtus's tunic. Snorting, he put his arm around her, pulling her close as he turned his back on Braxtus. She didn't dare look behind her, but heard Braxtus swim to put some distance between them.

23

KOSTAS

The rest of the day was just as miserable. Hunger gnawed at Kostas's insides, the chill prevailed, and his head spun with thoughts. What made it all worse, though, were the angry and depressed emotions of everyone else pressing on him. It was an effort to push it all aside and focus on the labyrinth.

The map he'd been forming in his head had been ripped to shreds with his new understanding of walls materializing. Slowly, he began piecing potential new maps together, but there were too many possibilities and variables for him to have any surety. The only consistent thing about the labyrinth was its inconsistency. Illusions continually existed in places that contradicted everything he remembered. No matter which direction they went, the shafts looked the same—as if the entire labyrinth flipped around to confuse them.

The puzzle was maddening, and he had no leads. Rather than attempt to lead the group back to the beginning, he began studying everything about where they wandered, trying to lock down the rules of the walls.

"'The only way out is the least likely route,'" he muttered to himself, running fingers through his hair absently. "What are we missing?" No one responded, used to him talking to himself.

They swam in silence, emotions tight like a bow string. Auras were all dark grays and blues, the only accents flashes of red. When the anger flared, Kostas's headache grew worse.

He watched from the corner of his eye as Galene swam with her arm around Iyana, comforting her. Guilt, confusion, and sorrow seeped from Iyana. Galene was compassionate and sensitive, but anger flared in her, too, just as it did in Braxtus and Demitri.

He rubbed his temple and turned his thoughts back to the riddle, back to everything they'd tried and all the things they hadn't.

"What if we mark the passages we travel down?" he suggested.

The others thought it was a brilliant plan, and so Demitri drew his hunting knife and chiseled into the smooth stone wall. Just a small nick in the perfect structure was all he could manage. He did it about four times before the labyrinth seemed to catch on. Fear snuck back into the group as every single passage they turned into already had that nick, that tiny flaw; passages they most certainly had never been down, as well as passages they hadn't seen since they'd first entered.

"I don't understand this!" Kostas exclaimed, unable to contain his anger for a moment. "Honestly, I think it has a brain."

"We all feel the same way. We don't need it constantly dredged up," Demitri said.

"Kostas," Galene muttered, "it's been about a week since we entered the sea. What if Anyss catches up?"

Kostas rubbed his eyes. "I don't know. We just need to keep going."

Galene tugged the end of her braid, distracting him slightly. Her expression was thoughtful, her aura clearer than it had been all day.

"What are you thinking?" he asked as Demitri struck onward, Braxtus and Iyana following.

"'The only way out is the least likely route,'" she recited. "We're in a labyrinth at the bottom of the sea. Where would we go to be in a worse place than where we already are?"

Kostas met her eyes, feeling as if their minds were working

together. *The* least likely *route,* he thought. *So, somewhere we wouldn't want to go, yes, but somewhere we wouldn't think of going, either.* Something clicked and his eyes settled on the floor. *Deeper.*

"Galene, you're amazing," he breathed.

"What did I do?" she asked, amusement and hope coloring her aura.

He just smiled at her and dove.

"Hey," Braxtus called back, "what are you doing?"

Kostas didn't answer, mind racing. "The walls are illusions," he told Galene as he reached the floor. "We've been trying routes that we'd normally stay away from—places that make us afraid, but it hasn't been enough."

Galene gasped and he looked to see her eyes light up. She'd come to the same conclusion. Kostas reached down. His fingers met more cold stone. He frowned.

"Not *all* the walls are illusions," Galene said. She kicked her feet up, then began swimming forward, testing out the floor as she went. Kostas turned and went the other way, toward their group.

"Galene, don't go too far!" Iyana shouted.

"What are you *doing?*" Braxtus demanded.

Neither of them replied. The stone stayed solid, and he was about to rethink their idea when one of his hands vanished through the floor.

His heart leapt. *"Look!"*

Galene was by his side in an instant, staring down at where his hand had been. She looked at him, eyes shining.

The others crowded around him.

"'The only way out is the least likely route.'" Demitri shook his head. "We were swimming, so we hardly ever touched the floor."

"An illusion." Braxtus rubbed his beard in disbelief. "Another illusion."

Kostas was rather disappointed in himself for taking so long to think of it. "It's the last place we'd think to travel in a labyrinth at the bottom of the Aegean Sea."

"You're a genius." Galene grinned, grabbing his arm.

A smile sprang onto his face.

"Do you really think this is it?" Iyana breathed. "I mean, it won't just be another tangle of passages and dead ends?"

"Only one way to find out." Demitri looked around once, then without further hesitation, dove past Kostas and Galene through the floor.

Hope seared through Kostas's chest. He was the first to follow.

The tunnel was pitch-black, smaller, and slimy. It was no labyrinth.

Kostas let out a breath, thrilled to be clear of the chilling, sinister maze. He stretched his hands out and touched the slippery, round walls of the tunnel on either side.

He heard a groan behind him and looked to see Braxtus's aura orange with nerves, quickly mounting to panic. Kostas offered a pat on the shoulder.

"We're making progress. We'll be out of here in no time."

His words didn't seem to help much, but Braxtus wrestled his fear to a dull amber aura.

"All right, let's go." Demitri took off through the tunnel in the lead, and Kostas looked back to make sure the others followed. They used the close walls to push and kick off, propelling themselves forward.

The tunnel wound around, twisting until Kostas had no sense of which direction they were facing. Soon, though, the tunnel took to a steady incline.

"I feel the open sea!" Galene called. "Hurry, we're close!"

They kicked faster. The tunnel became steeper until they swam almost straight up a vertical shaft.

There was a soft *thwack*, and Kostas knew Demitri had surfaced into vegetation. "We made it!" Demitri called, sounding delighted.

Kostas shot up toward a gentle light, launching out of the tunnel and tangling in long, silky seaweed. He turned to offer a hand to help Galene out, eyes drifting to the new scene around them.

They had emerged beneath a giant dome of coral. Sunlight peeked through small holes everywhere, shining in rainbow hues, and colorful fish weaved in and out of the beautiful living shelter. Anyone traveling above the coral would have no idea of the space below, and no way to enter if they did.

Braxtus breathed relief, pushing past to kick out of the plants. Almost immediately, though, Kostas felt his discomfort resurge. "Still trapped."

Iyana followed, laughing as Demitri grabbed her hand and towed her along.

Galene started ripping up some seaweed. "I am so hungry."

Kostas joined her, smiling as she caught his eye. "We're going to make it."

She just stuffed some of the seaweed in her mouth and started chewing. He laughed, thoroughly enjoying watching the happiness spread from her face to her aura.

Braxtus made his way over, sighing deeply as he settled beside them. Galene handed him some seaweed, which he took without the slightest complaint, wolfing it down. The three of them sat in silence as they chewed, eating their fill.

Kostas watched them both.

None of them had been able to sleep in the labyrinth, but Braxtus looked awful. He radiated emotional exhaustion, and his posture was continually hunched.

"How are you doing?" Kostas finally asked him.

Braxtus moved to float on his back, eyes closed. He just grunted.

"Has being underwater gotten any better for you?" Galene asked.

Braxtus scrubbed his face. "Don't worry about me. I'm managing."

Kostas and Galene exchanged a look, but didn't push it.

Demitri and Iyana swam by, picking seaweed for themselves. Braxtus's aura shuddered with violet humiliation, and Kostas felt the pang of it.

Iyana's emotions had finally lightened and Demitri's anger had soothed, melting back into his common bloom of golden love, tainted yellow-green by the ever-present shade of possessiveness. Demitri's emotions had never settled right with Kostas. He had a lot of them, many selfish, held in check by his impassive face and feigned nonchalance.

Kostas looked to Braxtus. *He would love her better.*

Braxtus grumbled something about exploring the coral and swam off. This was the first time they could get a safe distance between each other, and Kostas was glad Braxtus was taking the opportunity for solitude.

"What's it like," Galene asked, "feeling everyone's emotions?"

He turned his gaze back to her. She was playing with the reeds, absently braiding different strands. "I don't know what it's like *not* to feel everyone's emotions," he replied. "But . . . it can get noisy."

Her blue-green eyes blinked slowly, her lashes dark and curling. "Is it ever hard to distinguish others' feelings from yours?"

"It has been the last few days." He smiled. "Back on Olympus I could just retreat to my temple, where I was alone."

Galene nodded. Attraction was there again in her aura, along with caution and . . . did he see fear?

"I don't usually need to stop and analyze my own emotions," he went on. "Most of my life they've been very straightforward."

"But you've felt that need recently?"

She can read me almost as well as I can read her, he thought in mild panic. He swallowed. When had his heart started racing? "I suppose, in one area."

"What area is that?" Her voice was quiet, and her eyes fled back to her fidgeting hands.

The more he thought how to respond, the more lost he got. *To Tartarus with this.* "You."

Her aura flared and Kostas was hit with relief, excitement, joy, and even more nerves. It suddenly felt like a violation to be reading her like that. He tried his best to block it out, to ignore it, but it had ignited his own emotions. His insides fluttered.

"It's not fair—you've been able to read all of my emotions," she said. Her voice wavered, her eyes still down.

It was getting harder to breathe. "Do you want to know mine?" And with that, he mustered every ounce of courage he had left in his pounding chest and took her hand.

Her aura bloomed and swirled as she stared at his hand over hers, then she laced her olive fingers through his.

He couldn't tell where his emotions ended and hers began. She met his eyes again, trying not to smile, but the longer they looked at each other the wider it got. She ran a thumb over his, sending electricity up his arm.

"Look," Braxtus called.

Kostas's euphoria faded as Galene's fingers slipped from his. She turned toward where Braxtus waved. Reluctantly, he followed suit.

The chill settled back into his bones.

A dark, looming cave stood at the far end of the coral dome. It was bleak and uninviting, but somehow beckoned at the same time. The four of them swam to Braxtus.

In front of them, tangled in seaweed, was another marker. Braxtus kicked down to touch it. The next part of the riddle illuminated on the gold and silvery surface.

Coils of death guard the cavern where the globe of prisoners may be obtained. But a prisoner may remain.

Kostas felt a united shudder run through the group.

"Lots of ominous words in this one," Braxtus commented quietly.

Kostas repeated the final section of the riddle in his mind, quickly memorizing every word.

"Let's just get this over with," Demitri growled.

"Wait," Galene sighed. "We really need a rest. Let's break here, eat, and tackle the final test tomorrow."

After two days without food, no one opposed. They ate and explored until the waters turned dark. Tethering themselves once again to the seafloor with the seaweed, they settled down for a good night's rest.

24

IYANA

Iyana tightened the seaweed around her waist and curled up. Sleeping underwater was becoming more familiar, but she still didn't like the way her body shifted and rocked all night long. Hopefully, she was tired enough that she'd sleep through the night this time.

She closed her eyes, waiting in the darkness for sleep to overtake her. One by one, she heard the others' breathing deepen. Just as she thought she might sink into oblivion, Demitri's fingers ran down her arm.

He wants to talk about today. She bit her tongue.

"Iyana." He spoke in a quiet voice.

Slowly, she uncurled and turned to look at him.

"Listen." He scanned her face, a contrite expression in his gaze. "I'm sorry I lost my temper when you wandered off in the labyrinth."

Dark stubble had grown on his jaw since they left Olympus, and his blue eyes caught a glint of filtered moonlight. *Why do you always have to look so perfect?*

She turned her head, not wanting him to read the emotion on her face. "Well . . . it's true, isn't it? I keep getting us in trouble. I'm making things harder."

"You know I only said those things because I care. I just don't want you to get hurt."

"I wish I could just protect myself," she muttered.

"But you don't need to—I'm with you. I promise I'll take care of you." He pulled her into his embrace, and she breathed deeply. The familiar scent of oak was still there, but faint, mingled with the brine of the ocean. "I should have been the one to find you and pull you back, not Braxtus."

She tensed in his arms.

"Didn't I tell you I was concerned about his motives?" When she didn't answer, he continued. "He didn't stay with us to help Galene or stop Poinê. He stayed for the same reason he came. For *you*."

She took a breath, wanting to defend Braxtus's intentions but not sure how.

"I know you were friends. I get it. But this isn't healthy. It's an obsession. It drove him all the way out of Olympus, potentially into exile, and it concerns me." He drew her up, scanning her face. "I'm worried he's going to get to you—drive a wedge between us. I'm not sure how to protect you from that."

She swallowed the lump in her throat. "Demitri, he won't."

"Can you promise me that?"

Her heart panged, and she brushed the hair from his eyes. "You've done everything for me. I'm here. I'm not leaving you, no matter what Braxtus says or does."

"Good," he breathed. "Then do one thing for me."

"What?"

"Stay away from him."

She frowned. "That's pretty difficult in such a small group."

He took her head in his hands. "Just don't allow him to continue to engage you. Avoid him all you can." He lowered his head and kissed her. His lips were warm and soft against hers, and after a moment, he pulled back just enough to look in her eyes. "Please."

"All right," she whispered.

Giving her a gentle smile, he tucked back a strand that had

come loose from her braid. "Thank you." He released her. "We should get some sleep."

Iyana lay in the dark waters for a while, long past when Demitri's breathing grew deep and even, matching the sounds of sleep around her.

An obsession. The words grated against her, sounding wrong. She knew Demitri was concerned and understood why. She'd probably be upset, too, if a goddess had left Olympus to follow Demitri. But Braxtus was good and kind . . .

To her right, he mumbled something in his sleep, shifting and pulling taut against his seaweed tether.

She pressed her eyes shut. She'd waited for Braxtus to say something for so long. She'd been there for him, had cared deeply for him. And he'd said nothing. He'd taken her for granted. She figured he'd seen her only as a friend.

And Demitri really *had* done everything for her. He had *exiled* himself for her.

She twisted in the water to turn her back on Braxtus, determined to get some rest.

DARKNESS PRESSED IN from every side, so deep Iyana couldn't see the hand she waved in front of her face.

She sat up, and a ceiling brushed against her head. She reached out. Her fingers touched cold walls on either side of her, but the way forward and backward was open. She was in some sort of tunnel.

A low creak and a few whispers trailed past. She started, heart beginning to pound. The whispers grew.

"In the deep shadows, where Apollo's sun never reaches . . ."

"Endless—"

"Iyana . . ."

Iyana's heart leapt at that last, familiar voice. "Galene? Is that you?"

"Iyana." A new voice.

"Kostas!" she called back. "What's going on? Where should I go?"

"Turn around." Their voices spoke in unison. Iyana obeyed, scrambling onto her hands and knees. "Travel that way."

She started crawling down the tunnel, shivering. "How far do I—"

She crawled right into something stringy, thick, and sticky.

A shriek escaped her as she backtracked, tearing the web from her face and hands. Immediately, she pictured an enormous spider bearing down on her and backed up even farther.

"Keep going!" Galene called.

"Into a giant web?"

"It's the way you need to go," Kostas insisted.

She shook her head, shuddering.

Two more familiar voices started murmuring. After a moment she recognized them—Demitri and Braxtus. Their voices blended with a few other haunting cries, but finally Braxtus's rose above them.

"There's a different way out, Iyana. Turn left."

"But—" she started, feeling the wall. To her surprise, it cut inward, a passageway opening up. Her fear eased, and she turned down it.

"That's it," Braxtus encouraged. "You're going the right way."

But when her hand next touched the stone, searing hot pain shot through her arm.

She screamed and jerked back, falling against the side wall. That, too, was scorching. It burned through her tunic, scalding her shoulder. She pushed away, crying out as she crawled on her burned hand to get back to cool stone.

"What's going on?" she choked. "Braxtus, it burned me!"

"It's okay. You were going in the right direction. Don't give up."

"I can't go that way! It hurts!"

"Iyana!" Demitri's voice rose, clear enough to hear, though not as loud as the others. "Iyana, I can get you out of here. You need to go back the way you came."

"Don't do it, Iyana," Galene whispered. "Don't turn around again."

"You're so close," Braxtus said.

"No, listen to me." Demitri's voice was forceful, but earnest. *"Turn around and go back."*

Confused and desperate, Iyana slowly turned. A sob escaped her lips as she started back the way she came. Her hand and shoulder pulsed in pain, the people she loved all giving conflicting directions, their voices clearer and stronger every minute.

"Stop it, Iyana!"

"What are you doing? Don't you trust us?"

"Keep coming."

Iyana passed where she had started, moving in the opposite direction as she listened to Demitri. The tunnel widened. The darkness remained.

"You can stand now," Demitri told her.

Cautiously, she did so. *"Am I almost out?"*

"No!" Braxtus, Galene, and Kostas cried at the same time Demitri said, *"Almost!"*

She swallowed, then continued forward, cradling her injured hand to her chest.

"Iyana," Demitri said. *"Stop!"*

She skidded to a halt, feeling pebbles roll away from her feet. She listened as they seemed to drop off something and land far below her with a clatter.

"What . . . what do I do now?" She hated how her voice trembled.

"You jump for the other side."

She froze.

"Are you crazy? Don't listen to him, Iyana!" Galene shouted.

"Why are you listening to him?" Braxtus demanded. But Iyana felt her burned hand throbbing and pushed away their voices.

"Demitri . . . I . . . I can't see a thing, I don't know how far to jump—"

"Iyana, you need to jump."

"I'm serious, there's no way—!"

"The cliff you're standing on is going to collapse! You have to trust me, Iyana!"

She trembled. *"I . . . I do trust you,"* she whispered.

"Then jump!"

She backed up, then ran and leapt.

Right as her feet left the ground she heard a crunching, moaning sound as it collapsed beneath her. She arched high into the air, reaching out to grab onto something, anything—

A hand caught hers. Light pierced the scene, and she stared up into Demitri's face as he held her whole weight from the edge of a cliff. With one heave, he pulled her up.

Shaking, she threw her arms around him.

Iyana gasped, jerking awake.

Another moment of panic surged at the darkness around her. It was nearly as impenetrable as it had been in her dream, but she blinked and forced herself to relax as she faintly made out her surroundings.

She put her arms around herself, trembling as her mind raced through her dream. It had been as vivid as her other recent nightmares, but even more detailed.

"Iyana?" someone whispered. "Are you awake?"

She looked up as Braxtus swam over. He'd untied himself from the seaweed, and though she could see the outline of his broad frame, his face was swallowed in shadow. She cringed, remembering the pain of the burn, his voice leading her there. She shook her head to clear the lingering effects of the nightmare.

"Why are you up?" she asked.

"Nightmares. You?"

She rubbed her hand. "Dreams for me, too."

He hesitated. "Do you want to talk about it?"

"No . . . I'd rather just forget it."

"All right." He nodded in understanding, and as her eyes began to adjust, she looked at him closer. He was a wreck—exhaustion pulled at the lines of his face, and his eyes were swollen and bloodshot.

"Do *you* want to talk about it?" she asked cautiously.

He seemed to struggle with himself, then said, "I haven't been sleeping much."

"I'm so sorry. Sleeping underwater is *awful—*"

"Not that." He rubbed his beard. "I mean, that, too. But on top of it I've been plagued with these nightmares." He gave an audible shudder.

She paused. "What did you dream tonight?"

"They're all pretty similar. Usually, it starts good. I'm on land, but when I try to use my fire, it burns me. And I can't put it out, so I go to water, and then I'm dragged down, and I can't breathe . . ." He swallowed. "Sometimes you're there, but you never hear me when I call out."

She felt a sudden urge to reach for him, but resisted. *It's this water. Being separated from our element is getting to the both of us.* She looked up at the coral dome above them. There was so much water and rock between them and the sky.

"Remember when my father took me training?" he asked, voice quiet. "He said I needed to face my fears. He took me to the Eastern stream to fight Tereine."

I remember.

Tereine was the most powerful naiad currently living on Mount Olympus. Iyana had worried about this particular training session. She'd gone to watch.

Braxtus had stood alone in the center of the rushing stream, wearing nothing but his tunic. The naiad had raged from the rapids, sending water crashing over and over the flames he desperately used to shield himself. Iyana felt familiar anger at the memory. Though he'd looked mildly sympathetic, Apollo had just watched. He'd let the naiad bludgeon his son until Braxtus lost his footing and his head went underwater.

"He hadn't trained me enough. I'd never been more helpless, or terrified, or humiliated." Braxtus gestured to his chest. "That feeling—that's how I feel *all the time* underwater."

"Me too," Iyana whispered.

They locked eyes, and an understanding passed between them. His face broke with relief and gratitude, and her barriers crumbled. Reaching out, she drew closer and wrapped her arms around his waist.

His arms went around her immediately, drawing her against him. He buried his face in her hair, tangled a hand in it.

Chills ran down her arms—her heart raced. Her breath hitched, and she knew he heard it.

Oh, Kronos.

Avoid him all you can. Demitri's words flooded her mind.

Demitri had done everything for her. She could give him the one thing he asked for.

She unwound her arms and disentangled herself, pulling back. Cold water filled Braxtus's place, but a line of heat kept them connected, coursing between them. There was a brightness in Braxtus's eyes. She breathed hard.

After a long silence he said, "Listen, about today . . ."

"Thank you for pulling me out."

"I just meant, what Demitri said—"

"He shouldn't have said that," Iyana interrupted. "He apologized to me, and I think he'll apologize to you if I ask—"

"Iyana . . ." He moved closer, a pained expression crossing his face.

She retreated until the seaweed around her waist stopped her. "No, Braxtus, listen. I chose Demitri."

He stopped, looking at her as though he could see right to her stupid, traitorous heart. "Why did you? When you clearly still have feelings for me?"

"I . . ." She swallowed, then tried again. "We never talked about our feelings."

A flash of surprise crossed his face. "I didn't think we needed to," he said hoarsely. "Everything was natural."

She stared at him, then shook her head. "I'm sorry I blind-sided you, Braxtus. I really am. But I'm with Demitri now."

His pain-filled eyes burned into her. "And your feelings for me?"

She cursed the heat on her cheeks, the tears she felt rising to her eyes. "I chose him." She turned away.

She curled up next to Demitri's sleeping figure. After a long, painful moment, she heard Braxtus quietly retreat.

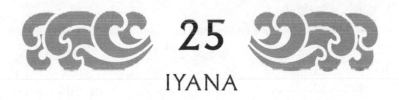

25

IYANA

The darkness of the cave reached toward them with icy fingers.

They all cringed backward, and Iyana huddled closer to Demitri. She breathed in and coughed. If water could be dusty, this was.

"'Coils of death guard the cavern where the globe of prisoners may be obtained. But a prisoner may remain,'" Kostas recited. "I think we'll know the 'coils of death' when we come to it, but . . ."

"'But a prisoner may remain'?" Iyana questioned.

Kostas grimaced. "That sounds like a trap to me."

A freezing current washed over them, shepherding them toward the abyss.

She clutched Galene's arm and felt her jump. "Are you doing that?" Iyana asked.

"No."

Iyana shuddered. The darkness ahead seemed to retreat and advance simultaneously.

"Let's just *do* this." Braxtus started forward, but Kostas caught his arm.

Iyana had done her best not to look at Braxtus all morning, but she'd sensed the subtle shift in him. His brown eyes were still bloodshot, his face drawn, but his fear had settled into a hardness. A drive to get through

He was reaching his breaking point—Iyana knew it. They had to finish this soon.

"Maybe we should make a plan first," Kostas said. "We barely survived the last two tasks, and this one blatantly says it's a trap—"

Braxtus groaned.

"We have to go in sometime," Demitri pointed out, for once on the same page as Braxtus.

Iyana balked at the currents that pulled her forward, tightening her grip on Galene's hand.

"We'll be blind."

Another current washed over them. Kostas shook his head, but Galene put a hand on his arm.

"I don't think we can plan for this. I'll be our eyes in there."

He nodded and caught her hand, then let the water tow him forward.

Iyana reached out for Demitri, who laced his fingers through hers.

Kostas, on the other side, swam forward, grabbing Braxtus's hand to finish the line. "Let's just play it safe."

"Galene said she could sense things just fine," Braxtus mumbled, taking Kostas's hand all the same.

As the light from the opening faded into a dim glow behind them, the darkness quickly became impossible to penetrate. Iyana swallowed, reminded of her pitch-black dream. They drifted forward, huddled together. A shiver trembled through Galene's hand, and Iyana bit her lip.

"If it's this dark the whole way through, the *avyssos* could be right under our noses and we'd pass it," Demitri muttered.

"No, I have a feeling we'll know exactly where it is when we get there," Kostas said darkly.

"Wait!" Galene hissed. Iyana froze, watching the darkness ahead. "I see something, there!"

"What is it?" Kostas asked.

"A light. Don't you see it?"

Iyana squinted through her lashes. "It's pitch-black. I can't even see you."

"It's right there! Look—"

"Maybe you have special powers of sight underwater, Galene, but the rest of us—" Demitri started.

"No, wait! I see it, too," Braxtus said, cutting him off.

Silence fell. In the distance an eerie white point of light bloomed to life, then sank into nothing.

"What is it?" Iyana whispered.

"Let's find out," Braxtus said.

Iyana heard a snarl and Kostas snapped, "We're staying together."

She kicked quicker to keep pace with the others as they sped up, moving toward the light.

The flicker gleamed ahead of them again, but it seemed to flee their approach, leading them deeper into the cave with every soft glow.

"This is definitely a trap." Demitri's usually collected voice was tense. But what else could they do but follow? As one, the group moved faster, cold currents still washing over their backs.

The light vanished. They kept moving forward, unsure of what else to do. When Galene winced, Iyana realized she'd been tightening her grip on Galene's hand.

"Watch out," Galene said quickly, but there was a thud and a grunt.

Braxtus, who was presumably in the lead, grumbled, "Too late."

"I'm sorry. It's harder to feel the currents in enclosed spaces."

"Dead end?" Kostas asked.

Iyana released Galene and stretched out a hand, completely blind, and felt the smooth surface of the wall. "Where did the light go?"

Another gleam answered her question, this one bluer. Everyone turned to see a tunnel, the muted light breaking through swaying reeds that grew all the way to the ceiling. Galene took Iyana's hand again.

Iyana let herself be pulled through the slippery reeds. The tunnel twisted around a few corners, but the light, now constant, led them on, glinting off the smooth black walls. They finally rounded the last corner, and Iyana caught her breath.

The entire cavern was filled with shining, swaying creatures. Algae and sea sponge lined the reflective floor, faintly illuminating the scattered rocks around them with different hues of blue and purple. The twisting eels and fish could only be distinguished by the random stripes of pale light that marked their presence. Long shadows were cast in every direction, but despite this, Iyana judged the size of the cavern to be as big as the arena, and everything was glowing, moving, whirling gently through the mysterious currents.

"What are they?" Kostas asked.

"Luminescent creatures," Galene breathed. "There shouldn't be this much life in so much darkness—it's evidence of unnatural power influencing this place."

Iyana glanced at the others. Their faces were lit up by the ghostly, pale light; it was an eerie image that raised the hair on her arms.

"They don't . . . they don't *seem* dangerous," she said, releasing her grip on Galene.

"They can be poisonous," Galene cautioned. "The eels especially."

"They're not attacking us." Demitri narrowed his eyes at them.

"Look at the size of that thing!" Braxtus pointed at an eel. It rippled as it moved, the stripe of light on its side almost three times the length of Iyana herself. She shivered, and the whole group huddled closer together.

"I don't see any more tunnels," Galene said, "so the *avyssos* must be in here somewhere."

"Let's get looking." Braxtus glanced around, then dove toward the reeds and coral on the cavern floor.

"Stay close!" Kostas ordered.

Galene and Kostas swam up high, looking for shelves and crevices where the *avyssos* might be hidden. Iyana moved to the wall to start along the edges. Demitri stayed nearby, doing his own search as Iyana trailed her hand along the stone. It had patches smooth as glass and others that were rough and jagged. She hissed as a particularly sharp edge pricked her finger.

Below her, Braxtus glanced up at the sound, then away again. He'd been giving her space, but she felt his presence like a physical weight.

She moved around a section of wall that jutted out. The rock here was smooth again, but had thin rivets lightly carved into it in some kind of pattern, almost like . . .

The wall shifted beneath her hand, restricting and flexing. Iyana pulled back as the scaly side of something enormous slid past her.

"Demitri," she whispered, throat tightening.

The dim light glinted off the thick, round body that was a good six feet high. As it trailed by, the body grew thinner. Her eyes darted in the direction it was moving.

"Demitri," she hissed more forcefully.

A hand touched her back. "What—?" Demitri cut off as he saw the thing.

She could barely voice her question. "Where's the head?"

Demitri grabbed her arm and drew her backward. Iyana grunted as her back hit something.

The small, light-giving creatures darted away into nearby hiding places, darkening the scene.

Very slowly, they turned around. Her heart stopped.

Two large, milky eyes glinted down at them from a diamond face. Spines rippled over the creature's head and down its

183

powerful, slick body. The jaws opened, revealing rows of long, needle-sharp teeth, each thick as an arm. A forked tongue snaked between them.

"*Iyana!*" Braxtus yelled.

The sea serpent lunged.

Iyana screamed, kicking back. Demitri swung his twin swords. They rang against the serpent's teeth as they snapped down just shy of Iyana.

There was a roar, and Braxtus launched into her vision, raising his shield and ramming hard into the beast's head. The serpent reeled back, coiling, then lashed at Demitri.

He swung away just in time, swiping again, but the creature twisted its muscular body around them, cold scales pressing Iyana against him. Demitri jerked his arms up to avoid cutting her, then put his forearms on her shoulders and shoved her down. She slipped free of the crushing body, watching it tighten around Demitri.

All light was blocked out by the giant serpent, and horror closed her throat. *Coils of death.*

Somewhere above Braxtus yelled, Galene shrieked, and Kostas's bow twanged. There was a small opening as the snake whipped around, and Iyana struck out, pulling one of her spikes free.

I'm no good underwater with my spikes. I can't throw them here.

Galene came into view, her scimitar in her fist, but it glanced off its hide as it crashed into her, shoving her into the cavern's wall. She cried out at the impact.

Kostas fired arrow after arrow, shooting absurdly close to the creature for maximum impact. His quiver was almost empty by the time it moved, releasing Galene. The motion gave Demitri enough room to wiggle free, and he dove out of sight.

The sea serpent went for Galene again, but Iyana felt the swell of the currents as Galene pulled on them. She kicked off the wall to dodge, the water accelerating the beast forward. The serpent rammed into the rock, and Iyana had a flash of Galene's Immortality Trial.

The creature backed up, its pale eyes giving a haunting glare.

Iyana kicked forward and slammed her spike down with all her strength. Her bones shook as the steel hit scales and ricocheted off.

Galene shot through the water, her scimitar poised to plunge into the beast, but again the scales deflected it like armor.

"We can't pierce it!" Iyana yelled, swimming away as the serpent thrashed.

"Of *course*," Galene groaned.

It swung its head and snapped its jaws at everyone in reach. Kostas and Braxtus focused on its head, Kostas firing into its mouth and Braxtus swinging his sword at its eyes.

"Where's Demitri?" Kostas cried. "We need him!"

Iyana looked around frantically, but Demitri was nowhere in sight.

Galene swam up to its side and put her shoulder against it. Then she wedged her scimitar between two scales and shoved.

The beast roared. Iyana had to cover her ears to stop her skull from rattling. The serpent whipped around.

"Get ready!" Demitri yelled, and Iyana turned to see him swimming up along the wall. "There's a passage down there, behind that coral."

He didn't finish explaining, just hefted his javelin, aimed, and threw it. It spun through the water and sank deep into the serpent's eye.

The jaws tore open as a shriek like Iyana had never heard shook the water.

"*Come on!*" Iyana grabbed Galene's hand, and the two of them dove for safety.

Braxtus kicked ahead of them, searching for what Demitri had found. "*Down there!*" He pointed at the crevice, plenty big enough for them, but too small for the monster. They kicked for the chasm, Kostas swimming up behind them.

Braxtus waited by the side, waving them in, but Iyana stopped, looking back for Demitri. He was struggling to get past the thrashing creature, jabbing it with his javelin.

"Get in!" Braxtus shouted, but she didn't move.

Demitri finally struck free. The beast jerked its head in pain but lunged after him.

"Move!" Demitri shot past them into the crevice, followed by Braxtus. Kostas dragged Galene in, and Iyana threw herself after them.

The gaping mouth slammed against the wall behind them, teeth caging the opening like bars.

26

GALENE

Jaws snapped at the entrance. Iyana squeaked, pushing herself deeper in, up against Galene, and they wiggled farther into the tunnel.

The solid walls were far too close to Galene's shoulders.

Reaching up, she felt the ceiling barely a hand's width above them. She shifted forward in the darkness, but ended up pressed against Kostas, Iyana closing the limited gap behind her. "I don't like this."

"Would you rather be back with the sea serpent?" Braxtus's muffled voice drifted to her.

Galene's heart quickened, and she found herself pushing at Kostas. "Move."

"I'm trying." His voice showed his surprise at her sudden demand. He inched forward. Her discomfort mounted to panic as the walls seemed to close in. Despite logic telling her otherwise, the possibility of being stuck in that tiny place forever seemed far too real. Her breathing accelerated.

"Galene?"

She pushed harder, a slight whimper escaping her lips.

"Whoa, Galene." Iyana grabbed her shoulder. "We'll be out of here soon. There's got to be a way through."

"You don't know that," she gasped. She couldn't feel the open sea. In a state of near hysteria, she pounded on Kostas.

"Galene!"

She turned around. "I'm going back."

"No!" they all cried, Iyana blocking her way.

"Galene," Kostas tried again. She felt him shift, and then his arms wrapped around her.

Even the shock of his touch didn't distract her for long. "Don't hug me, get me out!" she protested, but he wouldn't let go.

"All right, we're moving. I'm going to get you out." He wiggled, but she didn't feel him move far.

She shook her head. "Get me in front," she mumbled into his shoulder.

"What?"

"Get me in front!" Pushing him up against the wall, she pressed herself up to him, wriggling to get past, despite the sharp rock scraping against her backplate.

She ran into Braxtus, who pressed himself against the wall without comment, letting her somehow squeeze by his impressive build. Demitri, in the lead, gave a grunt of surprise, but she forced her way past him, too, diving forward. Her fingers trailed along the walls, and she willed the water to push her out. She inched through the tunnel, sometimes through spaces she was sure *she* wouldn't fit through, let alone Braxtus and his shield.

Her head hit rock. Crying out in surprise, she reached out to feel the way forward. The floor had not dropped, but the ceiling had fallen dramatically. Panic began overpowering her again.

A moment later Demitri pushed her hips to the floor and shoved her forward. She shouted in protest, barely fitting into the tiny space he had crowded her into. Summoning what clarity she had left, she began pulling herself forward, clutching the rocks and inching her way through. Just as tears rose to her eyes, she saw a light.

With one last burst of determination, she angled herself to take advantage of the available space, braced her feet against the walls behind her, and pushed.

Pain clawed down her arms as she squeezed through the rocks.

"Help me!" she snapped, and Demitri's hands returned to help her through. She tasted the ichor in the water, but her arms were soon free. Her hips stopped at the opening, the scimitar and daggers strapped to her belt not helping. Reaching to either side, she grabbed the walls and pulled, tearing her skin even more, but releasing herself from torture.

She went limp, hugging herself and breathing deeply. She heard pounding, and grunting, then, after a while, a crack as stone shattered. Her friends emerged from the black dust, and Kostas came to her side.

"Are you all right?" he asked. His fingers danced gently along her skin as he checked her wounds.

She managed a nod, suddenly realizing all she wanted to do was fling her arms around him. Everyone's watching eyes made her pause. Iyana moved beside her, so she hugged her instead.

"You're scared of small spaces?" Iyana asked. "I didn't know."

"Neither did I," Galene mumbled. There weren't many of those on the mountain. Just thinking about it made her long for home.

"Look." Demitri gazed at their surroundings, wonder on his face. She looked up.

They were in another huge cavern, this one twice the height of the first. The water gleamed in the light of the small fish and eel, magnified by the millions of crystals that coated the rock walls.

Each of the crystals sent different rays of light glancing across the room. The floor reflected the colors off its black, obsidian surface. A tall, thick pillar rose in the center of the cavern.

Obsidian like the floor, scattered crystals and dark gray coral glowed and glittered over its surface. Seaweed sprouted from small cracks, and some seahorses darted into them. At the top of the pillar sat an enormous clam.

It was chalky white in the surrounding darkness, radiant ridges running over the top, jaws locked firmly together.

"Well," Kostas breathed, "who thinks we've found it?"

Braxtus gave a weak chuckle that was quickly stifled in the silence.

"I'm going to get it." Demitri pushed off the wall, propelling himself toward the giant clam. Galene winced as Iyana grabbed her arm, digging her nails harder and harder into her skin the closer Demitri got. She gently eased open Iyana's fingers and took her hand in her own.

Demitri approached the clam, circling it to assess the problem. Finally, he took his favored approach, drawing his dagger and lodging it into its jaws.

"Demitri!" Galene moaned.

He heaved downward on it, but merely managed to propel himself upward. Grabbing the edge of the column, he pulled himself back down and braced himself with his knees to try again.

"Stop that!" Galene cried, unable to watch anymore.

He raised an eyebrow at her. "Do you have a better idea?"

She bit her tongue to stop the insult that flew to her lips. "Actually . . ." She scowled.

He let go, the dagger wobbling in the clam's mouth.

She swam up to him, and he moved aside, motioning for her to proceed. Taking hold of the blade's hilt, she teased it out, handed it back to its owner, and placed her right hand on the clam's crown.

"I am Galene, Daughter of Poseidon." To prove it, she called for a gentle current to rush around them. "I have been sent by my father to relieve you of your duty. We thank you, earnestly, for your diligent protection of the *avyssos*." She held her breath.

There was a moment of tense silence. Nothing happened, and her heart began to sink. Demitri grunted. "Did you expect it to ans—"

There was a deep creaking sound, and Galene's hand flew backward to silence him. The wavy jaws began to open. A shimmery pink cushion could be seen through the rising jaws, then upon it . . . a glow of something . . .

Demitri drifted forward and stretched out a hand. The clam froze half-open, and Galene shot him a look that was all daggers. He retreated, eyes dark.

The clam resumed its opening, light spilling from within. A small, perfect globe swirled with a hypnotizing array of silver and gold, glowing brightly. The luster dimmed, and Galene, filled with awe, reached out and picked it up. The *avyssos* rolled into the palm of her hand, smoother than glass, winking innocently and sending beautiful colors dancing across her face and arms.

"Don't look at it too long, Galene!" Kostas called.

Hearing the wisdom in his words, Galene tore her eyes away and curled her fingers around it.

The obsidian walls began to tremble, cracking. A couple loose stones fell down into the passage they had come through.

Kronos. She moved, but Demitri moved faster, diving and seizing Iyana's wrist, pulling her toward it.

Crack!

Iyana shrieked as a line splintered through the wall above the opening. With an ear-splitting groan, it widened, and the rocks above the entrance fell harder.

Galene stopped, watching in horror. "It's caving in!"

Iyana started to pull back as Demitri towed her along. "It's our only way out!" He shoved the smaller rocks out of his way, starting in. "Hurry!"

"*Stop!*" Galene screamed, but Braxtus came barreling in. Shield out, he rammed into Demitri and Iyana, sending them careening out of the way.

The ceiling in the chasm collapsed.

Rocks thundered down, plummeting around Braxtus. Galene heard his shout but quickly lost sight of him in the whirling dust and cascading stones.

"No!" Before everything had finished falling, Iyana threw herself at the rocks and tried to pull them loose. Kostas rushed to her aid, knocking the final tumbling rocks aside before dragging out what stones he could.

Galene pulled herself out of her shock and swam down to help. By the time she got there, she heard a distinct groan.

"Get this boulder *off* me."

Iyana let out a choked sob of relief, and Kostas and Demitri both shoved one of the largest rocks until it tumbled free and sank. Beneath it was Braxtus's shield. "Stand back," Braxtus commanded, voice muffled.

He shoved hard, sending more rocks rolling, then emerged from the wreckage. "Ow," he complained, slinging his shield on his back and rubbing his arm.

"Congratulations," Demitri spat. "You successfully prevented *any* of us from getting out." He gestured at the crevice, which was still solidly blocked from top to bottom.

Galene groaned silently as Braxtus rounded on him. "I think you mean *thank you*! You never would have made it."

"We were so close. We might have."

"You know, I just might have let you kill yourself, but when you're dragging Iyana with you—" Braxtus fumed.

A soft red glow caught Galene's eye, and she turned to look into a split that the tremors had opened in the obsidian. She blinked, apprehension crawling up her spine.

"Stop it!" Iyana pushed in front of Demitri so he couldn't get to Braxtus.

"Look!" Galene tried to claim their attention, but no one listened. *Seriously? Now?*

"It doesn't matter what would have happened!" Kostas glared between the two of them. "We're all stuck here together, so let's just find a way out, all right?"

The red glow brightened.

Braxtus seethed. "Fine. So was that all that was intended? To trap whoever got the *avyssos* in here?"

"'A prisoner may remain,'" Demitri quoted darkly. "I think that was the intent, yes."

Galene couldn't believe they hadn't noticed the blaze yet. With a jolt of frustration, she sent a wave rippling through the cavern. "Listen to me!" They all looked at her. She pointed to the crack.

"What on Gaia now?" Iyana muttered, kicking upward to become level with it.

"It's hot in here." Kostas's voice grew tense.

Galene blinked at him, realizing the truth of his words. The temperature of the water had indeed risen. They exchanged glances. There couldn't be fire underwater, but . . . her eyes rested on the shining black walls. Obsidian.

"Um"—Iyana stared into the glowing crevice—"I know what it is. I can see it."

But Galene didn't need Iyana to tell her what it was. She had just understood, dread squeezing her heart.

"What is it?" Demitri and Braxtus moved to join her, but before they could reach her, she backtracked to put distance between herself and the glow.

"Lava."

As soon as she said the word, a glob of thick, red liquid pushed itself through the gap, crusting over and fading to a dusty gray as it slid down the wall.

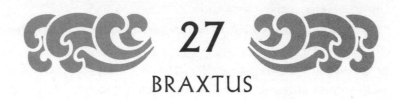

27

BRAXTUS

A searing torrent of bubbles hissed to the cavern ceiling as lava crusted over and sank through the water. The crack widened from the heat and pressure until it was bigger than him, and the seething flow steadily increased.

Braxtus turned to see his friends backing up, looking for a way to escape the building temperature. Kostas and Galene moved against the cool obsidian on the opposite wall. Demitri put himself in front of Iyana, trying to block her from the heat that didn't remotely bother Braxtus.

"We have to get out of here!" Galene choked. "That lava is going to heat this cavern to boiling point."

"Can you, I don't know, blow the rocks aside with the currents?" Iyana asked Galene, pointing at the caved-in entrance.

Galene glanced doubtfully at the rocks, then closed her eyes. A moment later she opened them again, shaking her head. "Maybe if it was open water, but I can't get that strong of a hold all the way in here."

"There has to be a way out," Kostas muttered, scanning the ceiling for an exit.

Braxtus swallowed as he saw their panic, then swam toward the flow of lava that was starting to waterfall over the rocks below.

"Braxtus, what are you doing? It's too hot over—" Galene stopped herself mid-sentence as she realized her mistake. He grabbed the edge of the crack in the wall to pull himself closer and investigate.

The fiery liquid piped up a vertical shaft from a chamber far below and blazed through the tear in the wall, already filling half the crack. Bubbles lifted from the surface of the lava, careening upward through the water and higher along the tube. He stuck his head in and looked up to see how far the shaft climbed, but couldn't see much with the bubbles and dim light.

He withdrew, frowning in fierce thought.

"There's no way out," Demitri said flatly. Everyone looked at him. He had given up a search for escape shortly after starting one.

"Don't say that," Kostas growled, still looking.

"There's no point, Kostas!" Demitri snapped. "The walls are too thick. I'm telling you, there's no way out except the way we came in."

"So you'd have us give up?" Iyana rounded on him, fire catching her eyes that Braxtus hadn't seen in a while.

"No, just . . ." He trailed off, pressing his fingers to his forehead.

"'A prisoner *may* remain.'" Galene turned in a circle. "There has to be a way out—we just have to use our heads. Block the lava, wait out the eruption, dig our way back out . . ." Her words were unconvincing, and Braxtus shook his head.

"You won't survive this heat," he said. "I guarantee it."

"How would you know?" Demitri scoffed.

"Heat may not bother me, but I'm an expert in it." He looked back at the glowing lava pouring from the shaft, cooling and collecting as rough gray rock on the ground below them. "There's too much lava. There have to be shafts filled with it. This volcano was rigged to blow the moment we got the *avyssos*, and this cavern is the target. You'll boil within the hour."

No one, not even Kostas, argued with his logic.

"But," he continued, heart thumping, "I might be able to find a way out."

"How?" Demitri asked.

Iyana's beautiful eyes went wide. "You want to go through there." She pointed to the shaft.

Galene's mouth opened. "Are you crazy? You can't go through the lava tube! Even if you don't die, we can't follow."

"There's no other way out of this cavern. Who knows where that shaft could lead?"

"How will you get us out?" Kostas's dark eyes locked on him, and Braxtus looked back helplessly.

"I'll break in to you somehow. Through the thinnest wall I can find."

"Braxtus, you can't *breathe* lava." Iyana sounded strained. "It could go over your head." When he didn't answer, she whirled on Kostas. "You're not going to support this, are you? It's almost impossible! He could die!"

"Almost impossible is our best chance," Kostas said. Even Demitri nodded, watching Braxtus. "We'll all be dead if he doesn't try."

Braxtus looked between them, noting in alarm how quickly the ichor had risen to their faces, flushing them gold. "I'm not going to stay here and watch my friends boil, Iyana. Not if there's a chance."

"You know . . ." Kostas faltered, face tightening, then tried again. "You know we're going to have to try to block up the entrance behind you. To give ourselves as much time as possible."

Braxtus understood. Once he was through, there was no coming back that direction. He nodded once, and Kostas returned the silent note of fellowship.

"Braxtus." Galene swam toward him. "In case you can't get back to us"—she extended her hand and revealed the shining *avyssos*—"you should take this. If the rest of us don't make it . . . well, you probably can't capture Poinê on your own, but maybe the Olympians will listen to you."

196

He stared at the gold-and-silver orb. Cursing the sudden tremor that ran through him, he reached out and took the *avyssos*.

"I'll do my best." He sucked in a breath and tucked the orb away into a pouch at his belt.

Galene smiled and nodded in gratitude.

If he couldn't get back to them, it would be *entirely* up to him to save Olympus. *And if I don't make it* . . . A rush of feelings he couldn't quite name rose. Kostas paused, watching him, clearly reading his churning emotions.

Come on, Kostas. Please understand what I need. Braxtus let his eyes flick to Iyana, and Kostas followed his gaze for an instant before turning away.

"Demitri," Kostas jerked his head. "Help me gather some rocks so we can fill the hole."

Demitri nodded, swimming off with Kostas. Braxtus released a breath, and in that brief moment of freedom, turned to Iyana. Her eyes caught his, bright blue and shining. He wanted to pull her into an embrace, but resisted.

Tell her. Before he could change his mind, he made himself speak.

"I'm in love with you."

Her lips parted.

"I have been for a long time. I should have told you before." He paused, searching her face, afraid of what he'd find. "I just needed you to know."

Iyana just stared at him, cheeks flushed, chest heaving. "Be safe," she whispered.

"Time, Braxtus," Galene murmured, sounding desperate.

He tore himself away from Iyana and grabbed the jagged edges of the crack in the wall, kicking his feet into the mounting lava to propel himself into the shaft.

The thick liquid sucked at his legs, dragging him down the tube. Braxtus threw his hands out to either side to brace himself on the obsidian walls. He stopped sinking, but bubbles swarmed around him, making it hard to see, and . . .

He choked. Hard to *breathe*. The mixture of water and bubbles was exactly like the maelstrom, where he'd nearly drowned. The bubbles left a foul taste in his throat, stinging his lungs. He held his breath.

Using the wall as leverage, he pulled himself up until his feet were free of the lava, then struck out, swimming upward with the rising bubbles. He swam for several long seconds, pressure building in his chest and anxiety mounting, before his head burst through the surface of the water.

He tried to suck in a breath, then burst into a coughing fit, gagging until his lungs were clear, breathing in something thinner, but still humid. Something *natural*.

Air.

Braxtus laughed weakly as he paddled to stay afloat. This volcanic air pocket wasn't the reunion with air he'd been hoping for. Heavy steam rose around him, and below the bubbling water, the lava blazed red, lighting up the otherwise dark shaft and obsidian walls with a harsh and bloody light. *Looks like Hades's realm.*

He moved to the side of the shaft closest to the cavern and felt along the side of the wall. The obsidian was cracked in places, making for tiny handholds. It took him a few tries, but painfully, he lifted himself from the water and began to scale the wall.

Water poured off him, his water-logged clothes weighing him down even more than his armor and weapons already did. He gritted his teeth, squinting to see the wall through the steam. Droplets stung his eyes. He kept climbing. *Swimming would have been a whole lot easier.*

As he moved, the lava rose beneath him. The water level seemed to stay the same, evaporating faster as the lava caught up to it.

The wall he scaled began to slant, easing his climb. He picked up speed, until all at once it flattened enough for him to stand.

He straightened, head brushing the top of the tunnel, and his heart leapt.

The tunnel kept going, curving as though it followed the outline of the cavern where his friends were waiting. The soft glow of lava barely illuminated the dark shaft.

He called to his element, and sweet, blessed fire raced up his hands like gloves. "Hello, my friend." The comforting light flickered against the obsidian, showing him the way.

He scrambled up the slope, almost putting out the flames on his hands as he occasionally pushed off the floor. It leveled as he climbed, but he still gasped for breath, knees trembling with every step in the effort to propel himself upward.

He looked behind him at the soft red blaze where the lava was climbing after him. Falling to his knees, he pressed his toes against a crack to stop himself from slipping. *This has to be above them.* He begged silently to the Fates that he was right, swung his shield off his shoulder, and slammed it into the ground with a loud crack.

He threw it again.

And again.

The floor shuddered at the impact, black chips flying as they caved to his blows. He continued for a minute, but the progress was slow, so he threw his hands to the floor and searched the cracks frantically, his fingernails splitting. He dug his fingers in and tore at them, switching to push with his palms, deepening them.

The lava came back into view, lapping at the obsidian as it crested the hill. Braxtus retrieved his shield, turning it on its edge this time before he brought it back down.

He smashed it at his knees again and again. The walls shook, the floor shook, and his shield vibrated his entire arm and back. The ground chipped away like shards of glass, and he increased his vigor. Somewhere in the back of his mind he registered pain, but ignored it.

There was a hollow sound of breaking rock, and a surge of hope pulsed through him.

Crack!

He almost fell through the hole that split under his final blow. Water came through, sloshing over his knees, and his heart stopped beating when it steamed.

Dropping his shield, he dove straight into the water.

His lungs protested at the transition again, and it took him a moment to orient himself, twisting in the glowing water as he tried to get a view of his friends.

There they were. His heart lurched. "Kostas! Iyana!"

They didn't respond. Stripped of armor, they drifted in just their tunics, weapons, and sandals, skin golden. They didn't even look up as Braxtus shouted their names.

They're overheated.

Heart pounding, he propelled himself toward them and seized Kostas's arm. Kostas turned to look at him, and utter relief shone in his black eyes a moment before they rolled to the back of his head.

"Braxtus," Galene panted. She seemed the most alert, holding Iyana's arm. Iyana struggled to stay conscious. Demitri's eyes were closed, and he didn't move.

Braxtus threw his best friend on his shoulder, turning to kick to their escape. "Follow if you can!" With enormous effort, Braxtus hoisted Kostas through the hole, then pulled himself up after. He held his breath as he emerged, not wanting to make the transition. Below him, Galene and Iyana moved lethargically, Galene supporting her best friend. He reached down and hauled them up through the hole by their arms, one at a time.

As soon as he heard them coughing the water from their lungs, he dove back in.

Demitri was still out of it. Braxtus clenched his teeth as he grabbed the god around the waist to drag him to the surface.

When Braxtus forced his head through the hole, Galene and Iyana were there, reaching down to help pull Demitri through.

They spread him out on the rocks, next to Kostas, and Galene pounded his back until he, too, choked up water. The gods lay there, breathing normally, still unconscious.

Braxtus turned to the goddesses. "You okay?" he asked hoarsely.

Iyana combed back her wet hair. "We're fine now. They burned up faster trying to block the hole, but"—she shook her head in amazement—"I can't believe you made it."

"We're not out yet." Galene looked around them.

"But your armor—" Braxtus started.

"It's scorching. We don't have time to let it cool."

He nodded. "The lava's coming this direction. We have to move."

Iyana bent down to pull Demitri to his feet, but was too weak. Galene moved to help her, and together they hoisted him up. He sagged sideways. Iyana gave him a shake, and his eyes fluttered. He groaned, and the goddesses put their arms around his waist to support him.

Braxtus slung his shield on his back and crouched. Lifting Kostas, he pulled him on his shoulders and stood. Kostas was heavy but manageable, for now.

"Let's go." He cast an anxious look over his shoulder at the pursuing fire, then took off in the lead, his friends stumbling in his wake.

The path was still an upward climb, which at first proved nearly impossible for the struggling three. He stopped twice to let them catch up, concern mounting to near panic as the light behind them brightened. The longer they raced on, however, the more sure-footed they all became, until Demitri shook off the supporting arms and marched along on his own. Kostas still hadn't moved.

The tunnel came to a dead end. Braxtus stopped. Galene

pushed by him and pressed her body up against the rock, moaning in appreciation.

"The sea is here," she said, patting the wall. "I can feel it."

Braxtus glanced at his cut-up hands holding Kostas in place. "Then we'll have to break through it."

"The lava," Iyana warned. Turning to look back, they watched the liquid below them climb with a fevered frenzy. Braxtus set Kostas down and took his poor, damaged shield from his shoulder.

"We'll need to do this together."

"This wall is thick." Galene hit it with the flat of her hand. "If the sea hasn't broken through already, what makes you think the four of us will be able to?"

Braxtus scowled at her sudden pessimism. "All right, I'll heat the rock, and you, Galene, see if you can get the sea to push from the other side." Galene opened her mouth, looking unsure. "We have to try!"

She closed her mouth and nodded.

He stepped up to the wall and pressed his hands against it, channeling all the fire and heat in his body. It poured through him into the cold stone, flames lighting under his fingers.

"You three try to break it. I'll bring up the colder currents," Galene said as she moved beside Braxtus. "The contrast in temperatures might help the rock crack."

Braxtus's hands and arms started glowing, followed by the rock around them. "Are you ready?" he asked. It probably hadn't been long enough, but if the growing light was anything to go by, they didn't have much time.

Iyana and Demitri stepped up, and Braxtus brought his shield forward.

"One . . . two . . . *three!*" All three of them slammed into the wall together. Braxtus felt his tunic rip as his shoulder smashed into it, but he ignored it, stepping back.

"Again! One . . . two . . . *three!*" They pounded over and over.

There was a deep crack.

"One more!" Demitri yelled. They threw their entire bodies onto the wall.

"Watch out!" Galene screamed.

The rocks crumbled, and a tsunami slammed into them. Iyana's scream cut short, and they were blasted off their feet, knocked backward from the sudden, crushing impact.

Kostas! Braxtus lunged in his friend's direction. He thought he touched him for an instant, but then it was all a white, pounding blur as he tumbled down the slope toward the lava.

The water level dropped, the flow stemming.

He windmilled once, then regained his feet.

Galene was standing in the middle of the shaft, her face screwed up in concentration as she held the tidal wave at bay. The hole was a window to a wall of water, begging to crash through. Steam rose up from behind them as water met lava.

Demitri pulled Iyana to her feet, and then another person staggered upright, dripping and shaking his dark curls.

"Good to see you awake, Kostas!" he shouted.

Kostas's face broke into a wide grin. "You did it."

"Let's get out!" Demitri shouted over the hiss of steam and the roil of water behind them. He and Iyana staggered for the exit, and Braxtus sloshed behind in pursuit.

For the first time in his life, he happily threw himself into the cold, blue sea.

28

IYANA

Iyana's heart raced with the thrill of freedom, of *safety*.

Galene used her currents to carry them far and fast. Whenever Iyana glanced back, she could see black bubbles flaring with red from the sloping rocks behind them, a cloud of darkness staining the water. They wouldn't have lasted another five minutes.

When they'd gained some distance, a laugh burst from Kostas. They slowed and everyone pulled up, gathering in a circle. Braxtus whooped and clapped his best friend on the shoulder.

Iyana felt a smile tug at her lips. Demitri slung his arm around her and pulled her into him, kissing her temple. Her heart panged, but she kept her smile on, looking around at her celebrating friends.

"You did it, Braxtus!" Kostas turned to him.

Braxtus shook his head, but his dimples showed his pride. "We all made it happen."

Except for me. Iyana's smile became harder to fake. She'd been no help. Again.

"Here." Braxtus pulled the shimmering orb from his pouch and gingerly extended it to Galene. "I'm *so* glad I didn't have to take this to the Olympians! You should be the one to do it." His hands were cut and stained with ichor, but his warm eyes laughed as Galene happily returned the *avyssos* to her pouch.

He said he's in love with me.

Heat rushed through her at the memory of his words, the feelings she'd locked away swarming her full-force again. She sucked in a small breath. Demitri, who still had her pinned to his side, glanced down at her. She flushed deeper under his gaze, hoping he wouldn't be able to read her.

He cleared his throat. "Where's the closest island, Galene? I believe it's time to find some land."

Braxtus smiled even wider.

Galene nodded and closed her eyes. The currents around them rocked harder as she focused. "We can make it to the closest one in a few hours. Let's head there to sleep and plan our next steps."

"Will we swim the whole way?" Braxtus asked.

"No. I'll take us on the tides."

"Are you sure?" Kostas studied her. "We're all tired, and that's a long way."

"I'll be fine." Galene smiled at his concern. "Let's head toward the surface. The tides are easier to control up there."

They complied, kicking for the surface with unbridled enthusiasm. It took several long minutes, but soon the glare of the sun appeared rippling on the water above them. Rays of light scattered from a passing school of silver fish. Iyana was surprised the sun was still up. Time had been hard to track since the labyrinth.

She longed to swim the last several feet and break through into the air, to feel it rush into her lungs, to wake her gift and play with the wind. *Not too much longer,* she told herself. She was hopeful she'd get to feel the sun on her skin before they rested for the night.

Water swelled around them and pulled them along. Iyana let it, trying to adjust herself so she didn't drag. They seemed to move faster this time. Iyana suspected it was both because Galene had gotten better with her ability, and because they were much lighter without their armor. Braxtus, still wearing his, had to paddle along to keep up, but he wasn't complaining. She kept her eyes averted from him, busying herself watching animal life. Schools of fish darted through the water, their weightless, synchronized movements reminding Iyana of birds navigating the sky.

Birds. Her heart soared at the thought. She never imagined she'd be so excited just to see a *bird.*

Their good moods lasted a while, then faded back into exhaustion. Galene's face tightened as the afternoon wore on. Suspicious that it wasn't *all* tiredness, Iyana propelled herself to her.

"Are you worried?"

Galene nodded.

"I can't imagine Anyss making it past that volcano. I think we're in the clear."

"Unless she realizes we already got the *avyssos* and goes back. Then we'll have all of Chrysander's people on our tail."

Iyana bit her lip. "Maybe . . ."

"The next steps are just as scary, you know? Not only do we have to figure out how the *avyssos* works, capture the rebels, and convince Chrysander to run, but then we have to return to Olympus and convince them to hear out our story without getting struck down on the spot."

"We've gotten this far." *Despite me. You haven't needed me one bit.* "We can make it." She kept her voice even, so it wouldn't betray her emotion.

Galene took a breath. "I feel selfish even wondering this now, but . . . Even then, after we save Olympus from destruction, what if it's not enough to retract their sentence of exile? The prophecy still stands against me."

Iyana touched her shoulder but didn't know how to respond. *My worries are nothing compared to hers.*

Galene fell silent, her focus returning to the tides.

Over the next hour, the seafloor sloped up. It rose, all tangled reeds and rocks, pushing them toward the surface until Iyana exhaled all the water from her lungs and burst into the sun.

She gasped and coughed a little, blinking water from her eyelashes as the others surfaced around her. It was cooler than she'd expected, the sun hanging low on the horizon, but she reveled in it. The blue sky was clear and welcoming. Ahead was a small island—a sandy beach leading to a rocky black cliff that jutted into the sky.

The tide dragged Iyana forward until her sandaled feet touched down on sand, the water retreating to her waist.

Galene spread her arms. The tide rushed forward in response, white foam cresting the small waves, smacking into them to propel them forward. Iyana's hands hit the sand and she struggled to get to her feet, but before any of them rose more than halfway, another wave crashed into them, sending them back to their stomachs.

Braxtus spat out a mouthful of sand. "We can walk!"

Galene nodded feebly, and the tide slunk away from them, leaving them deposited on the shore.

Iyana staggered to her feet, legs shaky from going so long without weight on them. Demitri caught her arm, helping her regain balance. "Thank you," she mumbled, wiping the worst of the sand from her attire.

Wind swirled around her almost before she'd realized she'd beckoned it, like an instinct. She welcomed the rush of the air on her skin, closing her eyes. But the chill cut through her thin tunic. Goose bumps rose on her arms, and her teeth began to chatter. Regretfully, before anyone could complain, she stilled the breeze.

"We can find some shelter against the cliffs," Kostas suggested.

"High tide is coming in," Galene protested, voice weak, "and I can't hold it at bay."

"Up the cliff, then." Demitri pointed to a steep slope that led up to the top of the cliffs. Iyana's heart sank at the trek.

The woebegone group trudged through the sand, but after only a few steps, Galene stumbled and collapsed.

"Galene!" Iyana hurried over, dropping to her knees. Kostas stooped to help her back to her feet, but she wouldn't, or couldn't, get up.

"Imallright," she mumbled.

"She didn't tell us how much energy she used traveling on the tide," Iyana groaned.

"She probably hadn't recovered from overheating before she started." Braxtus sounded worried, too, as he crouched beside Iyana. "She should be fine with rest, though."

Without another word, Kostas gathered her into his arms, lifting her from the sand.

Braxtus collected sticks as they trekked uphill, and eventually, exhausted as they were, they made it to the top of the rocky slope, overlooking the sea two hundred feet below.

Completely soaked and caked in sand, Iyana dropped to the ground, huddling close to the others. Kostas lay Galene down carefully, brushing her hair back from her face under Iyana's watchful eyes. She felt a small twinge of jealousy at their simple, new affection.

The cold that sank into her bones was almost enough to make her wish they'd stayed underwater, but Braxtus arranged his firewood and lit it with a sudden burst of flames. Heat radiated from the little fire, and Iyana shivered in delight, then loosened her hair from the braid it had been in for far too long.

"Sleep tonight, hunt and plan tomorrow?" Kostas suggested wearily.

They gave murmurs of agreement. Despite the hard rocks, Iyana was sure she would sleep more soundly than she had the entire journey underwater. Hopefully, Braxtus could catch up on some much-needed sleep, too.

She raised her eyes to him. A jolt went through her as she found his already on her. Heat flowed between them, not from any fire, and she dropped her gaze back to the flames.

She'd wanted him to tell her his feelings for so long.

Like he could sense her thoughts, Demitri moved closer to her and ran his fingers through her wet hair, gently untangling it. Iyana rubbed her eyes and curled up on the rock, acting too tired to reciprocate the affection. He didn't say anything, just pressed his lips to her jaw before stretching out beside her.

What am I supposed to do?

One by one, her friends dropped off into slumber.

She had been wrong about her good night's rest: Both discomfort *and* her racing mind battled the exhaustion that had seeped into her bones. After a long time on her back, staring at the stars and trying to clear her mind, she rolled onto her stomach and watched the sticks smolder their way down to embers, savoring the last of their warmth as she listened to Braxtus's soft snores.

Demitri stirred.

Iyana stilled, not really wanting him to know she was awake. She heard him get up and peeked through her hair, seeing his vague silhouette in the dim light.

His feet were sandaled, and his footsteps seemed too loud as he moved past Braxtus and Kostas, over to Galene's sleeping figure. Demitri knelt by her side and swiftly untied the pouch on her belt. Iyana raised her head an inch off her arms, bewildered.

He felt through the pouch, then withdrew his hand as he found what he was looking for. She caught a glimpse of the gleaming *avyssos* before his fingers curled over it. Galene didn't stir as he tied the pouch back on her belt.

She opened her mouth to call to him, but sudden, unexpected fear prickled at her. There was something in his furtive movements, in the way he stood and surveyed the scene, that made her keep her mouth shut.

Demitri rose to his feet and turned away. He didn't look back as he walked off, his footsteps and silhouette fading into the darkness.

Iyana stared after him, nerves and uncertainty rushing through her. *What is he doing?* She got to her feet and looked at her friends. She moved past Braxtus, who had plenty to dislike Demitri for already. Past Galene, who she knew would never trust him again.

"Kostas," she whispered, gently shaking his shoulder, "Kostas, wake up."

His head lolled, his breathing deep and even, but he didn't stir.

She shook him harder. He gave no response, so she smacked his cheeks. Nothing. *What on Gaia—?*

She grabbed Galene's arm and shook it. "Galene?" Her voice trembled as new fear gripped her throat. When she didn't respond either, she turned to Braxtus. "Braxtus, get up! Braxtus!" She seized his face, hands cupping his cheeks. "Braxtus!" she pleaded quietly, searching his face. His expression contorted, and he looked troubled, but he didn't open his eyes.

She let go and straightened, mind racing. Then she laced her sandals and gripped her quiver of spikes, swinging it onto her shoulder, just in case. Before she could change her mind, she turned, running quietly in the direction she had seen Demitri go.

Mist coated the ground, clinging to a vast expanse of black rock that stretched out ahead. She couldn't see the horizon line, just the darkness rising up until the glimmer of stars, blurred by fog, interrupted it. It took a few minutes of a light jog in the direction he had gone before she spotted his silhouette and slowed.

He stood at the edge of the cliff, staring out at the sea. His arms were crossed, and as she crept closer, she could see the tightness in his shoulders. She paused, watching him. And waited.

Come on, Demitri. Do something, Iyana silently begged. *Test out the avyssos's powers or something, so I know what's going on.* But the longer they stood there, the more her suspicions mounted and her fears increased.

Before she thought to stop it, a breeze responded to her anxi-

ety, first ruffling her long hair into her face, then reaching Demitri and catching his tunic. He dropped his crossed arms and
half-turned toward her, blue eyes cutting through the darkness.

"Hello, Iyana."

He didn't sound surprised, or concerned in the slightest, that
she'd followed him out here.

Taking a breath, she gathered her courage. "What are you
doing?"

He beckoned to her, and she cautiously stepped up beside him,
despite the dizzying drop now at her feet. Far below, a narrow
strip of beach hugged the cliffs, thinning as the tide rolled in.

"We have to talk," he said, taking her hand.

She waited for him to speak, watching his face as he watched
the sea.

"I have a plan for us," he said quietly, "and I need you to trust
me and listen to what I have to say."

Nerves twisted her stomach, and she followed his gaze. Then
narrowed her eyes. There, sitting on the gently tossing waves, was
a large, dark shadow. Long and thin, with a wide sail.

"Demitri, is that a *ship*?" She tightened her grip on his hand,
turning to look at him. "Do you see that? Who would be coming
here?"

His eyes did not shift from the sea. "Come with me tonight,
Iyana. We have the *avyssos*. Within the month, we will fix everything. No more tyrannical Olympians. A new regime." He finally
turned to look at her, a strange light in those blue eyes. "You can
be part of this with me."

She looked from him back to the ship. A small boat was
lowered over one side, two dark figures in it. Her hand began
to tremble in his. "Demitri," she whispered. "Tell me that's not
Poinê."

"It is." He squeezed her hand, as though trying to be reassur-
ing, but it felt like a trap closing.

"You . . . you brought them here?" She shook her head, trying to clear it. *This can't be real.* "You're working with Chrysander. You've been with them this whole time."

"Yes." Demitri still sounded calm, but there was an undertone of intensity there. He released her hand, only to catch her chin and look her directly in the eye. "This is the right thing to do, Iyana. You know the Olympians are cruel. You'll never go home, never gain immortality under their rule. Come with me."

"Demitri, we talked about this." Her voice came out strangled. "We had a plan, remember? We can prove ourselves to the Olympians by turning Poinê in. It could improve so many things for us—"

"Could isn't good enough."

"But the chaos, the violence. You said yourself it was all too extreme—"

"We *need* extreme. This is justice."

"Galene—"

"She doesn't understand." He cut her off. "She's grown up trying to make them proud of her and is still under the illusion that one day she can."

Iyana gaped at him, struggling to find something else to say. Below her, the rowboat slid onto the sand.

"When we have the new regime set up, Galene and the others can come back," he soothed. "We'll need people like Galene to take over for Poseidon on the seas . . . She'll thank us later. Leave them behind tonight so we can do this for them. Do it for everything you believe in."

She wanted to resist him, her mind screaming logic about death and destruction, but a small voice in her whispered that his plan made some kind of sense. And Demitri was her rock. He'd always known what was best.

"Trust me, Iyana." He put his hand between them, palm up. "Take a leap of faith."

A strange feeling flooded through her at his words, his out-stretched hand. It was so familiar, like she had lived this moment in another life, and if she only reached out and took his hand she would complete the parallel . . .

Her recent dream came flooding unbidden into her memory.

"Iyana, you need to jump."

"I'm serious, there's no way—!"

"The cliff you're standing on is going to collapse! You have to trust me, Iyana!"

She trembled. "I . . . I do trust you," she whispered.

"Then jump!"

She leapt.

Staring at his hand in shock, Iyana's mind spun through her other dreams. Him protecting her from the taraxippi. A memory that wasn't a memory, when he disappeared and the arrows struck.

"I've been having dreams," she whispered, meeting Demitri's eyes again. "But you knew that, didn't you?"

He watched her grimly, lowering his hand. That was enough confirmation.

"You've hidden a second ability from us all this time. You can manipulate dreams, can't you?"

His expression didn't change. Rage grew hot in her. "You've been manipulating me!" Her voice rose to a shout. "Why would you plant ideas in my head? To make me dependent on you? So I would come with you tonight?"

"They were just dreams, Iyana," he said placatingly. *Come now, Iyana,* his voice seemed to say. *Don't be dramatic, Iyana.*

She stumbled back, everything he'd ever said warping in her mind. Could she even trust the feelings she had for him? Had he always been pulling the strings? She racked her brain, trying to think of any more dreams he could have twisted to his advantage. *Braxtus.* Her anger lurched even higher. "You gave Braxtus nightmares. Terrible ones, keeping him up all night!"

He just gave a slow blink. She wanted to shatter his calm, make him beg for forgiveness. *What else did he...*

It hit her like a charging bull. The dream that had started this whole mess. She swayed, feeling her face drain of color. Demitri looked like he was bracing himself, completely aware of what she had realized, but at first she couldn't even get the words through her teeth.

"Apollo," she managed. "You twisted his prophetic dream to show Galene. *You* stole the Decks of Fates and created the beasts."

"Iyana—" Demitri started, reaching for her.

"Am I wrong?" She took another step back.

His eyes flashed, and he drew himself to his full height. "No."

Footsteps sounded from beyond Demitri, climbing up the cliff from the opposite slope. She looked past him, eyes making out two distinct figures stepping through the fog—a young god, and a tall goddess with long, midnight hair.

"Demitri!" Chrysander called. "Do you have it?"

"I have it." Demitri kept his eyes on Iyana as he called back.

"Then hurry up, will you?"

Hatred, shock, and fury pounded through Iyana. She whirled toward their camp.

"Traitor!" The wind snatched her words, tearing back toward her friends. *"Demitri is a traitor!"*

29

GALENE

asping for air, Galene jerked awake.

Wind whipped the hair from her face. Her heart pounded, head spinning as words echoed through her mind. *Demitri's a traitor.* She blinked away the darkness of her nightmare, the words fading as she turned over to fall back asleep. Her eyes fell on the vacated stone.

She jolted back up, smacking Kostas in the process. He gave a light groan as she spun to look into the cold night.

Beneath the starry sky, the misty scene was still.

Kostas sat up. "Galene, what's wrong?"

"Where are Demitri and Iyana?"

He looked over to where they should've been sleeping, his eyes clearing as he tried to make sense of the situation. They suddenly flashed. He leapt to his feet. "Galene, you have the *avyssos*, right?"

She blinked, then grasped at the pouch on her belt. It folded under her fingers, empty. Her heart skipped a beat, and she plunged her hand inside, but her fingers groped over nothing. She rolled away to search where she'd been sleeping, frantic. Kostas watched in silence.

Braxtus jerked and twitched in his sleep, muttering under his breath. "Betrayal," he breathed. Galene froze, listening. "Demitri's a traitor."

The words triggered a jolt up Galene's spine. She locked eyes with Kostas, his mouth a hard line.

"No," she whispered. "He wouldn't . . ."

But Kostas was already by Braxtus's side, shaking him awake. Galene scrambled to her feet as Braxtus grunted and opened his eyes.

"Iyana's calling us." He stared vacantly at Kostas. "I heard her voice."

Kostas grabbed his arm and pulled him to his feet. "Come on, there's trouble."

Snatching only their weapons, the three of them took off barefoot and armorless over the rocks.

An almost full moon shone just above the horizon, and a breeze swept away the mist, clearing their visibility. Even so, Galene had a hard time making out much in the darkness as they ran across the clifftop.

"I'm such an *idiot*," Kostas hissed. His eyes gleamed. "I should have known, I should have figured it out sooner. All of Demitri's emotions, since Poinê's camp—I misinterpreted them all."

Galene sucked in a breath as her foot scraped against a particularly sharp rock. "What do you mean?"

"He was good." Anger shattered his usual unbreakable calm. "He disguised what he felt, twisting his fear of being caught to blend with situational fear. And back at the camp, do you remember, he approached with Chrysander, then appeared to knock him out. They were together from the start!"

Dread clenched her gut. *So Chrysander got through to you after all, Demitri.* She tried to run faster, but exhaustion hindered her. *Where are they?*

The silence was the most ominous part of all. Galene withdrew one of her throwing knives from her belt, waiting to hear something, anything . . .

A shrill scream split the night, and Galene immediately regretted her thoughts. She snapped her gaze ahead of her, to the right. There, at the edge of the cliff, stood four figures. One of them grabbed Iyana's small frame, hauling her away in the opposite direction.

No. Galene took off. Kostas's and Braxtus's footsteps pounded behind.

A wall of wind slammed into her, sending her hair streaming and eyes watering. Her lungs burned, her legs shook with fatigue. She gasped, but try as she might to hold her pace, Braxtus and Kostas soon outstripped her.

The downward slope ahead led back to the beach, where a small ship waited just off the shore. Braxtus and Kostas ran down toward the four figures.

Braxtus skidded to a halt as Demitri turned to face him, splitting his staff into two swords. Kostas stopped farther back, hurrying to nock an arrow. Galene's eyes fell onto one of the figures beyond him, and she stumbled to a stop.

Chrysander.

Beside him stood Poinê, dark hair free and flooding over purple robes, gripping Iyana close.

She drew a dagger, clenching her hand around the hilt.

Demitri's eyes flicked to Kostas, then to Galene, then back to Braxtus. Nobody moved.

"Hello, Galene." A bucket of ice seemed to drop down Galene's spine as the dark-haired beauty spoke, a smile curving her lips. "I believe I owe you thanks."

Galene continued running toward Iyana, but Demitri hefted a sword. "Go. And steer clear of Olympus until we've usurped the Olympians."

She halted next to Kostas.

"You have no idea what you're dealing with, Galene." Chrysander had flint in his gaze. "Get out of here, or someone will get hurt."

"He's right." Poinê's eyes were as black as Kostas's, but where his were the midnight sky, hers were empty caverns. "In gratitude of your . . . ah . . . *efforts* on my behalf, I'll let you leave with your lives. But if you become unreasonable, you just might force my hand."

Iyana twisted furiously in her grip, but the goddess didn't seem to notice.

"You've been double-crossing us since the camp," Galene growled at Demitri, fury rising.

He looked her square in the eye. "Actually, no. It's been since Chrysander left the mountain. Before you were even exiled. Before I *set you up* to be exiled." He said the words with relish, as though he'd been waiting to take ownership of his actions.

The world reeled. "How?" She couldn't get her voice above a whisper.

"He's been hiding a second gift, and it has nothing to do with war!" Iyana spat. "It's *dreams*. He manipulates them to influence others. He manipulated Apollo's *vision*."

Galene's mind spun wildly as the pieces fit together. "Apollo's vision . . . you . . ." She felt like she didn't have enough air.

Demitri twisted his lips into a mocking smile. "Based on what Chrysander kept telling me over the years, I'd expected more from you, Galene. Truly, how naive can you get to believe all of this"—he swept his hand holding the *avyssos* aloft—"had been orchestrated by the Fates? So much went into this. Iyana nearly messed it all up by exiling herself, too, and I had to fix the problem. You might not have left her behind alone, so I decided to come along, just in case."

Behind him, Iyana sucked in a breath. Torment swam in her eyes.

"And then I thought, if we could *all* go . . ."

"My father gave me that boon," Galene said through gritted teeth.

Demitri's eyes glittered. "Why do you think Poseidon thought of it? Because I planted the idea in his head with a dream."

Hot, angry tears Galene didn't even know had risen spilled onto her cheeks. "That's why you framed *me*. Because I can breathe underwater. So I could get the *avyssos* for you."

"We hoped you'd join our cause, but we had a plan to make you go even if you refused." Chysander stepped forward, watching her. "I figured you'd be too *noble* to just step aside and let Olympus fall, so we told you we had another who could go instead. Anyss, remember?" He snorted. "She can only make it rain. There was no one else but you, Galene, and all you needed was the motivation to get it."

Galene's rage erupted. She threw her dagger at her brother.

Her throw was weak and he dodged easily, but she ran at him, drawing her scimitar. It felt too heavy in her arms, but she didn't care. He freed his blade from its scabbard just in time to stop hers, and they met with a clash of steel.

"*You ruined my life!*" She pulled back her sword and swung it forward with her trembling strength. "My own *brother!*" The words came out as sobs.

He ducked under the blow. Galene spun and kicked Chysander in the stomach, but as he doubled over someone hit her, tackling her to the ground. Demitri pressed one of his twin swords to her throat.

Kostas cried out and Iyana screamed. From the corner of her eye Galene could see Braxtus start to charge.

"Stop!" Iyana yelled. "Everyone *stop*! Demitri, let her go. Let her go and I'll come with you willingly. I'll do this with you."

"No!" Braxtus yelled.

But the blade eased up on Galene's throat, Demitri's eyes going to Iyana. Poinê released her, and she ran to Demitri. Tears clung to Iyana's eyelashes, and she threw her arms around him, crying into his shoulder. He pulled back from Galene, rising, letting him hold her and keeping his blades safely away.

Galene felt sick, renewed hatred bubbling under her skin. How much had Demitri hurt Iyana? What dreams had he been putting into *her* head? Galene watched, wanting to tear them apart. Were Iyana's thoughts even her own anymore?

"It's okay, Demitri," Iyana soothed. "We don't need to fight. Please." She pushed up on her toes to kiss him.

Galene gripped her scimitar tighter, and she heard Braxtus growl.

"Leave them be," Iyana said as she pulled back, "and let's go."

Demitri nodded slowly. He slid his two swords back together into a staff, and guided Iyana toward Poinê.

Galene felt her heart fracture as her best friend walked away with a traitor.

He had never deserved her.

Then, in one quick movement, Iyana shoved Demitri to the ground. She ran, a glow of silver and gold shining through her clenched fingers.

30

KOSTAS

Everyone understood what had happened at the same time. "Get her!" Poinê yelled.

With a curse, Demitri launched to his feet and took off after Iyana, steaming with red and green. Chrysander moved to follow, but Galene lunged at his knees, hauling him to the ground. "Run, Iyana!"

Kostas followed Iyana's projected path—to the cliff's edge. *She's going to throw it into the sea.* Where Galene could carry it away, back to the depths.

Kostas aimed one of his last arrows at Demitri, but Braxtus moved in the way, crouching to tackle him. Without missing a step, Demitri grabbed Braxtus's shoulder, leaping to roll across his back. He landed smoothly on his feet again and continued running.

Kostas fired. The arrow whistled through the air, but before it hit home, Demitri spun his staff, deflecting it.

He shot again, but once more, the son of Ares cut the missile from the air. Kostas started running.

Demetri was gaining on Iyana.

Kostas reached back for a third arrow, but his fingers groped at nothing. He tossed aside his bow and *ran*. Demitri's eyes shifted to his.

Iyana was a stride from the cliff's edge and its dizzying drop.

Kostas skidded between her and Demitri, Iyana's hair whipping his neck as he raised his arms to shield her.

Demitri grabbed Kostas's shoulders and, with all his momentum, shoved him sideways, catching Iyana's arm mid-throw.

Kostas staggered back, one step, two steps—

His foot met no ground, and his stomach lurched as he fell backward off the cliff.

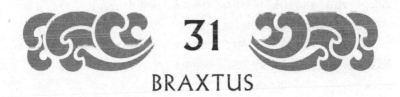

31

BRAXTUS

Braxtus felt as though he were falling beside his best friend as Kostas disappeared over the edge. Galene screamed.

Wind howled to furious life, rocking Braxtus as Iyana leaned out over the cliff against Demitri's grasp.

Catch him, Iyana!

Distantly, he heard Kostas strike the ground two hundred feet below.

Braxtus swayed.

Iyana's knees buckled, and Demitri dragged her back to safety, tearing the *avyssos* from her fingers. He glanced down once, then turned away, lip curling, as though pushing Kostas off a cliff had been mildly distasteful.

Iyana crumpled to the ground, a sob breaking from her. The sound tore through Braxtus's shock, and he staggered in their direction, broadsword almost slipping from his shaking hand.

A rush of dark hair and violet robes swept past him, and Demitri left Iyana crying in the dust, meeting Poinê and handing her the *avyssos*. She took it with a jerk. "Return to the boat, Chrysander, and signal the ship to prepare to leave." Her voice was stony.

Behind him, Braxtus heard a tussle, then someone running down the slope. He glanced back in time to see Galene struggle to her feet and take off after her brother.

He turned back and met Demitri's cold eyes.

Fury and pain wracked him. He bared his teeth, lifted his sword, and hurled himself at the treacherous god.

Demitri planted his feet as Braxtus reached them, letting Poinê move away. Braxtus swung, but Demitri moved like lightning, blocking Braxtus's blade with his staff. Demitri's ice eyes were lit with energy. "I'd say don't be a fool, but that's exactly what you are. All of you."

"You *murdered* Kostas," Braxtus snarled.

Demitri snorted. "Kostas. He was the biggest fool of all. Even with his gifts he was blind to my role."

"You bastard." The handle of his broadsword grew hot in his grip.

But there was something about the way Demitri pushed back, making Braxtus retreat, that made him pause. *He wants to distract me from Poinê and the* avyssos.

With enormous effort, Braxtus shoved away his anger. He attacked, trying to find a way past, but Demitri matched his every move. Braxtus took his sword in a two-handed grip, striking more furiously, but Demitri twisted his staff back into two thin swords and easily held his ground. Braxtus retreated a step.

Then, with a fierce battle-cry, someone came hurtling out of the mist, tackling Demitri from the side. Shock crossed Demitri's features an instant before he crashed to the ground. Iyana wrapped her arms and legs around him in a practiced grip to keep him down. Demitri twisted in Iyana's vice, but seemed reluctant to fight her.

Braxtus hesitated for an instant.

"Go!" Iyana shouted at him, redoubling her efforts. "Get the *avyssos*!"

Braxtus ran.

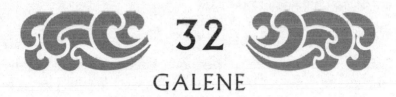

32

GALENE

It was too much. All of it was just *too much*.

She raced down the hill after her brother, bare feet slapping the rocks. Tears blurred her eyes, and her heart wouldn't stop *pounding*. She could hardly breathe as she pushed her body to its limit, sobs still shaking her lungs.

Kostas. Gaia, Kostas had fallen.

She wanted to scream.

Dashing a hand across her eyes, she tried to concentrate. *I can't let any of them leave.*

Chrysander was way ahead of her. His feet hit the sand of the short beach. A small rowboat waited to take him, Poinê, and Demitri to the ship. Chrysander stopped before it, waving his hands to the crew at sea, signaling.

Galene's ankle twisted as she sprinted onto the hard, wet sand. Barely managing to avoid spraining it, she staggered forward. "Chrysander!"

He ignored her. Done with his message, he put his foot on the rowboat, waiting.

The sea rushed in, grazing her toes. High tide was fast approaching, but Galene threw out her hands, shoving the sea back with all her might. The water fled, leaving Chrysander's boat stranded on the sand.

"Galene." He finally acknowledged her.

She kept the water out, holding the fighting tide at bay as she turned her attention to the ship.

"Galene!"

She kept her focus on the sea, ignoring the pain—her heart aching, her lungs burning, her brain begging for reprieve, and now the strain of holding the tides. She let it go and yanked at the water, willing it to rock the ship.

The surf came crashing in, cold water rushing over her ankles. She pushed it back out, gritting her teeth and shoving, then hauling the tides toward her again. The water rushed higher, to mid-calf. She released it to flow back, only to bring it hurling in. The ship began to sway.

"Stop!" A force hit her, gripping her shoulders and shoving her down into the solid sand.

It took all of Galene's concentration to not lose her grip on the sea. She ignored Chrysander holding her down, ignored him as he yelled into her face. She just pushed and pulled. The tide soaked her tunic and hair as it washed over her. The tremors in her muscles redoubled with shivering. Her mind went fuzzy.

"No, Galene!" He shook her, lifting her a foot and throwing her back against the sand. "Stop it!"

She couldn't, she wouldn't. This was the last thing she could do for them. If Braxtus and Iyana couldn't get the *avyssos* back, she was the only thing standing between Poinê's band and their escape, the *only* thing stopping them from bringing an army to Olympus. Gritting her teeth, she closed her eyes. She could feel the ship tilting, but it needed more.

"Stop it, Galene, you'll kill yourself!" Only then did she hear the panic in Chrysander's voice. He slammed her down again, the tide striking her face, flooding into her nose. It washed back. "Galene, *stop!*"

Just a little more, she told herself. *Just a little longer.*

33

BRAXTUS

The mist on the ground turned the rocky clifftop to an eerie reflection of the Land of the Taraxippi. Braxtus lit his free hand violently enough that the flames shot up over his head. He scanned to see where Poinê had disappeared.

A dark shadow formed in the mist. He spun toward it, raising his broadsword.

Crack! With a flash of pain, a welt opened up on his shoulder. Braxtus put out his fire, swinging his shield off his back and raising it in defense. *Crack!* Something snapped against it, jarring his arm. Poinê laughed, and Braxtus risked a quick glance over his shield.

She looked different. Her skin had tightened over pointed bone, and fully black eyes glinted from hollow sockets. She stood with a now clawed hand curled protectively around the *avyssos*, the other holding a whip by her side. She smiled at him. "Come now, do you think you can stop me?" Her voice sounded like hissing.

The next two strikes he caught again on his shield. *I'll never get within reach of her. Not with those whips.* He sheathed his sword, lit his hand, then hurled a ball of fire at her.

Poinê darted out of the way. Braxtus threw another, but she was gone again. "Kronos!" he swore, trying to keep his shield up and still see where she went. He lobbed a few more fireballs in her direction. Her laughter rang around him.

A blaze sprang up where a fireball hit, brighter and fiercer than his original sparks. *Did something catch fire?* He lowered his shield a bit to see better, but the moment of distraction cost him.

Crack!

His cheek split open, pain shooting through his face. Reeling backward, he fell, smacking his head on the rock. Stunned, he fought to sit up, vision swimming.

"Thank you, Braxtus," Poinê cooed. Her silhouette stepped up to the flames. Extending her hand, she dropped the *avyssos* into his fire.

"What are you *doing?*"

Ripples of silver and gold spun out from the blaze, painting the air until it seemed to shimmer. Poinê's beastly face looked distant, focused. Braxtus barely caught her whispered words. "I release you from your prison, Gryphiekin."

His stomach seemed to drop through his body. The fire went out, leaving the glimmering dust behind. In stark contrast to the settling glitter, darkness converged, swelling where the fire had been. It morphed and grew, solidifying.

Poinê scooped the *avyssos* from the ground, pocketing it. She half-turned toward Braxtus. "I gave you a chance, and you decided not to take it. Farewell, Braxtus. We have a mountain to storm."

Braxtus didn't watch Poinê rush away. He staggered to his feet, keeping his eyes locked on the shadow that rose, darker than the night, until it obliterated the stars. A steady *thrum, thrum* filled the air as sharply curved wings beat heavily, lifting the enormous beast from the ground. Air buffeted his face, an elegant neck arched proudly, and a beam of moonlight gleamed off a wickedly hooked beak.

"Right," he muttered. "King of the Gryphons."

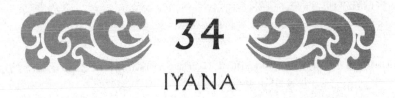

34

IYANA

Iyana hit the ground on her side. She let out a growl and lunged at Demitri again. Her arms strained from repeatedly trying to keep him down, but she *had* to stall him. He was humoring her, but even that delayed him from joining Poinê.

She twisted his arm behind his back, yanking it upward. A sound of impatience escaped him. "Iyana, honestly—"

Fast footsteps sounded as Poinê raced through the darkness to their side. Iyana's heart dropped. *Braxtus failed.*

"Time to leave." There was a gleam in her dark eyes as she tucked the *avyssos* into a fold of her robes. She beckoned once, then started down the hill.

Before Iyana knew it, Demitri had twisted free again, gripping *her* arm instead. "Come on, Iyana." He started to pull her after Poinê.

She dug in her heels and jerked her arm out of his grasp. "After everything you've done you think I'd stand by you?"

Frustration crossed his face. "Stop being ridiculous and *come on*. It's not even about us right now. Your life is at stake. I'm saving you, once again."

Anger and disbelief pounded through her. "No. I'm not going."

"Iyana—" He started forward, reaching out to drag her.

"Are you *deaf?*" she shouted, backing up. "I said no! Get away from me!"

Demitri's blue eyes widened, her words seeming to finally

sink in. Shock and anger roiled in his expression, and she felt a glimmer of satisfaction.

"Demitri," Poinê called forcefully, looking back. *"Now."*

"Have it your way," Demitri spat at Iyana. "If you survive tonight, one day you'll come running back." He turned, jogging after the Goddess of Retribution. "You need me."

"I don't need you!" she screamed at his retreating back. She reached for a spike, but he was quickly swallowed in the darkness.

Lightning flashed, thunder cracked just a second behind, echoing around her. She looked up.

The sky had blackened to an empty void. Lightning illuminated it again, splintering between swirling, dark clouds. Wind that was not her own picked up, rushing with the unnatural storm. *If you survive tonight.* A chill rose on Iyana's arms. *Where's Braxtus?*

She turned and started running in the direction he'd gone. The scent of rain filled her nostrils, but none fell. Clouded night cloaked everything, making it hard to see beyond a few feet in front of her. "Braxtus?"

"Stay back, Iyana!"

She skidded to a stop.

With a flash of lightning, a monstrous figure lit up against the night sky.

Iyana's mouth went dry.

She knew the Gryphiekin instantly. Glossy, golden eagle feathers interlocked like armor, smoothly transforming to fur halfway along his back. Massive wings beat to keep him aloft, and his powerful body ended with a whipping lion's tale. The jutting, lowered brow made his gleaming orange eyes angry, fierce.

The lightning vanished, taking the image of the Gryphiekin with it, but now that she knew he was there, she could make out his silhouette.

And something else—a thrumming power that emanated from

him. Ancient. Strong. A physical force that summoned the storm crackling above them. A piece of Zeus's power.

Her control of the wind was dwarfed in comparison to what she now sensed.

Sudden amber light blazed to her left. Iyana looked to see Braxtus standing ahead of her in a ring of his own fire, chest heaving. He held up a battered shield, sweat and ichor trickling down the side of his face, but he stood tall as he faced the Gryphiekin.

Iyana choked on a sob. He was as good as dead.

Not knowing what else to do, she ran for him as he made his futile stand. The Gryphiekin pounded the air with his wings as he circled once, then plunged, massive, curved talons stretching open for his prey. Braxtus roared and his fire shot higher, but it didn't faze the beast. Claws descended and snatched him, swooping back up in the air, climbing quickly.

A scream stuck in Iyana's throat as the Gryphiekin dropped him.

35

GALENE

"You can't do it, Galene, just give up!" Chrysander was still shaking her. At some point he'd propped her onto his knee. Her head lolled against him. She could hardly feel the sea anymore. Were the waves still moving? *The ship.* Was the ship still upright?

"Please, please, just stop. You're hurting yourself."

Was she?

Her mind fluttered in and out of lucidity. Chrysander's face was above hers, screaming. Crying. *Crying?*

"Kronos, Galene." That sounded like a sob.

Her hands fell, hitting the beach. Water washed over her shoulders, then hurried away. The sound of hissing waves ebbed and flowed in her ears. The water met her again, rushing up higher, brushing her chin. The tides were still moving, but her mind was quiet.

My gift is working without me.

It was sapping her energy, draining her life, triggered by what she had called it to do.

Galene summoned every ounce of concentration she could, then severed her hold on the sea. Her muscles relaxed with the water around her, which rushed out to settle in the sea. When the tide came back, it only lapped against her legs.

Chrysander sighed and slumped.

She rolled onto her hands and knees, wet sand splashing onto her wrists. Seeing was difficult, but despite her blurry vision, she made out the rowboat in shallow water, and behind it, the ship bobbing right side up, unharmed. Galene collapsed.

She'd failed. Her power cowered within her, and blackness coaxed her mind toward submission. She was tempted to let it take over.

"Galene." Chrysander's face appeared above hers again. He shook her shoulder. "Galene, you need to go."

Go where?

"Poinê and Demitri are coming, you need to get out of here. She won't spare you anymore."

Light flared in the sky, thunder cracking.

Poinê and Demitri. Iyana and Braxtus. Head throbbing, muscles shaking, Galene pushed herself up. Hands helped her to her feet, but she swayed.

Chrysander nudged her away. "Go," he urged.

She blinked, staring at the slope. Two figures ran at them. Sudden fear struck her. Were Iyana and Braxtus even still alive? She couldn't see anything at the top of the cliff, just stormy darkness.

"*Go!*"

Chrysander pushed her, and she staggered, somehow keeping her footing. Her feet kept moving. Every time they hit the sand, she felt the weight of the world slamming down on her. How was she still standing? Where was she going?

The sea was a cold, shadowy, useless mass to her left, the cliffs rising like a threat to her right. Above her, storm clouds roiled in anger. There was no one she could run to—she had to stay out of sight of the boat before she climbed to the top of the cliff for Iyana and Braxtus. And Kostas—

Kostas.

Galene's staggering steps broke into a run. She hugged the cliff wall, scanning the sand desperately. What if he was still alive, somehow? The hope that fluttered in her chest hurt almost as much as watching him fall.

Then she saw him—a crumpled form in the sand, curls getting soaked by the waves. "Kostas." Her voice was barely audible, even to herself. "Kostas!"

How could she be moving so slowly? She was running, wasn't she? Had it started raining, or were those still her tears? She stumbled, fatigue nearly crushing her again. *Kostas.* The thought revitalized her. She pushed herself just a little harder and his face came into view.

Galene fell, a sob tearing from her lungs.

Gold ichor pooled around his head, his bare arms and legs stained with deep golden bruises. His eyes were closed, his lips parted, his body still.

She clawed her way to him, shuddering with sobs.

"Kostas!" Her voice was raw. She should have tried to help Iyana save him, should have used whatever strength she had left to catch his fall with the tide.

Hunching over him, she brushed her fingers across his skin, searching for the smallest sign of life. His chest seemed motionless, but she moved her trembling fingers to his lips.

"Please, please, please," she begged the Fates. "Please, please, please."

The tiniest feather of warmth brushed her hand.

Falling over him, she sobbed into his broken chest. *He's alive. He's alive.*

But for how long?

Everything had gone wrong. She thought she had been doing what was right. Instead, she'd handed them the very thing they needed to destroy her home.

She looked up just as another flash of lightning illuminated Poinê's ship, pulling away from the island.

"What do I do?" she whispered into the night. "What do I do?"

36

IYANA

Braxtus tumbled head over heels toward the ground.

Not again, not again!

She threw her hands out, heaving on her ability. Wind swept in. The fall wasn't as high as Kostas's had been, and the wind steadied him, but Braxtus still hit the clifftop with a crack.

He still didn't rise.

Something within Iyana crumpled, an overwhelming helplessness crushing her where she stood. Kostas was gone, Galene had chased after her brother, now Braxtus had fallen. She was alone and hilariously outmatched.

The Gryphiekin dove to finish Braxtus.

How many times was she going to stand by, helpless?

Iyana called to her wind once more. She pulled back her spike, then hurled one, two, three, one after the other, into a mighty gust. The silver missiles streaked toward the beast and struck his enormous shoulders.

The impact probably felt like nothing more than small stones to the creature, but she got his attention. He rotated in the air, swiveling to look at her with one amber-gold eye.

Iyana blasted air at him again, as much as she could muster. His feathers ruffled slightly, and the beast swooped up, angling in her direction. Heart jolting, she scrambled a few steps back. His claws stretched forward . . .

Thunder cracked at the same time he landed before her, setting the ground trembling as he tucked his wings by his side.

She was an ant, nothing more, in comparison to this magnificent creature. Another glimmer of lightning illuminated his body, glinting in his shrewd eyes—eyes that were locked on her. He lowered his head, as though analyzing a strange phenomenon. His head was bigger than her. Staring back into that vicious creature's gaze, Iyana understood. He recognized her for what she was: Zeus's kin. Another who had claim to the skies.

His electric power thrummed against hers.

The storm quieted.

From the stillness rose a shout. *"Iyana!"* The distant, anguished cry floated up from below, somewhere at the base of the cliff. "Iyana, are you alive?"

"Galene," Iyana whispered.

The Gryphiekin lifted his head as he lost his focus on her. With one sudden move, he bunched his muscles and launched himself off the ground, scattering rocks with the beat of his wings. He swept over Iyana, heading for the voice.

Galene is defenseless. She'll die!

Iyana turned and ran, feet pounding on the rock ground. Ahead of her, the Gryphiekin beat his wings once more, then dove down beyond the cliff. Iyana ran straight for the jagged edge, harder and faster than she ever had in her life. Her heart leapt to her throat, but she didn't think.

She threw herself over the edge.

She fell, air rushing past her. Wind streaked to her as she called it, but this time it was pushing her *down*, making her fall *faster* . . . below her, glossy feathers and sleek hair raced closer. Iyana stretched out her hands . . .

And hit the back of the Gryphiekin.

Her arms and legs seared with burning energy at the contact. She was electrified by the strength of his power, blinded by the piece of Zeus in him. She gasped, sinking her fingers into the Gryphiekin's feathers. Her blood sang. The power pulsed. It felt drawn to her, as she was drawn to it.

Distantly, she heard the Gryphiekin's bellow. He twisted beneath her, and she got a glimpse of Galene's pale face as they swept past.

The Gryphiekin went berserk, swerving back and forth to get Iyana off. The beast's back was too wide for her legs to get a good grip, so she clung all the more tightly to his feathers, pressing her forehead to him. If she fell, she would have a similar fate as Kostas and Braxtus. Her wind just wasn't enough.

But this *power.* Iyana reached out to it with her mind the way she reached out to her wind. It responded, zinging against her.

The God of the Sky had placed a piece of his power inside the Gryphiekin. So why couldn't she, as his daughter, take it back out?

She pulled on it.

The Gryphiekin yanked the power back. Another cry escaped his beak as he fought her. She lost her grip on the power and the feathers, slipping back a few feet before catching hold of the lion hair on his back. She gritted her teeth and twined her fingers through it. Then she closed her eyes and dove back after that power.

I am Zeus's daughter. I should have had this power. I claim it! Thunder cracked, wind screamed, and Iyana heaved, calling it to her.

The Gryphiekin held on, the strength of Zeus remaining captive within.

"You will give me this power!" Iyana screamed, though her words were swallowed in the wind. "I am capable of defeating you!" She pulled, pulled, *pulled.*

Her body went hot. She cracked her eyes open.

Everywhere she touched the Gryphiekin, her skin glowed a brilliant white. The power slid into her—she felt it pooling inside her, and it began to seethe, crackling into a storm. The glow spread across her body, up her arms and legs until she shone like an Olympian, like her *father*. Her mind seemed to expand, offering her a chasm full of new potential. She kept pulling, feeling as though she was going to burst. It was almost all there . . .

The Gryphiekin spun like a corkscrew, and her fingers finally slipped. She tumbled backward through the air.

And smiled.

Stretching her hands to either side, she unleashed the tempest inside her.

er best friend fell through the air, glowing white against the stormy sky.

Tears of horror blurred Galene's vision—her whole body trembled as she held herself up against the cliff, watching helplessly.

Iyana spread her arms to either side, and wind erupted.

Iyana swept upward, carried by the gale that whipped her hair and tunic. It lifted her higher. She passed the Gryphiekin, who was buffeted to the side. The massive, midnight shadow screeched, a sound that drowned out the thunder, ringing in Galene's ears. He beat his wings, pumping up toward his challenger.

Galene waited for Iyana to drop again, for the unstable wind to fail her, but it did not. Iyana swooped farther up over the sea, arms outstretched, hair whirling around her like a furious halo. She was flying.

Galene's heart leapt, hope and wonder coursing through her.

Iyana was *flying*.

"Get him, Iyana!"

Wind snapped harder at Galene, and she caught her breath. The storm clouds began to retreat from the horizon line, pulling in toward Iyana. The low moon reappeared, casting an eerie light on the beast. He bellowed again, fighting the wind to climb to Iyana's height.

Iyana floated, holding the gaze of her opponent. The wind screamed as it rushed by the cliff. Water spat up at Galene, loose sand stinging her skin, whipped by the torrent. She had to squint through fiercely growing winds to the dim, tumultuous scene above.

A gust hit Galene, which would have tipped her if she hadn't been gripping the cliff. She quickly glanced at Kostas to make sure he was still safe. She had never felt Iyana create a wind so strong, let alone have the control to concentrate it like this.

Iyana raised her hands above her head, and fear stung Galene's chest again as the clouds above began to twist, spiraling. Iyana's winds snapped, circling tighter and tighter until a dark funnel was pulled from the black, roiling clouds. It lowered around Iyana until her best friend was little more than a faintly glowing spot of white in the darkness.

Galene reached down and gripped Kostas's arm, preparing to use her last reserves of strength to keep them from being dragged into the whirlwind. The tornado touched down several feet from Galene, sucking water and sand into the base of the funnel, but its confined winds did little more than toss Galene's hair. Above her the giant gryphon pitched and struggled.

The Gryphiekin flung out his wings, pushing back from the cyclone and righting himself to circle upward, finally getting above Iyana.

He dove.

Galene screamed a warning, but air erupted in a shock wave. It caught the enormous creature, buffeting him back. His pounding wings flared and strained, but Iyana sent another massive surge, and he flipped backward, barely pulling away from the storm.

A choked, twisted laugh escaped Galene. Iyana was doing it. *She was doing it.* Galene's hair whipped against her cheeks, and she wanted to hide her face from the stinging water and sand, but couldn't tear her eyes away.

The tornado spiraled thicker, darker, faster. The Gryphiekin toiled against the pull inward, toward the vortex.

Iyana floated in the middle of the growing rage. Through the wind, Galene could still make out the Gryphiekin's trembling, straining wings a second before a powerful draft overwhelmed him, dragging him into the cyclone. His enormous body whipped around in the storm, snatched like flotsam. He screamed, still struggling, still fighting with all of his might.

"Give up," Galene urged through gritted teeth.

Everywhere the creature turned he hit a wall that threw him back. He fought to break through time and time again, then cried out. He twisted his giant head, and Galene caught a flash of fear in his orange eyes as he passed.

The tornado tore asunder, winds scattering into nothing. Water and sand dropped like rain back to the beach, drenching Galene. The storm above was no more, the stars and moon shining bright.

The Gryphiekin was tossed, and he tumbled—straight toward her and Kostas. Panic rocked her body into motion. She shoved from the cliff, swaying dangerously as she yanked Kostas's arm to haul him away. He was heavy, and the wet sand resisted her efforts.

The Gryphiekin was too close and moving too fast.

Air blasted upward. Galene fell as Iyana's wind caught the Gryphiekin, slowing his descent and heaving him backward.

He stretched out his back paws and landed heavily on the beach, sand cascading around him, some of it spraying Galene. Iyana floated down gently, until she stopped above the ground before his eyes.

The Gryphiekin cocked a tired head as he observed her, then made a rumbling sound deep in his throat. Slowly, Iyana reached out and placed her hand on his beak.

Galene's jaw slackened. She pushed herself back to her feet, slowly, painfully. Her best friend touched down on the sand, and with a small smile, turned away from the resting Gryphiekin. The godly light emanating from Iyana softened, then disappeared, like she'd never been glowing at all. But a new light shone in her eyes, as if she'd absorbed the storm's lightning into them.

Her smile faded as she saw Galene. She broke into a run.

A sob escaped Galene, followed by a genuine smile as Iyana skidded to her side, catching her arm to keep her upright.

"You did it! Gaia, Iyana. You can *fly!*"

"I know—I can't believe it." She shook her head, then her eyes shifted to Kostas. "Is he . . . ?"

"He's still alive, but I don't know for how much longer." She scrubbed her eyes with her free hand. "I should have brought in the tide to help save him. I should have stopped Poinê and Chrysander. I tried, but I'm completely useless like this." More tears leaked from her swollen eyes.

Iyana stepped closer. "You never have been and never will be useless, Galene. We've done this together, and we will finish this together." Galene saw the brokenness in her best friend's eyes, brokenness that fueled a fearless conviction. She marveled at the change.

They embraced. Galene wanted to laugh, to yell, but all she seemed to be able to do was keep crying.

Distant footsteps sounded, and they broke apart, turning. A figure was making for them, feet slapping in the rising tide. Braxtus limped heavily, stained with ichor. Iyana sucked in a breath and dashed to meet him. "Thank Gaia you're all right! I'm sorry I left you. I—"

"I saw you jump from the cliff." Braxtus cut her off. Galene followed his gaze to the Gryphiekin, whose golden chest rose and fell as he lay in the shallow water. "And almost everything after." He shook his head in amazement. "You claimed that power of his, didn't you?"

She nodded.

"Unbelievable. I've never seen anything so brave." He and Iyana locked eyes, and something electric passed between them. After a moment, he tore his eyes from her. "Where's Kostas?"

"Here." Galene gestured. Iyana helped him over. Dropping by Galene's side, Braxtus leaned down to assess his best friend's condition. A sigh of relief escaped from his mouth when he found a heartbeat.

"Has he stirred?"

Galene shook her head, unable to verbalize an answer.

Braxtus took Kostas's arm and began prodding and squeezing along the limb, then continued to do so across his body. "Broken bones," he murmured to himself. "These bruises . . . *Kronos*." He blinked furiously.

The golden bruises dappling Kostas's body were dangerously prominent against his dark skin. Galene dropped her face into her hands. "What are we going to do? Kostas is on the brink of death, and Chrysander . . . Demitri . . ."

Braxtus rubbed her back, but she could feel his hand shaking, too. "Kostas will make it, Galene. He *will*. He has to."

"We'll all make it." Galene looked up to see Iyana half-turned away. "We'll fly back to Olympus."

Galene blinked. "Iyana, are you strong enough to carry all of us?"

Iyana shook her head. "Not me. Him."

Galene's stomach dropped as Iyana pointed to the giant gryphon. He gave an exhausted bird-cry, and sand surged around him as he shifted, fluffing his feathers.

"The Gryphiekin can take us home. We will ride on his back as he rides on the back of my wind to get us there fast. He'll do it. I don't know how I know, but I do." She looked back at them. "It's the only way to possibly beat Poinê and Chrysander and . . . Demitri back to Olympus."

Galene swallowed. "Iyana, you've done so much. Are you sure

you have the strength to keep the wind under the Gryphiekin's wings the whole way back?"

Iyana nodded. "I only have to call it once, then I can rest. It will keep driving in the right direction."

Galene nodded and looked to Braxtus.

He gave them a strained smile. "Then let's not waste another second."

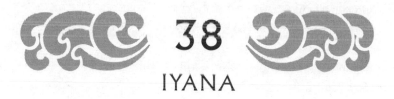

38

IYANA

With a few encouraging gusts of wind, Iyana coaxed the Gryphiekin up. He lurched to his feet, suddenly towering over her, twisting his sharp head as he looked around at Iyana's friends.

At a mere thought, air twined around her feet and ankles, lifting her upward. It wasn't flying, exactly. Not in the way the Gryphiekin flew. But the wind held her nonetheless, steady and sure. She rose to the Gryphiekin's eye level, making soothing noises.

He snapped his sharp beak a few times, but held still, and Iyana glanced down at her friends, nodding to them that it was all right. Braxtus carried Kostas, he and Galene carefully making their way to the creature's side.

Iyana levitated herself to his back, kneeling there. "Hold still," she said, then closed her eyes. She focused on the air, guiding it to sweep around and under Galene and Braxtus. Galene let out a squeak of discomfort as she rose, but Iyana reached out and caught her hand, pulling her onto the Gryphiekin behind her.

Braxtus and Kostas landed in the rear. The back was too broad to straddle, so Braxtus propped Kostas up carefully in front of him, keeping him as straight as possible. He wrapped one arm around his friend's torso and gripped the Gryphiekin's feathers with his free hand. His face was still covered in ichor and sweat. Iyana didn't dare look too closely at Kostas.

Galene entwined one hand into the creature's feathers and wrapped her other arm around Iyana.

She looked them over, checking to make sure they were in place, and then leaned forward. "Take us home to Olympus," she whispered. She called to the wind, letting it swirl his feathers, urging him to fly.

He crouched, and his wings rushed upward. They hung there for an instant, then drove down as he flung himself into the sky.

Galene gave a shout as they shot up with a violent lurch; in only seconds they had risen high above the rocky cliffs. Turbulence buffeted them, snatching the breath from Iyana's lungs, exhilaration racing through her veins.

Galene's arm tightened around her waist, and her best friend lowered her head against her shoulder. "Is this payback for keeping you under the water so long?"

Iyana smiled despite herself, though she couldn't blame Galene for being so nervous. Swirling gusts from the Gryphiekin's wings battered them, and its flexing muscles rippled under their legs, making them bounce sickeningly.

They climbed at a shallow incline for several long minutes. When they finally leveled out, Iyana brought the wind back, the power within her humming.

She took another breath. It was not just more power than she had ever felt, but *control.* She closed her eyes, and the world painted itself in her head. She could *see it* in the wind; the way it flowed around obstacles, diverging from its path and seamlessly reconnecting with itself on the other side. She was aware of everything, from her friends behind her to the rippling waves below.

She focused on the Gryphiekin. Air moved over and under his wings, the air underneath pushing against them, giving him lift. She pulled more air for his wings to catch. It rushed to her call, and he glided toward Olympus, only occasionally flapping.

Between the wind roaring in their ears and their exhaustion, they traveled in silence, gliding northwest. Iyana rested her head against the Gryphiekin's neck, but didn't dare fall asleep. She was too worried that one of the others would become unseated, and she'd have to catch them.

She probably couldn't sleep if she wanted to. Try as she might to shove Demitri's face from her mind, it appeared time and time again. *Trust me. They were just dreams, Iyana. One day you'll come running back. You need me.* She gritted her teeth, seeing his burning blue eyes filled with so much derision. He hadn't even left Olympus for her. He'd done it so she wouldn't foil his plan.

A hatred born from deep hurt simmered in her.

Galene's arm went slack, and Iyana spun just in time to steady her. Her head lolled, freckled face pale. Iyana looked up and met Braxtus's eyes.

"She's out cold," she called over the wind.

He shook his head, face tight. One arm was still clamped around Kostas, the other holding the Gryphiekin's feathers. The cut on his face had swollen his eye.

Kronos. We're all in bad shape.

She held on to Galene as they flew.

The sky slowly lightened, then the sun broke over the horizon line to their right. She blinked in the light. The sea unfurled below them like a great blue-green map. The earth looked so far away that it seemed impossible to fall that distance.

The cold wind numbed her face from the heat of the rising sun, but she was sure she was burning anyway. She put her head back down, watching the earth race by.

"Iyana," Braxtus called when, hours later, her muscles cramped miserably. "Look."

She lifted her head. A towering silhouette, pale gray against the light blue backdrop, rose before them. Above the tree line, it was all crags and cliffs, erupting through the distant clouds to the heavens, looking like some castle floating in the sky.

She let out a breath and squeezed Galene's arm, glancing back at her. Galene groaned, and her eyes fluttered open.

"We should be there in another hour or so," Iyana told her.

Galene swallowed, a sudden clarity entering her green eyes. "Will . . ." She hesitated, then voiced the question Iyana had been thinking. "Will they even let us in?"

She didn't answer, turning forward again.

Iyana sat there, eyes wide, watching Olympus come ever nearer. Though there wasn't an exact moment when things came into focus, eventually she could make out shapes among the green and gray she thought she recognized at the top of the mountain: a section of gold that could only be Zeus's domain; a long, winding stretch of blue and yellow and white that she could've sworn were Persephone's perfect flowers; a patch of circular brown that could be the hard-packed dirt in the arena, and a glint of a shimmering dome barrier . . .

Home, she thought fiercely. *Oh please let us in. Just listen to us.*

Iyana dropped most of the wind and guided the Gryphiekin with slight pressure. He obeyed the direction in which her wind ushered him, navigating toward the open plains on the Southeastern slope. Iyana braced herself as the boundary drew closer. Not twenty feet from the barrier, the Gryphiekin flapped, then reared as he landed, claws digging into the earth.

Between the guard towers, behind the magical boundary, half a dozen guards gaped, waiting for them.

"I think they were alerted to our approach," Braxtus said wryly.

Iyana's throat was tight, and she locked eyes with Galene.

"Now what?" Galene asked.

There was a brief moment of silence, then Iyana pushed herself up and flew from the back of the Gryphiekin, toward where the guards were drawing their weapons.

She recognized their faces, and the faces of others running down to join them. They all knew her, too, but as their eyes darted among the ragged group, they always fell back to the creature behind her. Few of them even gave more than a glance to Iyana as she stopped before the barrier, only feet in front of them.

"We need to speak to Zeus," she told them. "It's urgent."

They exchanged glances. The head guard muttered instructions to Myron Unnamed, and he ran off.

The next few minutes stretched for eternity. Then . . .

"Iyana Unnamed."

She jumped. The voice was clear, magnified far beyond its normal capabilities. Even the trees seemed to recoil from the power behind it.

Iyana straightened, a sudden determination steeling her weary body.

"Father."

"Did I not remind you of the consequences of exile?"

"You did." Iyana gradually released the wind that supported her and touched down on the path. She scanned the open space of Olympus before her, trying to pinpoint her father's location.

"Did you not make the decision to walk away from Mount Olympus?" His voice was stiff, with an undercurrent of anger. "Knowing full well you would not be allowed to return?"

"I did, Father. But—"

"Begone." He dismissed her more harshly than she had anticipated. "I will not hear what you have to say."

"But you're in danger!" Iyana raised her voice, letting the wind carry and amplify it. "Galene was framed as part of a plot to overthrow Olympus—"

A derisive laugh rang out over Iyana's words, and she ground her teeth, knowing instinctively who the voice belonged to. Hera would do her best to keep her husband's daughter off Olympus forever.

"It took you all that time to come up with this story?" Hera sneered. "I'm amazed you didn't run home sooner."

Braxtus groaned, and Iyana clenched her fists. "It's the truth. Give me a chance to explain—"

"I have stayed my hand this long only because you're my daughter, but the laws of Olympus won't allow me to let you linger much longer," Zeus cautioned. "I command you again to depart."

"At least let Braxtus and Kostas in!" Iyana said desperately. "They're here with us, and they are not exiled. Kostas needs immediate help, and Braxtus can explain our story."

"Braxtus Unnamed left Mount Olympus and joined the exiled," Hera returned coldly.

Iyana sucked in a breath, glancing back at him. His jaw was set as he returned her gaze. "He left with Kostas, God of Games. He was escorted by an Immortal."

"Does Kostas speak for him?" Zeus asked stoically.

Iyana's stomach clenched.

"Zeus, King of Olympus." Braxtus raised his voice as well. One arm was still around his best friend to keep him from slipping. "Kostas is on the verge of death. He cannot speak at *all*. He needs to see my father, Apollo, for healing."

There was a long silence before Zeus spoke again.

"Leave Kostas where you are, then depart. We will take him back in, heal him, and hear his story. Depending on what he has to say, we may contact you. In the meantime, do not return to Olympus again."

Galene's shoulders slumped. Iyana shook her head, a sick feeling settling in her gut. *We don't have time for that.* A furious wind rushed around them. The Gryphiekin raised his head, closing his eyes in enjoyment.

The Gryphiekin. Zeus hadn't said anything about him . . . which meant he didn't know. He wasn't looking at them. Her father was probably speaking from his throne through one of Iris's messageways.

Iyana raised her hands and the wind grew stronger. Her hair rushed into her face as she made one last attempt to get her father to hear her.

"Zeus, *Father,* though you can't see us, you must have sensed the power we brought with us. We flew here on the back of the Gryphiekin."

The silence stretched so long that Iyana began to fear he'd stopped listening.

"The *Gryphiekin?*" More than anything, Zeus sounded amazed.

"The Gryphiekin has been banished to the *avyssos* for eons," Hera hissed.

"Come see for yourself," Iyana invited. It probably wasn't the best time to mention she had taken the power Zeus had given the Gryphiekin.

"You have the *avyssos!*" Hera screeched. "That is further proof of their treachery! Zeus, take it and expel them—"

"We don't have the *avyssos,*" Iyana corrected loudly. "But that is part of our story. Let me explain. Please, Father. Olympus is truly in imminent danger."

"No—" Hera started.

"Hera." Zeus silenced her with one word, and Iyana's heart leapt. She knew she had him. If what she had to say involved the Gryphiekin and the *avyssos,* it was obviously important.

It wasn't immediate. Every second felt like an eternity as she waited for his decision.

Then the translucent boundary rippled vibrant blue, humming and shimmering before fading back to its usual color.

"Iyana, you have been granted temporary access to Mount Olympus," Zeus announced. "Enter. Bring Kostas, God of Games. Tell us your story. If it's plausible we'll grant the rest of you temporary admittance until we have confirmed the truth."

Iyana felt a jolt of nerves that her father had chosen her to speak for them instead of Braxtus. She looked at him and Galene again. They gave her encouraging, hopeful nods, and she raised her hand, calling her wind to lift Kostas from Braxtus's arms. It swept under his body and supported him. She focused on keeping him steady as the billowing wind guided him to her.

She faced Olympus. "Thank you, Father."

"Straight to the throne room."

She nodded, then, keeping Kostas afloat beside her, crossed through the barrier back into her home.

THE OLYMPIANS LOOKED down coldly at her from their golden thrones. She felt like a bug; a tiny insect they were considering, ready to squash. Zeus, who had gone to the boundary line to see the Gryphiekin in person, was the only one absent.

They all waited for his return in silence. Zeus's empty throne seemed to glare at her as much as the eyes of the others. It took so much effort just to stay standing, Iyana worried if she would be able to get through a whole hearing.

Finally, the door opened and her father swept in. His gray eyes landed on Iyana as he dropped onto his seat. They searched her, and she forced herself not to fidget. "Speak."

Iyana ignored the pain shooting through her head and the weariness in her bones, then began.

"Poinê, the exiled Goddess of Retribution, recruited Demitri Unnamed to set Galene up to be exiled."

A few mutters rose, but Zeus didn't speak, watching her intently.

"You're back at this argument, are you? Have you so quickly forgotten the vision that proved Galene Unnamed guilty?" Apollo asked.

She bowed her head in respect before speaking. "The vision you recieved, Apollo, was inaccurate." He stiffened on his throne. "It was twisted by Demitri Unnamed."

Silence fell as the Olympians considered her words.

Finally, Ares scoffed. "*My son, with power to manipulate prophecy?*"

"Dreams," she corrected. "Apollo's prophecy came to him in a dream. Demitri never declared a second ability, but he has tampered with my dreams as well. And others. He admitted all of this to me."

"Even if that were true, why would Poinê want Galene exiled?" Athena questioned.

Iyana took a steadying breath. "Because Galene had the ability to steal the *avyssos*." She hesitated. "Which she—we—did."

A commotion rippled through the gods, Hera's outcry louder than the others. "Once exiled, you turn immediately to *steal* one of our most guarded artifacts, and now you ask us to trust you?" The Queen angled her scepter toward her threateningly.

"You must listen to our story!" Iyana shouted above them. "I will explain it all."

Zeus raised a calm hand. A hush fell upon them and the eyes of the Olympians, more burning and untrusting than ever, stared expectantly.

Iyana flew through their tale, from the encounter with Poinê and Chrysander, to their plan to save Olympus from the rebels, through the race to the *avyssos* and all the trials they had faced.

Then, swallowing hard, Iyana finished. "Demitri must have prearranged a meeting with Poinê on an island where we stopped to rest. He betrayed us there. Poinê and Chrysander arrived, and the truth came out. He admitted to everything, how it was he who created the beasts, he who twisted Apollo's prophecy to show Galene in his place." There were many raised eyebrows, but no one stopped her. "He decided to join me in exile when I was a potential threat to his plans, and"—here she looked apologetically at Galene's father—"twisted a dream of Poseidon's, planting the idea to give Galene a boon. That way we could all travel with her underwater."

All eyes turned to the Olympian with the long, dark silver hair. Poseidon blinked his sea-green eyes at her, then nodded slowly. She let out a breath, legs trembling.

"We did our best to stop them and take back the *avyssos*. Kostas was pushed from a cliff." Her head started to get fuzzy. "They . . . they got away. They left us to die fighting the Gryphiekin, which Poinê released from the *avyssos*."

She paused, looking uneasily at her father again.

His lips twitched. "And, if I might take a guess, you bested my creation by claiming the power I'd given him as your own."

She ducked her head, but Zeus didn't seem to be angry. The power thrummed inside of her quietly. "Yes, Father."

When he didn't say anything further, she addressed them all. "We're here to warn you that Poinê is drawing everything willing to fight from the *avyssos*. She plans to wage war against Olympus within the month."

Athena appraised her. "That is quite the story. Saving Olympus is the perfect way to redeem yourselves. The only way, in fact, after your friend tried to destroy it."

Her head throbbed distantly and black fringed her vision. She was too exhausted to protest.

"I do not believe this is a fabrication," a new voice said suddenly. Iyana turned to see Hermes, with his dark skin and black eyes, staring at her. Hermes, Kostas's father and God of Thieves, didn't speak often. The other Olympians hushed to listen. "This can't be from her imagination. People lie to be believed. If this is a lie, she would have thought of a better one."

The Olympians looked at each other.

"If this does not sway you," he continued, "look at what she and my son have been through. Kostas has a long recovery ahead of him. They have obviously faced many challenges."

Silence. Then Ares spoke. "Battle leaves a mark. I sense its presence."

The gods considered this.

Zeus nodded. "We shall allow Galene and Braxtus Unnamed in for now, and send scouts to see how much of their story we can confirm. All in favor?"

Iyana didn't see the results of the vote. The last, feeble dregs of her energy depleted, and her knees buckled.

39

KOSTAS

Kostas shifted on the bed. His head throbbed in unison with his aching ribs. Despite holding back his groan, Galene's aura clouded with worry. She studied his face.

"I'm fine," he assured her for the tenth time.

She scowled. "When any certified healer tells me that, *then* I'll believe it."

"I'm healing quickly. I'm in good care. I'll be out of here in no time." He stroked his thumb across her palm and felt her emotions blush, soothing her worry, but not dissipating it.

"You were on the brink of death when we got back here. Skull fracture, broken ribs, internal bleeding in your abdomen *and* brain, along with a few other broken things. It's only been two weeks, and you've been ordered to stay in bed for at least one more." She sniffed. "I'm only here so often to make sure you don't go running off prematurely, because *you* think you're fine."

"Come on, we both know I'm smarter than that. That's just your excuse to spend time with me." He winked.

She smacked him.

"Watch it! I'm still healing."

She rolled her eyes but couldn't hide her amusement.

"I just hope I'm healed enough to fight when the time comes." His eyes drifted to the open door where there was a constant, unusually high amount of bustle—a stream of gods and goddesses coming in for physicals.

The Olympians had sent their scouts to track Poinê, and as pieces of their story came back confirmed—the missing *avyssos*, movement in the Land of the Taraxippi, and a small ship along its coast—battle preparations began. Their first move had been to summon all gods and goddesses back to Olympus to fight. They had started trickling in from all over the country, leaving their established temples to answer the call. The entire mountain was readying for war, and Kostas could only watch from the window.

"I'm just glad you're alive," Galene said softly.

He met her eyes. He was being selfish, wasn't he? He *was* lucky to be alive. Lucky his friends had survived, too, and managed to get back to Olympus. Lucky they'd let any of them through the gates. Especially Galene.

He smiled. "How's my temple? Braxtus isn't raiding my Linked Chamber, is he?"

"No more than is to be expected." Humor lit her eyes.

"Good. And you and Iyana are comfortable in the guest rooms?"

Though the Olympians had not revoked Galene's sentence or Iyana's self-banishment, they had allowed the three of them to stay in Kostas's temple. It was heavily guarded, and they had a curfew, but Galene, Iyana, and Braxtus could move about freely otherwise. Kostas suspected it had something to do with needing every available arm to train and fight.

Iyana and Braxtus were practicing now. They spent most of their days that way, Galene pretending to grow tired sooner than the others to visit him. "Yes, thank you."

"And everyone is recovering well?"

"Braxtus is nearly at a full sprint again," Galene reported. "Iyana is practically blooming, loving her new power. She uses it constantly, sometimes just to see what she can do. Yesterday she tried to float a pitcher full of water to the dinner table and pour it into our glasses." She chuckled. "The goddess can nail a target with a spike, but that did not end well."

Kostas smiled. "And you?" he asked.

Her eyes rose to the high windows as she took in a deep breath. "I'm well."

Physically, he knew she'd recovered from her ordeal, but . . . "But you're not content."

She hesitated, and her unease washed over him. "I'm home but, not really. Not yet." He nodded. She was still a prisoner, still a suspect in what had triggered all of this. They were all still under suspicion until further notice. "And can anyone be content knowing a war is coming to their doorstep? It's just a waiting game."

"Tell me about it." Kostas could empathize with that aspect of things at least.

"But games are your specialty."

He pressed his lips in a tight smile.

Galene smirked, then sighed, settling deeper into her chair. "Well, hopefully soon, everything will be back to normal."

"I hope not." She gave him a quizzical look, and he clarified. "Demitri and Chrysander are wrong in their methods, but things *do* need to be different here. Hopefully, this opens the Olympians' eyes."

It was her turn to offer the tight-lipped smile. "Maybe they'll change their minds, and I won't have to wait ten more years before re-attempting my Immortality Trial." She was hopeful, but he could sense her reeling back that emotion, not wanting to be disappointed in the future.

"They'd be insane to ignore everything you've done over the past few weeks. You're more worthy than anyone I know of becoming an official deity."

"Thank you," she said, leaning in to give him a peck on the cheek. She'd started doing that since he woke up, and every time she did, his insides warmed like coals.

"I really should be thanking *you*. Not only for saving my life"—

she rolled her eyes, but he pressed on—"but for starting me on the greatest adventure I'm sure to ever go on."

Her smile turned crooked. "If you don't recall, I was framed, and you left of your own accord."

"Fine," he conceded, taking both of her hands in his. "Then for being there for it."

40

BRAXTUS

Iyana looped around Braxtus once in the air before landing on her feet in front of him. "Again."

Braxtus couldn't help but smile at her, decked out in battle-armor, hair pulled back tightly into a braid, which meant she was serious. They stood in a private section of the training grounds, away from the hordes of other practicing gods and goddesses.

After just two days of rest, Iyana had asked Braxtus to help her train. They'd been out every day since.

Braxtus was more than a little worried for her. Anger threatened to boil out of him every time he thought of how Demitri had manipulated her, but Iyana hadn't even mentioned his name. If Braxtus didn't know better, he'd assume she wasn't grieving his betrayal at all. But she had loved him, and every once in a while he saw the shadow in her eyes that proved it. Every time he caught a glimpse of her pain, Iyana threw herself back into practice with fiery dedication.

They hadn't spoken of his love confession, but he felt it hanging there between them. And he was happy to leave it there for now. Until she processed her grief and decided what she wanted, he would give her all the space she needed.

At least she knew.

Iyana's power had increased tenfold with what she'd gained from the Gryphiekin. He could still picture her besting the creature in his mind's eye, white-blonde hair swirling as she hovered in the midst of a storm.

She quickly proved to be a newfound master at target practice, using her detailed control to perfect every throw of her spikes. From there, they had moved on to offensive combat.

"There's only so much I can teach you, you know," Braxtus reminded her. "You're going to have to adapt everything to your abilities."

"I know," she said, flipping one of her long spikes in her hand. "I can get out of reach of any opponent easily if I need to. I just want to gain confidence up close."

"All right." Braxtus settled back into his fighting stance, raising his broadsword in a two-handed grip. "Come and get me."

Iyana's face became incredibly focused, her mouth pulling to a thin, determined line. She spread her hands out, ran a few steps, then leapt into the air. Wind swirled around the arena, battering Braxtus as she got close. She tried to drop down above him, but he swept his blade up. She dodged him nimbly, then dropped to the ground on his other side.

Braxtus turned and struck out, but she caught the blow on her long, thin spike. Using the momentum of the hit, she spun around and stepped inside his reach—a maneuver he had just taught her.

Excellent, he thought proudly. *Let's pick up the intensity, then.*

He backed up, trying to keep her at bay, but she went for him again and again, matching his pace. He deflected a spike, then saw an opening on her right and struck.

Wind caught his arm like a rope, holding his swing back. He gaped, and Iyana swung her spike up, stopping it at his neck.

"Point for me," she said sweetly.

Braxtus let out a low whistle. "With tricks like that, you'll be lethal on the battlefield."

She positively beamed at him. "Next time you should use—"

A warning horn rang out, echoing down the mountain. Two short blasts, repeated three times. Braxtus's stomach jolted. It was a signal: enemies were approaching Olympus.

Commotion rose from the neighboring gods and goddesses. Braxtus sheathed his sword. Iyana met his gaze with wide blue eyes, then called the wind again.

He lurched as powerful ribbons of air wound around him, pushing up against his arms and feet to lift him into the sky. His hair blew upward, and Iyana rose beside him. He felt a brief rush of exhilaration, somehow trusting the supporting wind. A smile broke across his face.

They rose above the arena, then higher. The wind under his feet seemed to twist, turning him to look across and down the mountain, southeast. With their view now clear for miles, his joy vanished.

Approaching the base of Mount Olympus was a vast, unorganized army. A monstrous army, built from the exiled, the forgotten, the legendary. The very gates of Tartarus seemed to gawk open before them. The creatures came in every size and shape—enormous, small, winged, fanged, horned, snarling, and screeching. He scanned the masses, picking out the largest of the monsters: cyclopes, minotaurs, chimeras, dragons.

Braxtus knew about monsters. He had studied them, fought a few, built his own in Beast Maker . . . but what he saw now made his knees want to buckle. Every creature trapped in the *avyssos* must have been there. With one glance, he knew that Olympus was hopelessly outmatched.

Iyana's face froze in an expression of terror and dread. He reached out, but was too far away to touch her and dared not shift too much while standing in the sky. "Iyana," he whispered. "Let's go." She didn't move. He tried again. "We should go."

She nodded slowly, turning around in the air. The wind began moving them again, lowering them in a steep descent toward the path outside the training grounds. They dropped faster, and the air was snatched from Braxtus's lungs. They hit the ground running.

Iyana could have flown to the infirmary faster than he could run, but Braxtus was grateful they were together when they burst through the door to Kostas's room.

Kostas sat up in bed, wincing. Galene rose to her feet beside him. "We heard it."

"We *saw* it," Iyana told them, catching her breath.

Galene sank back down onto the edge of the bed. "It's bad, isn't it?"

"It's really bad." Braxtus's stomach churned. "I didn't know how many people and creatures had been trapped in the *avyssos*."

"How soon will they get here?" Kostas asked.

"They're practically here already." Braxtus met Kostas's eyes. He knew his best friend well enough to see the agitation there, as best as he tried to hide it.

The door swung open, ethereal light entering the room. They all turned as his father, Apollo, stalked in in a rush of power, a golden cape around his shoulders, bright brown eyes lingering on Braxtus before moving over the rest of them intently.

"Father," Braxtus said respectfully, dipping his head as everyone else bowed.

Apollo stopped. "So. You've heard."

"We saw it ourselves," Braxtus explained.

Apollo breathed out through his nose. "Your story has been confirmed, at least to some extent. Galene Unnamed, consider yourself temporarily exonerated. Since what you have told us has so far proven true, we are lifting all punishments until we get to the bottom of this."

Temporarily exonerated? As though an army marching on Olympus isn't proof enough? Braxtus almost opened his mouth to protest, but Galene caught his eye with a soothing expression.

She nodded. "Of course. I assume you intend to question Poinê or Demitri personally?"

"We do," Apollo growled. "Your exoneration will be made public

263

after we have done so. And Iyana Unnamed, you will not be bound to the law that keeps you exiled from Olympus."

Iyana stepped over to Galene and clasped her hand.

"Report to Athena's temple for battle assignments," Apollo continued. "We need every able arm." He eyed Kostas, who set his jaw. No one needed to tell him he wasn't fit to fight.

Galene rose, looking sympathetically at Kostas. He wouldn't meet any of their eyes, staring at his linens. Apollo gestured them out, and Braxtus stepped aside to let them pass him until he was left alone with his best friend.

"Are you going to be all right?" he asked.

Kostas leaned his head back. "I'm not a fighter at heart anyway."

"That doesn't matter. Of course you'd want to stand with us, after everything."

Kostas ran a hand through his hair, nodding. "It just doesn't feel right, somehow, to not finish this. Like I'm letting down my team, or leaving a game of petteia one capture from a win."

"Kostas, you've done enough. Maybe this time you can let us win without you."

Kostas frowned at that, and Braxtus left him to his thoughts. He stepped out, finding Iyana and Galene waiting for him. Together, they left the infirmary and started up the mountainside.

It wasn't easy—the recent mayhem of Olympus had reached a critical point over the past few days. Camps had been erected in the fields, between temples, and off the paths. It seemed he could hardly move without bumping into gods, goddesses, demigods, or other allies of Olympus hustling up and down the path. Dryads gathered at one end of Demeter's wheat field; gods sparred at the other end. Directions were shouted out, supplies were moved, and there was a quiet urgency in the way everyone prepared.

Iyana touched his arm, and his skin tingled at the contact. "Look," she murmured, nodding her head to someone farther up the path.

Braxtus observed the broad shoulders and long, dark hair. "That's not . . . is that . . . *Perseus?* The demigod?"

"That's him."

Awestruck, they followed Perseus himself all the way up to Athena's temple. He, Iyana, and Galene stopped outside, near the olive grove, where different groups stood, waiting for direction.

Perseus strode through the open, gilded doors. Inside, Braxtus could see golden tables strewn with scrolls. Athena convened with Zeus and Ares, pointing to various pages and speaking intensely, wearing her battle-helm. Hermes shot around the room in his winged sandals, passing information.

There was Orion, the Nephelai with their strangely translucent skin, and a regal centaur he thought might be Chiron. A tall, thin god with smoke trailing from his tunic caught Braxtus's eye, darkness seeming to emanate from him, contrasting the Olympians' light. He sucked in a breath. "*Hades* is here!"

"What?" Both goddesses turned to stare through the open doors, looking for the God of the Underworld.

"I don't think I've ever even seen him before!" Iyana hissed, gaping.

"Come on, let's not gawk." Galene tugged on their arms, and Braxtus reluctantly turned away, following her to join the other Unnamed.

There were nearly a hundred of them. He was older than the majority of the Unnamed, but they still seemed particularly small. Weren't some of them a little young to be summoned to battle?

He caught a few of their eyes, smiling at some of his friends and acquaintances. A few smiled back, but most shifted away, eyeing Galene. Murmurs spread through the group, and a few disgusted glances were shot their way.

Braxtus felt his face go hot and glanced at Galene. The animosity was not lost on her. She stiffened.

"They haven't been told you're innocent yet," he said quietly.

"Combine that with the news that my brother is partly responsible for the attack, and they have plenty of reason to hate me." She kept her eyes forward, holding herself with dignity.

Iyana scowled at them. "They'll know the truth soon enough."

A few minutes later, Aphrodite came out to address them. Her strawberry blonde hair was clipped back, and she looked around at them all with eyes that matched Demitri's in shade, but were somehow so much softer.

"I'm here to assign you to your battle positions," she said, pulling open a scroll. "Those of you fourteen and under, return to the Common Temples, collect some supplies, and move to Hestia's temple. You will be housed there until the battle is over. No exceptions."

Braxtus let out a breath of relief as the youngest broke away and headed back down the mountain.

"The rest of you have been sorted by your ages and declared abilities."

She began to read aloud from the scroll. Some were assigned to medical, some were to join the archers. Braxtus was one of the few assigned to be in the direct waves. Galene was put on a strike team. Iyana was the only one called to be a sentry.

Aphrodite rolled up the scroll. "A reminder. Poinê, Goddess of Retribution, is leading this army. She has refused all messengers. She is ruthless. She holds the *avyssos*, and if she, Chrysander Unnamed, or"—a flash of pain crossed her face—"Demitri Unnamed are spotted, you are to report them to a superior. Do not engage them." Braxtus glanced at Iyana, but her face was stoic. Aphrodite paused. "As for the rest of the army, they are mostly the daemons and beasts we sealed in the *avyssos*, paired with several dozen exiled gods and goddesses. They were all sealed or exiled for a reason. There will be creatures like you haven't seen before. We will need to fight in large groups to take them down."

The Unnamed were still, stiff with anticipation. Aphrodite looked around once more. "They're making camp for the night and gathering the full might of their army. We suspect they will attack at dawn."

41

GALENE

The sun still hadn't fully risen when Galene left Kostas's room. She tucked her helmet under her arm as she walked out of the infirmary to where Iyana waited in the cool morning air. The rising sun barely touched the wispy clouds high above.

"How did that go?" she asked, falling into step beside Galene as she headed to the main road. They were dressed to match—short tunics shielded by Olympian breastplates, stripped leather skirts, arm and leg guards strapped tight. As a sentry, however, a helmet would only hinder Iyana's view, so she simply wore her silken hair braided back.

Galene sighed, shrugging. "He's so unhappy about having to stay behind. I feel like a traitor just leaving him there."

"If the situation were reversed, you know he'd do the same."

"I know." Galene chewed on the inside of her cheek. She still wondered if the Olympians should have brought Kostas in on their council or something. He would have been useful. *Everything is a game.*

She shifted topics. "How are you feeling?"

Iyana's eyes were ablaze. "I'm ready for a fight."

Galene didn't doubt Iyana would bring a storm to the battlefield. "You've grown so much." Galene grimaced. "If only it hadn't taken all of this to get us here."

Iyana wrapped her arm around Galene's. "Blessings in disguise," she murmured. "It would have taken me forever to figure out Demitri's true nature, and to break free." She paused, then added quietly, "It still might take me a while to recover."

"Take your time," Galene told her. "A betrayal like that is going to leave scars." An image of Chrysander rose in her mind, and she pushed it away.

With the roads so empty, it felt like they were the last ones making their way to the battlefield. Down the winding roads and through the temples, Galene could see Olympus and its allies, gods and creatures alike, gathered, starting to organize and move into formation. Dryads, satyrs, and several centaurs were scattered throughout the ranks. They passed through the barrier like it was nothing—the Olympians had removed the restrictions for all allies today. The clamor and chatter of the gathered soldiers sounded above the distant roar of the enemy.

After a few more paces, Galene pulled Iyana to a stop. "I could never ask for a truer friend, Iyana. And . . . I'm so grateful you came with me."

Iyana grinned. "I told you you wouldn't regret it." Then her tone grew more serious. "Not even the Fates could end this friendship."

Galene pulled Iyana in and hugged her tightly. "Stay safe . . ."

". . . but fight hard," Iyana finished.

With a last smile and a nod, Iyana called her winds, launching herself into flight toward the gathering sentries.

Galene turned, searching through the crowds for her assigned strike team.

GALENE DARTED THROUGH the trees on the slope beyond the boundary line. Around her were the dozen other comrades chosen for the strike team led by Dionysus.

Though not known as a fighter, the God of Wine and Madness

was as physically fit as any of the other Olympians, and his sword looked just as sharp. When she'd joined them, he'd held each of their gazes. "Remember, you were chosen for this because of your unique abilities. Use them to wreak havoc any way you can. Confuse them, torment them." His eyes gleamed with mischief. "Move into enemy lines to unleash your gifts. That is your only order."

She allowed herself a rueful smile. Causing chaos—her specialty.

They kept out of sight as the two armies marched toward each other across the fields to her left. Though Galene could hear only drums and pounding feet, she knew the air would soon be filled with cries of pain and the clash of weapons.

Dionysus signaled for a halt. He scanned the scene with narrow eyes.

Looking between the branches, Galene caught her first real glimpse of the battlefield. The golden armies of Olympus faced the ugly, dark forces of the *avyssos*.

Galene's strike team was equally spaced between the two, waiting hidden on the invisible line where they would meet. Far away on the opposite tree line, somewhere in the deep morning shadows, another group waited like them, preparing for the battle to start and chaos to ensue.

Ares himself led the armies of Olympus, standing at the front of the first of three waves. Columns of warriors were stationed behind, ready to advance after the waves charged. She squinted, trying and failing to pick Braxtus out of the identical soldiers lining the front of the second wave. Her gaze shifted up, above the battlefield. Several dots in the sky marked figures flying, and among them was a slight goddess with white-blonde hair.

She looked toward Poinê's army, scanning the front lines, but though dark gods and goddesses were scattered between the creatures, Poinê herself was nowhere to be seen. *Coward.*

Galene took a deep, steadying breath. Closing her eyes, she quickly made a mental note of the larger water sources nearby.

Behind them was a river that tumbled toward the base of Olympus. There were also smaller streams and ponds scattered around that she could also pull from.

She drew her scimitar.

Ares drew his sword. From somewhere at the front, a long, loud blast sounded. Ares raised his blade, looked behind him, and thrust it forward, crying his fierce, thundering battle-cry. Olympus charged.

Like a shadowy reflection, Poinê's army advanced.

A blaze of light shone behind Olympus's soldiers, and Galene looked back to see Artemis floating above her ranks of archers in a silver chariot. She raised her bow, the arrow tip glowing with fire. One hundred hands moved as one, drawing their bowstrings back, every arrow dancing with flames. *That's where Kostas would have been.* The archers shifted their bows, raising them to target the sky, then a wall of flames rose toward the clouds just below Iyana and the other sentries. The volley arched down and plummeted into Poinê's ranks. A few dozen enemies fell.

Ares charged before the others, the army narrowing to a point. With a thunderous crack, the armies collided.

Another volley of flaming arrows fell upon their foe. More fell. Some creatures roared in pain, raging forward.

"Now!" Dionysus cried.

Galene sprinted out of the trees with the rest of them, adrenaline coursing through her as she headed for a fanged wolf.

Before she reached it, it shrank into a crouch, ears flattening, eyes darting everywhere. Galene took advantage of its distraction, leaping into the air and driving her scimitar into its side. It fell, thrashing. She jerked her scimitar free and looked at Dionysus.

The creatures and gods all around him screamed, terrified of something, though nothing was there but him. Gods dropped their weapons and ran, some back, some in circles. Others fell to the ground in a stupor as Dionysus cut them down. Galene caught a glimpse of his eyes—a spiraling mess of red and purple, spotted with yellow and black.

She tore her gaze away.

A thick root shot from the earth at her feet, tackling an enemy goddess and wrapping her in tight coils. Jumping over her, Galene drew one of her knives, hurling it at a harpy. The creature fell, the blue hilt protruding from its chest. Galene retrieved her weapon, fleeing back to the woods.

Reaching out with her mind, she seized the waters from the river behind her. She hauled on it, feeling it respond, racing for them. *It's not the ocean, but it'll do.*

The rest of the group was in the battle now, too. Some stayed in the trees, manipulating things from a distance, some ran into the army and chaos followed them.

Eris moved like a nightmare. The Goddess of Chaos seemed to teleport around and through Poinê's soldiers in a veil of shadow, not even fighting, just moving. Like Dionysus, wherever she went, creatures ran amok—screaming, raging, falling with no apparent cause.

Huge monsters lumbered among the army, like giant pines amid scraggly oaks. A third of the strike team converged on a giant cyclops. Persephone twisted her wrists to coax thorny branches from the earth. They snatched its ankles and arms, pulling it down as others peppered it with attacks. The earth trembled as it toppled to the ground.

The thunder of moving waters filled her ears. She had to move or she'd catch her comrades in the tidal wave.

Galene ran down the line. A daemon woman leapt at her. Her sword glanced off Galene's helmet as she ducked, setting it ringing, but she sliced her scimitar across the daemon's chest, sending her down hard. She kept running.

Galene pulled the waters after her as she hurried farther along

Poinê's ranks. The water was almost there, a huge mass of it rushing through trees and undergrowth. She heard the roaring, the snapping and creaking of branches somewhere behind her.

Galene turned to the open field. A two-headed dog charged her.

She squared her shoulders, focused, and hauled her wave forward.

The water parted around her, then crashed into Poinê's army. The dog went under. Gods and goddesses flattened like reeds in the wind, monsters struggling not to be swept away by the powerful currents.

Before too many of them could recover, Galene ran in, slashing and stabbing the dark creatures before she staggered back into the trees, reaching out to the river again.

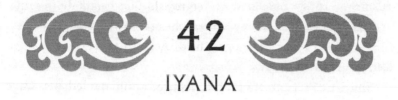

42

IYANA

Rows of Olympic warriors slammed into Poinê's army of monsters.

The power and momentum of the first waves looked promising—Iyana was even able to make out Braxtus far below her, charging into the enemy line, driving a sphinx back with scorching fire—but it quickly proved not to be enough. The beasts reared, some of them taking to the skies, all flashing teeth and guttural roars. A dragon dove into the ranks, spitting blue fire and swiping with massive talons, wrecking a hole in the formations. It took nearly fifty deities to ground and overwhelm it.

Behind Iyana, a few of the Olympians had spread out before the boundary line, some at the base of the towers, others hovering in the air. All focused their unique, substantial power on the enemy forces. Athena stood on the closest tower, watching as the sentries reported to her, calculating and strategizing on her own. The earth down the mountainside rumbled, throwing ranks into disarray as Poseidon stretched out his hand. Hephaestus stood by in smoking armor, releasing whirring artifacts and creatures in intricate battle-gear as he saw fit. But to Iyana, her father was the most impressive.

Zeus's figure had grown larger, fingers glowing with charged energy. He towered like a giant on the back of his equally massive steed. The Gryphiekin was now fitted with gleaming armor, and he swept past Iyana along the perimeter. He turned his orange eyes in her direction, as though he sensed the power she had taken from him. Zeus noticed and looked over, nodding her way.

She'd spoken to her father briefly before the battle, seeking him out with a strange sense of urgency. Zeus had taken one look at her and knew what she was going to ask.

"You saved your friends when you took the Gryphiekin's power," he'd reminded her.

"Yes, but . . . I kept it, too. I *wanted* it." She didn't add that she still wanted it, that she dreaded its loss if he asked that she return it. But she had to know.

Zeus had contemplated his response, then said, "Iyana, the Gryphiekin is a mighty creature, but he's still a creature. He doesn't miss it. Besides, that power was part of the reason he was dangerous enough to be put in the *avyssos* to begin with." A smile tugged at the side of his mouth. "You wear the power well. I think you were meant to have it all along."

Remembering the bolstering words, she raised a hand at her father in good luck.

Iyana turned back to the battle. Athena had given her direct and specific orders: watch the strike teams and report the resulting casualties, but more importantly, search the army for signs of Poinê and the *avyssos*. She shot toward the right flank of the army, eyes narrowed against the wind.

The battle grew uglier by the minute.

Iyana called out many times to report to Athena, letting the wind carry her voice, but the numbers grew harder to track, and the awful sight of blood and ichor below made her stomach churn. There was very little glory in what she saw—weapons hitting other weapons and bodies; screams of dying monsters, creatures, and gods; formidable strength and speed and anger.

Dwarfing it all, destructive forces clashed. Zeus targeted their ranks with well-placed strikes of lightning, but with all the explosions, flashes of light, shadows, and elements rising up in battle, it was hard to tell what came from which side.

Far down the mountain Iyana could see the last of the warriors of the *avyssos*, bottlenecked by the forest on either side as they all tried to push up into combat. Olympus had long since run their last wave, and nearly everyone they had was in the thick of the fight.

They were losing ground, being pushed slowly up toward the boundary line.

Iyana raised her hands, calling on the power within her. Air rushed around her, eager to be released. She refined it into a hundred spear-like shafts and hurled them all at once into the untouched enemy lines.

A few rows of smaller monsters smashed into the ground at this unforeseen challenge. Some staggered to their feet after a moment of shock, others were trampled by allies that pounded on. Feeling slightly gratified, Iyana looped back around to update Athena on the side assaults, getting close enough that she would be able to hear Athena's response.

"Most of Dionysus's strike team no longer has the cover of the woods," she called into the wind. "They're deliberately cut off and being pushed back toward Olympus with the rest of the army. They're holding their own, for now. Persephone is out of commission, but she's made it to medical. Permission to join and help them?"

Athena didn't take her eyes off the battle as she answered. "Fighting is not your responsibility, Iyana Unnamed. Focus. We need you to find Poinê and the *avyssos*."

Frustrated, Iyana swept back out again. *I thought I'd be able to help more,* she thought. *Eventually, I'm going to watch people I love get cut down.* She took a deep breath. *Find Poinê, like Athena said. That will help.*

It's not like she wasn't trying. Poinê hadn't exactly been drawing attention to herself, and there were so many people to search through. Though she could see most of the battle, the enormity of the field made it practically impossible for her to make out individuals. She raised her hands to call her wind again.

The air currents moved through the battle, tripping and tumbling over and around numberless creatures of every size. The picture it painted in her mind was overwhelming. It was an entire sea of swinging, yelling, moving warriors. How was she supposed to find Poinê?

She sent it out again, this time focusing on one area at a time, trying to ignore all those without human shape. *Kronos, I don't know! She could be anywhere!*

She flew over the ranks of the enemy army, heading toward the back lines. Maybe she was directing her forces from behind.

The end of the army was in sight, her wind showing her monsters and gods alike, racing to get a piece of the action. Few of Olympus's soldiers had fought their way this far back. No one stood out as Poinê.

With a curse, she turned away.

Then her wind, almost like an afterthought, showed her three beings trailing behind the army, keeping their distance.

She turned, eyes searching, until she saw them.

They were nothing more than dots at this distance, but to her they were unmistakable—Poinê, Chrysander, Demitri. Iyana's hands shook. Not with fear, not even with anger, but with restraint as she turned from them, instead following orders and looking for the closest Olympian.

Ares was easy to find, roaring and single-handedly battling a chimera. Iyana dove, streaking toward him, willing the air around her to swell and move her faster.

"Ares!" she shouted.

He flipped around, cutting his battle-ax toward her in the air. With a gasp, Iyana swerved to miss it and pulled back, hands up. "It's Iyana Unnamed. I found Poinê!"

His blood-red eyes seemed to focus for an instant. "Where?" he growled.

Iyana just pointed to the outer edge of the battle. Ares's eyes followed her finger, then he took off, throwing people out of his path as he barreled toward the Goddess of Retribution.

Somehow, Iyana doubted she had done the right thing, but she raced back toward the tower like an arrow, shouting into the wind to Athena as she did so. "I found Poinê! Ares is after her."

A moment later, she could make out Athena leaning over the tower wall, searching with her eagle eyes.

A crack like thunder rang across the battlefield, followed immediately by a shock wave. Iyana lurched forward as it hit her, and she tumbled through the air for a moment before catching herself again, swinging around to gape at the battle below.

Nearly everyone had been knocked off their feet by the blast, and the air . . . Iyana's breath caught. The air was shimmering with streaks of silver and gold. The same hues and transfixing colors of the *avyssos*.

A roar of triumph went up from the enemy lines, and beasts and dark gods surged forward, cutting through their opponents with a sickening, renewed energy. Iyana turned to look back at Athena, who was still leaning out over the tower. She appeared to be shouting something. Iyana reached out with her wind and snatched Athena's words, carrying them to her.

"She trapped Ares in the *avyssos*!"

Iyana's stomach jolted. Their best warrior, gone in an instant.

She flew higher to try to get another glimpse of Poinê, and her eyes landed on a flying chariot pulled by pegasi racing to the back of the battle. Artemis stood, raising her bow.

"Artemis saw where he went, she's going after Poinê, too!" Iyana yelled to Athena.

The response on the wind came instantly. "Tell her to pull back! Now!"

Iyana shot toward Artemis. *"Artemis, Athena says to pull back!"* She threw her words forward on the wind, but she seemed too far away to hear.

The Goddess of the Hunt fired a slew of arrows at Poinê.

The three small figures dropped, Chrysander and Demitri raising their shields to defend their leader.

Artemis dove closer.

Then vanished.

The pegasi swerved in the air, unsure where to go.

Boom.

Another shock wave hurled Iyana backward, silver and gold painting the air.

Two Olympians gone.

Iyana twisted the air around her, righting herself as the armies below heaved back to their feet.

"Give the order to retreat!" Athena's words cut to her on the wind. "Have them pull back inside the boundary!"

Two of the other sentries—Nephelai, who had been circling the tower—scattered to obey. Iyana dove, streaking toward where she'd last seen Apollo, eyes searching frantically. She found him glowing, covered in blood and ichor. Braxtus fought at his side, teeth gritted, swinging furiously. The two of them were surrounded on most sides, barely holding their ground. "Apollo, Braxtus!" she shouted. Braxtus's eyes flicked up to her, but Apollo only grunted his acknowledgment. "Retreat to the boundary! Hold the line there!"

"Retreat!" Apollo bellowed.

Iyana shot off again, but the Nephelai had already spread the word. As the entire army of Olympus retreated step by step, Iyana flew back to the boundary, touching down beside Athena.

Athena's eyes looked restless, but she held her composure well as Olympus's warriors started to back up through the barrier, the top ranks passing unharmed. Monsters and gods roared as they hit the shield, trapped on the other side. The quiet behind the barrier seemed like a sigh of relief, and gods and ally creatures lowered their weapons as they made room for more to enter to safety, savoring what little rest they had.

"Athena," Iyana started. "Poinê is still—"

A shaft of dark purple light shot over the ridge and shattered against Olympus's shield wall. It rippled in their direction, rolling off the front of the tower.

"What was that?" Iyana demanded.

Another arched down and cracked against the barrier.

"Hecate," Athena said darkly. "Goddess of Witchcraft and Doorways." She placed her hands on the tower wall, and white light seemed to flow from her fingers, seeping into the shimmering barrier, slowly strengthening it . . .

But Iyana looked up just in time to see an entire volley of purple light coming for them a moment before it pummeled the defenses.

Iyana fell to the floor as the world shuddered, and with a sound like breaking glass, Olympus's defenses between the two towers crumbled.

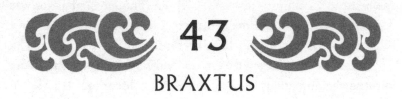

43

BRAXTUS

Olympus's barrier burst, shattering and dissolving to dust between the two Southern towers, so close Braxtus could have reached out and touched it.

With only an instant to react, he swung his shield up, shoulder to shoulder with his fellow Olympic warriors. They rushed to lock their shields in defensive formation.

A wave of triumphant monsters surged past the boundary line and slammed into him.

Braxtus roared, leaning into the assault even as he slid backward from the impact. He'd traded his broadsword for a spear, and now used it to thrust over the shields. Sweat dripped down the side of his face as he jabbed and shoved, the monsters before him a tangle of snouts and fangs and talons.

"Hold the line!" Zeus swooped in, the Gryphiekin's claws snatching monsters below. A flash of lightning raised the hair on Braxtus's arms, and the smell of burning flesh hit his nose. The pressure against him eased. A few soldiers cried out with renewed courage, and their line staggered forward a few feet.

But the enemy came again, a wall of harpies, boars, gorgons that pounded into his shield. Just beyond them he could see even bigger creatures—a manticore leaping for them, scorpion tail rising behind its lion's body.

Someone dropped from the closest tower, directly in front of the creature.

Athena, in all her deadly precision and battle-glory, swung at the beast in a cold fury just ahead of him. Though slight, she was agile, leaping and tumbling. The manticore went down.

A minotaur barreled in to take its place.

His father Apollo leapt over the shields to join her, glowing with power. Braxtus lost sight of them in the chaos. He dug in his toes and thrust again. *Just hold the line.*

As Braxtus buried his spear into a gorgon, the weapon snapped. He let it fall from his fingers, focusing on keeping his shield up. He didn't dare use his fire so close to his comrades.

A Calydonian Boar, several heads taller than the shield formation, swung its mighty tusks. It cracked against Braxtus's shield and would have thrown him back but for the soldiers behind him, keeping him pressed up against the enemy. His neighbor fell. Braxtus gripped his arm, pulling him back up and into a tighter formation.

To his right, the line was breaking.

We're not going to be able to hold them.

44

KOSTAS

Through the shimmering waters of Iris's Rainbow Glass, Kostas watched the line holding the enemy at the barrier break. He gripped the edge of the bowl until his fingers hurt, trembling with fear and fury as creatures and gods tore through the hole, flooding onto Olympus's soil.

Whirling, he staggered past the amphoras of Ares and Athena, already empty at his feet, to seize the pitcher on Apollo's stand. Making it back to the glass, he sloshed the new liquid into it.

"Show me Braxtus."

The image zoomed in, blurring through warriors to focus on a god now surrounded by enemies. A few younger deities fought beside him, slamming shields and swinging blades at a group of traitor gods. Ahead of them, a giant lumbered forward. Kostas's heart stumbled.

He'd seen Ares and Artemis get captured. Somewhere at the very back of that dark army, Poinê was wielding the *avyssos*. It was a good strategy—stay in the back as the army rampaged the Olympic forces. Capture anyone who came near. And then, when they were weak and overwhelmed, walk through with the *avyssos* and finish them off.

He took a deep breath. *This battle cannot be won with straight-forward combat.* By the looks of things, it wouldn't even last a few more hours.

Before the image in the glass faded, Kostas was moving. He

hobbled as quickly as he could out of his mother's grove, breathing labored due to the bandages still cinched around his chest. Dressing himself in the infirmary had been difficult enough, let alone what he was about to attempt. *There's no choice.* Kostas went over his plan, again and again, making tweaks and adjustments as new questions popped into his mind.

He'd almost forgotten about the pain in his head and chest by the time the arena came into view, the armory sitting quietly before it.

Kostas's skin prickled as he walked around the side, following the same path Demitri had taken when he framed Galene that night. Kostas approached the same door he had—the room that held the Decks of Fates.

Removing his belt with quick fingers, Kostas isolated the middle pin of his buckle and stuck it in the lock. After a painfully precise amount of wiggling, the lock clicked open, and Kostas pushed into the room.

The light from the doorway spilled onto a single marble table, four Decks stacked neatly on it. He snatched the main Deck of Fates—full of earth-based traits—and ran back out.

The main doors to the armory had been left unlocked, and Kostas hurried in, moving down a short hallway to the archery weaponry. Grabbing a standard bow and full quiver from their hooks on the wall, he readied himself for battle.

The stable was next. Most of the stalls were empty, as many leaders had ridden horses into battle, but among those remaining, Kostas chose a huge, black Olympian stallion. He grumbled and cursed as he struggled to saddle the creature. Finally, muscles aching worse than before, Kostas mounted, kicking into a gallop, riding along the barrier toward the Southeastern end of Mount Olympus.

He heard the battle before he saw it. The dull roar ahead turned to horrifying screams, the painful clash of metal on metal, and worse, metal on flesh. Trees blocked most of his view of the army, but as he drew closer, monsters appeared, scrambling against the invisible shield beside him.

Kostas spurred his mount faster, and the full scale of the battle came into view on the plains.

The split in the barrier, visible as slightly clearer air, was like a window to the terrors storming up from the battlefield below. Warriors and Olympians filled the hole from tower to tower, trying to slow the stream of monsters getting through, but more kept making it in. Those who did started up the path toward the temples, and no hands could be spared to stop them.

Dizziness made him sway in the saddle.

Braxtus, he reminded himself. *Find Braxtus.*

He looked to the pack of golden Olympus soldiers still struggling at the boundary line. That's where his friend had been last, closer to the right side.

Kostas rode to the fight. The roaring of war was almost deafening, and it was near impossible to pick any single person out in the chaos. Kostas looked for signs of fire, but a huge dragon was spraying so much of that, he soon gave up.

"Braxtus!" he yelled, barely hearing his own voice above the din. "Braxtus!"

For minutes he swept his eyes over the armies, moving his horse back and forth behind the break in defenses. An enemy god in haphazard armor broke through the line ahead of him and charged with a yell, sword raised high. Kostas palmed his bow, drew an arrow, and fired, the fletching sprouting from the god's neck. He quickly turned his eyes from the body, stomach churning.

Where is Braxtus?

He longed to ride in there, to help fight, but he wasn't an idiot. In his condition, he'd be dead in minutes. A sudden fear seized him. What if Braxtus had fallen?

Kostas kicked his horse, riding farther up the line, searching even harder.

"Braxtus Unnamed! Has anyone seen Braxtus Unnamed?"

"Headed toward the healers' tent," a goddess finally called back to him.

Kostas didn't stop to thank her, just dug his heels into the horse and flew up the mountain, on a smaller path where the tent had been erected. He scanned the faces of the injured staggering along the path, of everyone on stretchers, some of their eyes closed. He caught sight of a blond, curly head barreling back down toward the fray.

Kostas's heart thundered painfully against his ribs, but he relished the relief that flooded him. "Braxtus!"

Those golden-brown eyes met his, and the god's face turned to fury. "Kostas, you ass! Get *out of here!*"

"What are you doing up here? Are you hurt?" Kostas pulled his horse to a stop as Braxtus drew close.

"I helped carry Evadne up. I'm heading right back in there and you are heading right back to the infirmary."

"Braxtus, I need your help."

"I'm not helping you kill yourself!" Pulling his helmet back over his head, Braxtus made to march past the horse, but Kostas jerked the reins, intercepting him.

"We're losing."

"And you think *you're* going to make the difference?"

Kostas gave him a flat stare. "Yes."

Braxtus let out a bark of laughter. "You're barely keeping yourself upright in the saddle. You're no use to any of us dead." His eyes turned full of sorrow. "Please, Kostas."

"We're *losing*, Braxtus. We can't win this battle with soldiers anymore. We need a different strategy. Two of the Olympians have already been captured, and any others who get close to Poinê will be, too."

"Do you think I don't know that? I'm the one who's been out here, watching it with my own eyes." He rubbed a fist across his face, as if trying to scrub those images away.

"Someone needs to get the *avyssos* out of her hands. If we could take it back, we'd change the direction of this war."

"And what's to say she won't immediately suck us into that thing as well?"

"I have a plan." That seemed to make Braxtus even more exhausted. Kostas clenched his jaw, glaring down at his best friend. "You said that I should let you win this game without me, Braxtus, but I'm the *God of Games*. You *can't* win this game without me. Either this plan works or Olympus falls."

Braxtus's mouth formed a thin, determined line. He nodded, then gripped the back of the saddle and hauled himself up behind Kostas.

"I suppose if anything's going to work, it'd be one of your crazy plans."

Kostas smiled and spurred the horse toward the forest right of the raging soldiers.

45

GALENE

Galene released another wave onto the enemy's ranks. She could see the end of the army from here, as most of them had pushed up closer to the barrier.

How are we going to win this?

Her stomach had turned to lead when she saw Olympus's shield break and the enemy push through into her home. The armies of Olympus looked so small now; small and caged, backed up against a wall.

A cyclops only a head taller than herself came for her. Numb to it now, Galene sidestepped the beast's falling club and stabbed it through the eye with her knife. Its putrid scent burnt her nose, but the battle had turned the air foul long ago. Yanking her blade free, she hurried back to the trees, calling another tidal wave.

She hid behind a pine as the waters approached, catching her breath and lifting her helmet just enough to wipe her sweat. Once the summer sun had fully risen, it beat down relentlessly—even the shade of the trees didn't offer much reprieve.

Most of the strike team had either been cut down or pushed back with the army. She gritted her teeth. She had no idea where Dionysus had disappeared to. Eris was still there, appearing in and out of the trees as she spread her chaos, relishing the fight.

Galene refused to look down at her weapons, at her hands. She'd seen too much blood already, and the red-gold mess caked on them only made her stomach twist more.

The wave rushed closer, and Galene steeled herself to jump back into battle when a new sound caught her attention. Not from behind her, where the water rumbled and snapped branches, but up the slope. Hoofbeats.

She slowed the wave, holding it back as she scanned the shadowy wood. *Who would be riding down here? An enemy retreating?*

She lifted her scimitar.

The Olympian stallion appeared through the trees, two gods riding it. Galene stepped cautiously closer to its path, careful to stay hidden. The horse pounded closer, weaving easily through the trees, dancing around a pine tree not ten feet from Galene to reveal . . .

She almost dropped her blade.

"Kostas? Braxtus?"

The stallion thundered past, neither of its riders seeing her or hearing her shocked outcry.

She stumbled after them. "Kostas! Braxtus!" *Where on Gaia are they going? Why is Kostas here?*

Determination more than anything gripped her. She dropped the tidal wave she had been hauling, taking off in a sprint.

She might not be able to keep up with a stallion, but whatever Kostas was surely planning, she *would* get there to help pull it off.

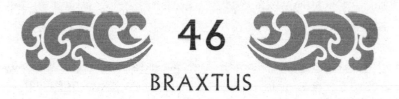

46

BRAXTUS

Trees rushed by, the stallion nimbly dodging them as it cantered down the slope. The hooves hitting dirt jarred Braxtus's aches and pains, but he was sure it was nothing compared to what Kostas was feeling. Mingling scents of sweat, earth, and scorched grass hung in the air. To his left, he caught flashes of the raging battle through the branches. The fight was every bit as desperate here as it was at the boundary line—he clenched his jaw as he watched some of his allies fall.

Nothing you can do. There was only Kostas's plan now, whatever that was.

The fights grew more sparse, then trickled off. Kostas steered the stallion out through the trees, back onto the plain, then let him come to a stop.

The army had left flattened grasses, a few small fires, and corpses in its wake. Braxtus forced his eyes from a mangled centaur, and noticed for the first time three solitary figures walking up the slope toward them.

Chills ran down Braxtus's arms. Poinê walked in the middle, her long, dark hair pulled back into a high ponytail, wearing a breastplate over her violet robes. To her left was Chrysander, to her right was Demitri, both decked out in full battle-armor from helmets to greaves, armed to the teeth. Her own personal bodyguards.

Loathing rushed through Braxtus, followed by fury. He wanted to leap off the horse and charge Demitri. He gripped the saddle harder.

Poinê touched Demitri's arm, saying something to the two of them. They looked over, and Braxtus felt their focus land on him and Kostas.

"Plan?" he asked.

"I need to talk to Poinê—to get as close as possible without getting trapped in the *avyssos*. If those two won't let me do that, we need to take them out."

Chrysander and Demitri pulled out weapons and started running.

Braxtus let out a breath. "I was hoping you'd say that."

Kostas kicked the horse again, riding out to meet them. He pulled an arrow from his quiver, nocking and raising his bow. Ahead of them, Demitri pulled something back.

"Kostas—"

He fired, and at the same time a dark streak shot at them. Kostas tried to swerve, but the stallion wasn't fast enough. Demitri's javelin buried into its thigh, and the horse went down, whinnying in pain.

Braxtus dove, dragging Kostas with him. They rolled when they hit the ground, and Braxtus helped Kostas to his feet. The horse struggled to rise, blood leaking down its leg, dark eyes wide. It would survive, but it'd be no help in this fight.

Chrysander and Demitri were still running for them. A tremor pulsed through Kostas's body as his friend raised his bow again.

Braxtus cursed. "Don't let Chrysander get close to you." He pulled out his broadsword, swung his shield from his back, and sprinted out to fight a son of Ares.

Demitri locked eyes with him, and Braxtus's fury reignited. He wasn't stupid—he knew that Demitri was better than him. But if he could just land a good blow . . . make him hurt for what he'd done, distract him while Kostas pulled off his plan—

Chrysander broke off, heading for Kostas, and Demitri slowed. Reaching back, he pulled his staff free and cast it to the side. He unsheathed a broadsword, then unbuckled his belt, from which hung a slew of daggers, and dropped it to the dirt. Lastly, he pulled the shield from his back.

The message was clear: He was so confident in the outcome he would even fight to Braxtus's strengths.

Taking a flying leap, Braxtus raised his blade above his head. Demitri held his blade horizontally to catch Braxtus's strike.

With a thundering crack, steel hit steel. Demitri shoved back against the impact, and Braxtus dropped in front of him, swinging his blade at Demitri's chest. Demitri blocked him, moving to a side swing at his neck.

Braxtus ducked. Using his downward momentum, he drove his sword toward Demitri's legs, but Demitri sidestepped, bringing his sword down on Braxtus's arched back. It bit into his armor, slamming him to the ground.

Snarling, Braxtus flipped onto his back. He pulled his shield up to block Demitri's thrust toward his chest, then kept rolling until he regained his feet.

He was forced on the defensive as Demitri delivered blow after blow. He barely managed to block each one in time, shield raised as he was driven back.

Demitri pulled his sword back, and, seizing his opening, Braxtus leapt into the air, heaving his sword down. Demitri raised his shield just in time, and metal crashed.

Demitri pivoted with the force. Braxtus landed, but Demitri unwound, ramming into him. He reeled sideways, and Demitri thrust forward. Braxtus caught it on his shield, but the head-on slam threw him backward. He staggered, but kept his feet.

In his peripheral, he saw Kostas and Chrysander, locked in an impasse with Kostas's bow raised. He blinked against the sweat that stung his eyes.

"Come on, then," Demitri called, eyes glittering. "Let's finish this."

Braxtus lit his hand on fire, sending flames dancing up the hilt of the sword, and charged in again.

Galene's lungs were fit to burst as she tore toward the group at the back of the battle. She gasped through the stitch in her side, taking it all in.

Demitri and Braxtus were locked in a brutal fight. The heat from Braxtus's flames warmed her face as she ran by, scorched grass burning her nose. She almost stopped to help, but Kostas was shaking, arrow drawn back, aimed straight at Chrysander.

Galene's heart stammered at the sight of both of them.

Her brother stood several feet away from Kostas, arms raised, but still clutching his sword. He barely flicked a glance her way before focusing back on his challenger. Behind them, with the audacity to actually look *bored*, stood Poinê.

"Kostas!" She skidded to a stop at his side. "Explain."

He kept his eyes on Chrysander, but let out a breath. "Glad you made it. Can you distract him for me?"

"Why?"

"I need to talk to Poinê."

"*Why?*"

A vicious tremble racked his already shaking frame. "You're going to have to trust me."

Braxtus was fighting *Demitri*, son of Ares. She was to fight her brother. So Kostas, the weakest among them, could speak to the leader of the entire enemy army.

"I trust you," Galene sighed, drawing her scimitar. "Do what you have to."

He gave her a half-smile.

Her throat constricted as she heard him step away. Her focus settled on Chrysander.

Kostas appeared in her side vision, skirting the two of them toward the awaiting dark goddess. Every step he took, Galene matched, moving closer to her brother. Chrysander's eyes darted between the two of them. He took a step toward Kostas, but Galene leapt closer—the more imminent threat. He met her gaze. "This has been a long time coming, hasn't it?" he asked. His voice was quieter than she'd expected.

She swallowed, stopping a few paces away. For the last few years, she'd suffered the shame and ridicule he'd put on her. He'd schemed to get her exiled, had lied to her, cheated her, and hurt her. Galene longed to strike him with her blade, but despite it all . . . he was still her brother.

He's not your brother anymore, she told herself. But she barely believed her own words. He was standing right in front of her like a warped reflection, with a face she'd seen thousands of times, with eyes she knew like her own.

He drew a second sword from his back, and Galene gripped one of her daggers, a chill running through her.

"I wish we didn't have to do this, Chrysander." A tremble in her voice betrayed her emotions.

His eyes flashed with what might have been hope. "We don't have to."

But Galene thought of the war around her—what Braxtus and Kostas were now forced to do, the countless number of allies now dead, and Iyana, lost to her somewhere in the battle. A furious, pent-up anger exploded in her chest. "Yes we do."

She leapt forward.

He charged at her with two swords raised. Galene lifted her

scimitar in time to deflect one of them, spinning to the side. Chrysander swung in front of her. She tried to jam her scimitar in through an opening, but he blocked.

She deflected his returning strike and kicked him in the stomach. He let out a grunt as he hit the ground, rolling to get back to his feet. "You've grown, Galene." He came at her again.

She just managed to catch each of his blows. "I have. You missed it." She spun away, letting his momentum carry him forward, and lashed out with her scimitar, but he deflected it.

This was not the young man who had run away from home—this was a seasoned warrior. Galene threw her dagger, but at such close range it hit his armor awkwardly, spinning to the ground. He hardly flinched.

She yelled, raising her scimitar and swinging it with all her strength.

The blow skitted off Chrysander's blade and nicked his arm. He didn't pause, leaping at her.

She deflected one of his swords with her scimitar, but the other was coming for her. She threw her hand up, catching it on her arm guard. It screeched up the metal, biting into her wrist.

Gritting her teeth against the pain, she kicked him and thrust his blades away, taking only a moment's breath before lunging back into the fight.

48

IYANA

Iyana hovered above the battle and raised her aching arms to the sky.

Wind howled down again, battering the enemy. Some staggered at the power, but it wasn't nearly enough, so Iyana hurled her spikes at the monsters below. The wind perfected her aim, sending them slicing through the least protected parts— wings, legs, necks—then returning the weapons to her, dripping with blood, to be thrown again. Here and there a creature dropped from the blow, but she mostly angered them, distracting them so others could finally, painfully, take them down.

Athena, thick in the fight, had long since stopped giving her orders. Iyana had taken that as permission to engage. As she fought, a few beasts had tried to combat her in the air, but they were nothing compared to the Gryphiekin. She grounded them with wind that battered their wings and shoved them downward. She kept a gust swirling around her, knocking aside the occasional arrow that targeted her.

She pulled the last of her spikes back up into her hand and swept her gaze over the chaotic ranks. It was getting harder to tell friend from foe, harder to know where to aim her spikes. Beyond the seething knot of warriors at the break in the barrier, higher on the mountain, smoke rose from a few distant temples.

Part of her yearned to stop those who had broken through, but a scream of pain changed her mind in an instant, dragging her back to the battle below. She needed to stay and help. She pulled back another spike, aiming for a minotaur—

"Iyana!"

Somehow the commanding voice rose above the din, and she spun in midair. Athena was locked in battle with a boar, seizing its tusks and driving it back with shocking brute strength.

Iyana swooped over to the Olympian.

Athena threw the boar to the ground and drove a sword through its chest. "We're losing!"

Desperation flooded Iyana. "What do I do?"

"We need more soldiers to hold this line. Send them our way!"

"But eventually you'll be overrun—"

"Unless someone gets the *avyssos.*" Athena met Iyana's eyes. For an instant the battle seemed to slow around her, and she understood. Athena wouldn't risk sending in another Olympian. They were too valuable, and the fight was too desperate. But Iyana, while talented, was disposable.

And if Demitri was with Poinê, they might let her get close. She had a better chance than anyone.

A flinty resolution ignited in her chest. An itch to *fight,* to really do something. She nodded. Athena threw herself back into battle.

Iyana dropped her spikes into her quiver, then launched higher into the sky.

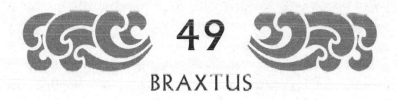

49

BRAXTUS

Red-gold flames rushed from Braxtus's hand along his blade, shooting outward at Demitri. His opponent raised his shield, the fire rolling harmlessly off to each side.

Braxtus charged, then swung his shield like a blade over the top of Demitri's. It crashed into his sword, sending it reeling to the ground. Demitri crouched and smashed shield against shield.

Braxtus staggered away again, but stayed on his feet. Demitri turned for his fallen blade, and with a sudden surge of recklessness, Braxtus hurled his shield.

It struck at just the right angle, slamming Demitri's shield out of his grasp. The traitor grunted, and Braxtus guessed he'd deadened an arm in the process.

"Clever," Demitri spat, "but not good enough."

Weaponless, he sprang at Braxtus. His knee collided with Braxtus's stomach, and he seized Braxtus's wrists just above the flames, twisting them. He was forced to drop his broadsword as they went down, the slam jerking his helmet free. Fire raced up his arms, and Demitri snarled, jerking his hands back and pinning them with his knees instead. Braxtus thrashed, but Demitri struck him in the face, once, twice, three times.

Pain tore through Braxtus's skull, blinding him. Rage seared, and he forced his arms free, grabbed Demitri's breastplate straps, and hurled him off.

Demitri was on him again like an animal, but Braxtus roared, blazing with fire and shoving back, rolling until he was on top. The acrid smell of burning flesh filled his nose. He reached a flaming hand for Demitri's throat, but Demitri twisted, expertly hooking his leg around Braxtus to flip him.

They rolled for their weapons. Braxtus snatched his sword from the dirt, spinning to his feet and wiping the ichor from his nose. Demitri grabbed his sword and rose with his back turned. Braxtus threw himself at his foe, about to swing, but without even turning around, Demitri brought his elbow back, hard.

It smashed into Braxtus's chin, and he bit through his lip, lurching away. Hot ichor dripped down his neck, his head splitting with pain. Demitri turned around, eyes cold.

There was nothing for Braxtus to do except retreat as Demitri released the full force of his skill. Braxtus knocked each blow aside, barely escaping being sliced to ribbons. Demitri feinted right. Braxtus moved to block, and Demitri twisted his broadsword down, driving it into his left thigh.

The edges of Braxtus's vision went black. He cried out. In his moment of distraction, Demitri crouched and threw his whole weight into Braxtus's right side. With the sword still embedded in his flesh, Braxtus toppled to the dust.

Demitri dropped and pressed his knee onto Braxtus's chest, drawing his blade out slowly, maliciously. His vision swam, and despite himself, he screamed.

Ichor slid down the edge of the metal. Demitri reached for Braxtus's own broadsword. His flames had gone out, and the pain overwhelmed everything else.

Demitri pried the sword from Braxtus's fingers. He crossed the blades, looking down at him.

"And this is how it ends." Demitri drove toward Braxtus's neck.

Braxtus caught his wrists, straining to keep the blades from his throat—

"Stop! Demitri!"

Braxtus vaguely recognized Chrysander's voice, bellowing at them. Demitri kept the blades by his throat, but eased up on the pressure.

"Demitri, we need him! We'll need someone who can control fire!"

A snarl twisted Demitri's face. "Why him?"

"Because Poinê said so, you idiot! And because he's the only one we've got."

Demitri jerked the swords back, pulling out of Braxtus's grip. Then he kicked him hard in the stomach. With a burst of excruciating pain, Braxtus flipped over twice in the dirt, sprawling on his back again.

He looked up through streaming eyes as Demitri pulled the *avyssos* from a pouch.

No.

Braxtus fixed his eyes on the orb. Demitri had it, not Poinê. Did Kostas know? It was so close, but as he lay there, shuddering with pain and unable to stand, it had never felt farther away.

Demitri glowered from behind his helmet, angry red burns running up his arms to his neck. "I hope you rot for a few millennia before anyone pulls you out."

"Fates damn you to Tartarus," he snarled.

Demitri extended the *avyssos* and spun it.

The world dissolved into silver and gold. Nothing existed except Demitri's cruel face and the revolving orb in his hand. The metallic colors grew blinding as they swirled in time with the *avyssos*, around and around Braxtus. The *avyssos* grew larger, and then even Demitri dissolved from his sight.

The silver and gold blurred.

And then there was nothing.

50

KOSTAS

The blast struck Kostas, knocking him flat to his stomach. His ribs exploded with pain, and he shoved against the ground, rolling onto his back.

What just happened?

He stared up at the gold and silver dust falling through the air. Roaring filled his ears. Someone else had the *avyssos*.

Every inch of him aching, Kostas pushed himself up on his elbows. He scanned the trodden battlefield before him. Galene and Chrysander had also been thrown to the ground. Demitri stood alone, breathing heavily, fingers curled around something small.

Oh, Gaia. Nausea struck him and his head swam. *No, no, no.*

Galene ripped her helmet from her head, as though needing to be sure her eyes weren't fooling her.

He's not gone, Kostas told himself, forcing himself to sit. *He's trapped, he's not gone.*

Braxtus had done this for him, for his plan.

Sea-green eyes met his, and Kostas focused on Galene. Her sorrow, her sympathy, her sudden doubt cascaded over him. Time seemed to slow as their emotions intertwined, amplifying.

Demitri moved, and Kostas's eyes sliced to him. The traitor who'd exiled Galene from Olympus, who'd tried to kill them, and now . . . Kostas shoved to his feet. The traitor who had trapped Braxtus in the *avyssos*.

Anger roiled within him, burning away any other emotion, any other thought. *No. This will work. I'm going to kill Poinê and get my best friend back.*

"Demitri." Poinê's voice rang out, sending a shiver through him.

Kostas turned to see the goddess's smooth, pale hand extend gracefully. Demitri rolled the *avyssos* once, then tossed it. Kostas's stomach lurched as the glass orb flew through the air, catching the light and flashing as it fell into Poinê's waiting palm. Poinê curled three of her fingers around the *avyssos* and in the same motion, jerked her index finger from Demitri to Kostas in a silent command.

Demitri's sharp blue gaze found Kostas. He hefted his sword.

With shocking speed, Galene lunged. Not for Demitri, for Chrysander. She was on top of him with a knife at his throat before Kostas had blinked.

"You move, Demitri, and I'll kill him. Don't you think I won't, that I haven't been waiting for this opportunity for *years*."

It was dangerous. So, so dangerous. Demitri could call her bluff any moment. But he faltered.

Kostas didn't waste the opening she'd just given him. He took a step toward the Goddess of Retribution.

"Poinê! I challenge you to a duel."

She looked at him slowly, and a sheen of blackness veiled her eyes at the open threat. Her high, clear voice carried far. "You? A duel?" A glimmer of amusement spun through her aura.

Kostas took another step toward her, taking in each of her emotions: frustration, disdain, a twinge of disbelief. He could work with those.

"If you're so confident, accept my challenge."

The goddess looked him over. "I imagine lots of people want to kill me, young god. I don't intend to fight them all individually. This is war, child." She spat the last word and Kostas could practically *feel* the venom she laced it with.

He forced himself to stand taller, to ignore the throbbing in his chest. He forced himself to chuckle. "War is just a game, Poinê. And I am the God of Games." He cocked his head. "I think you're afraid to get your hands dirty. That's why you keep Chrysander and Demitri close. That's why you hide. You're not powerful enough to stand on your own."

Poinê wasn't remotely beautiful anymore. Her skin—now a pale greenish color—tightened over the sharp bones in her face, giving her a horrifying, gaunt look. Fury dominated her emotions, but to his grim pleasure, he detected a note of humiliation. Deliberately, threateningly, Poinê exposed the *qvyssos*.

Real laughter jumped out of him now. "See? Here you are again, relying on something *else* to do the job for you. Even now you're going to use the power of the Olympians instead of your own. Understandable, I suppose, since you clearly have none."

She bared suddenly sharp teeth. "Don't tempt me to prove you wrong. I would crush you."

"Then *do* it." Kostas raised his voice, feeling his anger flare. "Let's prove to Olympus once and for all who's stronger—a lowly son of Hermes, or the Goddess of Retribution."

Poinê hissed again, and goose bumps raised on his arms. Her fury blurred her aura a deep red.

She moved, lunging toward him with animal-like power, her terrifying face suddenly inches from his. A clawed hand clenched around the strap of his quiver, and she held him there with frightening strength. His heart thundered, but he stood his ground.

"Accept, if you want to fight!"

Poinê did not move, her black eyes narrowing.

"Take your revenge in a duel," he whispered. "Just you and me."

With a curse, she hurled him away from her. He barely managed to catch himself on trembling legs.

"I accept!" Poinê snarled. "Choose your weapon, as it is your right."

He withdrew the Deck of Fates from his pocket. They grew warm in his hand, a familiar comforting weight. "Beasts."

Poiné's outrage struck him, her scowl morphing to an ugly mask as she realized Kostas's meaning. "No," she spat. "This is a fight between you and me. We won't be hiding behind puppets."

Kostas raised his eyebrows. "Believe me, there won't be much hiding. Everything that happens to the beast, will happen to us. One creature will die, and one of us will die."

Her rage flared, and Kostas had to force himself to keep looking at her now hideous, fanged face. Her pitch-black eyes tried to swallow him whole. "Forget it. You're a cheat."

"As soon as you accepted my duel, you became bound to fight me, and to fight me my way. I haven't broken any rules—my choice of weapon is sanctioned."

The red of Poiné's anger slowly waxed dark.

"You really are clever," she said so he could barely hear. "But pray for strength, God of Games. You are as good as dead."

51

IYANA

There had been another shock wave.

Another had fallen to the *avyssos*. Either someone else had charged Poinê, or she was growing more daring.

Strands of Iyana's hair whipped free of the tight braid as she shot down the mountainside. She yanked on her wind, and it supported her, racing over the final ranks. There had only been one more group she'd intended to tell to retreat, but the moment the shock wave hit, she'd left them. It was time to stop Poinê.

Her only plan was to use Demitri's feelings for her to her advantage. If that didn't work, she was going to have to improvise.

The last of the ranks fell away behind her, and she narrowed her eyes as she saw a group of . . . not three, but five people.

Allies or more enemies?

As she flew closer, she made out a young goddess with copper brown curls, a dark-skinned god—

Her heart stopped. Galene and Kostas.

Gaia.

She hurtled toward them at a dangerous speed. Galene had her brother pinned, a knife to his throat. Kostas stood facing Poinê. She pulled up and lowered herself, landing a short distance away and running the last few steps. "What's happening?"

Galene looked up, and in her moment of distraction, Chrysander threw her off. They rolled in different directions, then stood. Galene's eyes shifted between him and Iyana. "Kostas has a Deck of Fates. He's battling Poinê in Beast Maker."

Her eyes snapped to Kostas. The real game of Beast Maker. Of course. She should have known he'd have a plan—

"Iyana."

The sound of his voice felt like a punch to the gut. Slowly, she turned to face Demitri.

She thought she'd been prepared to see him. She'd tried to brace herself to withstand her pain—to use him to get the *avyssos*. But nothing prepared her for the wave of fury that rocked her when she met his piercing blue eyes.

His jaw was hard, anger simmering dangerously beneath the surface. "What, are you running back now? I mean, now that everyone knows we're going to win this whole thing, I don't really blame you . . ."

She curled her hands into fists so tight that her fingernails bit into her skin.

Kostas wanted to deal with Poinê and the *avyssos*? Fine. She had a score to settle.

Wind rushed at Demitri, a quick, powerful gust that shoved him backward. He staggered a few steps away. She sent another one at him, then another. She stalked toward him, driving him away from the rest of the group, until they were isolated on an empty stretch of battleground.

Snarling, he planted his feet and braced himself, so she changed the direction of the wind, throwing him sideways. He caught his balance again and crouched lower.

Iyana trembled with the strength of her turbulent emotions, reaching back to palm two long spikes.

"What do you think you're doing?" he sneered.

She lunged for him, wind lifting her inches off the ground. He snatched his staff from his back, but she spun inside its reach. He blocked her first blow. The next whistled over his head as he ducked.

"Stop! Iyana, stop!" he commanded, deflecting each blow with his staff.

"Why?"

He shoved back against her spike, and she stumbled. "Because you don't stand a chance against me," he snapped. "And because all of this was for you."

She feinted, then swung again more viciously, and he jerked back before the tip of the spike could slice open his cheek. "Don't you dare pretend like you were doing me any favors! You exiled my best friend, lied to me—"

"Iyana—"

"—manipulated me . . ." Demitri whipped his staff around, and she was forced to fly backward, the wind lifting her off the ground. "Pushed Kostas off a cliff . . ."

He clenched his jaw, but there was amazement in his eyes as he tracked her movement through the air. "Believe it or not, I still don't want to hurt you."

"Funny," she growled. "Because I *do*."

She pulled back and let a spike fly. Demitri dodged its trajectory, but her wind redirected it. It sliced through the air, scoring his cheek and nicking his ear.

He raised his hand to touch it, looking shocked that she had actually drawn ichor. Anger and resolve flashed in his eyes, and he split his staff into two swords.

She streaked in.

And he underestimated her.

She pounded him with wind from different directions, catching his wrists with ropes of air to slow his blades. His eyes widened as he fought the pressure around him, barely deflecting her. She swung and struck from a foot in the air, scoring a few cuts to his arms. He stumbled, and she had a clear opening to his neck.

She hesitated. Did she really want to kill him?

Demitri dropped a sword, leapt for her wrist and caught it,

yanking her back to the ground. His grip was like stone, and he twisted her arm so hard that she gasped, dropping her spike.

He pulled her close, eyes blazing. His dark hair was damp with sweat, and dirt smudged across his cheek and down to his neck, where angry, red skin blistered.

Iyana's heart stopped.

His tunic was singed, too, and now that she looked more closely, she saw similar burns across his arms, on the hand that gripped her wrist—

"Where's Braxtus?" she whispered.

Leaning over her, he tightened his hold. Her fingers began to go numb. "I told you I would protect you. And I did. Even from him."

She struggled to make sense of the words, staring at his face, twisted into an ugly sneer. "You . . . what?"

"He's dead, Iyana. I killed him."

Time froze. The world went silent and dark for a moment that lasted an eternity.

Braxtus was dead.

No. No no no no no no no—

Something erupted inside of her.

She slammed her fist into Demitri's jaw.

He reeled back, grunting in pain and letting go of her arm.

She threw her hands out, and a hurricane ripped to life, catching Demitri's arms and flinging him into the sky.

Demitri thrashed against the wind. As he writhed, he ripped free of ribbons of air, hindering her from pushing him upward. So she held him in place, wind swirling around him in a tight fist to keep him suspended twenty feet in the air.

Her breathing grew heavy, not from effort or strain, but from the pure loathing that roared in her brain. She picked up the spike she'd dropped and hurled it at him, aiming directly for his neck. A breeze kept her missile on target.

Demitri swung his sword, somehow, impossibly, knocking the spike aside.

She threw another. Harder. Faster.

A flash of panic lit his blue eyes, but he stopped that one, too. *Fine.*

She cut the wind, then pounded him from above. He dropped, slamming against the ground.

Wind came back as she called it, wriggling under him and tossing him back into the sky, lifting him until he started fighting again.

She dropped him again.

And again.

"Stop, Iyana!" Demiti's voice was weak, panicked, as she launched him skyward once more. "I lied! I didn't kill Braxtus— he's alive!"

Hot rage pounded through Iyana. She slammed him back to the ground, then kept the wind pummeling him, pinning him to the earth. She leapt, soaring through the air to land on his chest.

He groaned, and she seized his helmet, ripping it off to see his face. He flinched from the heat of her glare, ichor trailing from his lips. The wind still rushed downward, pulling her hair fully free from her braid and snapping it against his cheeks.

She wrapped her fingers around the last spike in her quiver and drew it slowly, making him hear the sound of it dragging across the leather. Making him see the flash of it against the sky. She pressed it under his chin.

He swallowed, chest heaving.

"You have lied to me too many times to count," she hissed.

"It's the truth." His voice came out hoarse. "Poinê needed him. I didn't kill him. I trapped him in the *avyssos.*"

The words knocked the breath out of her. She sat up a little, delirious hope expanding in her chest. It made *sense.* There had been the blast, and there was no sign of his body . . .

"Listen to me, Iyana. I love you."

She snapped her eyes back down to Demitri's pain filled face, and saw that somewhere in his twisted heart he really believed his own words. It only disgusted her more.

She pressed the tip of the spike in harder. "You don't get to say that anymore. You don't know what love *is*."

Real fear and horror crossed his face. "You're angry, I get it, but you love me, too. I know you—"

"Shut up, Demitri, I'm warning you—"

"If you kill me, after everything we've been through, you'd never get over the guilt—"

Iyana struck with all of her strength.

Demitri slumped and fell still.

She leaned close to whisper in his ear. "I'm done with your games."

52

KOSTAS

Fury, hatred, and betrayal rushed over Kostas—a seething, nauseating tide he couldn't keep at bay. He doubled over, watching Iyana thrust her hands forward, battering Demitri away with her wind. She stalked after him, reaching for her weapons.

Good luck, Iyana.

As they moved away, her emotions faded, replaced by Galene's terror.

She stood apart from Chrysander, hair stuck to her cheeks and neck, a knife still in her hand. Silver rimmed, those sea-green irises moved from Iyana to him. She was so scared—scared for him, for Iyana, for Olympus.

Kostas closed his eyes and took a couple of deep breaths. Running his thumb down the Deck of Fates, he crouched and set the cards onto the dirt at his feet. He removed twenty-six, placing thirteen on one side of the deck, thirteen on the other. They glowed as he finished the setup, recognizing the game he wanted to play. Their arena was set.

The air seemed to vibrate. Kostas backed up until he stood an equal distance from the cards as Poinê. He held his breath.

Cards erupted into the air, gleaming as if on fire. Easily over a hundred hovered by the time every card had left the ground. Then they blasted outward, forming one giant ring between Poinê and Kostas. A ripple of energy engulfed him, a tie binding him to the game. The cards were casting their own magic, forcing the players to stay until the game ended.

They whirled in front of him. Kostas's stomach clenched—this is where luck came into play. Blank, random cards flashed out to bob at his side. He watched them, counting in his head until thirteen flicked into place.

He steeled himself for the worst, watching as images and words blossomed to life on the cards' faces.

Hearing of a gorgon, Strength of a hellhound, Poison of a manticore. He focused on the best cards, and his heart resumed beating. This was a hand he could work with. Images of a potential beast began to form behind his eyes. He had cards he needed to get rid of, too, but he was confident it was within his ability.

Sensing Poinê's emotions, he tried to gauge how good her cards were. She remained fairly neutral, with twinges of both excitement and disappointment.

The ring of cards between them slowed. A picture appeared on the surface of one, and Kostas watched as it flashed by, rounding the circle to show Poinê. The image of a centaur, the word beneath reading *brains.*

Whatever his creature became, it needed that kind of genius to stand a chance.

Furrowing his eyebrows, he looked back through his hand. *What am I willing to risk?*

Slowly, he selected one and held it out to the ring. It tugged free of his fingers and flew to the center of the circle, joining a card Poinê had chosen from her hand. Together, the two cards rose into view, rotating to show everyone.

Kostas's card: Strength of a hellhound.

Poinê's card: Talons of a harpy.

His shoulders relaxed. The card he gambled was obviously the better of the two, and so he won the new card. *Brains of a centaur* whizzed into place by his side, and he exchanged it with his worst card, the determination of an orc.

Poinê glowered at him as her card rushed back into the ring and a random one flashed out to take its place in her hand. Nothing but fury and hatred seeped from her.

This opportunity to gamble for better cards would only come a few more times before they were stuck with their ending hand. This is where the game was played, this is what ultimately decided if Kostas would be the winner, or if he would lose . . . and die.

As they played, Kostas tried keeping track of Poinê's emotions, but the strain of it only added to his fatigue. His legs began to shake again, his chest and back aching mercilessly as he strained to hold himself upright.

He focused on his cards.

Size of a satyr.

I still have to get rid of that.

Rage of a dryad.

My worst card. With a dryad's temper, his beast would more likely forgive Poinê's creature for every strike than fight back.

But then his prize. He carefully kept the grin from his face.

Speed of the Ceryneian Hind. Artemis's sacred deer was said to be able to outrun an arrow in flight.

He looked up in time to see a card flash by, *Determination of Laelaps* inked under the picture of a black dog. Laelaps was destined to catch whatever he hunted. That, too, was a powerful card. Kostas glanced through his, and when his gaze rested on the dryad's rage, he paused, thinking. Maybe it wasn't such a bad card after all. If it was coupled with Laelaps, that would give him a beast that was outwardly calm, but coldly determined to kill.

He looked at Poinê, reading her emotions. She, too, wanted that card. The only one of his he was sure would trump any of her cards was the Cerynelaii Hind, and that would reveal his most powerful asset . . .

"It's worth it," he muttered, seizing it and thrusting it at the ring.

The cards flew above the ring, and Kostas won. He could feel Poinê's silent fury, twisted with a second of fear that she quickly smothered.

With a breath of relief, he got rid of the size of a satyr. *Now if I can only get rid of the sight of a cyclops . . .*

But as soon as the thought crossed his mind, the cards in the ring sped up, then imploded into a tight group. They flew in a pack toward Kostas, piling themselves back into a neat deck at his feet.

He gazed at his now final thirteen cards. Poinê looked over her own to appraise him, and he met her black gaze.

"Are you ready, Kostas?"

He clenched and unclenched his sweaty hands. Now the beasts would be created from their cards and fight. And Kostas would take every blow with his beast. He was confident in his hand—on a day when he was healthy he'd be sure of his imminent victory.

But he could hardly stay on his feet. It wouldn't take much injury to his beast to bring him down.

I am the God of Games. I can do this.

His cards started to vibrate. They flew away from him to form their own circle, each trait on the cards facing the center. On the other end of the arena, Poinê's cards did the same.

In turn, each card shot a blinding ray of light onto the ground at the center of the circle. Kostas's eyes watered at the brightness. When all thirteen cards were lit, something began to writhe in the dust at the center of the beams.

The light shifted, roiled, morphed, grew, shaping itself into something blazing and solid. A beastly cry rang from Poinê. The light grew too painful, and he screwed his eyes shut.

And then everything dimmed, and he looked up.

Before him stood his beast.

Short tusks curved elegantly down around the lower jaw of the skeletal head. Long, powerful legs with rippling muscles held up the roughly horse-like body, and the broad, muscled chest heaved in and out as the beast breathed. Three rows of spines grew from the blue-green, scaly hide, running from the forehead along the back, down the tail that forked into two gleaming spikes. Its feet were wide, with long toes that ended in claws. They curled into the ground, breaking up the dirt beneath.

A thrill of pride went through him as he looked over the magnificent creature, but he assessed its possible weaknesses. The sight of the cyclops had been distributed between two milky blue eyes, and so it was obviously nearly blind, but when he snapped his fingers it jerked its thin head in his direction. The dark holes on the side of its skull offered fairly good compensation.

He turned to face Poinê's beast.

Two sharp, dark eyes were set on top of the head that ended in a short snout, its entire body covered in hard sea monster scales: the armor of Campe.

Kostas was amazed at how lizard-like the creature looked, from its wide belly to the short legs he could barely see. His relief at the beasts' height difference was short-lived, for at that moment, it unfurled two huge, white, feathery wings that more than tripled its size. Pegasus wings.

So Poinê had managed to hide her secret weapon from him.

The creatures locked eyes, and nothing else mattered.

Poinê and Kostas backed away. He could feel her anxiety: wanting to leave, bound to stay.

His beast crouched down, long legs bending backward under it, giving it a distinct birdlike appearance. It went still, alert and focused on its opponent.

Poinê's beast had its wings out to either side of it, flared but inactive, and slunk forward, hissing and snarling.

The muscles tensed under his creature's scaly hide as its opponent got nearer and nearer. Only a few steps away now . . .

His beast sprang. Its powerful hindquarters propelled it into the air, directly on top of the lizard-beast.

It bucked and howled as his beast sunk its teeth into a shoulder blade. Poinê cried out and convulsed. Ichor stained the robes at her shoulder. Scarlet drops flew as her creature shook itself, and then the wings flared even bigger. With a sudden heave, it reared. His beast flew through the air, twisted, and slammed on its feet.

Poinê's creature launched into the sky. Even its belly was plated in armor.

It swung around nimbly in the air. Its claws flexed, sharp and bright, and it plunged downward, talons outstretched.

Barely two feet away, his beast's tail flashed up, as quick as a scorpion's, slicing across the flying creature's jaw.

It shrieked but didn't retreat, scoring Kostas's beast across the side of the neck with its claws before kicking off its shoulders to spring back into the air.

Heat coursed through Kostas's body, and three long, shallow gashes ripped open along the side of his neck. The weight of a boulder seemed to crash onto his shoulders and he stumbled, just managing to keep his feet.

Nausea rose again. He pressed a shaking hand against his neck to stanch the bleeding and fixed his gaze on Poinê. Ichor dripped from her jawline and her fangs were exposed, but her black eyes focused only on the battle.

Her creature circled above, snapping its teeth in agitation. His beast looked unperturbed, despite the pain Kostas knew it was feeling. Its toes dug into the ground again, pulling up clots of dirt. It turned its head from side to side, viewing the world through its ears.

In one fluid motion, it rose on its hind legs and hurled a rock at the beast with toes as capable as hands.

Poinê's beast swerved, but the rock slammed into its right wing. It careened in the air, a few feathers bent, but then another rock struck the beast in the wing joint. A snap echoed around them.

Poinê gasped.

It flapped harder than ever to stay aloft, but swerved and hit the ground in a clumsy landing.

Kostas's creature charged, and the lizard's wide, white wings flipped up and around itself like a shield. It launched forward, running on quick feet directly at his charging beast.

His creature reared up to attack, but before it could hit, a snout emerged from the feathers to seize a leg with its teeth and twist . . .

Kostas's creature toppled, emitting a sound like a bugle as it fell, pinning a wing under it in the process. Holes opened up in his leg, the markings of teeth. He hissed, bracing for more, but the pain of a broken leg didn't come.

His beast moaned again, struggling to stand.

Or . . . *pretending* to struggle.

Her beast twisted and slammed its tail against his creature's back. Its wing slid free, and, a moment later, it pushed back into the sky. Though it couldn't fully fly, the creature reached an astonishing height, and Kostas knew it wanted to strike the death blow while his creature was down.

His beast feigned well, trembling, throwing its tail into the ground for extra support. Kostas saw its front knees bend, but not straighten, as Poinê's beast dove once more.

His beast tensed, shoving its tail deeper underground. Hers gave a cry of triumph as its claws descended.

Faster than lightning, Kostas's beast propelled itself high into the air, straight up. Poinê's beast missed his by inches, slamming into the ground right where his had been. A split second later, his beast landed on a wing.

The other creature screamed, trying to bat it away, but Kostas's beast held firm. It anchored one foot on the wing and slammed the other onto its spine.

Poinê's beast writhed, lashing its tail, but could not escape. With one swing of his beast's mighty tail, it plunged the spikes between its opponent's shoulder blades.

It roared and flailed, and Poinê screamed. Kostas saw the silver agony that ripped through her aura. She swayed, but forced words through her lips.

"*You!* Trickster!"

A blast of light exploded from where Poinê's beast had been lying. As the light faded, Poinê fell forward, corpse hitting the dirt.

Kostas's beast swiveled its head until it was staring at him, and then gradually, it melted away, vaporizing into dusty light.

Black spots blurred his vision, and Kostas let himself collapse. The game was over.

53

GALENE

Galene sprinted to Poinê as she hit the ground, Chrysander right on her heels. Without even checking to make sure the goddess was dead, she dove for the prostrate body, clumsy hands delving into the pockets of Poinê's robes. Her fingers closed around the icy touch of the *avyssos* as her brother seized her shoulders.

Chrysander hauled Galene away, but she tightened her grip on the orb, letting herself be flung to the ground.

Madness lit a fire in Chrysander's eyes, and Galene's heart jolted. She tried to scramble away, but he leapt on her, pinning her down.

"Give it to me!"

"Chrysander, she's dead." Galene wriggled and ripped her hand from his grasp over and over.

He fought her. "The war is still undecided. I can still capture the Olympians."

"I won't let you!" Managing to flip onto her stomach, Galene shoved her hands under her body and curled around the *avyssos*.

Chrysander scratched and pulled, trying to pry her arms away from her. Finally, he gripped her upper arms and lifted her clean off the ground.

She kicked backward, her heel colliding with his knee. He staggered, loosening his grip. She spun in place and, with every last ounce of her strength and resolve, decked him in the jaw. Chrysander's eyes rolled and he fell back, deadweight.

Galene hesitated only an instant, just long enough to take in his slack face, then sprinted for Kostas.

He wasn't moving—his eyes were closed, his skin beaded with sweat. *No no no no no.* His face was contorted into a mask of pain. Ichor soaked his tunic and pooled beneath his neck.

She dropped to his side and brushed his cheek. "Kostas?" Tears welled against her eyelashes. His eyes opened, and a weak smile spread across his face.

"Sorry to scare you," he whispered, reaching up to tuck her hair back. Galene clasped his hand and held it to her trembling lips. "It's going to be okay."

She smiled and nodded, holding up the *avyssos* so he could see. "You did it."

"Yes, I did," he groaned. "I told you. You and Braxtus."

"I'm going to get him out."

His head flinched in a nod. "You have to save Olympus." His eyes fluttered and he groaned. "I . . . think I'll take Apollo's advice now. You know, stay out of the fight. Rest. Recover."

She let out a choked laugh and leaned over quickly, sweeping down to kiss his forehead. "We'll get you taken care of."

"First things first," he said, sending a pointed look to the *avyssos.*

"First things first," she agreed.

Galene let his hand fall from her fingers, then stood, looking up the mountain.

The army above her roiled, somehow more chaotic than before. She took a step toward the enemy masses. A roar rose from the trailing end of Poinê's ranks, a shout that was taken up and passed among them, rising higher along the mountain. "Poinê is dead!"

Chills ran down Galene's spine as the end of the army shifted their focus, turning toward her. She tightened her fingers around the cold orb.

She had to get the *avyssos* to the Olympians. *But they're all the way at the boundary line.*

"Galene!"

She spun toward Iyana as her best friend rushed in her direction. Sweat stuck her hair to her neck, and her hands were stained with ichor, but she looked relatively unharmed.

"Iyana!" Galene ran the last few steps to her and clasped her arm. "You're all right!"

"I'm fine. Kostas?" She looked past her, eyes widening.

"He'll survive. What happened to Demitri?"

"I left him back there." She jerked her head, and Galene looked over her shoulder at an unmoving figure in the dirt beyond her.

"Is he—"

"He's alive. We need him to clear your name."

Galene nodded gratefully, though she wasn't sure she would feel any worse if Demitri had been killed. She glanced back up the mountain.

A few dozen of Poinê's soldiers had broken away from the back of the battle, drawing quickly closer.

There was no way she and Iyana could fight them off by themselves. And more would soon follow, fighting over the *avyssos*.

"Iyana, we need to get Braxtus, Artemis, and Ares out of here." She raised the *avyssos*. "We need their help protecting it until the Olympians can take over."

Iyana's face lit with relief and joy, tears gathering in her eyes. "So he *is* in there. Demitri didn't kill him."

Pain stabbed Galene's heart at the thought of Iyana believing, even for a moment, that Braxtus was dead. "I saw Demitri trap him in it, but I have no idea how to—"

"Braxtus saw Poinê open it on the island," Iyana interrupted. She looked around sharply. "We need fire."

Between the dragons and Braxtus's battle with Demitri, fire was not hard to come by. Leaving Kostas behind them, they ran until they reached a flaming patch of grass.

"Drop it in," Iyana ordered.

Galene gaped at her. "What?"

"That's what he said she did. Drop it in the flames!"

Galene looked at the fragile orb between her fingers, but stepped forward, stretching out her hand to toss the glimmering *avyssos* into the fire.

Gold and silver erupted before her eyes, swallowing the rest of the world. A great void opened up within her mind. Endless. Desolate.

"Galene?" Iyana's voice was distant, but it was there.

Where was she?

Iyana cried out and she heard the roar of wind. "Galene, hurry! Find Braxtus!"

Braxtus. As soon as she thought of him, her mind involuntarily shifted through the space, moving through the nothingness until it wasn't empty anymore. She sensed something. A familiar presence.

Braxtus?

Galene?

Galene's heart took flight as his weak voice echoed through her mind. She focused, the *avyssos* creating a link between them. Unsure if she was doing the right thing, Galene took a deep breath and, with a surge of willpower, pulled.

Galene felt Braxtus's consciousness slip by, filtering through to escape his prison. Galene shook her mind out of the *avyssos* and blinked back into reality.

A roaring tornado swirled with dirt and grass all around them, barely holding back a ring of enemies. Blades and pulses of power broke through the wall of wind on every side before being swept away. Iyana stood, arms out, hair flying, face screwed up in concentration. Between them, Braxtus solidified, coalescing into a form that slumped to the ground. Bruises and ichor stained his face, and he clutched his left leg, groaning in pain.

"Iyana!" Galene yelled, scrambling over to him. Iyana made a desperate sound through clenched teeth, but otherwise didn't respond.

Braxtus used Galene's arm to pull himself up, hopping into a shaky stance beside Iyana.

Flames erupted from his hands, sucking into Iyana's cyclone. Blazing light flooded the area as the tornado turned to fire, gold and red streaking by, scorching heat bearing down on her.

The monsters on the other side reared back and cried out, but they did not retreat.

Iyana and Braxtus looked at each other, flames dancing in both of their eyes. "We've got this, Galene," Braxtus shouted. "Get the others out!"

Galene grabbed the *avyssos*, now lying in blackened grass. Throwing it into another patch of flames, Galene opened her mind to the gold and silver rain, diving into the metallic void and calling out for Artemis. She heard her enraged war cry and felt her within. Seizing her with her consciousness, she yanked the Olympian free. She emerged, silvery blonde curls tossing from the firestorm around them, immediately assessing the situation. Galene scrambled in front of her for the *avyssos*, then jumped back in.

Ares's consciousness was livid, his bellows becoming all too real beside her, eyes blood-red.

Without missing a second, Ares hauled a giant shield from his back and leapt through the firestorm, breaking the wall just long enough for Artemis to draw a slender sword and charge after him. Galene took an instant to wonder if he had even noticed being trapped, then looked through the fire up the mountain.

Through the occasional break in the flames whipping by, she saw the enemies of Olympus turning. They must all have finally caught on, word spreading about their leader's death and the *avyssos* falling into Galene's possession. Though Ares, Artemis, Iyana, and Braxtus valiantly held off the few dozen swarming around them, they wouldn't be able to withstand the entire army.

A raging mass began charging toward them.

Galene looked to the flaming winds, Braxtus and Iyana working side by side to fight off nearly half of the host themselves. They poured their energy into sustaining such a massive force, but their frames shook, sweat pouring down their faces. They were close to falling.

She looked down at the globe in her hand.

"Spin it!"

Galene turned to the voice shouting above the din. Braxtus's eyes locked on the *avyssos*, and he managed one more time, "Spin it!"

Galene obeyed, taking the delicate object and spinning it on her palm.

A sudden power emanated from the *avyssos*, racing up her arm and into her head.

In her mind's eye she saw the life surrounding her—Braxtus and Iyana keeping the tornado alive, soldiers and creatures battling Ares and Artemis, fighting to get to her through the flames. The power zapped, wanting to lash out.

She directed it at a raging minotaur.

It seized the beast, drawing it in. Galene *saw*, in that picture in her mind, as it vanished just beyond the whirling flames.

Immediately, a buildup of energy inside the *avyssos* threatened to unleash a shock wave.

Galene let out a gasp. It was a tide like the ocean's. Drawing something into the *avyssos* pulled with it a power that now fought to be released. Give and take. It explained the shock waves that erupted when gods had been trapped.

The understanding vibrated through her. It suddenly felt like her *right* to control the *avyssos*. She gave a grim smile, holding back the *avyssos*'s shock wave like she would a tide. She wasn't done yet.

Tightening her grip on its power, Galene reached out for more monsters, and found the *avyssos* had a limit. The power couldn't stretch to the army charging down the mountain—it reached only the dozen or so enemies still fighting in the ring of the battle around them, but she snatched those within her grasp.

Those she targeted vanished, and the pressure came to a peak. She let it go.

The detonation blasted the firestorm outward, flames racing across the battlefield. The wave of energy flattened everything in its path, down the mountain and up to the towers of Olympus, toppling the army.

No one could doubt she had the *avyssos* now. Instead of fear, confidence bloomed in her chest.

Iyana helped Braxtus to his feet, the two of them gasping, the flaming whirlwind completely gone. She turned to Ares, only to find him charging, running sword-first toward the wall of an army coming for them. Artemis put her fingers to her lips and let out an unnaturally loud whistle. Far up the mountain, a chariot drawn by four pegasi launched into the sky.

Athena's magnified voice swept down the mountain and rang in Galene's ears. "Hold your ground. We're coming for the *avyssos*."

Hold your ground. Galene stared down at the *avyssos*, then her eyes drifted to the army, back on its feet, maybe only a minute out.

"Come on," Iyana panted to Braxtus. "One more time, just long enough for the Olympians to get here." She raised her arms.

"No." Galene stepped forward. "You've done enough. I can take care of this."

They stared at her, Artemis eyeing her suspiciously, but Galene flexed her fingers into a tighter grip around the *avyssos*.

Then, alone, she strode toward the entire advancing army.

Gods and monsters hurtled toward her like a bellowing storm

cloud, ready to devour her. Dragons took flight, roaring flames into the smoky sky. Harpies and gryphons soared over the army, overtaking those on foot. But Galene did not retreat.

She could see the whites of their eyes, the teeth behind their snarls. She raised her hand and spun the *avyssos*.

As soon as she sensed the end of the orb's reach, monsters came crashing through it. Suddenly within her grasp, Galene used the new power racing through her to latch onto the enemy, and a crescent of monsters about fifty feet around her vanished into the *avyssos*. The resulting shock wave leveled the army.

Before they had fully risen, Galene called on the *avyssos* again. Another wave of enemies was drawn in. Another blast knocked them down.

With shrieks and bellows, the army of the *avyssos* began to flee. She snatched more and more of them, slowing their escape.

"Galene." Somewhere outside herself, she heard the voice—calm but commanding. She pulled out of the *avyssos*'s power.

Artemis, mounted in her moon-silver chariot, swooped down beside her. The rush of pegasi wings swept the hair from Galene's shoulders. "Get in."

Galene climbed up beside her in the chariot. With a lurch, the pegasi leapt into the air and her stomach dropped as she watched the earth fall away.

In a moment of surprise, Galene realized they were not flying up toward the boundary, to the other Olympians, but out, chasing a group of the fleeing enemy.

Artemis was getting her closer, flying her around so she could finish off the whole army.

With a small, cold smile, Galene spun the *avyssos*.

Olympus felt shock wave after shock wave as she collected Poinê's army. Artemis flew with acute precision, swooping low over the largest clumps of enemy soldiers. From the boundary line, having regrouped, the allies of Olympus charged the stragglers.

The other Olympians launched into the skies or darted through the trees, helping.

Artemis directed the chariot back down the slope, to where a few were trying to escape the mountain. Galene closed her eyes, letting the *avyssos* paint the picture in her mind, reaching out—

The range of the *avyssos* enveloped a familiar, motionless enemy, wounded but still alive.

Chrysander.

Galene hesitated.

There was only one sentence the Olympians would give to a leader of this attack.

I can't let him be killed.

She trapped him in the *avyssos*.

Exhaustion settled over her, and she gripped the rail with her free hand.

She and Artemis soared back up toward the border. Olympus broke into cheers, whooping, hugging, and crying at the shimmering boundary line.

They had won the war of the *avyssos*. Relief seeped through Galene, but she didn't feel like celebrating. Not yet. Not as her vantage point showed her the hundreds of bodies littering the fields of her home.

54

BRAXTUS

Braxtus stared out at the battlefield, devoid of all enemies but the dead. Toward the boundary line towers, he could faintly see Galene in Artemis's chariot, regrouping with the other Olympians.

They'd done it.

A breeze caressed his face, like the slightest touch of a comforting hand. He felt Iyana's gaze on him before he turned and met her eyes.

Her windswept hair caught the light, her cheeks were flushed gold, eyes shining. He stopped breathing, taking her in.

She took a step toward him, then ran the last few feet and threw her arms around his neck. Sliding her fingers up through his hair, she pulled his face down to hers and kissed him.

Her kiss was fierce, demanding, but her lips felt soft against his mouth. Fire stoked in his chest—his heart swelled to near bursting. He skimmed his fingers over her arms, down her back to where her armor ended at her waist, pulling her against him. He kissed her back deeply.

She tasted like the wind, like a mountain spring. She tasted like home.

Iyana leaned into him, and the sudden extra pressure sent a jolt of agony tearing through his leg. He groaned, and Iyana jerked back.

"I'm so sorry!" She winced, then scowled as she looked at his leg. Fresh ichor began trickling down the side of it.

"It's fine," he said weakly, the heat of their kiss still thrumming through him, but she shook her head. Grabbing the hem of her tunic, she tore a strip off the bottom. He grimaced as she looped it around his thigh and cinched it off.

Iyana slid an arm around his waist to support him, and he leaned into her gratefully. She nodded up the mountain. "They're coming."

Braxtus looked up. Ares still seemed filled with bloodlust, snarling and prowling through the corpses, searching for more opponents. Beyond him, the rest of the glowing Olympians were streaking toward them, Zeus, Hermes, Apollo, and Artemis in the sky, the others on horseback.

The Gryphiekin landed in a cloud of dust, Apollo and Artemis close behind in blazing chariots. Galene leapt out and rushed over to them. Hermes shot past in his winged sandals, heading for one of the bodies on the ground farther down the mountain.

"Hermes is getting Kostas. He says he'll bring him right to the healers," Galene told them.

Braxtus expelled a breath as Hermes landed and scooped up an unconscious figure. "He's okay?"

"He should be fine."

"Where's Poinê?" Athena asked as she rode up.

"Dead," Galene pointed. "Somewhere back there."

"And Chrysander Unnamed?"

"Also dead."

Braxtus and Iyana both looked over at Galene in shock. She set her jaw.

Athena looked at Iyana. "What about Demitri Unnamed?"

She met her eyes. "I left him alive for questioning."

Braxtus's stomach jolted, and he followed Iyana's pointing finger to a motionless lump in the grass, one he'd missed among the corpses. Iyana had bested Demitri, then left him alive. Her face was stoic, but sudden emotions churned Braxtus's gut.

Bloodstained and grim, Apollo swung to the ground and walked over to Demitri, easily hoisting him off the ground by his armor, twisting an arm behind his back. "Shall we do this now?" he asked Zeus.

Zeus nodded, the rest of the Olympians stepping closer to form a formidable half-circle around them. Apollo's hands began to glow once more, and after a few long moments, Demitri jerked his head up with a gasp.

His sharp blue eyes flashed to take in the scene, and Braxtus saw Apollo's grip tighten on his arm. "Don't try anything."

A shadow of fear crossed Demitri's face, then it hardened once more into a mask of defiance as he stared at the Olympians. Iyana's grip tightened around Braxtus's waist. Aphrodite took half a step toward her son, then faltered.

"Demitri Unnamed." Zeus pinned him with his stare. "Did you or did you not plot to overthrow Olympus?"

He raised his chin. "I did." His voice came out raw.

"And did you or did you not, as part of that plot, launch a violent attack on Olympus and frame Galene Unnamed?"

Galene stiffened beside him.

"I did." Demitri narrowed his eyes. "I killed Endymion and created the beasts. I changed Apollo's vision to frame Galene. Chrysander and I tricked Galene into retrieving the *avyssos* so we could wage war."

"Why?" Aphrodite breathed.

Demitri didn't even look at his mother, still glowering fiercely at Zeus. "*Why?* Are you genuinely asking? Do you need me to spell it out for you?"

"Zeus—" Hera started, but Zeus gestured for Demitri to go on.

"In the name of *fate*, you've stacked the Trials to prevent those with real power or ability from gaining immortality or status."

"*You* stacked Galene's Trial," Demeter protested.

Demitri let out a bark of dry laughter, no real humor in his face. "Stop feigning innocence. I did nothing of the sort. I just capitalized on your continued tyranny."

A few Olympians shifted uncomfortably, and Braxtus glanced at Galene. Confusion and distrust battled on her face.

"You have denied your children, your *kin*, proper mentors to prepare for the Immortality Trials," Demitri continued, starting to twist in Apollo's grip. Apollo snarled a warning, but he ignored him, rage bright in his eyes. "Which, by the way, are absurd. Why should every god have to showcase battle-prowess to prove they're worthy of aiding the humans?"

"I think that's enough," Artemis snapped, but Braxtus read the uneasiness spreading over many of their faces.

"You have unjustly exiled hundreds of gods and goddesses over the years." Demitri's voice raised to a shout, and he twisted more furiously. "Then you hunted and killed those who dared interact with humans. All to keep a threat to your thrones at bay."

Apollo lifted him clean off his feet to stop him from charging the gods. "One day, the world will stop bowing to you!" Demitri bellowed. "One day they'll *all* fight back!"

A blinding white beam of light erupted from the end of Hera's raised scepter, streaking to Demitri and hitting him square in the chest.

An expression of horror froze on his face, and Apollo dropped him.

By the time he hit the dirt, the life had vanished from those cutting blue eyes.

Galene let out a strangled sound that rang loud in the sudden silence. Iyana's arm dropped from around Braxtus's waist and she jerked half a step forward before freezing. Her face was white as she stared at Demitri's corpse.

Conflicting emotions warred inside Braxtus—shock that Demitri was gone, understanding for his argument, sadness for Iyana, confusion with where it left them, when, even though she'd kissed him, there was such pain in her eyes . . .

He shifted his gaze to the surrounding Olympians.

Anger left two golden spots on Hera's cheeks. She lowered her scepter slowly. Beside her, Zeus's expression was astounded, and a few silent tears ran down Aphrodite's face.

Hera let out a breath, sweeping her brown hair back from her shoulders. "It needed to be done. He was at the root of this disgusting rebellion."

"Good riddance," Dionysus spat in agreement. "The madman was responsible for the entire attack."

Iyana sucked in a quiet breath, and all of Braxtus's mixed emotions morphed into fury that seized him in a tight grip.

"Congratulations," he growled. "One more voice is silenced, to your advantage."

"Excuse me?" Hera said slowly, turning on him.

He met her cold eyes. "That's your history isn't it? Silencing, overriding voices like Chrysander, Iyana, Demitri—"

"Braxtus," Apollo barked. A few Olympians hissed, others simply gaped at his nerve. Iyana looked up at him, a flash of surprise widening her eyes.

"You're using Demitri as a scapegoat for your own offenses. Demitri—bastard that he was—was the by-product of your own oppression."

"You *did* stack my Trial against me, didn't you?" Galene asked, eyes on her father. "I thought it was Demitri, but . . ."

Poseidon wouldn't meet her eyes.

Disgust filled Braxtus, but Galene just shook her head, sadness and exhaustion etched on her face. "I had so much faith in you. Even when you exiled me, I defended you." She paused. "Maybe that's the irony. Maybe in the silence of Demitri's death you'll finally hear what so many have tried to say."

Zeus looked between the three of them.

"The rage of so many brought an army to Olympus," Aphrodite murmured to him. "We have not ruled the way we pledged."

A lingering pause. Iyana turned her gaze back on Demitri's body and stood still as a statue.

"Clean up this battlefield," Zeus finally said in a low voice. "Get the injured to the infirmary and surrounding temples. We will discuss this in depth later."

One by one, the Olympians dispersed.

Braxtus, Galene, and Iyana didn't move for a long time, standing in the silence that stretched far beyond Demitri's corpse, all the way across the bloodstained battlefield.

55

IYANA

The infirmary bustled with healers, rushing from room to room.

Iyana slipped by them, scrubbed clean and well rested, dressed in a new tunic with her hair spilling over her shoulder. She hugged a bouquet of perfect, golden flowers to her chest as she squeezed between a cart and a healer. Turning the corner, she reached a door and opened it just a crack, peeking inside.

Sunlight flooded through the window into the private room. Braxtus lay on top of the bed linens, leg bandaged tightly, brow furrowed as he read a scroll.

"You trimmed your beard."

His face lit up as he looked toward the door, dropping the scroll. "Iyana!"

She let herself in, smiling at his enthusiasm, then placed the flowers on the bedside table. "I thought these would brighten your room."

"You've already done that."

Her cheeks warmed, but her smile grew bigger. She sat down on the stool by his bed and nodded to his leg. "Is the pain bad?"

He glanced down at it. "It could be worse, all things considered. It's the same damn leg I fell on when the Gryphiekin dropped me. I'll have quite the scar, but they say it'll be another full recovery." He shook his head. "They're only keeping me in a private room to see if there were any lingering effects of being trapped in the *avyssos*. Turns out they hadn't ever bothered to pull anything out, so Ares, Artemis, and I are under close watch."

It wasn't hard to believe, considering the size of that army. "What was it like, trapped in there?"

He rubbed his beard. "Cold. Empty. Dark. It feels like a dream now."

Dreams. A shudder ran down Iyana's spine, and her eyes fell back to his leg. "Demitri did that to you, didn't he?"

Braxtus nodded slowly. "What happened?" he asked. "I mean, Kostas told me about Beast Maker and how Galene ended up with the *avyssos,* but you . . . how did you find us? How did you beat him?"

She tugged at the end of her hair. "Athena sent me to try to get the *avyssos* because she couldn't risk losing anyone else. And I figured I had to try. And then Demitri was there, and I just . . . snapped." She closed her eyes. "I fought him, and he was angry, and he told me he'd killed you. And I . . . I . . ." How could she put into words how she felt, what had happened? "I almost killed him, Braxtus. I was so close."

His warm, rough hand enveloped hers. She opened her eyes to find him watching her, pain and uncertainty in his gaze.

"I didn't kill him, though. Because we needed him to testify to the Olympians. But also because . . ." She faltered, then swallowed. "I didn't want it to be my hate and vengeance that brought him down. I wouldn't have wanted to live with that. So I decided to let it be the Olympians' judgment instead."

Braxtus searched her face long and hard. Then, expelling a breath, he released her hand. "Iyana, we can't do this."

Fear twisted inside of her at his words. "What do you mean?"

"You and I. Not yet, anyway."

The fear twisted harder. "What? Are you suddenly doubting how I feel about you? Gaia, if you knew what it felt like when I thought he'd killed you—"

He let out a strained, dry chuckle. "I know you have feelings for me. The way you kissed me after the battle said it all."

"Then is it *your* feelings?"

He groaned. "No. I told you I love you, and I meant it." He laced his fingers together, muscles straining, as though trying to resist reaching for her. "But I saw the look on your face when you watched Demitri die. You loved him."

Iyana sucked in a breath. "I loved who I thought he was. I loved a *fantasy*. I don't even know how much of those feelings were even real now."

He took a moment, formulating his next words. "I just want to be sure I'm not pressuring you into something you're not ready for. It's not fair of me. You need time to heal. Take it. I'll be here."

Despite the earnestness in his expression, despite his obvious good intentions, Iyana felt a sudden spike of temper.

She stood up and leaned over the bed. "Don't tell me what to do."

Surprise crossed his face.

"I've had enough of being told what I can and can't handle," she continued. "Leave that to me to figure out."

The surprise in his eyes morphed immediately into respect. He sat up straighter. Taking her arms, he guided her to sit on the edge of the bed. "You tell me, then," he said. "What are you ready for? What do you want?"

His brown eyes searched hers, intent for her answer. People often spoke of the color of eyes, as if it mattered at all. His would have been beautiful in any shade. She was drawn to the warmth in them, nothing like the flint that had so often come with Demitri's. From Braxtus's eyes came honesty, gentleness.

"I want you. Now." The world went blurry, and it took her a moment to realize she had tears in her eyes. "I love you. I have this whole time, and yes, I cared about Demitri, but I turned to him in the first place because I was scared I was just a game to you—"

He caught her face in his hands, cutting her short and leaning forward. "Say that again," he said huskily, breath brushing her face.

"I love you," she breathed. "I always would have chosen you, in the end."

His eyes went from soft to burning, and his thumb stroked her cheek. Her heart stuttered, then raced as he leaned in. Lips brushed hers, and that light touch sent shivers through her nerves, shivers that made her whole body tremble . . .

The door flew open, and both of them leapt in shock. Braxtus fell back against the pillows, and Iyana twisted to look at the doorway.

Kostas had Galene by the hand and was leading her in, neck and shoulder bandaged. He froze after two steps, eyes locked on them. Galene looked thrilled to see them, but Iyana knew Kostas had just been bombarded with the heat of the moment. He hesitated, a light of understanding entering his eyes as he read their intense emotions.

A grin spread across his face.

"Iyana!" Galene pulled away from Kostas and rushed to her side. "We thought we'd find you here."

"Why are you out of bed?" Braxtus accused Kostas, glaring at him for what Iyana knew was more than his lack of restraint. Iyana let her hair fall in her face, trying to hide her blush.

"I'm allowed the occasional walk." Kostas was still grinning.

Galene gave him a reproachful look. "He really shouldn't be this far from his bed, but we wanted to tell you . . ."

"Tell us what?" Iyana asked.

Galene's sea-green eyes sparkled. "The Olympians have called for everyone to gather on the field of victory in three days. They asked us specifically to dress in our finest."

Iyana frowned. "When you say us . . ."

"The four of us." Kostas raised his eyebrows meaningfully, and they all exchanged glances.

"I guess this means we're cleared of all charges," Braxtus offered.

At that moment Apollo swept into the room.

Kostas froze guiltily.

Apollo sighed through his nose and pointed out the door.

Kostas shot them an apologetic look as he contritely backed out.

"Everyone else, too," Apollo said. "Even you, Iyana. I'm bringing in a team of healers to work on his leg. Come back tomorrow."

Galene gave Braxtus a cheerful wave, then followed Kostas. Braxtus's gaze lingered on Iyana. She met his eyes, a smile playing on her lips, but with his father watching she, too, stood up, trailing after them.

56
GALENE

A shimmering, glorious mass spread out below Galene. She stood with the Olympians and her friends on a dais before the boundary towers. Thousands of gods, goddesses, and friends of Olympus stood on the cleared battleground, wearing their best robes or armor. Bright flowers and branches of laurel waved among the crowd. Everyone was silent, reverent, as they awaited the King of Olympus's words.

Zeus glowed in majestic, golden robes with a crystal crown that crackled and flashed like real lightning.

"Children," he began. "Brothers and sisters. We gather here to revere all of those who fought and gave their lives in defense of our home. Five hundred and forty-two have been buried within our mountain tomb, their spirits now set among the stars. Let us remember their sacrifice, and always honor their lives and heroism."

Heads bowed, and the following silence weighed on Galene's shoulders. In the crowd, she could see many tear-streaked faces. Zeus himself tilted his face to the sky, as if seeing through the blue to each one of those new glittering stars. He turned his gaze back to the mountain. "The battle led by Olympus's own children created a scar on this land, and it is something that we will not forget. Because of this, we are instituting some changes." He paused for effect, and a soft murmur rippled down the mountain. "The Olympians have come to the decision that

Unnamed gods and goddesses will not be required to complete the traditional Immortality Trial to become official members of the pantheon."

A shock went through Galene. She looked to Iyana and found her friend gawking, mirroring what must have been her expression. She turned to the Olympians.

Though most looked proud or satisfied with this change, it was clear that a few weren't at all pleased. Galene realized with a jolt that Hera wasn't even present. Her eyes found her father's, and he smiled at her.

"Though our children still must be proven worthy, if they wish to petition a different path to prove their worth, we will allow it."

Cheers rose up, scattered through the masses until it became a roar. Braxtus thrust his fist into the air with a whoop, and Galene couldn't keep the grin from her face.

"Great time and effort will be spent preparing for this change," Zeus continued with a small smile, "and we will be seeking input from many."

The crowd buzzed with chatter and excitement, particularly from the Unnamed, who stood together in a clump. "In accordance with this change"—Zeus raised his voice slightly to regain silence—"we have found a select few who have proven both their capability and worthiness outside of the Immortality Trial."

Iyana's hand slipped into hers, and she squeezed it.

"It is clear to us that Galene, Braxtus, and Iyana Unnamed are prepared for their titles and immortality."

Galene's heart leapt into her throat. Tears welled in her eyes, and she struggled to maintain composure. Iyana danced on her toes. A hand touched her back, and Galene didn't need to look to know how proud Kostas was feeling.

Zeus turned his eyes on his daughter. "Iyana, my child, come forward."

Galene dropped her friend's hand, and Iyana stepped out to

339

meet her father. She knelt, sitting back on her heels and smiling up at their king.

"Daughter, you have proven your fierce strength and unyielding devotion. You have endured much and overcome trials most here will not face in an eternity. I crown you a Hero of Olympus." He placed a laurel wreath delicately on her shining hair. "I name you Goddess of Winds. May that wind ever guide and protect the human realm."

Her expression turned to awe, and she bowed her head with smiling pride. Iyana rose, eyes sparkling as she returned to their group.

"Galene," Zeus called, gesturing for her to approach.

Taking in a deep breath, she stepped forward and knelt.

She looked up and was surprised to see Zeus tip his head to her. "Daughter of Poseidon, I am humbled to offer you an official apology of the Olympians. We have deep gratitude for your actions that led this group to deliver Olympus. You have shown composure, respect, and exceptional resilience through your trials." Poseidon appeared beside his brother and, with a proud smile, passed a golden laurel wreath to Zeus. Galene bowed her head. A tear slipped onto her cheek as the crown was placed there.

Poseidon replaced Zeus and beamed down at her. "My daughter, with becoming a Hero of Olympus, I give you your title. I name you Goddess of Tides, Tamer of the Seas. May you continue to calm turbulent waters throughout the eternities."

Galene blinked back her tears as she rose, giving him a bright smile. She started to turn around.

"And, Galene," he added. She looked back, and he pulled something out of his robes. It glowed silver and gold in his hand. "Since you have proven yourself so capable, might I ask you to put this *back*?" He extended the *avyssos* to her, humor dancing in his eyes.

Is he serious? She scrambled for a response. "Wouldn't it be safer here?"

"Didn't you realize why the *avyssos* was placed underwater?" Poseidon asked, cocking an eyebrow. "It needs air and fire to be opened. Neither of which are likely to be found at the bottom of the sea."

Galene blinked at him.

Her father chuckled. "I'll give you a few weeks. You can solicit your friends' help again, if you wish."

She accepted the *avyssos*, a reluctant smile returning to her lips. "I suppose I deserve that."

"I'll show you a shortcut," he promised.

She returned to her friends. Iyana and Kostas were smirking, but Braxtus looked downright horrified.

Apollo came forward, beckoning his son. Braxtus's expression morphed to pride as he strode out. He dropped to one knee but kept his chin high.

"Braxtus," the Olympian began. "Strength, resilience, but most of all your inspiring loyalty have proven you worthy to be named a Hero of Olympus." He placed a laurel wreath on Braxtus's head. "With this honor I present to you your title. Rise, Braxtus, God of Wildfire."

Chest puffed, Braxtus rose, radiating with the honors given him.

Next, Hermes stepped up holding a laurel wreath. "Kostas, my son." Kostas took a knee before his father. "You have already earned your title and temple, but for your bravery and great sacrifices, I am *proud* to crown you a Hero of Olympus."

Galene's heart swelled as Kostas bowed his head and Hermes placed the laurel upon his dark curls. He stood, bowed to his father, and walked back. Galene held his gaze, feeling the pride and joy flooding from his glistening raven eyes.

Without faltering for a moment, Kostas stopped in front of her, wrapped an arm around her waist, and kissed her.

Galene's mind exploded into stars at the soft pressure of his lips against hers. She felt his heart beating, fast as hers, as he hugged her close. Cheers and whoops from the crowd echoed through her fuzzy brain. He broke away, fixing her with one last, dizzying stare before turning and taking her free hand in his.

Heat coursed through her, pooling in her cheeks as she tried to avoid the gaze of a thousand jubilant gods and goddesses. But a smile bloomed on her face and didn't budge. It could probably last forever.

Zeus retook the center of the dias. "Iyana, Galene, and Braxtus, with your titles and the approval of Olympus, you are now ready to obtain immortality."

Kostas trailed his fingers through hers as he stepped back.

The other ten Olympians gathered in a half-circle around their king. In one motion, they raised their right arms out to the three of them, and the ethereal glow emanating from them seemed to collect, channeling into their palms. Beams of light shot out, engulfing Galene and her two friends.

For a moment she was afraid, but then she felt it. A warm, electric tingling flooded her being, every inch of her. She seemed impossibly energetic, alive, charged with Olympic power.

The light faded and Galene looked to Iyana and Braxtus. Their eyes gleamed, and they looked radiant, emanating a soft glow.

"Olympus," Zeus bellowed, "I give you your heroes."

Never before had Galene heard such a joyous uproar. Flowers and laurels flew into the air, raining down upon the cheering gods of Olympus. Tears she didn't know had gathered tumbled freely down her cheeks.

They had done it. She was welcome. She was *home*.

ACKNOWLEDGMENTS

Our idea for *The Immortal Game* started at a sleepover in seventh grade. This book has come a long, long way since slumber parties and pajama pants, and a slew of people's help and support shaped this story into what it is. A thirteen-year stretch of support is a long time—but we'll do our best to list everyone!

Thank you, Ben Grange, our awesome agent, who helped us navigate the exciting new world of publishing. Thank you, Holly West, Val Otarod, and Lauren Scobell, our stellar editors, who came up with amazing new ideas! Our book wouldn't have made it this far without you, and without you believing in this story. Special thanks to Liz Dresner (our talented designer), Mandy Veloso (production editor), Celeste Cass (production manager), and Jean Feiwel (publisher of F&F and Swoon Reads). Thanks to our publicist and marketing teams, and everyone else who turned this book from an unformatted Google doc into a beautiful creation, and launched it into the world.

Thank you, Brandon Sanderson, for being a teacher and inspiration in so many ways. Thanks, too, to Isaac Stewart, for your amazing publishing advice and for connecting us to Ben.

So many thanks to Talia's wonderful mom. You never doubted us and supported us with a fierce passion, despite the fact you don't quite "get" fantasy. ;) You helped us write our first-ever query for this book and gave us endless, amazing advice. We love you!

ASHLEIGH:
I have so much gratitude for everyone who read and gave feedback over the years: Chelsea Holdaway, the best of friends, who read and

edited all of my first drafts. Camilee Belloli, for all the hours of hiking, brainstorming, and talking stories. Jay Gould, who was always excited about my latest project and fell in love with this book. Ethan Fullwood, for being my first friend, fan, and supporter. My husband, Ken, for being my biggest cheerleader as we struggled through hours of edits. My parents, the first ones to read my young, messy writing and who've encouraged me to always climb to greater heights.

Thank you to everyone in all my writing groups through the years who've helped my writing get to this point.

Finally, thank you to all my students, for celebrating with me when I first got the call, in the middle of third period, that this book was getting published.

TALIA:

Thank you to the people who read and loved it first:

My dad, who believed in my dreams. Cairo, who really thought this story was special. Stephen, who let me read it to him. Amanda Friend, who read the printed, fat, original manuscript and gasped aloud at all the appropriate places. And my mom, again, who loves with her whole heart and is my biggest inspiration.

Thanks to Heather Merkley, who gave it its first review on Swoon Reads. You're a stellar friend. Thank you SO MUCH, Michelle, for cheering me on from the sidelines my whole journey. I love you forever.

Thanks to my amazing writing group—Lee Sandwina, Nicholas Binge, Lia Holland, and Eleanor Roth Imbody—for being the best writing support and a solid group of friends. Thanks, too, for all the last-second help on this book.

Thanks to my husband, Nathanael, for being my dear friend and confidant, for listening to all the woes and triumphs of writing.

Check out more books chosen for publication by readers like you.

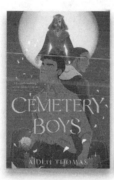